Anna Bell

'Unputdownable. I loved reading every page of this funny romance story'
I READ NOVELS

'Another cracker from the lovely Anna Bell – highly recommended!
ON MY BOOKSHELF

'A fresh and fun read'
ALBA IN BOOKLAND

'Modern, fresh, charming, warm and very exciting . . . a wonderful romantic comedy, full of unique moments and scenes'
SIMONA'S CORNER OF DREAMS

'A wonderful and relevant book'
KATIE'S BOOK CAVE

'I definitely recommend this book!'
CHAPTER AND CAKE

Anna Bell lives in the South of France with her young family and energetic labrador. You can find out more about Anna on her website, www.annabellwrites.com or follow her on Twitter @annabell_writes.

Also by Anna Bell

The Bucket List to Mend a Broken Heart
The Good Girlfriend's Guide to Getting Even
It Started With a Tweet
Don't Tell the Groom
Don't Tell the Boss
Don't Tell the Brides-To-Be

IF WE'RE NOT Married by THIRTY

Anna Bell

ZAFFRE

First published in Great Britain in 2018 by
ZAFFRE
80–81 Wimpole St, London W1G 9RE
www.zaffrebooks.co.uk

A CIP catalogue record for this book is available from the British Library.

ISBN: 978–1–785–76478–3

Also available as an ebook

1 3 5 7 9 10 8 6 4 2

Typeset by IDSUK (Data Connection) Ltd
Printed and bound in Great Britain by Clays Ltd, Elcograf S.p.A.

Zaffre is an imprint of
Bonnier Books UK
www.bonnierzaffre.co.uk
www.bonnierbooks.co.uk

To Jane and Ollie.
Thanks for the inspiration – of course Kerry and Jim are
nothing like you . . . except maybe the rhubarb

Prologue

Saturday, 6 June 2009

The sounds of 'Agadoo' drift round the corner of the marquee and I let out an involuntary groan. When I get married, I'm going to dictate the set list to the DJ. Or maybe I won't even have a DJ. Maybe I'll elope. Yes, that's a better idea. Then I won't have to put anyone through the pain of wearing a ridiculous bridesmaid dress or having their hair sprayed with so much hairspray that they fear it may never move on its own again.

I wrestle with the top of my dress that was tight at the start, before the canapés, three-course meal and countless drinks I've downed since the wedding began. Yes, I'd definitely not put anyone else through this pain.

'Hey, I wondered where you'd got to. You're missing our mothers pushing imaginary pineapples and shaking trees,' says Danny.

I cautiously look around to check that he's alone, and breathe a sigh of relief when I realise he is.

'Oh my God. They're so embarrassing. I told Kerry that she shouldn't do Pimm's as the welcome drink.'

'Doesn't she remember what happened at my mum's fiftieth?'

'I know,' I say incredulously. 'That's what I said. But she and Jim had snuck off somewhere early on and missed our mothers getting up to mischief.'

My sister thought I was exaggerating when I told her Mum was dancing on tables at her best friend's birthday party. Let's hope the tables in the marquee are more sturdy than the ones at Hazel's house. I've never seen plastic buckle like that before.

'Are you coming back in? I bet it'll be "the Macarena" next. Or maybe "Oops Upside Your Head".'

I shudder at the thought.

'Come on,' I say, holding my hand out for him to pull me up. 'I'm desperate for a drink. There's a pub next door. Do you fancy coming for a quick pint?'

'I'm pretty sure there's alcohol in the marquee. Besides, it's your sister's wedding and you're a bridesmaid.'

'And I've fulfilled all my bridesmaid duties. I kept her sober until after the ceremony. I've ensured that she has a change of clothes and a toothbrush in her hotel room and I've held her dress up inside the toilet cubicle at least twice so she could pee. I think I've earned a cheeky pint before she needs the loo again.'

Reluctantly, he takes my hand and yanks me up.

'We'll come back soon. Just a quick drink,' I say winking.

We walk across the rock-hard grass towards the fence. It takes me a few strides to realise that I still have hold of Danny's hand. I blush a little as I let go and hope he won't see my glowing cheeks by the light of the moon.

'Lydia, where are we going?'

'Here, there's a hole.'

I push at one of the wooden posts of the fence and it swings open.

Danny gives me a look.

'Jim plays cricket here and Kerry and I come to watch, but it goes on for so long that at some point we usually sneak off for a drink. Only,' I say, getting stuck in the gap, 'I hadn't quite factored this dress into the equation.'

It might not be as big as Kerry's wedding dress, but it's poufy enough to get me stuck between the fence panels.

Danny very helpfully gives me a little shove, and I find myself in a tiny courtyard at the back of the pub. I'm met with glares from those sitting around the one wooden table that makes up the tiny beer garden.

Danny flies through the fence after me, almost knocking me over.

'Oh, sorry,' he says, brushing himself down.

'Come on,' I say, dragging him in the back door.

The inside of the pub is lit up like Blackpool Illuminations, or at least that's what it feels like. My eyes have been used to the moonlit sky and the pub's neon fairy lights around the bar and flashing fruit machines are practically blinding me.

I try to ignore the watchful eyes of the locals who are giving me funny looks and I can't work out if it's because of my dusty-pink bridesmaid dress or the tiara in my hair. Whatever it is, I don't care. I order a pint of Foster's. Thankfully there are no older female relatives to tut and call me unladylike.

'Let's go round the corner,' I say, sipping as I walk. We find ourselves on an old sofa at the back of the bar area. We're far away from the stares of the locals and noise of the fruit machines. I sit down and, for the first time today, I let myself relax. Who knew going to your sister's wedding could be so exhausting? Of course it's not just been today; the run-up's been going on for months. I'm lucky I've been away at uni and missed most of it.

'This is better,' says Danny. 'I mean, not saying Kerry's wedding isn't fun or anything, but I'm more of a pub man.'

'Me too. I was thinking earlier that I'd hate a big wedding like that.'

'Really? I thought you'd love it. Aren't you the one who wants to become some big party planner?'

'Yes, but I want to be behind the scenes. I wouldn't want to be centre of all that attention. Have you seen how many times Kerry's had to pose for photos? What? Why are you looking at me like that?' I say, as Danny's got this weird eye thing going on.

'Nothing, it just surprises me, that's all.'

I like the fact that after all these years of knowing him I can still surprise him.

'So, you're holding up well despite the amount of booze you've consumed,' I say, changing the subject.

'Am I ever going to live my mum's party down?'

'No,' I say, laughing at the memory of him being a pathetic but sweet drunk. Danny is always so confident and self-assured, so it was nice to see him less than perfect for once. 'You were so funny rambling away.'

'I just wish you'd tell me what I was rambling about.'

'And what, ruin all my fun?' I say, sinking into the couch. To be honest, Danny was pretty incoherent that night. But I'm not going to let him know that.

'Bloody Pimm's. I had the worst hangover the next day.'

'Probably like the one I'm going to have tomorrow.'

'So was I talking on one particular topic or . . .?'

'Stop fishing, Whittaker. I'm never going to tell.'

He goes a bit pale and I wonder what he has to hide.

'So,' says Danny finally giving up. 'Are you going to tell me why you're hiding from the wedding?'

I try not to laugh at the foam moustache on his upper lip.

'I'm not hiding. I was getting some air, and now I'm getting a pint.'

'Uh-huh, both of which you could have done at the wedding. I was looking for you for ages.'

'It's been a frantic few days; I just wanted to be by myself. And the pint, well, I got fed up with all the tutting from my aunts.'

'Hmm,' he says, raising an eyebrow. He knows I'm lying.

I hate the fact that he knows me so well. Mine and Danny's friendship is a by-product of our mothers being best friends and us spending a lot of time together when we were growing up. We've both been away at university so we haven't seen a lot of each other over the last few years, but he still knows when I'm keeping something back.

'What's the real reason? Is it the wedding? Aren't you happy for Kerry? I thought that you got on well with Jim.'

'I do. Jim's great and I'm so happy for them – honestly, I am – it's just ...' I say, sounding so insincere. I don't mean to. I'm genuinely happy for them and I'm not even the tiniest bit jealous of my sister as she truly deserves every happiness.

'It's just what?' asks Danny, when I don't reply.

'I guess I'm sad because I'm nowhere near that, you know?'

'What? Nowhere near marriage? We're only twenty-one.'

'I'm actually still only twenty. I've got another two months until my 21st,' I say, thinking that makes me sound even more pathetic. 'I definitely don't want to get married yet; I know I'm way too young. I just worry that it's never going to happen.'

'Lydia, you're being ridiculous. Of course you're going to get married.'

'But it's not only the marriage thing; it's the whole love thing too. I mean, I've never even been in love. Look at Kerry and Jim. They met at sixth form and have already been together for a decade. Then there're my uni friends. All of them have had their first love already. And, OK, some of them might have been with total knob heads, but at least they've had that whole giddy-in-your-belly-butterflies thing going on. I've never had that. I just want to know what it's like.'

'What? That rumbly feeling in your belly? There's this Indian round the corner from my old flat that I'm pretty sure would leave you feeling the same way.'

I pull a very attractive face to tell him how much I don't appreciate the sarcasm. 'I'm being serious,' I say. 'I want to know what it's like to have someone who loves me. Someone who would do anything for me.' I pick up my pint and start drinking until

I realise I'm in danger of downing it. 'I mean, have you ever been in love?' I ask.

Danny looks at me as if he's shocked I've asked him such a personal question. Of course he is. In all the years that I've known him I've never talked to him about stuff like this, despite us being so close. Our friendship might have been forced upon us, but being roughly the same age, we always stuck together. From the times when our older siblings were throwing rotten apples at us from their tree house, to the time when we saw in the millennium together, huddled in his bedroom terrified of the computer downstairs that we thought was about to go nuts with the millennium bug. We might talk – or, more accurately, argue – about politics and other things that we don't really understand, but we never talk about love or sex or feelings, aka personal stuff.

The look in his eyes, however, says it all. Of course he's been in love. Everyone at our age has; everyone except me.

Fran? Camilla? Jane? I wonder which of his many girlfriends he'd fallen for.

'You see, I've been missing out. Well, obviously I haven't been missing out on *everything*,' I say, in a rush. I don't want him thinking that I'm saving myself for 'the one'. 'I have had a very good time at uni, if you know what I mean.'

Danny's giving me a look as if to tell me to stop talking. He clearly knows what I mean.

My cheeks are actually burning and I can only imagine how red they must have gone.

'I don't even know why you're worrying about this,' he says. 'Of course you're going to find someone.'

'But what if I don't?' I look down at my pint only to realise I've finished it.

'You will.'

'But what if I don't?' I whine again. 'I'll be like Bridget Jones at the beginning of the film where she's singing "All By Myself" and I'll be meaning every single word.'

'I haven't seen it, but I'm guessing by the end she's not still single.'

'Well, no, but that's so not the point,' I say, pouting. 'The point is, I could be Bridget Jones. Except I won't be shagging Hugh Grant and I won't end up with Colin Firth. I'll be a spinster forever. Not in love and unloved.'

Danny rolls his eyes at me. 'Weren't you the one who was saying earlier that you didn't want to get married?'

'I don't want a big wedding, but I still want to get married. I guess I just want to know that I'm going to have a husband at some point in the future.'

Danny sighs. 'Look, if it'll stop you crying into your drink, why don't we do one of those pact things? You know, if we're still single at thirty we get married.'

'So you think I'm still going to be single at thirty?'

'No,' says Danny. His messy eyebrows lodging into the bridge of his nose as he scrunches up his face. 'I meant, if you do happen to be single still, and I am too, then we give it a go.'

'When you're thirty or when I'm thirty? You're eight months older than me.'

'You, then.'

'As long as you're not married already.'

'As long as I'm not married already,' he says slowly, as if it needs spelling out for me.

'Oh great, so my only chance is to hope that you're as much of a loser in love as me?'

Danny shakes his head and I wonder if he's regretting even mentioning it.

'Come on, you're like "Mr Lover Lover",' I say in my best Shaggy impression. 'You've always got some girl on the go. There's no way you're going to be single. I'm doomed. I'm never going to get married. I'm never going to be kissed in that swoony way. I'll never know what those rumbly feelings in my belly feel like. I'll—'

WTF? Danny is kissing me. Like, properly kissing me.

Danny who I have known forever. Danny who's seen me through every stage of my life – nappies, braces, acne outbreaks. Danny who's giving me butterflies. Danny who's actually an amazing kisser.

When eventually he pulls away, I'm left leaning towards him, my lips still puckered, confused by what just happened.

I stare at him as if I'm seeing him for the first time. I've had a crush on Danny forever, but I've never even thought of acting on it. I always thought that he'd never be interested in me. He's so smart and funny and sexy, and, oh boy, am I now in trouble.

I'm still too shocked to say anything and I see Danny's face fall as he thinks I didn't like it.

'Hey, no,' I splutter. 'That was – where the hell did that come from? It was . . . It was . . .'

My mind is racing through all the possible scenarios. Was it a one off? Will he do it again? Would it be that mind-blowing if we had sex? Are we going to start dating? Is the pact still on?

'It was amazing,' I say finally.

He laughs and he takes my hand in his.

'Is that something you want to do again?' I ask, dipping my toe in the water.

'Like this?' he asks, before he leans over and kisses me once more.

This time he takes hold of my waist and his fingers brush my back. I'm tingling all over with anticipation.

'I'm sorry,' he says, when finally he pulls away again. 'I know this is really bad timing, what with me going travelling for the summer . . .'

'Travelling?' I say. This time it's my turn to scrunch up my face.

'Oh yeah, didn't I tell you? I'm going to South East Asia for a few months before I start my graduate scheme. I leave on Monday.'

'As in *this* Monday?'

'Uh-huh, as in tomorrow's Sunday, then Monday evening I fly out to Thailand,' he says, wincing.

I look at Danny. We've been friends for years, why the bloody hell did he have to kiss me hours before he flies ten thousand miles away? We've been at the most boring family parties where a snog or a fumble would have made it far more entertaining. Why did he have to wait until now?

'Why don't you come with me?' he asks.

'What?' I say, not understanding.

'Come with me, to Thailand,' he says, his face lighting up.

I start to imagine it, lolling about in the waves with him. It'll be just like *The Beach*. Although without all the scary stuff that happens at the end. And most importantly I'd get to find out where that kiss was leading. I'm just wondering where I'm going to buy my backpack from when I think back to my temp job.

'I can't, I'm heading back up to Newcastle for the summer. One of my lecturers has pulled some strings and got me a job at an events company for the summer.'

'Are you sure you wouldn't prefer to come to Asia?'

'Danny, you're far too impulsive for your own good. Of course I'd love to come, but I can't. My lecturer did me a huge favour and I can't turn down a job.'

I let out a long sigh. 'So how long are you away for?'

'Three months.'

'Well, that's not so bad,' I say, thinking that'll pass quickly when I'm working.

'And then I start my graduate scheme in London, so maybe once your summer job is finished you could get a job there?'

Thoughts of the kiss linger in my mind and for a moment I'm tempted.

'There's talk that the temp job could lead into something permanent. I don't want to make any promises I can't keep.'

'So you'd be in Newcastle and I'd be in London?'

'I guess there's always long distance,' I say, unenthusiastically. I've never known anyone to successfully have a long-distance relationship.

'There is, but my graduate scheme is going to be relentless. Apparently, I'm going to be working ridiculous hours.'

'Which would make a long-distance relationship a tad tricky,' I say sighing. 'You bloody arsehole, Danny Whittaker. Why the hell did you go and kiss me like that? Why flipping now?'

'I'm sorry. You were going on about not being kissed and not being loved, and all that talk of marriage.'

'Bloody weddings,' I say, half laughing. 'It brings out the horn in people. Look at Monica and Chandler.'

Danny's face is blank.

'Come on. You're telling me still, after all these years, despite all the repeats on E4, you haven't watched *Friends*?'

He shrugs his shoulders and gives me a look. A look which suddenly makes me want to jump his bones. That kiss has changed everything . . .

'What are we going to do?' I practically whisper.

'I don't think there's much we can do. I'm going travelling and then I'll be in London and you'll be in Newcastle.'

I nod. 'Bastard timing.'

'But hey, we'll always have our pact, right? Maybe I'll kiss you again in nine years when we get hitched.'

'Don't laugh about that,' I say, prodding my finger into his chest. 'I'm going to need that pact. So if you could just stay single until then.'

He laughs and I feel my heart burning a little, which is ridiculous as up until ten minutes ago this was Danny, and now he's *Daaaaaaaaaaanny*. It's like I could cope with my crush when I thought it was unrequited, but now that there's a hint that he likes me too, it's become unbearable.

I look at my empty glass suddenly needing more to drink. 'Same again?' I ask.

'We should get back to the wedding. People will be wondering where you are.'

He's right. I snuck out of the marquee well over an hour ago. I'm sure that Kerry's bladder is almost at bursting point given the rate she was drinking her vodkas earlier.

'I guess we should.'

I squeeze his hand and he squeezes mine back.

'Are you staying over at the hotel?' I say, a fleeting thought popping into my mind.

'I'm sharing a room with Stuart. How about you?'

'My cousin, Clara.'

We groan again. Destiny is not on our side.

Reluctantly we stand up and weave our way through the pub and back to the little fence.

I'm pleased the courtyard's empty and I turn back to face Danny.

'You can't kiss me at the wedding,' I say, firmly – more to myself than to him. 'If either of our mothers saw, you know what they'd be like. We'd never hear the end of it.'

He nods his head.

I can't resist him now, though, and I lean up and kiss him. I grab hold of his suit jacket and he wraps his arm around me. I hear the whizz of fireworks going off round my ears. Fucking hell. First butterflies. Now fireworks. He's like the don of kissing.

'Fireworks,' mutters Danny as he pulls away.

'You felt them too,' I say, as a massive bang goes off and I look up to the sky to see twinkling red lights.

I close my eyes, feeling like such an idiot. Of course they are actual fireworks. My sister planned them for ten-thirty.

'I felt it too,' he whispers against my ear, before he pulls out of the embrace and gently drops my hand. 'We'll always have our pact. It's only nine years away.'

'Nine years' time,' I say, and we both laugh, although the laughter doesn't reach our eyes.

He pushes the fence panel and holds it open for me to squeeze through before he follows me. We stand there looking at the marquee, neither of us making a move towards it. I look at him trying to convince myself that he's just the same old Danny he's always been. I need to forget how that kiss made me feel if things are going to go back to how they were before. Only I wonder if they ever can.

Chapter One

My mum told me on the phone tonight that it's Kerry and Jim's first wedding anniversary. This time last year, huh? Who'd have thought I'd be living in a tiny apartment in Tokyo with a toilet that squirts warm water and you'd hob-nobbing with celebs at your fancy job in London. Don't think that just because we live in different time zones I won't be invoking the pact, only another eight years to go . . .

Email; Danny to Lydia, June 2010

23rd December 2018

I'm scanning Instagram, as I always do in my break, wondering why I do it to myself. I mean, I love looking at all the beautiful photos, yet it always leaves me feeling a little bit empty. Why is my version of real life nowhere near as glossy?

With only two sleeps till Christmas nearly every photo on my feed is themed appropriately with copious amounts of glitter and sparkle and there's always a perfectly decorated Christmas tree in the background.

I study an old school friend's photo. She's surrounded by a large group of girls, their arms draped around one another, and they're all dressed in knitted Christmas jumpers. I read the hashtags and groan: #besties #LoveMyFriends #blessed #SquadGoals #LivingMyBestLife – I don't know which hashtag offends me the most.

I plump for #LivingMyBestLife; what does that even mean? Who knows, if she hadn't routinely bunked off business studies to fool around with Matthew Cook, she might have ended up as some hugely successful CEO. And by who's yardstick are we measuring this 'best life'? To some, spending an entire Sunday morning watching *Sunday Brunch* rather than going out for actual brunch with real-life people might be sad, but to me there's nothing I love doing more than curling up on the sofa and vegging out after a long week at work.

I quickly google 'How do you know if you're living your best life', wondering if there's a quiz I can do. Bingo! Found one, what a perfect way to spend my break time:

Question 1: Do you love your job?
I poke my head round the corner of the giant lollipop that I'm hiding behind and look out across the sea of guests who are being offered canapés by waiting staff wearing Oompa-Loompa costumes. It makes me smile and reminds me I have the potential to love my job. I just wish I was managing these events, not spending most of my time pushing the paper behind the scenes.

Question 2: When was the last time you did something spontaneous?
Let's see now, last Tuesday I ordered a Chinese from a different takeaway to the one that I usually use. That's got to count for something, right?

Question 3: Are you happy in your love life?
What love life? Since I broke up with my long-term boyfriend Ross five months ago, things have been a little quiet in that department – make that non-existent. Next . . .

Question 4: Have you ever taken a risk and completely changed your life?
Aha – now this I have done. In my early twenties I moved to London to work at a swanky events company. Unfortunately, it wasn't the best life decision I've ever made. The job was awful, I was flat broke (not that it mattered, as I had no time off to spend money) and to top it all off the guy who had been a huge factor in me taking the job moved to Tokyo before I even got to London . . . I'm not sure that's the best advert for taking a risk.

Question 5: When was the last time you tried something new?
Since I broke up with Ross I've tried to do new things as I'm searching for something that's going to put the sparkle back into my life. I've done a taster pottery lesson, played one game of netball and found a Pilates class. The fact that I didn't go to any of them more than once isn't really the point.

Question 6: When was the last time you ticked something off your bucket list?
Is it wrong to admit that I don't actually have one? Maybe that's my problem; I don't know what I really want out of life.

I sigh heavily and I put down my phone. I'm clearly not quite living my best life. I broke up with Ross because I had the feeling that it wasn't right and that something was missing from my life, and yet in the five months we've been broken up I've not been able to work out what would make me happy.

It's New Year next week and I'm quite looking forward to seeing the back of 2018. I usually love making New Year's resolutions – but I never stick to them. Perhaps this year I'll think of things to do that'll sort my life out that I will absolutely, 100 per cent, definitely stick to. I mean, I have to, or else I'm going to have to stop using Instagram once and for all.

'Lydia, we need some ice over at the factory gates,' comes a crackle in my earpiece. I guess that time's up on my break.

'I'll be right there,' I say as I push the button on my lapel to make my walkie-talkie work.

I always feel terribly important when I'm wearing the earpiece and in my head I imagine my role to be as important as a secret service agent guarding POTUS, rather than a lowly event co-ordinator usually guarding the alcohol-supply cupboard should guests mount a daredevil raid on it.

I climb out from behind the giant lollipop and straighten myself up as I slip back into work mode. I jump over the river that's supposed to look like chocolate and navigate my way through guests who are already well on their way to being wasted. I smile as I walk past the waitresses dressed as Oompa-Loompas, relieved that I'm dressed in a black top and skirt so I can blend into the background. Or at least I could, if the background wasn't bright pink and orange.

Charlie and the Chocolate Factory might not have been the most obvious choice for a Christmas party theme, but the guests here seem to be lapping it up.

'You're just in time,' whispers Helen as I find her over by the faux factory gates. I see just why she needed ice. There's a man who looks like he's stepped off the front cover of *GQ* magazine getting dressed up as Willy Wonka in the photo booth. Hmm, if he's Willie Wonka – where are those golden tickets . . .

'I mean,' Helen says, fanning herself with her hand and wafting alcohol at me in the process. At first I don't believe the fumes could be coming from her. There's so much booze in this place that the smell could feasibly be coming from anywhere, but as I edge closer to her, the smell gets stronger. There's no denying it's on her breath.

We don't drink when we're working events. OK, correction, we don't drink *very* much when we're working. We have been known to have the odd little glass of wine or bubbles to get us in the party mood, but we never ever get over the drink-drive limit. Helen must have had quite a lot for me to be able to smell it.

I look at her a little bit more closely and she's actually swaying along to 'Driving Home for Christmas'. This is not good. Helen's the event manager and she's supposed to be alert during the whole event to do as her title suggests – manage it. She's got to orchestrate the running order as well as insure that the performers, caterers and guests are all in the right place at the right time. Which means reacting to any little problem as well as acting as babysitter to the adults. She needs to be able to think quickly on her feet, like last year when the theme was Winter Wonderland and the CEO of a large multi-national got his tongue stuck to a giant ice sculpture in the most inappropriate place, or the year before that when the aerial acrobat's ribbon snapped and she ended up kicking a man in the head and knocking him out. Whilst on big events like this there might be more staff around to help, the buck ultimately stops with her. Only right now I can't imagine she'd even know what a buck is.

'Here you go,' says Tracey, the Operations Director (aka our big boss) as she walks up to us with a bucket of ice. 'Is this going to be enough?'

Helen and I stare at the bucket in confusion before it dawns on me that she's on the same radio channel and heard our conversation.

I don't think Helen has made the connection. She wrinkles her face up and opens her mouth to say something and I grab the bucket before she can. I don't want Tracey to realise that Helen's been drinking.

'Um, yes, thanks. It's just to put under the chocolate sculpture in the lobby as it seems to be melting under the lights.'

'Good thinking,' she says. 'Have you seen Willy?'

Helen points, open mouthed, at the *GQ* model.

'The real Willy? I wanted him to do a photo op before he does the call to dinner and he seems to have gone AWOL.'

'Um, I did see him a while ago in the shrinking space,' I say, thinking that, of all the parties we've thrown, this *Charlie and the Chocolate Factory* one seems to be the most surreal.

Tracey gives a little nod of the head in appreciation and clip-claps off in her skyscraper heals.

'Ice?' I say, holding the bucket with a smirk. 'I forgot she was on the radio loop tonight. I guess we better watch what we say.'

Helen and I only work together if it's one of our large events, like this one where we've got almost two thousand guests on site. It means that the two of us get a bit carried away with our headsets and over the years we've honed a discreet radio code. *I need some ice over here* is code for this guy is so hot I need some ice to cool down. *The hotel has confirmed the reservation* is for people who are getting down and dirty and are in danger of needing a room imminently. *Time for the rubber gloves* means that someone's about to throw up. *Have you seen Mary Poppins* is for when someone's as high as a kite.

It might sound a bit childish, but it helps get us through the night. And when we're managing fifteen nights of work Christmas dos, we need all the help we can get.

I spot a man crouched on all fours bending down towards the chocolate river.

'Excuse me,' I say, pulling him slowly up to standing, 'it's not actually chocolate. But if that's what you're after, we've got a chocolate waterfall near the entrance, or the chocolate liqueur luge by the fairground rides. They taste much better.'

The man nods and staggers off in the opposite direction to where I pointed.

'I can't say I blame him. It does look delicious. This whole place does. It's giving me the right munchies tonight,' says Helen, and I grab her arm as I think she's about to make a lunge for the river herself. The company that supplied it have done too good a job with the clever lighting projected onto water – it really does look like chocolate.

'Have you eaten tonight? Maybe you need something more.'

I don't know what's got into her. It might be our last Christmas party of the year, and the event staff know what they're doing blindfolded by now, but that's no reason to be slacking off.

'I was on my way to get something from the kitchen, when I bumped into Willy Wonka – not that man obviously, but the real one. Well, not the real one, as the old guy died, didn't he? And Johnny Depp's not here. But the Willy Wanker from here. Oops! Willy Wanker – ha! That so would have been a better character name for him –'

'You were on your way to get food when you saw the guy who's acting as Willy,' I say trying to follow the babble and keep her on track.

'Right. Willy W-O-N-K-A', she says, enunciating it carefully and suppressing her giggles, 'was drinking this cocktail. Of course I told him that he shouldn't be drinking on the job.'

'Of course,' I say, wondering if that was before or after she'd drunk the rest. I just hope that he's in a better state than Helen, who's turned away from me and is licking one of the fake giant candy canes. I don't want to point out that she's probably not the first person to have done that this party season.

'They look so real, don't they?' she says, as if she's surprised that they're not, despite the fact that she was the one who came up with the concept and sourced the props.

'I know, they're so impressive. It's going to be a hard theme to top next year. What do you reckon Tracey'll pick?'

I'm trying to keep her talking to gauge how drunk she is.

'Maybe *Fifty Shades of Grey*.'

She's turned back to stare at the *GQ* model again and I can tell exactly what's on her mind.

'We could have chains hanging from the ceilings, and whips and riding crops as props.'

'Hmm, perhaps,' I say realising she's further gone than I thought.

Kylie's version of 'Santa Baby' starts playing through the speakers, proving to me once again that Christmas music is the only part that doesn't gel with the party theme. I'm about to say this to Helen, when I realise that she's got her leg draped around one of the giant candy canes and she's about to swing round it like it's a stripper pole.

'Helen,' I say, catching her after the candy cane begins to bend. Of all the things I risk assessed it for, having a woman try to hang off it with her thighs hadn't been one of them.

The real Willy Wonka breezes past us on stilts, ushering the guests to the dining room. He's swaying slightly and it's hard to know whether that's just because he's so high up or whether he's been affected by the cocktails too. I'm hoping it's the former as right now I've got enough to deal with looking after Helen.

'I guess that's our cue to check everyone's in position,' I say to her loudly, in an attempt to remind her that she's supposed to be working. She just smiles blindly back at me. 'Do you want to take the acrobats and I'll take the catering staff?'

She nods, but not before she thrusts her phone at me and tells me to take a photo. She slips her arm round the *GQ* model and grabs one of the photo booth props. Of course she picks the giant #LivingMyBestLife sign.

I take a photo of them grinning wildly and drag her away from the man, nudging her in the direction of the acrobats. I watch her walk away – she's doing an over-the-top swagger as if she's trying very hard to walk normally. I can only hope she sobers up.

I needn't have worried about the caterers; as this is the last party of the season it's the fifteenth time they've done this menu, so they've got it down pat. They've just started clearing the main-course plates and I've got time to find Helen. I hurry along, weaving my way through the giant candy statues, wondering if she'll be back to her normal self.

As soon as I go out of the back of the tent I get my answer: a big fat giant resounding no. She's currently waving the acrobats' long ribbons whilst spinning around and trying to make them fly out.

'Helen,' I say, rushing over and holding her up as her body tries to move in time with her spinning head.

'Lydia, are there two of you or am I just seeing double?'

She laughs as if it's the funniest thing she's heard, and I know then that we're in trouble. She was slurring a little before, but now it's unmistakeable.

'Are you OK, Helen?'

'Totally, totally fine.'

She is definitely not fine. What am I going to do?

The radio crackles in our ears. 'We have a situation with the chocolate river,' comes Tracey's voice.

I see Helen going to press the button on her lapel and I make a lunge for it and knock her onto her bottom.

'What are you doing?' she says, giggling.

'I'll get the chocolate river. You stay here and play with your ribbons.'

Her face lights up and she starts spinning around again, reminding me of a dog chasing its own tail.

I slide back through the door to the main tent and see a waiter carrying coffee.

'Hey, Angus,' I say, waving him over, 'can you give me a really strong cup of that, please?'

'Sure,' he says, pouring me one. 'Long night?'

'Something like that. Thanks.'

I quickly deliver it to Helen and tell her in no uncertain terms to stay put and make sure it's all drunk by the time I get back.

I practically run to the chocolate river where I find Tracey standing over it, a pint glass in her hand.

'Everything OK?' I ask, slightly red-faced and out of breath.

'I think someone's been sick in it.'

I look at it and there are definite lumps. My stomach lurches at the thought.

'And you want help clearing it?' I say, looking at the pint glass that she's handing to me. I'm assuming she wants it to be scooped out.

'I'd do it, but I've just had my nails done for Christmas.'

I look down at my own glossy maroon talons. I hadn't planned to redo them before Christmas either, but I guess they're not as intricate as Tracey's, which have little snowmen painted on them.

I approach the chocolate river and have a quick check to make sure there are no guests around.

'Let me know if anyone comes,' I say, finding a switch behind a fake hill. I flick it and the chocolate river looks like normal water again. I'm relieved to see that the sick is in fact just a selection of Dolly Mixtures that someone's dropped in there. I scoop them out with the pint glass and pop it on a nearby return station for the catering team to deal with.

'Sorry about that, Lydia,' says Tracey as I flip the switch back on, 'we probably could have left them there. I just didn't want anyone to see the lumps and feel queasy.'

Now she tells me.

'Where are they up to with the dinner?' she asks.

'They're just starting to serve coffees and the desserts with follow shortly,' I say, hoping that Helen's drunk hers.

She looks at her watch and nods approvingly. 'Everything's running like clockwork. Excellent. Looks like you and Helen are doing a great job as per usual.'

I can't help glowing with pride that she included me in that too, even though this is Helen's baby. It's nice to be appreciated. Before this job I worked for an events company in London for six months whose ethos was the polar opposite of here. It was a culture which thrived on snarking, shouting and belittling. So whenever I get a work compliment I appreciate it all the more.

'I'll probably be heading off soon,' she says.

Spurred on by the compliment I figure that I should ask her about my latest idea. I've been trying, unsuccessfully, to make the transition from events coordinator to events manager for the last year and I've come up with a plan. And who knows, if it goes right, I might be able to be #LivingMyBestLife in no time.

'Um, Tracey, I was just wondering if you'd had a chance to look into the proms proposal I sent over?' I'm holding my breath in anticipation.

'Ah, yes, as a matter of fact I did. I think it could be quite a lucrative new market. Thank you for suggesting it.'

'Great. So should I look into it in the New Year?'

'Actually, I thought I'd put Helen onto it. Hopefully, we'll have enough time to get some ideas in the planning before schools and colleges book them up.'

My heart sinks. I'm about to accept it and skulk away when I stop myself.

'Actually, Tracey, I had hoped that this would be my project and that I'd get to plan the events from start to finish. I've got some ideas for packages and . . . '

'Lydia, don't get me wrong, you're a fantastic events coordinator and we could not be more grateful for the work that you do in the support role. There is nobody that does an event risk assessment as well as you. Which is why I don't think we should add to your responsibilities.'

'But I could always research proms on top of my current workload.'

'I have no doubt that you could. It's just that Helen is such an experienced manager and she's the one who always has the creative ideas – the crazy ones, the kooky ones. Perhaps, with her being younger than you, she's got a bit more lust for life. You know? She'll tap right into that youth market.'

'Um, Helen's five years older than me,' I say, desperately trying not to take it personally that my boss has basically just called me boring.

'Is she? Well, look at her,' says Tracey, pointing. I follow her finger and gasp in horror. Helen is currently in the bright purple zorb ball rolling around a pen doing her best Violet Beauregarde impression. 'Have you been in the zorb ball, Lydia?'

I look over at it before looking back down at my pencil skirt. I mentally risk assess zorbing in this outfit: 1) risk of flashing my pants; 2) greater risk of splitting my skirt; and 3) knowing how uncoordinated I am there's a high risk I'd probably roll right over the pen boundary and knock the giant candy canes over like skittles.

I don't point out that the only reason that Helen is in it is that she's drunk as a skunk.

'You're a great asset to the team, Lydia, but I think it's important to stick to what we're good at.'

She gives me a firm look as if to indicate that the subject is now well and truly closed.

I start to feel tears welling up behind my eyes and I try and blink them back, wishing that I hadn't put quite so many layers of mascara on tonight.

'Oh dear, I think there's something going on over in that bed,' she says, nodding towards the double bed where people can pretend that they're Willy Wonka's grandparents sleeping top to toe. Only the two people in it seem to be recreating quite a different scene. Something you definitely wouldn't expect to find in children's fiction. I glance over at Helen, who's still zorbing around and decide she'll be OK where she is for another few minutes.

'I'll sort it out,' I say, relieved to have a reason to leave before I start sobbing in front of my boss.

I slump off blinking back the tears. It's not that I mind my job. I'm good at what I do and I enjoy it, which I know is the important thing, but I'm desperate for a promotion. I'd worked so hard to think of a new revenue stream and now Tracey's giving it to Helen because I'm too boring.

I almost take a glass of champagne from a passing wait-ress, figuring that if you can't beat them, join them, but then I remember that someone's got to be the responsible one. And I guess, as per usual, that'll be me.

'Um, excuse me,' I say, as I gingerly approach the bed, trying not to notice that only one of them has now got their head out of the cover, 'would you like me to call you a taxi so that you can go to a hotel? The dinner's about to end and there are going to be a lot of people heading this way – including your bosses, I imagine.'

A woman's head pops out from the other end of the bed and she gets out without saying a word. She pats down her dress and slides into the heels that she'd left by the side of the bed. She doesn't even acknowledge me as she pulls out a make-up com-pact and reapplies her lippy as she goes.

'Amy,' calls the guy as she totters off to the toilets. 'Her name was Amy, wasn't it? Or was it Emma?'

I hear a crash over on the other side of the room and I leave lover boy and head off to the zorbing. Helen's knocked over one of the chocolate trees. From the looks of it, no one was hurt and thankfully Tracey's nowhere to be seen.

I sigh as I cross the room. Boring Lydia to the rescue. Thank goodness this is my last day at work before the holidays, as at this rate I'm going to need a couple of weeks at home to get over it.

Chapter Two

Dear Scrooge, I know you hate Christmas and that you will have no decorations up, so here's one to melt that icy heart of yours during the most wonderful time of the year. Bet you never thought you'd see Santa giving Mrs Klaus a present like that, huh?

Parcel containing a naughty Christmas decoration;
Lydia to Danny, December 2010

It's Christmas Eve and I feel like I should be running round in a festive frenzy but instead I've cocooned myself in a blanket on the sofa and I've barely moved all day. The work Christmas dos I've been working at have turned me into the Grinch, and I've spent the day watching alternative Christmas movies: *Die Hard*, *Gremlins*, *When Harry Met Sally*.

I'm exhausted after last night's event, I didn't get into bed until well after 1 a.m. Tracey buggered off at 10 p.m. and I put Helen to sleep in Charlie's grandparents' bed, which meant that I managed the rest of the party by myself.

The irony wasn't lost on me that I'm trying to prove to Tracey that I'm capable of running events, and yet I spent the whole night trying to pretend I wasn't running that one as I didn't want to drop Helen in it. Poor old Helen, though. I don't know what got into her; it's so out of character. I had a text from her this morning apologising and saying she'd make it up to me. Hopefully she was just suffering from the holiday blues.

I hear a knock on the door to my flat and I groan before I heave myself off the sofa.

I roll my eyes as I answer the door. There, standing on the other side, is my best friend Lucy who's dressed in an elf costume.

'Why aren't you ready? We're already late for the party,' says Lucy, looking me up and down.

The party. I'd been trying to forget. Our friend Rob is having his annual Christmas Eve shindig. They were originally just for the five of us who used to live together: me, Lucy, Ross, Caroline and Rob. Then it evolved over time into this big party. This year will be strange for me as it's the first year that I won't be going with Ross as my boyfriend.

'Have you even showered yet?'

'I was going to get in the bath later.'

Lucy shakes her head at me and goes straight over to the tiny kitchenette in the corner of my lounge. She wastes no time pulling out glasses and mixing us drinks.

'Not the same and you know it. Nothing says let's get ready to go out more than a hot shower. Go on, off you trot.'

'Do we really have to go?' I say pleading. I'd hoped that Lucy might have wanted to snuggle up on the sofa with her fiancé tonight instead.

'Of course we do. It's tradition. As is the costume. I got you the same one as me.'

I stare at her hard. Horizontal red and white striped tights are no one's friend – except, of course, Lucy, who seems to be able to pull anything off.

'Just kidding. But you've got to at least put on something glittery so I don't feel too much like a dick.'

'Are you sure you don't want to see Ed tonight? I wouldn't mind, I've got this book that's getting to the good bit and it's a Christmas one so it'd be good to finish it before—'

'Bath, book, bed routines are for toddlers. Besides, Ed is coming to the party later on, after he sees his friends. Now, get your arse in that shower and let's get this on.'

'We could stay in and watch *Elf*.' It may go against the anti-Christmas films I've been viewing today but I know that it's one of Lucy's weaknesses.

I can tell she's tempted by the twitch in her eye.

'Nice try, Toots. Get in that shower and get those sparkles on. It's Christmas Eve, baby,' she says, shaking her head and causing the little bell on her hat to ring.

I give her a Grinch-like growl as I head towards the bathroom.

'What is this?' shouts Lucy. 'It's hideous.'

She's standing at the Christmas tree and she's found my latest decoration.

'Squeeze its body,' I say, already laughing. It's a skiing penguin and it's one of the tackiest things I've ever seen.

A tinny version of Wham's 'Last Christmas' rings out and Lucy screams with joy.

'Oh my God, where did you find it? I have to have one.'

'Danny sent it to me.'

She looks from the decoration to me, her eyebrow raising. 'Oh Danny boy,' she says in a husky Marilyn Monroe voice.

'He always sends me a decoration with his Christmas card.'

'Uh-huh,' she says, nodding. 'I don't get you two. Why don't you go and see him? You can't use the excuse that he's too far away now that he's back living in the UK. If I had some hot guy that wrote me letters and sent me presents, I'd have got off my arse to travel up to the Lake District to see him. Plus, you're single now.'

I've noticed that since I broke up with Ross five months ago she's been trying to matchmake me. Her criteria are very straightforward: male, under fifty, single, pulse.

I kick the floor with my slippers. If only it were that easy. I've always had a thing for Danny, but the trouble is, he doesn't feel the same way. I make do with the letter writing and the occasional meet up, although, to be honest, I try not to see him very often as it always reminds me of what I can't have.

'He's got some girlfriend. Diane or Diana or something.'

I know her name's Diana. I've seen her tagged in Facebook photos. Diana something posh sounding.

'I wouldn't like that,' she says, pressing the penguin again. 'If my Ed was sending letters and parcels to some woman.'

'It's not like that. We've just always done it. We're friends – nothing more.'

She gives me the look she always gives me when we talk about this, the one that suggests that I'm deluding myself. But it's true. I heard it with my own ears, years back when I went to London not long after he'd come back from travelling, *she's just a friend and that's all she'll ever be.*

'I just don't know why you don't at least try to be together. You always talk about that kiss being magical.'

'It was, but I think it was just in the moment. You know, weddings do that to people, don't they?' I say sighing at the memory. 'I guess we both just enjoy having a pen pal.'

Lucy rolls her eyes at me and squeezes the penguin again.

'It's probably a good job; imagine how tacky your house would be if you lived together.'

I smile; she's got a point.

'Go, on. Get your Christmas things on, we've got a party to get to!'

There's a collective shriek as Mariah Carey's 'All I Want for Christmas' blasts out of the sound bar and there's a rush to the make-do dance floor in the lounge.

I've been sandwiched between Rob and Gavin on the sofa for the last twenty minutes, but I'm forced up as they propel themselves off the sofa. I let out a small groan. Bloody work. I used to love all the Christmas songs, but my job has ruined them for me. Hearing them on a loop as I watch a fresh bunch of sparkly, drunk people at Christmas dos night after night for six weeks has ruined any magic the season used to hold. I feel very bah humbug as I leave the lounge and head towards the kitchen.

'Lydia!' shrieks a woman as I walk down the hallway.

It takes me a moment for my eyes to adjust to all the sequins on her top which are shining under the bright hallway lights.

'Roni,' I say, going up and giving her a hug. 'I didn't realise you'd be here.'

Roni and I used to work together before she left for a job at a hotel. She still lives nearby and we bump into each other occasionally. It's always so lovely to see her and we always vow we're going to meet up and never do.

'I came with my friend Rebecca, she works with Rob. And *you're* here,' she says looking over her shoulder.

'Rob was one of my old housemates.'

She nods and starts to steer me quite forcefully towards the lounge, but I can't go back there; not to Mariah. I might strangle someone with the tinsel.

'I was trying to stay in for the night, but my friend Lucy dragged me along. I was just heading to the kitchen for a drink,' I say, turning Roni back towards the kitchen instead.

'Here, have mine,' she says, shoving a half-drunk glass of Prosecco into my hand.

As much as a glass might be nice right now, I'd prefer one without the perfect red lipstick mark on the side.

'Um, that's really sweet of you, but I think I'll go and find a beer,' I say handing it back to her.

'I'll get you one,' she says, reaching her arms out so that her fingertips brush the walls, blocking my path.

'What's going on? Why won't you let me in the kitchen?' I ask, peering over her shoulder and trying to see what's going on in there.

'Nothing's going on. It's just you look tired. You should sit down in the lounge and I'll bring you a beer,' she says.

'OK,' I say, pretending to go.

She sighs with relief and heads towards the kitchen and I see my chance. I turn and push past her to make it there before her. I fling the door open and catch a glimpse of who's inside before Roni rugby tackles me to the ground. We land in a heap in the hallway and impressively she's managed to keep her drink upright and not spilt a drop.

'Sorry,' says Roni, 'are you OK?'

'I think so,' I say, pushing myself up to a sitting position. I rub my throbbing elbows.

'You can't go in there, Lydia. You wouldn't want to see.'

There's a look of panic in her eyes and she seems genuinely upset for me.

'What, you're worried about me seeing Ross kissing that girl?'

'Oh God, you saw? I'm so sorry. It's bad enough that he's cheating on you, but he's being so brazen about it all. I mean he's not even hiding it. Do you want me to knock him out? I've been learning jiu-jitsu.'

'It's fine. Ross and I broke up. Five months ago now.' Roni looks visibly shocked. 'It was mutual and we're still good friends.'

Perhaps good friends is over-egging it, but we're still friends at least.

'I can't believe it. You and Ross? You've been together forever.'

'It wasn't that long. Five years . . .'

'That's practically a life time. I just assumed that you'd get married. You seemed so perfect,' she says echoing the sentiments of my friends and family when we broke up. It doesn't help that we are part of the same close-knit group of friends. Although we're not the fivesome we once were – we've grown apart as people have become loved up, sprogged up and generally grown up – but the rest of the group were still more upset about our split than we were. Everyone feared it would be the end of the group, but so far so good. Ross's new girlfriend has even been welcomed into the fold with open arms, or at least with gentle handshakes.

'Both of us realised that we were more friends than anything else,' I say shrugging. It never gets any easier having this conversation. I've stopped saying that we broke up because it didn't feel right, as that sounded so vague. But there was something missing and neither of us could ever work out what.

'So brave. You're single now, then?'

'Uh-huh, so if you know of any eligible bachelors,' I joke. Blind dates are definitely not my thing.

'I'll keep it in mind. Such a fun time of year to be single though, isn't it? All these parties. All the mistletoe.'

'God love mistletoe,' I say, looking nervously up at the ceiling and remembering to take it into account when navigating the party. Rob and Gavin are well known for putting it in strategic places.

Roni laughs a little and swigs her Prosecco, and I'm almost blinded again, not by her sparkling top this time, but by the biggest, blingiest diamond ring I've ever seen.

'Bloody hell. Is that what I think it is?'

Her whole face lights up.

'Who are you marrying? A Saudi prince? I've never seen a diamond like that,' I say, grabbing hold of her hand.

'His name's Chris and he's just dreamy. We met at the sailing club.'

'Sailing?' I ask. I can't remember her being the outdoorsy type.

'Yeah, I took some lessons at the Outdoor centre, then I joined the club and I met Chris.'

'And he has his own yacht,' I say laughing along.

Her face cheeks go a little pink and I get the impression that she's embarrassed.

'And he has his own yacht?' I say, my eyebrows lodging themselves in my hairline.

'Well, not a yacht. It's not that much bigger than a dinghy.'

'Is it inflatable?' I say, knowing that her little fidget means she's uncomfortable.

'No.'

'Does it have a below-deck area?'

'Yes, but only for a tiny bed. Look, you're making me blush,' she says, fanning her cheeks.

'That's awesome. Not the boat, although I'm sure that's awesome too, I mean the fact that you've met someone and you're getting married.'

I've missed Roni. We used to have such a laugh working together. As I remember it, she was always very savvy about her finances and wouldn't be one to flash the cash, so it's ironic now that she seems to have found herself a wealthy husband.

'I know. I'm really happy. Not just because of Chris; I'm happy in myself too, you know?'

I nod, but I don't really know. She's naturally glowing and you can hear the enthusiasm in her voice when she talks; I can't remember the last time I was like that. I haven't seen my sparkle in a long time.

'Did you know that I've started my own business?'

'No, I didn't.'

'Yeah, I decided to do my own thing. Domestic party planning. Golden wedding anniversaries, children's birthday parties, the odd wedding. It's hard work and I pretty much only just break even, but I don't care as it's all mine. I have a tiny little office in Chichester. It's smaller than a shoebox, but I love it.'

'That's great. Exciting times,' I say, genuinely feeling happy for her.

'I know. So, are you still at Blank Canvas?'

'Yes, for my sins,' I say, trying to pretend that she's looking at me with something other than pity. Everyone else's lives are moving on and mine's staying exactly the same.

'How long have you been there now?'

'Um, seven years, I think.'

'Wow. Is Rebecca still there?'

'No, she works for a marketing agency in North End now. Although she's on maternity leave at the moment. She had a little baby boy a couple of months ago. Harry.'

'Ah, bless her. I can't imagine her with a baby, she was always so wild.'

'Yes, she was,' I say, thinking of the countless times she'd go missing during events and I'd find her in a shots drinking competition with the clients. Helen's behaviour yesterday was tame in comparison.

'Do you remember the time that we caught her in that Arctic display?'

'Oh my God, I'd forgotten that,' I say, erupting into a fit of giggles.

'How could you forget that look as she walked out of the tent with that guy?'

We'd held a party for a defence contractor where they'd built different operational climates and we'd found Rebecca in a display about Arctic warfare training getting acquainted with a guest in one of the tents.

'That was nothing. Were you still there when she was teaching that celebrity guest speaker how to give body shots?'

Roni's eyes light up. 'No, but that does not surprise me. How was she never fired?'

'The clients loved her and the bars always took a fortune. Tracey, our new boss, wouldn't stand for it though. The last I heard of Rebecca she'd become teetotal.'

'No!' says Roni.

'Uh-huh, true story.'

'So did you take over her job?'

'No,' I say, shaking my head. 'Helen's doing the parties now. I'm still an events coordinator.'

'You were always good at it,' she says.

I inwardly sigh. I thought Lucy promised me this party was going to cheer me up, but all it's doing is depressing me by making me realise how much of a rut my life is in.

'I miss the big place sometimes. I miss working with you all now that I'm on my own. But I do love being the boss. Oh, there's Sandy. We really must go for that drink, Lydia,' she says as she spots someone she knows coming out of the lounge. I nod and excuse myself to get that beer.

I walk into the kitchen and I'm relieved to see that Ross is no longer snogging the face off Wonder Girl, as I affectionately call his new girlfriend. He's standing all alone by the booze, lost in thought.

'Penny for them,' I say as I walk up and get a beer out of an ice bucket.

'Hey you, merry Christmas,' he says as we shift uncomfortably on the spot, not knowing if we're supposed to kiss hello or not, but the moment passes and we don't.

'Merry Christmas to you, too. Having a good time?'

He nods. 'Not the same as it used to be, though, is it?' he almost whispers.

'No. But then again we're all different now. I mean, Caroline's in the lounge dancing with a baby in a sling for starters.'

'I know. I miss the old gang sometimes,' he says surprising me. 'Remember what it was like at the beginning when we all lived together?'

I cast my mind back to that shared house we had. It was a great time. We were in our mid-twenties and went out most nights and crawled into work the next day with hangovers. None of us had real work or home responsibilities. I miss those days.

'We had some good laughs,' I say, realising that the danger lights are flashing. I don't really want to spend the night travelling down memory lane with my ex. 'What are you up to tomorrow?'

'I'm going to my parents' house.'

'Oh,' I say with a low whistle. Ross's parents are formal, stuffy, joy killers.

'I know, but I guess I've had a good run over the last few years with your family. I'm escaping to Jules's parents' on Boxing Day.'

'That's good,' I say, sipping more beer.

'And you? Going to Kerry's?'

'Well, now that I only have to walk upstairs, it seems rude not to,' I say, jokingly, but really it's not like I've got any other offers.

'I'll miss Jim's roasties,' says Ross. 'And the inevitable trivial pursuit argument.'

Jim and Ross were always ultra-competitive and I can't help but smile at the memory of the two of them squaring off over their pie pieces. The year that Kerry won after a fluke guess at a sports question led to the boys sulking until New Year.

I hadn't thought what it was actually going to be like without him there, and I feel my heart sink.

'You do realise where you're standing, don't you,' says a girl I don't recognise, pointing up to the ceiling and laughing.

We both look up slowly and I cringe as I see mistletoe hanging right above us.

'You can't not kiss,' says the woman, as if we don't know the custom. She's standing watching us with her hands on her hips.

I turn to tell her to hold her horses just as Ross leans over for a kiss, and whilst I think he was aiming for a cheek, he kisses me smack on the lips. It catches us both by surprise and his lips linger on mine for longer than is necessary and I don't do anything about it.

The woman hollers 'get a room' and we immediately jump back, embarrassed.

My cheeks feel a little flushed.

'I guess we should have been more careful where we stood,' says Ross, taking a step back. 'Typical Rob and Gavin to put mistletoe where the booze is.'

'Sneaky,' I say. 'Very sneaky.'

I can feel my lips still tingling from the kiss. I don't have time to dwell on it as his new girlfriend Jules walks up and slips her arms around him.

'Lydia,' she says waving, despite the fact that I'm inches away from her. 'I didn't realise you were here.'

She leans over and gives me a hug and I try to plant a smile on my face.

'Jules,' I say. 'Having a good time?'

'Oh, the best. I adore Christmas parties. Don't you just adore Christmas parties? I mean, how can you not? All the music, and the glitter. I love glitter. Don't you love glitter?'

I can't fail to notice that she's wrapping her arms around Ross so tightly that she looks as if she's about to suffocate him.

'I heart glitter,' I say, and she beams at me as if I'm her soulmate.

I go to drink my beer and realise it's empty, so I grab another, relieved that it's a twist lid and I can start drinking quickly.

'So, are you all ready for Christmas? All your presents arrived on time? All wrapped up?'

'Yes, yes, and yes,' I say nodding. 'It'll be a quiet one. I'm just going to my sister's.'

I don't add that it'll be odd as it'll be the first time in four years that Ross hasn't been there too. I get the impression that the only reason she copes with Ross being friends with his ex is that we try not to talk about the fact that we were ever together. If we do, her eyes go all glossy and she gets even more squeaky.

'Lovely. That's really nice. Spending it with family. I think that's how it should be. Of course, I'm spending it with my family too. And Ross is going to come over on Boxing Day and then we're going to do it all over again. It's like two Christmas Days for the price of one. Isn't that great?'

'Well, it is until you get on the scales in the New Year,' I say, completely dead pan.

Jules looks down at her almost invisible belly in horror, as if she hadn't thought about that. She and Ross met at the gym and they share a passion for exercise. It makes me shudder even thinking about it.

'I'm kidding,' I say. 'We all know calories don't count at Christmas.'

Jules smiles again and laughs a little.

'You're so funny, Lydia,' she says, as if she's not actually sure what the joke was. 'I'm just so excited that Ross and I get to spend this wonderful holiday together. It'll be our first one, obviously. I'm so excited. Are you excited, Ross? It's just so exciting.'

Ross barely gets a chance to answer before she's off on a tangent again.

'I'm going to go and do some dancing. I hear there's dancing. I'm going to sneak Mariah Carey on, someone said that it's been on already but I don't think people will mind, will they? Everyone loves Mariah.'

'Of course they do. Especially Ross. You love "All I Want for Christmas", don't you?'

He gives me a look that when we were together would have resulted in me getting tickled in punishment. Before we started doing Christmas parties at work I used to play that song on a loop for the whole month of December. I know that he hates it as much as I do now.

Jules looks at him in a hopeful way.

'Do you want to come and dance?' she says, slipping his arm off her and taking his hand in hers. 'I know you don't really like to dance. But it's Christmas, so you have to get merry, don't you? Merry Christmas and all that. It's like the law.'

He shoots me a look-what-you-started face.

'Of course,' he says through gritted teeth. 'Unless . . . I don't want to leave Lydia on her own.'

'Lydia is fine without you. She doesn't need you,' she says, fixing her eyes on mine as if she's trying to subliminally tell me something. 'Besides, here's Lucy,' she says, grabbing her as she walks into the kitchen and pulling her over. 'I'm sure that Lucy and Lydia have lots to talk about. They always seem to have lots to talk about. Don't you have lots to talk about?'

'OK, then,' says Ross, as he lets himself be dragged away.

'What was all that about?' asks Lucy, grabbing a bottle of Prosecco out of the fridge as she passes.

'They had to go and dance. Everyone loves dancing. Do you love dancing? Dancing is super fun,' I say quickly, with a deranged look on my face as I do my best Jules impression.

Lucy passes me an empty flute and pops open the bottle.

'You're well within your rights to hate her, I can too, if you like. I don't think it would be difficult.'

'What are we talking about?' says Caroline as she fans herself with her hand, whilst swaying her sleeping baby in a sling on her chest.

'How Lydia hates Jules.'

'I don't hate her. I just wish she was a little less perky – in all senses of the word.'

I look down at my boobs, which seem to be a lot further away than the last time I looked. 'But I'm happy that Ross is happy.'

'Uh-huh,' they both say, smugly looking at each other.

'I am.'

'Then why don't you look it?' says Lucy.

Why can best friends read you like a sodding book?

'I don't know. I don't want him,' I say, deliberately ignoring that moment under the mistletoe and the confusion that it created in the moments after. 'I want him to be with someone, but it's just that there's something about her.'

'Don't worry about it, you're going to find Wonder Boy, soon.'

'Could you imagine a male version of her?' says Caroline.

I shudder at the thought, but then I start to think of just having a boyfriend. Would finding another one make me happy?

'I wonder if there are going to be any single guys at this thing on New Year's,' says Lucy.

I groan. I'd almost forgotten about New Year's Eve. I stopped looking forward to them a few years ago when going out started to feel like forced fun. But Lucy loves New Year's Eve almost as much as she loves Christmas Eve, and this year she's dragging me along to some club night her work colleague is DJing at.

'Come on, you need cheering up,' says Caroline grabbing my hand.

'Where are we going?' I ask, as she leads me down the hallway, topping up my glass as we go. 'I'm not going in there with all the dancing and Christmas music and—'

'And all the fun? Come on, you'll love it. Besides, I saw Wonder Girl dancing with Ross a minute ago and boy are you in for a treat.'

We just about wedge ourselves into the lounge. Everyone now seems to be on their feet swaying to the Pogues' 'Fairytale of New York'. All except Jules, who is dancing to a beat all of her very own. I'm almost worried she's going to break out into Big Fish, Little Fish, Cardboard Box at any second. Ross is caught in the middle, his arms around one person who wants to sway him and at the same time being tugged by Jules, who wants him to join her nineties rave.

Caroline was right. I did need to see this.

Roni drags me into the dancing and I slowly look around at everyone. Ed's arrived and his arms are wrapped tightly around Lucy. Rob and Gavin are gazing into each other's eyes. Ross is awkwardly half raving, half swaying. Caroline and baby Ethan are bobbing along. Everyone's life is changing and mine's staying exactly the same. If ever I needed an incentive to make a change this is it; this time next year I'm going to be standing here a completely new woman.

Chapter Three

I had a good, but busy, trip back to the UK. Stu's wedding went without a hitch, can't believe he's actually found someone who'd marry him. It was a shame that you couldn't make it – hope you had a good holiday. I bought this at the airport and read it on the flight. It reminded me of us – although hopefully I'm not such a wanker and you're not so whiny. And maybe we'll have a different ending . . .

Parcel containing *One Day* by David Nicholls;

Danny to Lydia, June 2011

I wake up to the sound of screaming and immediately sit bolt upright, trying to work out where the hell I am. Instantly, I fear that I'm in a war zone before my brain kicks in and makes me realise that the closest I've been to a war zone was when Ross dragged me to see *Dunkirk* – I say dragged me, but the fact that Harry Styles was in it meant I went voluntarily.

My head is killing me. I drank far too much last night at Rob and Gavin's party. In between the throbbing of the hangover from hell I piece together the vital facts. I'm asleep in my own bed – alone (phew!) – so it obviously didn't go too badly wrong.

There's another scream and I realise it's from my seven-year-old niece who has, no doubt, been up for hours opening presents, as it's Christmas morning. The light streaming in through the window means it's probably time to get out of bed.

At least I don't have to go to my mum's like I usually do. We've always had breakfast there before heading over to my sister's, but now that I'm living in Kerry's basement, Mum's coming to me. Kerry, of course, suggested we go upstairs early, but we declined – the official line is that we don't want to intrude on her family Christmas. But in truth we didn't want to cope with the present unwrapping frenzy that seems to turn my lovely little niece into a Tasmanian devil. I love Olivia, but does anyone *actually* love their niece on Christmas Day? All that chocolate. All those flashing, noisy toys. This way's much better. By the time we go upstairs at lunchtime she'll have been up for six or seven hours and will be starting to wear herself out. And in the meantime, Mum and I will have had a civilised bucks fizz with some Danish pastries.

I close my eyes. My hangover better disappear ASAP as the only thing worse than Olivia in Christmas mode is dealing with Olivia in Christmas mode with a hangover. I can already hear her banging around on the floorboards. I really hope I bolted the door at the top of the stairs. I'd better check on the way to the shower.

By the time I've finished in the bathroom I'm feeling slightly more human, but as I prod my skin in the mirror, I realise that I don't look it. I do my best to highlight and conceal with my make-up. I still don't look great, but it's the best it's going to get.

I scan the chaos in the lounge that I caused last night when I got in. Half-drunk glass of wine. An empty glass of what I hope was water. One high-heeled boot. Empty pizza box. Diet starts January, right?

I open the lounge window and start to tidy quickly. I have to keep stopping and sitting down to cope with the hangover. Luckily, with my flat being a studio, the bed and the sofa are never more than a few steps away.

There's a knock at the door and I kick the rest of my clothes under my bed.

'Darling,' says Mum as I let her in. Theatrically, she pulls me into a big hug, as if she hasn't seen me in years rather than the five days that it's been. 'Merry Christmas.'

My mum lives in Bedhampton, not far from Portsmouth, meaning that she drops in on us frequently.

'Merry Christmas, Mum,' I say, hugging her back.

I do a double take as I look at her. I still expect her to look like she used to. For as long as I can remember she'd always had bright blonde hair that she wore up in a style almost like a beehive – some days she could have stood in for Patsy in *Absolutely Fabulous* – but last year she had it cropped short and dyed brown. It suits her much better, but I do sometimes miss 'The Patsy', as we used to call it.

She waltzes straight into the lounge, plonking a bottle of Champagne down on the table, along with a box of Danish pastries.

'I forgot the orange juice. Have you got any?'

'Um,' I say, peering into my little fridge. 'I do, but I have no idea how long it's been open for. I'm fine with just fizz.'

'Me too,' says my mum, popping the bottle as I hunt around for some flutes.

There's a big crash above our heads and we both look up at the ceiling.

'How long do you think she's been up for?' asks Mum.

'The screams started half an hour ago, but I think that's because all the sugar's started to kick in.'

She shudders. 'I feel a little mean hiding down here. We'll have to go round to the main entrance to go in.'

'Yes, definitely. I'm surprised her present radar hasn't sensed that we're down here and brought her hunting for us.'

Mum laughs and looks around. 'Rough night last night?'

'Thanks. Does it show?' I say, sitting down on the sofa and diving straight in for some sort of apricot custard pastry.

'I nearly got knocked out by the fumes coming off you. Thank God you don't have to drive anywhere for lunch as you must still be over the limit.'

I eat my Danish more quickly.

'Yes, living in my sister's basement ticks so many boxes. I don't know why more people don't do it.'

Mum rubs my arm. 'I'm glad you had a fun night. After that disappointment at work.'

I'd told her on the phone yesterday about Tracey giving Helen the proms project.

'I'll just have to think of something else.'

'Good for you, and quite right too,' she says, as she swipes a pastry. I'm pretty sure that it's not her first as there seem to be a couple missing from the box already.

'So, did you have a good night, then?'

'Yes. Rob's parties are always fun. And Caroline popped in for a tiny bit too. She brought baby Ethan with her asleep in his sling.

'How fabulous. When you two were little, I always dragged you around with me to parties.'

I still have memories of that. Falling asleep on unfamiliar cushions and then being taken to the car when I was groggy with sleep before being transferred back into my bed when we got home.

'Speaking of those parties,' she says, a twinkle in her eye as if she's back there enjoying them, 'I've saved you the round-robin letters from my friends. I know you like to read them.'

She pulls a pile of printed letters out of her bag.

'Ooh, thank you,' I say reaching up and taking the pile from her as I finish the last mouthful of pastry. I wipe the residue off on my jeans before I pick up the first letter. It's from our old neighbour Marjorie. I scan read it, picking out the highlights. 'Ooh look, Charlotte's been scrapbooking and baking.' Charlotte's around my age, and my friend on Facebook, and, judging by the photos she posts of her nights out, I think scrapbooking's the last thing she's been doing – unless scrapbooking has another meaning on Urban Dictionary. I skip over the rest of Marjorie's letter as it's all bragging.

Here's one from my dad's cousin, Sandra. Her Henry's going to run the country one day, so it's always interesting to see what he's up to. 'Henry's decided to make an unexpected change in career path and is now working in finance. What's that about?' I ask, reading the letter out.

'He was defeated at the council by-election and now he's working in a bank.'

I laugh. Why do people always feel the need to embellish their lives in letters? Not that I'm any different. Danny thinks I live in my own flat and that I'm regularly hobnobbing with celebs at the glamorous parties I manage.

I know who the last letter must be from before I even open it. The different-coloured printer ink gives it away – only Hazel Whittaker does that.

I unfold it, wondering what Danny's mum has to say. I'm always apprehensive, even though I know that if there was any big news, he'd have told me about it in his letters.

I find it funny that, after all these years and after their weekly FaceTiming sessions, they still bother to send each other these round-robins, but I enjoy reading them.

Another year gone! Can you believe it! I may be older in number but I am, of course, not older in spirit! Let's hope that if we haven't seen you this year, we'll see you in the new year! So, this year we celebrated our tenth year in the Lakes. We couldn't be happier here in Hawkshead. Well, we could, if our friends and family from down South upped and moved here too, but you know what I mean! Brian is still working and in good health. As am I, and after a trip to the tarot card readers recently, where they told me that I had a gift for healing, I've signed up to do a course to become a reiki practitioner! Feel free to come up and be a guinea pig and have your chakras and your aura realigned.

I start to giggle – that's so Hazel.

'Reiki practitioner,' says my mum, rolling her eyes theatrically, knowing instantly what I'm laughing at. 'That is *so* Hazel.'

I nod and continue reading.

Stuart and Isabelle continue to live in Manchester with their two little ones. Lily (now 5!) and Harry (now 3!). Stuart's job is no longer under threat and he hopes there might be a promotion on the horizon (fingers, toes and everything crossed for that). Isabelle is also hoping to increase her hours back at work now that Harry is in preschool. Daniel is still in Ambleside, just down the road from us – a fact that never ceases to amaze me since he spent most of his adult life trying to live as far away as possible from us. We're still no closer to marrying him off, though. I'd almost visited the hat shop in Kendal when he started dating Diana earlier on in the year – but unfortunately they broke up in the spring. But, happier news for him, his business venture continues to do well.

Our house in Spain is still well used by all the family and it seems it was a shrewd move on Stuart and Isa's part buying in the same complex. It means we can all go out as a family together and enjoy it – meaning that Brian and I are roped into being babysitters whilst Stuart and Isa go out. Not that we're complaining – the little cherubs.

I stop reading as Hazel starts going into spiritual blessings for all her friends and family for the new year and instead I think about the fact that Danny is single. And that he has been for most of the year – at the same time as me. It's the first time since Kerry's wedding that we've both been single and living in the same country. Not that it changes anything. Danny only sees me as a friend. Proved by the fact that he's known that I've been single for months, since Facebook brutally advertised mine and Ross's demise.

So much for our if we're not married by thirty pact. He knew I broke up with Ross around my 30th birthday. Perhaps that's why he's never mentioned he's single and he's barely reacted to my break-up with Ross. Perhaps that's why I haven't seen him this year, he might be scared in case I'm going to take him up on it.

'Do you want some more champagne whilst it's still bubbly?'

'Absolutely. Champagne is just what I want,' I say, planting a fake smile on my face. I need something to help me to get over the shock. I guess I'd always hoped in my heart of hearts that Danny would change his mind about us only being friends and that if we were both single at the same time it might nudge him in the right direction.

'Everything OK, love? Are you sure Champagne's what you want? You look all peaky. Is the hangover getting worse?'

'No, it's fine. I think that, um, I just need a drink,' I say, as I hold out my hand, trying to keep it steady.

My mum doesn't know that Danny and I kissed. She knows we keep in contact, but she thinks it's just platonic. Which it is. Only I wish it wasn't. She doesn't realise that me finding out he's single and hasn't wanted me when I am too is just the blow I didn't need on top of everything else at the moment. Talk about #LivingMyAbsoluteWorstLife.

Mum fills up my glass and I sip the Champagne.

'How about I make you something more substantial than pastries? You've gone ever so pale,' she says, opening my fridge and picking out a packet of bacon. 'Bacon sarnie? That might put some colour in your cheeks. You know that Jim'll be faffing in the kitchen and we won't eat lunch until late.'

I nod. I try and give myself a pep talk as I'm being ridiculous. The silly letters we write each other are just that. They're not symbols of unrequited love, they're just a habit that we got into when we were young and which we've never grown out of.

I sip my drink and try to stop thinking about what a muddle my life is in. Next year I will sort out my living situation, I will find a new job and I *will* find my sparkle again.

'Toasted or untoasted bread?' asks my mum as the smell of bacon wafts over to me.

'Toasted please.'

I get up from the sofa and stand with my back leaning on the worktop facing my mum as she cooks.

She leans over and kisses the top of my head, greasy spatula in her hand. 'This next year is going to be your year, Lydia,' she says. 'I can feel it in my waters.'

I love my mum. She seems to always sense exactly what I need to hear. I try and blink back the tears and she either doesn't see or she pretends not to as she goes back to her bacon.

'Have you heard from your dad this morning?' she asks.

I give a spluttery laugh.

'I got a text from him last night to say Merry Christmas. I think the time difference is confusing him.'

'Yes, he never did well with foreign travel. Imagine, though, Frances has got him to the Caribbean.'

'And on a cruise too.'

'I know, I couldn't even get him to take me on the boats at Canoe Lake,' she says laughing.

I laugh too. My dad became a different man the day he married Frances. My mum and dad divorced when I was ten and it wasn't really a big deal. He wasn't very hands on – he worked a lot and went to the pub most evenings, so we didn't really notice a lot of difference when he left. Other than that we got two of everything: Two big birthday presents, two Christmas dinners, two trips to Thorpe Park in the summer. I still see him occasionally, but we always struggle knowing what to say to each other as we've barely got anything in common.

'So, when's he back?' asks Mum as she butters my toast.

'I'm not sure. New Year? I think they're going to New York on the way home.'

She shakes her head. 'Who'd have thought it.'

'I know.'

Mum hands me a freshly made toasted bacon sandwich and we go back over and sit on the sofa. She refills my drink instinctively.

'Are you seeing Keith tomorrow?' I ask.

Keith is my mum's fancy man. We call him that as she hates the word boyfriend – *Oh, Lydia, that makes me feel like a hormonal teenager*. She's been dating him for ten years or so now. We don't often see him as they tend to keep their relationship quite private. He's got daughters and grandkids that keep him busy.

'On the twenty-seventh. He's going to his eldest daughter's tomorrow.'

'And where's he today?'

'At his youngest's.'

'Don't you ever mind not being together at Christmas?'

'Not really. Not at our age. We've realised there are so many other important people in our lives. Like I have you girls and he's got his. We have the rest of the year to be together. It might not be like this forever. You'll have your own family one day and we'll all be split up.'

I splutter again.

'You will, Lydia. It's in my waters, remember,' she says, winking. The only thing in her waters right now is bubbles, given how much fizz she's downed.

'Careful, you're starting to sound like Hazel.'

'A reiki healer. That woman.'

'Is she coming down anytime soon?'

'Yes, next month, I think.'

I squeeze her hand. I'm not the only one to miss a Whittaker.

'Do you want another glass of bubbles before we go up?' I ask Mum.

She looks at her watch. 'We've got another half an hour. Go on, then, fill me up. But you'll have to explain to Kerry why I'm squiffy.'

I giggle. My mum's the only person I know who uses that word.

'I'll take full responsibility. So what did you get Olivia for Christmas?'

'Oh, did I not tell you the saga I've been through to get her a glittery unicorn? I ended up going to Asda at seven a.m. last Tuesday as I'd heard a rumour that they were having a delivery.'

'And were they?'

'No, but I did discover the black forest hot chocolate in the Costa next door and then I managed to find one in the Argos in Chichester.'

'Phew,' I say, knowing the pressure that we all feel to deliver our niece the right present.

'But, I get the feeling that she's not going to be the only one who's going to like her present this year,' she says, as she gives me an over-exaggerated wink.

'Ooh, you can't say that. That's such a tease.'

We don't open our presents until after lunch and that's ages away.

She shrugs her shoulders. 'Come on, get this drink down you, and that butty.'

I suddenly feel a little ripple of excitement. My mum usually buys me a voucher for a fancy spa trip, so the fact that she might have deviated from her usual has got me excited. Finally, I have something to look forward to – even if it is only until this afternoon.

Chapter Four

Happy Christmas! I've officially had the weirdest one ever. Apparently, nothing says Merry Christmas in Tokyo like a bucket of KFC chicken followed by an iced mini cake. I had to order such a delicacy two weeks ago. I am in absolutely no way jealous of the fact that you're about to tuck into turkey with actual cutlery. Also, I hope the decoration found its way through customs . . .

Email; Danny to Lydia, 25 December 2011

'Right then, are we ready for this?' asks my mum, touching her hair as we walk up the outside stairs at the front of Kerry and Jim's house. The Curtain twitches at Kerry's bay window and I see Olivia's little face light up when she sees us.

'Let's do it,' I say, preparing myself for the hysteria we're about to cause.

I love the main part of Kerry and Jim's house. It's so warm and friendly and it instantly feels like home to me.

'Grandma,' shrieks Olivia, as she launches herself on Mum as the door opens. 'Auntie Lydia. Come and see what presents I've got.'

I barely get to wave hello to Kerry, who's holding a large glass of wine in her hand, as I'm dragged down the wooden corridor into the lounge.

Holy moly. It's as if the whole world's been playing pass the parcel. I kick through the sea of paper to get to the sofa.

'Look at this, and this, and this,' she shrieks in too much of a frenzy to actually show me anything. 'Have you got me a present, have you? Have you? HAVE YOU?' she shouts.

I practically throw my present at her as if she's a rabid dog about to turn on me any second. She opens it and there's a pause. It's as if she's an X Factor judge about to deliver her verdict on an act. She's got a Simon Cowell look on her face and I'm cowering, fearing bad news, when she suddenly leaps up into an excited jump.

'Wow, Auntie Lydia, this is the best present EVER,' she screams. 'Thank you so much.'

I sigh with relief. I look over at my mum who's still got a look of fear on her face.

With Olivia distracted, I sneak out of the lounge and into the kitchen and I'm almost bowled over by how good it smells. I wave at Jim, but I daren't get close enough to give him a kiss hello as he's got a turkey baster in one hand, a large fork in the other and a look of super concentration on his face normally reserved for when he's playing Jenga.

Kerry, on the other hand, is looking super relaxed, setting the table with one hand whilst she sips a large glass of wine with the other.

'I don't mean to brag, but your daughter just told me that I bought her the best present ever,' I say, as I sit down at the table.

Kerry smiles. 'She says that about every present she opens.'

'Oh,' I say, the smile falling from my face. 'Any chance I could get one of those wines?'

'Sure, hair of the dog?'

'That obvious?'

'Uh-huh. The question is, is it from last night or what you and Mum have been drinking this morning?'

'Both.'

She puts down the last of her cutlery and walks over to a large bottle on the side and pours me a glass.

'This smells so good,' I say sniffing the air like a dog with a scent. 'It looks amazing too, Kez.'

'Thanks, I have been slaving over a hot stove all day, you know,' she says, waving her hand towards the cooker at the end of the kitchen.

'Bollocks you have. I cooked it and you bloody know it,' says Jim, walking over and whacking her on the arm with the tea towel that's draped over his shoulder.

Kerry giggles into her wine glass as she takes a sip.

Kerry and Jim have been together for almost twenty years now and I love being around them. They have all this playful banter and these affectionate jabs. Plus, Jim is an amazing cook and his roasts are legendary – his Christmas Day ones are just the best.

'Merry Christmas, Lydia,' he says leaning over and kissing me on the cheek.

'Merry Christmas, Jimbo.'

Kerry sits down at the table and the two of us sip our wine and enjoy a rare moment of quiet on Christmas Day.

It doesn't last for long as Olivia bounds into the kitchen pushing a doll's pram full of shiny plastic toys.

'Look what Grandma got me,' she shrieks. She thrusts it proudly at me and I take it, looking at it from all angles. Man that thing is ugly.

'Oh, wow, that's um . . . brilliant,' I say, nodding.

'I know. It's the best present EVER,' she shrieks. 'Is Uncle Ross coming later?'

Kerry almost spits out her wine and flashes me an apologetic look.

'Olivia, I told you not to mention him,' she says not so subtly.

'It's OK. I keep telling you, I'm fine,' I say to her and Jim as they both have concerned looks on their faces. 'No, sweetie. Ross isn't coming today.'

'He came last Christmas, and the Christmas before, and I can't remember the Christmas before that.'

I laugh. 'Yes, he did. But he was my boyfriend then and now he's not. So unfortunately he won't be coming today.'

I wonder why she's so bothered. We used to buy her a joint present so it's not as if she's missed out with his absence.

'Good. That's what Mummy said, but she's wrong about so many things that I thought I'd better check.'

'Olivia,' says Kerry, sternly. 'I am not wrong about a lot of things. That's Daddy you're thinking of.'

'Hey, she clearly said "Mummy",' says Jim, holding out his hand for a high five, which his almost seven-year-old daughter returns with gusto.

'To be honest, I reckon both of them are often wrong,' I say, weighing into the debate, 'but why are you pleased that Ross isn't coming?'

'I didn't like him,' she says, sitting down at the table. 'Are we eating, yet? I'm hungry.'

'In a minute,' says Jim, as he practically runs over to the other side of the kitchen to get the potatoes out of the oven – I'm guessing to avoid this conversation.

'Oh, um, that's good to know. Did you know she didn't like him?' I ask, glaring at Kerry. 'Olivia, why didn't you like him, sweetie?'

'He never listened to all my Sylvanian Families' names. He always drank that green stuff that looked like sick. And he made me eat that vegetable at your house – caw-caw.'

'Courgette,' says Kerry helpfully.

'Caw – jett,' says Olivia with distaste. 'It was super gross.'

I can't help but smile at her logic.

'I didn't used to like his courgettes either,' I say, with a conspiratorial wink.

'You've got to love a guy's courgette,' says Jim as he returns with a bowl of hot potatoes for the table.

Kerry takes the tea towel off his arm and whips him.

'You guys liked him though, didn't you?'

'Where's Mum? Shall I get her to sit up at the table?' says Kerry, suddenly standing up.

'Yes, I'll just make the gravy,' says Jim, walking off again.

Olivia starts dipping her finger into the cranberry sauce before shuddering at the taste.

'Come on. He's one of the good guys, isn't he?'

I still really like Ross, just obviously not enough to date him. Bar his protein-shake drinking and his mammoth gym sessions, there's nothing to hate about him.

'He's nice enough,' says Kerry slowly, as if she's choosing her words carefully. 'It's just that I don't think he brought out the best in you.'

'And he could be a little know it all – you know, when we played Trivial Pursuit and things,' adds Jim.

I smile, as he's just bitter that he never won when Ross was here.

'But we wouldn't say that we didn't like him,' says Kerry, nodding for reassurance.

'Well, I didn't like him,' pipes up Olivia again.

'Thanks,' I say to her, feeling just great about my ability to choose men. 'I promise the next man I date won't force you to eat vegetables.'

'And he'll learn all the names of my Sylvanians?'

'How many have you got now?'

'Eighty-six, thanks to the ones I got today,' she says proudly.

'Wow, that's a lot of names.'

Before I have to make promises I don't know if I'll ever be able to keep, Mum comes swanning into the room.

'We aren't eating yet, are we?'

'Well, I thought I'd make the most of our five a.m. wake up this morning and I put the turkey on early,' shouts Jim as he opens the oven and steam whooshes out.

Mum looks at me a little guiltily as if perhaps the bacon sandwich wasn't the best idea. But luckily all the booze I've consumed in the last twenty-four hours has made me ravenous.

My stomach starts to rumble.

'No complaints from me,' I say.

Mum shrugs and sits down. 'Who am I pulling a cracker with then?' she says to Olivia.

'Me,' she screams and we all go through the rigmarole of pulling a cracker with her and of course we let her win all the prizes. She's a fair winner though, redistributing anything remotely useful – tiny screwdrivers, needle and thread sets, mini tape measures – and keeping all the toys to herself.

Kerry puts *Now That's What I Call Christmas* on the CD player.

Jim keeps coming to the table with dishes that look truly amazing. They're met with oohs and ahhs as if we're watching a firework display.

'Let's get this Christmas started,' he says, when he finally sits down. 'Dig in.'

No one argues and we lunge for the serving spoons.

I look down at the last roast potato on my plate. I will not let it defeat me. I cut it up into four small chunks but as I put the first one in my mouth I know I'm beaten. I put my fork down on the plate in submission.

'Anyone for dessert?' asks Jim.

'Oh God,' I say, pushing my plate away. 'I couldn't eat another thing.'

'As no one has ever eaten my Christmas pudding, I've made a Christmas rhubarb crumble instead,' says Jim.

'Yuck, I'm not eating that. I saw Daddy pee on the rhubarb bush.'

'What?' says Jim as Mum, Kerry and I glare at him. 'I'm sure I didn't. I'm sure I would have walked into the house and used the toilet like a civilised person.'

I try not to laugh as that sounds exactly like the type of thing that Kerry would say to him when she's telling him off, and I guess that it's a regular point of contention.

'Well, you can just have the custard,' mumbles Kerry. 'Perhaps we'll all just have the custard. Have we got a back-up M&S Christmas pudding?'

'Oh come on. I wouldn't have actually peed on the rhubarb plant. Plus, if I had, I'm sure it was early on in the summer – the fruit wouldn't have even been out then.'

'Either way,' I say rubbing my belly. 'Can we postpone the dessert until later?'

'Yes, good idea,' says Kerry. 'How about we stick on *The Snowman and the Snowdog* and we can have some coffee and open presents.'

'Sounds good to me, then we'll clear up.'

We all groan as we look at the state of the kitchen. Jim's a great cook, but he's not a tidy one, and the kitchen looks more like a bomb's hit it than even the lounge.

Kerry shrugs her shoulders. 'Let's not worry about that now.'

'I'll make the coffee at least,' says Mum and she gets up.

Jim can't help taking away the turkey and covering it over with cling film.

I'm about to help but Kerry tugs at my arm and I'm too full to argue. I let her drag me into the lounge, where we collapse onto the sofa.

'You know Jim and Mum'll be in their element tidying – best to leave them to it.'

My mum was obviously hard at work before she came through; the sea of paper has been tidied away and the new presents neatly stacked near the Christmas tree.

Kerry tucks her feet under her legs.

'So, how's it been today?'

'OK,' I say, not too sure what she's getting at. 'Christmas lunch here is always great.'

'I don't mean that – that's a given. I mean, you've been a bit quiet since you got here and I wondered if you were OK about you and Ross.'

'Me and Ross?'

'Yeah, it's your first Christmas without him.'

'Why does everyone keep asking me about that? I really was fine with our break-up. He wasn't *the one*.'

I try not to think of Danny Whittaker and remind myself that he's not the one either.

'I know, but still, Christmas – it's that time of year which is every singleton's nightmare, isn't it? You know, like Valentine's Day?'

My sister's never had to go through this. She's been with Jim since she was a teenager so she's never really been single. Not Bridget-Jones-single-girl-about-town single.

'It's not that bad. I've got good friends and good family,' I say. 'Honestly, it's been much better waking up alone than waking up thinking that it's another Christmas I shouldn't be with the wrong man.'

'Was it the courgettes?' she says, giggling.

'Courgettes. What are you young girls like these days? You're all courgettes and aubergines and winky faces,' Mum says, as she breezes in.

'We were talking about his cooking,' I say, not wanting to discuss sex with my mother, something that she doesn't find as inappropriate as I do.

'Of course, of course,' she says squeezing in between Kerry and me, despite there being two perfectly good armchairs she could sit on.

'Do you think Olivia's going to fall asleep?' I say, pointing at her curled up on the rug in front of the fire. She's been playing with her Sylvanian Families but her head's been getting progressively closer to the ground.

'Let's hope so; that would be a Christmas miracle,' says Kerry.

'We could watch the Queen's speech in peace,' says Mum.

'Oh, please. If I get control of the TV remote, the Queen's speech will not be what I'm watching. No, I was thinking we could watch a Christmas movie. What'd be on? *Wizard of Oz*?'

'*The Great Escape*, surely,' says Jim bringing in a tray of coffee that we all help ourselves to.

I groan. 'Come on, the point of Olivia being asleep means we get to watch something decent on telly.'

We're having a little bicker about what we're going to watch, when Mum jumps up.

'Shall we do presents?'

Kerry and I instantly forget our argument and look up.

'Yes, please,' I say, clapping my hands. I go over and grab my bag of presents and hand them out. Kerry gives me a book, and I bet it's the same one I've bought for her. We pull the paper off at the same time, and, sure enough, we've given each other the new Marian Keyes novel. In the fallow years, when one of hers isn't out, then we're forced to get a little bit more creative with our choices, but we always buy each other books. It's tradition.

Mum hands us each an envelope – another tradition. Every year Mum gives us a voucher for a spa and we go all together to beat the January blues.

'Thanks, Mum,' I say, as I start to open the envelope, wondering what she meant earlier about a surprise. 'A spa day is . . . wait a second,' I say as I read the voucher. This isn't for a spa. This is a plane ticket. To Barcelona. For the 27th of December. Two days from now. 'Wow. That's great. Are we all going? I've never been to Barcelona.'

I'm all excited about a trip away, just the three of us.

'Hang on, Barcelona? I've got a voucher for the Four Seasons.'

'If Kerry's not coming, is it just you and me?' I say looking at my mum, wrinkling my brow.

'Actually, I'm not going either. It's just you,' she says, waving her hand as if it's no big deal. 'You've had a tough year with your break-up with Ross and working so hard. I thought you needed some time out.

'I thought that instead of mooching around in your flat over the holidays you should go and get some sun in Spain. Hazel's lending you her apartment. It's about an hour away from the airport by bus. She's emailed me all the details and the directions.'

'You want me to go by myself? But these dates,' I say, scanning them. 'They're over New Year.'

'Yes, I didn't know when you'd be able to take a holiday, so this way I thought that it would make the most of your leave over Christmas.'

'But what about Lucy? She'll kill me if I miss New Year.'

My mum waves her hand as if to bat away my worry.

'I'm sure she can spend it with her fiancé. Come on, Lydia. You know your mother always knows best. You need a holiday – trust me.'

I blow on my coffee before taking a sip.

'I think it'll be great. I'd love to go away by myself for a few days,' says Kerry. 'Hint, hint, Mother, for next year.'

'Well, I don't want you to feel left out. Here's Jim's present.'

Jim takes an envelope from Mum and jiggles his eyebrows at the mystery. He usually gets socks and a Jeremy Clarkson DVD.

'A night for two at the Four Seasons,' he says, reading it out like he's revealing the prize on a game show.

Kerry snaps her head round to look at our mum.

'Seeing as we're not all going to the spa this year, you can stay for the night after with Jim and I'll look after Olivia.'

Kerry practically knocks me out as she throws her arms around Mum.

'Thanks, Mum, best present ever,' she says, looking at me.

I look down at my plane ticket. I'm not entirely sure if I agree.

'You'll love it. Take some books and some box sets. Have a good think about everything,' says my mum, sounding sage.

'But what about Lucy?'

'Your problem is that you think too much about everyone else. Stop and do something for yourself, Lydia.'

'Trust me,' says Kerry. 'One day, when you've got kids, you'll look at that time you spent on your own and wish you'd done it more often.'

'But I've never been on holiday on my own before.'

'All the more reason to do it. Didn't you say that you were looking for new challenges?'

'But isn't it a bit risky travelling by myself?'

Responsible Lydia isn't known for taking risks.

'I'm sending you to Spain, not deepest darkest Peru. Think of it as an adventure.'

I stare down at the ticket. Wasn't I just thinking that I needed to do something to find my sparkle? Maybe this could be just the thing.

Chapter Five

So Kerry and Jim finally had their baby! Only a week and half late. They've called her Olivia Grace, cute or what? I've attached a pic so you can see her in all her wrinkled glory. I'm nipping into the hospital to see her later on – can't wait to give her a big squeeze. Then I'm jetting off this afternoon for a week in Majorca with my housemates Lucy and Caroline. Stand by for a new fridge magnet . . .

Email; Lydia to Danny, February 2012

'Thank you so much for giving me a lift. It was totally above and beyond, but so appreciated,' I say, as Lucy pulls into the airport complex.

'Please, I did it as much for me as for you. I had to get away from Ed's mum. Her ideas about the wedding were doing my head in. Anyone would think she's marrying Ed,' she sighs loudly. 'I was almost tempted to bring my passport and come with you.'

'You totally should have done.' I'd have loved nothing more than to spend a few days away with my bestie. I can't help being a bit scared about going away alone. I keep telling myself that it's nothing to freak out about, it's just a trip to Spain – no big deal – but it is to me.

'No, it's not fair. Your mum was right, you need some time to figure everything out.'

'But how am I going to figure everything out when I don't know what's wrong with me? I've got a good job, good friends and family, but I feel as if I'm missing out on something.'

'Maybe you need to move out of Kerry's.'

'Maybe. I don't know where I'd go though. I can't afford to rent somewhere nice by myself and I don't know if I can face a house share. It's just so confusing.'

I sigh heavily as I look out of the window.

'Do you think you're living your best life?' I ask as she turns into the short-stay car park.

She gives me a smirk as she takes a ticket. 'Totally. But then everyone is; it's just about how you look at it.'

I frown. I'm not so sure.

'Listen,' says Lucy, squeezing my hand as I try not to cry, 'I didn't want to upset you. This is a really exciting opportunity for you to have some time to yourself, I just want you to use it well and not spend the whole time watching *Modern Family* box sets.'

She knows me too well. She parks the car and we get out.

She opens up the boot and I pull out my case, then she hands me a little black bag with a bow on it.

'I thought we'd already done Christmas presents?'

'Just open it.'

I peel back the tissue paper in the bag and pull out a racy black basque. I hastily shove it back in the bag as a family goes past wheeling their cases.

'What the hell is this?' I say looking at her.

'Something to take with you.'

'Um, I'm going by myself. I've packed plenty of appropriate giant knickers.'

'Which is exactly what I thought you'd do. This is just in case you find yourself a sexy Spaniard. Have you packed any condoms?'

'Um no, as I'm going by myself,' I say again, slowly so that she understands.

'Yes, but if this was a rom-com, you'd meet the man of your dreams at the airport and he'd whisk you away to his chateau – oh no, hang on, what's a castle in Spanish – *castillo*?'

'My life is definitely not a rom-com,' I say, rolling my eyes and handing her back the bag. 'The only reason I would have packed condoms would have been for practical reasons, like our old geography teacher once said – they come in handy for all sorts. Like putting a used roll of film in just in case your back pack gets wet.'

'Right, since when do you have film in your camera?'

'That was just an example. I'm sure they work equally well for putting memory cards in.'

Lucy's trying hard not to laugh.

'Well, in case you have a film slash memory card slash sexy man emergency,' she says, pulling out a pack from her coat pocket and shoving them into my handbag.

'I guess it doesn't hurt to be prepared for any eventuality,' I say.

'Exactly, you never know when some sexy Spaniard will end up in your bed.'

I tut before laughing. I hadn't even thought about meeting anyone when I was in Spain. I try not to panic that I haven't had sex with anyone except Ross for five years and even then in the last year we barely did it. I'm bound to be rusty. Maybe I've forgotten how.

I try and banish such stupid thoughts. First, it's very unlikely I'll meet anyone to have sex with. Second, it's sex; everyone does it – so I'm sure it can't be that hard to remember how. Third, they have good wine in Spain, don't they? I can ply my man with rioja first so that he doesn't notice that I'm off my game.

Lucy takes the basque out of the bag and brazenly opens my case and slips it in. I do nothing to stop her; it's not as if I have to wear it, is it?

'So this is like the end of an era,' says Lucy, looping her arm through mine as she walks me towards departures. 'It'll be the first New Year in almost seven years that we haven't spent together.'

'So it will,' I say, thinking that makes me feel old.

'I hope you do meet your sexy Spaniard, I feel a bit bad at the thought that you're going to be spending New Year all alone.'

'It'll just seem like any other night,' I say, shrugging my shoulders.

'Do you think? I'll miss you though.'

'I know, and I'll miss you. But it'll be nice for you and Ed to spend it together. I should have insisted you do that anyway. Look how happy it's made him.'

'Maybe, but I would have felt like an awful friend, as you always came out with me and you never spent New Year with Ross.'

We walk into the terminal building and I try not to let the glaring lights dazzle me.

'I never spent it with Ross because I guess I didn't really want to kiss him at New Year.'

Lucy gives me a trademark WTF look.

'It's as if I didn't want to kiss him at midnight as it felt like I was pledging to spend the rest of that year with him. You're always so full of hope and optimism at New Year and for me it's all wrapped up in that kiss. In my heart of hearts I always knew it was wrong between us, which is why I was never with him. But that's exactly why you should be with Ed this year. You're getting married.'

'But I guess that's why I thought we should have had our last girls' New Year.'

'Come on, Lucy, don't you remember last year? We were in that awful club and we left before midnight?'

'Oh God. That awful techno rubbish.'

'Exactly,' I say, shivering at the memory. 'We haven't had an epic New Year's for ages. I guess we've got to accept things are changing.'

I'm trying not to let tears well up in my eyes again as I know it's true. Whether I like it or not, next year my life isn't going to be the same. My best friend's getting married and if I don't do something about my life soon, I'll be left behind. Everyone's right, I do need this holiday.

We reach my check-in queue and I turn to Lucy and give her a big hug.

'Thanks for everything.'

'Send me lots of pictures. I want you to make me jealous.'

'I will.'

I take a deep breath and give her a wave as I head over to the queue. I'm really doing this, I'm really going away by myself.

You know those glam women that you see at the airport. The ones who are dressed in light colours – you know, cream linen trousers, pristine white top, cashmere scarf draped around their shoulders, feet clad in delicate sandals, their make-up flawless and their hair neat – either up or down. Well, that is definitely not me.

I look down at my faded jeans that have yogurt stains all over them and my hoodie that's splattered with ketchup from the bacon buttie I wolfed down hours ago. My hair is a frizz ball. I straightened it last night but my early start coupled with the plane and bus combo has not helped matters.

I stop walking and blow at a section of hair that's strewn across my face, only it's stuck to the sweat that's broken out on the final ascent to the apartment block. I have to physically move it with my hand. The bus stop was all the way at the bottom of the hill and Hazel's apartment is near the top. I've become a sweaty mess, thanks to dragging my suitcase containing enough toiletries to start my own beauty salon and clothes for any eventuality – thanks, Lucy.

'Seventy-two, seventy-four,' I say trying to force myself on. I must be almost there. 'Where the bloody hell is seventy-six?'

This is my second loop of the apartment complex. I don't think my calves are up to a third pass and at this point I'm almost willing to start sacrificing my mini cosmetic bottles to make my case lighter.

I see a man walking out of an apartment up ahead of me. A person, a real, live person. I haven't seen one since I got off the bus.

'*Excuso*,' I shout, waving over-enthusiastically.

He turns and looks at me and I begin to panic. Not only do I have zero Spanish language skills other than '*hola*' and various tapas-menu items, but he's also devilishly handsome. Thoughts of the sexy Spaniard and the little black number that Lucy gave me float around my mind.

He walks towards me and I can feel my heart racing. I pat at my frizzy hair, wishing for the millionth time today that I was more like one of those immaculately groomed travellers.

I didn't think it was possible to feel any sweatier but now I can actually feel beads forming on my forehead. What am I going to say to him? Damn them for making me learn German at school.

'*Patatas bravas*,' I blurt out as he reaches me.

I close my eyes for a second in embarrassment. I open my eyes again, hoping that I've managed to hide myself in a giant hole, but he's looking at me and smiling.

'I mean, lost,' I say, enunciating each word slowly, in case he can understand me. I hold out my written instructions from Hazel and I point to the address, hoping he'll get the general idea.

'Oh, seventy-six. Yeah, it's a tricky one,' says the man, with a very English accent. 'Do you see that little alleyway there? There are some stairs and when you get to the top of them, seventy-six is up there.'

'Thanks,' I mumble, feeling like a massive arsehole.

'You know, if you fancy some good *patatas bravas*, you can always come and see me,' he says with a wink.

Oh dear lord. My cheeks are starting to burn. Have I accidentally stumbled upon a code word here in Spain? Is my favourite potato-based dish actually something naughty?

'Um, well . . .' I stutter, not knowing what to say.

'How about tonight?' he says. 'I'll have a glass of rioja ready and waiting. It looks like you've had a tough day. Seven o'clock? Los Toros? It's a little tapas restaurant on the edge of the complex as you go into town.'

I nod. I passed it on the way up. It looked cute. He looks cute. We'd look cute in there together. Totally postable on Instagram with #LivingOurBestLives.

'Sounds great,' I say flashing him a smile and stepping back gently in case my deodorant hasn't lived up to its twenty-four-hour protection promise. At least with a dinner date at 7 p.m., I've got time for a shower first.

'Perfect. Let me grab your case for you. It looks heavy.'

'Oh no,' I say waving my hand. 'I've got this. I'll see you later on. Oh, my name's Lydia by the way.'

'Steve,' he says, giving me a wave as he saunters off and I try not to check out his bum. He might not be a sexy Spaniard, but he's sexy so Lucy will be pleased with me.

I follow his directions and heave my giant suitcase up the stairs, wondering why I pretended that I didn't need him to carry it when quite clearly I did. I'm relieved when finally I see the little blue-and-white china tile stuck on the door with the number 76 on it. It might not have been quite the easy journey Hazel made it sound from her email, and the walk wasn't really a quick stroll, but I've finally made it.

I turn the key and push open the wooden door. I can't help but feel excited as I cross the threshold. The apartment is beautiful with its white stone walls and patterned tiled floor. The sun's streaming through the window over the top of the door and the overall feel is light and airy.

I breeze through the living room, glancing at the giant bookshelf crammed with paperbacks with a rainbow of different-coloured spines. There's no TV, but for once I'm not disappointed. I'll just have to keep the box sets until I get home and curl up with a book instead.

I peer in at the bathroom where there's a shower/bath combo, toilet and bidet, and at the bedroom, which has a large double bed with a white duvet covered with a brightly coloured crochet throw. I walk back through the lounge and as I push open the wooden door at the end of the room it reveals a small kitchen in dark wood with a tiny table wedged in the corner.

It's a lovely, small apartment – just the right size for me – but I can't help but feel a teeny tiny bit disappointed that there's no outside space. I try and remind myself that I should count myself lucky that I've got free accommodation, and the communal gardens, from what I've seen of them, looked lovely.

I take a deep breath as I look around the kitchen again. I've been concentrating so much on the journey that it hadn't hit me until then that I'm here; I'm actually here. What do I do now?

The silence of the apartment starts to deafen me and I feel a wobble coming on, but then I remember my date with Steve. I could start getting ready. I glance at my watch and sigh – it's only 4 p.m. I know it takes me longer to get ready now that my skin isn't quite so youthful and I have ever-increasing black circles under my eyes, but even taking that into consideration, starting this early is taking the piss.

I look around the kitchen and spot a kettle. Tea! Always a saviour. I flick the kettle on and whilst it boils I head back into the lounge and unzip my case to find my teabags and I see Lucy's present to me. I hold it up to the light and whilst the top might be somewhat supportive, the rest is totally see-through. I go to put it back in the case, but then stop myself. Perhaps this is where I've been going wrong all these years. If I'm really going to embrace change, then I need to put myself out of my comfort zone every now and then. Uncomfortable, yet more importantly, sexy underwear, here I come.

The kettle finishes boiling and I make myself a cup of black tea before scanning the lounge. My eyes fall on the giant book-shelf. I go over to try and decide what I should read first. Of course I brought books with me, but there's nothing more exciting than choosing a new book. I glance at the pink-and-pastel-coloured spines, wondering if I'm in the mood for romance. There are a few thrillers that I've heard are good, but I'm not sure that reading one when all alone in a foreign country is a very good idea. I'm a bit of a wimp at the best of times, so I should probably pick something a bit less scary.

I settle in the end for *Wolf Hall*. It's not a book I'd usually read, but this isn't my usual type of holiday either – and it gets me out of my comfort zone again. Maybe this is the holiday where I discover I want to be more intellectual. Maybe I'm about to reassess my whole life. I slip the hardback out of the bookcase, but I'm not prepared for the weight of it. Blimey, I'll be getting a brain and an arm work out as I read this.

I sit myself down in a comfy armchair and sip the tea before I open the book. I read the first few words and my eyes start to do that thing where they close and then spring back open. It has been a really long day; perhaps I should take a little nap? I wouldn't want to fall asleep in my gazpacho over dinner later. I drain my tea and pop the cup back down on the side before I close my eyes. I'll have a quick power nap before I spruce myself up for the date. I may have only been on this holiday for a few hours, but it's already going surprisingly well.

Chapter Six

Greetings from Singapore! It's so clean here and so ordered. It's so much less crazy than Japan, but still beautiful and amazing. It's technically closer to you so less of an excuse not to visit. I'm trying to tempt you with a fridge magnet – it's supposed to be of the famous Merlion (half mermaid half lion) and no, it's not projectile vomiting – unfortunate use of colour.

Parcel; Danny to Lydia, October 2012

I wake up with a crick in my neck and a numb foot. I wipe a patch of dribble away from my mouth as I push myself up. It takes me a second or two to work out that I'm in Hazel's apartment. It's now almost pitch-black aside from a sliver of moonlight coming through the window above the door.

I shiver involuntarily, as now that the sun's gone down it's cold in here. I realise that it must be late and I panic as I remember Sexy Steve. What if I'm late for the date? I flick the light switch on and try to find my handbag. I scramble to pick up my phone and I'm relieved that it's only 6.45 p.m. I breathe a huge sigh of relief. I've got fifteen minutes to get ready; that's plenty of time, right? RIGHT? All I've got to do is shower, shave my legs, pluck my eyebrows, find and apply my make-up and choose something to wear. Totally do-able.

I whip myself almost immediately into action. I crank up the heating before I have the quickest shower known to man. I choose legs over eyebrows and I don't deliberate over outfits like I usually would. I slip on Lucy's present to me followed by a pair of super skinny jeans and a flirty wool jumper that falls off one shoulder revealing the strap of the lacy black number underneath and finish the look off with my high-heeled, knee-length boots. I then slap on some make-up, shove some mousse in my hair and *voilà*. Stick a fork in me, I'm done. This is quite possibly the easiest getting ready I've ever done – I should definitely remember that less is more when it comes to time.

I quickly grab my bag and coat before I hurry off out into the apartment complex once more.

I'm practically skipping along, thinking how lucky I am to have found a holiday romance the second I arrived, when a thought hits me: no one knows that I'm going on this date and no one is expecting me home. I pull out my phone and WhatsApp Lucy:

Got a hot date tonight. Meeting at a restaurant called Los Toros. Will text you when home to let you know I'm safe. BTW thanks for the undies – I've got them on ;) x x

I'm just putting the phone back in my bag when I get the response:

OMFG – text me later – but he better see those undies x x

I laugh as I slip the phone into my bag and Los Toros comes into view. I can feel the butterflies starting to build up and I'm wondering if I've got the nerve to go through with this. I haven't been on a proper date for years. Lucy's been trying to convince me to join Tinder ever since Ross and I broke up, but I've resisted, hoping that I'll meet someone organically. Only I wish now I had as I'm a bit rusty and I wonder what one does on a first date these days.

'Come on, Lydia,' I say, giving myself a pep talk. 'You got this.'

I walk into the cute little restaurant and immediately I fall in love with it. It feels so quintessentially Spanish with its white-washed walls and dark wooden tables dressed with blood-red tablecloths. There are vaults running along the wall with large barrels set in them.

I look around for Steve but I can't see him. Apart from one other couple near the back the restaurant is empty.

'Ah, hello,' says a woman as she bursts through the swing doors from the kitchen. She marches up with a big smile on her face.

'You must be Lydia,' she says, in a thick Spanish accent. 'Steve told me all about you.'

'He did?' I feel so special.

'Ah, yes, he was pleased he ran into you. He was worried he'd have a quiet night tonight.'

'Me too,' I say, feeling flattered that he's so excited about our date.

'He reserved the best table for you, I have it ready. Shall I take your coat first?'

I slip it off and hand it to her, and she wanders down to the coat stand at the end of the room to hang it up. I stand there a little awkwardly, when the door jangles behind me.

I turn and see Steve and my stomach does a flip at the sight of him dressed in black trousers and a leather jacket.

I feel a bit underdressed in my jeans and jumper, as he looks as if he's made a big effort.

'It's cold out there, brrr,' he says with a theatrical shiver. 'Lydia, you're bang on time.' He leans over and gives me a kiss on each cheek.

God, he smells good. Whatever aftershave he's wearing it was worth every penny.

'You look great,' he says.

I pat my hair and feel proud of my fifteen-minute makeover.

'You don't look too bad yourself,' I say a little flirtatiously. I'm guessing things have to move fast in the holiday romance stakes.

'Why thank you,' he says, beaming.

'Hi,' says the waitress. 'I was just going to seat Lydia.'

'No need,' says Steve, looping his arm through mine. He leads me across to a table in the corner and pulls out my chair. He's so chivalrous. #Swoon.

I sit down and shake my hair over my shoulder so that my jumper slips down, revealing a bit of flesh. I don't know what's come over me; maybe the racy underwear is unleashing my naughty side or maybe it's because I'm on holiday, but I'm feeling less inhibited than normal. I'm pretty glad I popped on Lucy's little number as I'm feeling that it may well have an audience later tonight.

'So, what would you like to drink?' asks the waitress as she reappears with the menu. 'Rioja, sangria?'

I look up at Steve, wondering what he'd like.

'What do you reckon? Sangria?' I say with a wince.

'*Perfecto!*' he says with a wink. 'Liza makes the best sangria.'

'Do you want a glass or . . . ?'

'A jug,' I say, looking at how cheap it is on the menu.

She smiles and heads off to the kitchen.

Steve's still standing up, leaning against the back of a chair.

'Are you going to sit down?' I say, wondering if he's standing up simply so I get a better look at his bum, which in the tight black trousers he's wearing is no bad thing.

'Sure,' he says looking around the restaurant. 'I guess. So, how long are you here in Roses for?'

'Until the first, so just under a week.'

'Great, so I'm hoping in that time I'll see a lot of you.'

I'm having to pinch myself under the table.

'I'm sure that can be arranged,' I purr.

'Sangria,' says Liza, placing the jug on the table. 'Are you ready to order? I forgot my pad.'

She laughs a little and squeezes Steve's shoulders as she goes down to the bar.

I feel a ripple of jealousy come over me. I'm sure it's just the Spanish way to be touchy feely.

'Earlier, it looked like you'd had a busy day travelling. I'm sure you must be starving.'

'I am,' I say, glancing over the menu. 'It all looks so good. I'm never going to be able to decide.'

Liza walks up to us once again, pad in hand.

'Well, you want the *patatas bravas*, obviously, but also the meatballs are fantastic and the squid. Oh, and the Manchego. Perhaps the *gambas*. Liza also makes this thing with peppers which you have to try.'

Liza laughs. 'That's a lot of food.'

'It all sounds delicious,' I say.

'Shall I just bring you a selection?' she asks, writing it down.

'Yes, that sounds good, doesn't it?' I say looking at Steve.

'Absolutely.'

'Right, I'd better get back to the kitchen and cook it all,' Liza says, walking off.

I reach over to the pitcher of sangria and fill my wine glass before turning to the one across the table for Steve.

'Oh, I'd better not. Not when I'm working,' he says with a wink.

'Working?' I say.

'Well, it doesn't feel like work when I get to sit here and chat to beautiful women like you.'

I close my eyes as it starts to dawn on me what's going on. Oh, God. I'm not on a date. Well, I am, but it looks like I'm paying for it. I've somehow hired myself an escort. This cannot be happening.

'Um, I don't know how this happened,' I say slowly, as I try to work out how I'm going to get out of this. 'You seem like a really nice guy and I'm sure you're very good at your job, but I thought this was, you know . . .'

Steve's wrinkling his brow in confusion.

'I don't have the money to pay for it. I mean usually I don't have to, you know, pay for it. I usually get guys to take me out for free.'

'Oh,' he says, almost recoiling. 'I feel awful. I made you come and tempted you with the food and you can't afford to eat here.'

'What?' I say. Now it's my turn to wrinkle *my* brow in confusion. 'I can afford to eat here, I just can't afford you, I don't think. I mean, I don't know what the going rate for an escort is, but I don't really want to pay for one as, believe it or not, I can usually get men to date me for free. Not recently, but then I just broke up with my ex-boyfriend, well, five months ago, which is quite a long time, but I broke up with him as he wasn't the one, so I feel like I don't want to date just anyone and I—'

'Lydia,' says Steve before he bursts out laughing. There are tears coming out of his eyes. 'I'm not an escort, I'm a waiter.'

He slips off his leather jacket to reveal a neatly pressed white shirt.

I stare at him in horror.

'You're a waiter?'

'And Liza, the chef, is my girlfriend,' he says between laughs. 'I'm so sorry I gave you the wrong idea.'

'Ha ha,' I say with a fake laugh. 'You didn't at all; I was just a bit confused when you said you were working.'

'What did you think before that? Oh God, I'm sorry, did I make you think this was a date?'

'Not a date,' I lie, waving the idea away. 'I thought we were having dinner together. But no, not a date, obviously.'

My voice has gone all shrill and squeaky. I'm not being very convincing.

'How about I go and get you some olives, on the house,' he says as he gets up, taking his wine glass away with him as if to prevent further confusion.

'Great,' I say, gulping down the sangria. Oh dear Lord, that is strong. I look at the jug, which I'm now going to have to drink alone.

I hear my phone beeping in my bag and I pull it out to see that it's Lucy.

How's it going with the stud muffin?

I'm mortified. Damn me and my personal safety pro-activeness.

ME
   Aside from accusing the guy of being a male escort? . . . Let's just say I'm having a meal for one in a lovely restaurant, with a sexy waiter and his beautiful girlfriend.

LUCY
   OOOOOhhhhhhhh!!!! At least there's still time for a sexy Spaniard. Enjoy the meal x x

I feel like a right dick as a family walk in and Steve hugs and kisses them all. He's laughing and joking as he takes them to their table and I see that he's just as much of a charmer with them.

All I want to do is sneak back to the apartment and hide there for the rest of my holiday. Didn't I want lots of time for self-reflection?

I stagger a little on my way back to Hazel's apartment. Liza did suggest that Steve walk me home, but I thought I'd already made enough of a tit out of myself as it was. Knowing my luck I'd mis-construe him coming in for a hug and end up kissing him on the lips or something equally as embarrassing.

It was so mortifying tonight. Not that Steve minded. He found it most amusing and Liza said his ego wouldn't recover for weeks. I, on the other hand, practically wolfed down six plates of tapas and nearly a whole jug of sangria in record time and am back at the apartment at 8.32 p.m.

I open the door and I'm immediately hit by a wave of heat. I think I turned the thermostat up a little too much before I left. Man, it's hot in here – practically a sauna. I slip my coat off and turn down the thermostat.

I'm feeling pretty special after all that booze, so I go to make myself another cup of tea. Apart from the kettle, the apartment is silent and it's making me feel lonely. I find my handbag, pull out my wireless headphones and put iTunes on random on my phone. It's still roasting in here and I can feel myself get-ting clammy. I slip my big wool jumper off, and immediately feel ridiculous in the see-through underwear, so I start digging around my case for my pyjamas before I stop – even the thought of the flannel pyjamas bottoms in this heat is making me sweat. Instead I peel off my jeans and basque, put on to impress Steve, and I slip on a super-comfy pair of giant knickers with my pyjama vest top and a pair of woolly socks to keep my feet warm on the tiled floor.

I pop my noise-cancelling headphones on and turn the music right up, whilst I finish making my cup of tea. I'm just about to sit down when I realise I need another wee. Damn the sangria.

I head into the bathroom and I figure I might as well take off my make-up whilst I'm here. 'Like a Virgin' by Madonna comes on, and I start dancing around.

It's actually quite liberating being here by myself. I pick up the bottle of mousse from the side of the bath and I start to mime into it, before I remember that no one else is here so I start to sing. I'm getting quite carried away when I remember my tea's going cold and I open the door to the lounge. The floor tiles in this place are particularly excellent for sliding, which I imagine is going to do wonders for my dance moves. I slide out sideways singing the chorus and doing a big woo as I punch my arm towards the ceiling when I notice a draft hitting my legs. I look up, shocked to see a man in the doorway with his back to me, shutting the door.

He's blocking my only way out so I panic and throw the can of mousse I was holding and as he turns back round to face me, it hits him squarely in the stomach.

'Ow, fuck,' he says as he doubles over clutching his waist. And then as I get a better look at him, it's my turn to swear.

'What the actual fuck?' I say.

I wonder for a second if my mind (or that sangria) is playing tricks on me. But I'd know that face anywhere. 'Danny Whittaker, you scared the living daylights out of me.'

Chapter Seven

We're doing this event at work and Kylie Minogue actually played. I can never think of Kylie without thinking of you so I got her to sign a photo for you. So here you are 'Dani' – sorry, it never occurred to me to spell it for her, and I guess she's used to writing it that way.

Letter and signed photo; Lydia to Danny, May 2013

For a moment both of us stand stock still, staring at each other. He looks as shocked as I am and he seems to have lost all ability to speak. As have I. I mean, it's Danny – Danny is here and he's clutching my bottle of hair mousse which I just despatched as a not-very effective weapon.

'Lydia,' he says. His cheeks are a bit flushed and he's looking at a spot past my head as if he can't actually look at me. OK, so I know I just took my make-up off, but I don't look that shocking, do I? I might have been doing some dodgy out-of-tune singing to Madonna, but was it so bad that he can't even look at me?

It's then that I realise that my legs are feeling awfully chilly. I look down and jump in horror at the sight of the giant pants and pull a crochet blanket off the back of the armchair. I know that, technically, in my giant knickers I'm actually more covered up than I would be if I was sunning myself on a beach in a bikini, but somehow I'm more embarrassed.

'I didn't see anything,' he says, finally daring to look at me, now that I'm as decent as I can be.

'You forget that I used to play Monopoly with you when we were kids and I know when you're lying,' I say, my cheeks matching his in the red stakes.

He tries to suppress a giggle. 'I'm sorry, I couldn't look away quickly enough – those pants are pretty hard to miss.'

'Yes, thank you. I wasn't really expecting anyone to see them, and besides, they are super comfortable.'

He's grinning like a loon and I realise that I am too and it takes a moment for my brain to catch up with the situation.

'What the hell are you doing here? You scared me half to death,' I say finally.

'It's my mum's apartment. Shouldn't I be asking you that question?'

'She said I could stay here. My mum organised it for a Christmas present.'

'Oh God,' he says. 'I looked last week on the calendar and it was free and I didn't expect it to change.'

'It was a last-minute thing. Why didn't you ask your mum?'

'I didn't want her to know I was coming out. I was worried they'd all gatecrash.'

I can't believe that he's actually here. I haven't seen him alone for years. Of course, I would have preferred not to have been half naked with the world's most embarrassing granny pants on and zero make-up, but it's still great to see him.

He's changed a little since I last saw him two years ago. Grown up a bit. He's now got a tiny bit of salt and pepper around his sideburns and his hair's less spiky. He's also got a hint of stubble; too much for one day, but not a full-on beard.

I'm lost for words, which is crazy, seeing as this is the guy that I've been writing to at least once or twice a month for the last ten years. I know that I've seen him, but it's always been for some big occasion – his parents' 40th wedding anniversary or my mum's sixtieth – and we've always had partners in tow or been surrounded by relatives. This is the first time in almost nine years where it's just been the two of us and, suddenly, I'm a girl standing in front of a boy dressed in a pair of pants so large that I could eclipse the moon.

We both giggle as if we're suddenly embarrassed by the situation. I honestly don't know what to say to him.

'So why are you here?' I finally ask.

'Christmas with the family was getting a bit much so I thought I'd come out here for a few days.'

'You didn't get invited anywhere for New Year, huh?' I say, jokingly.

'You neither?' he says, still grinning.

That smile. I didn't realise how much I'd missed seeing it.

'Actually, I've got a friend who lives in Barcelona. He's having a New Year's Eve party and I thought I'd tack on a few days here before I went to see him.' He rubs his stomach where I hit him with the mousse. 'That bloody hurt, you know.'

'I'm sorry,' I say, wincing. 'I thought you were a burglar or something. Let me see.' I shuffle up to him, careful to keep the crochet blanket secure.

He pulls up his jumper and I try not to gawp too much at his taut stomach and instead focus on the red patch. I rub my hand over it and he flinches in pain.

'Good job you had all those layers on. Who knew that a can of mousse could be so lethal? Perhaps there's some ice in the freezer.'

'I'm sure I'll be fine.'

'Well, at least let me put some arnica cream on it,' I say, as I head into the bathroom and root around in my giant toiletry bag.

'Arnica cream? Who brings arnica cream with them on holiday?' he says, as I reappear.

'Someone who worries that they're going to injure people,' I say, as I squeeze the cold gel onto my finger before massaging it onto his stomach.

'Thanks,' he says, looking me in the eye.

My belly does an involuntary flip. All these years I've tried to tell myself that it was a silly little teenage crush, and that the kiss was the result of too much Pimm's, but the electricity between us is unmistakeable.

'You're here alone, then?' I ask.

I don't want to highlight his single status too obviously.

'Uh-huh, and you are too?'

I nod, biting my lip nervously.

We keep looking at each other for what seems like an age, and I wonder if he's going to make a move on me. I want him to. I want to forget about the time I went to visit him and what I overhead him telling his friend Gaz and, instead, I want to pick up where we left off all those years ago. But he doesn't. He turns and looks around the room, which now that I look at it, is a bit of a mess. It was such a rush to get ready to go out on my not-a-real-date and I've got half of my case emptied on the floor.

'I hadn't really expected guests,' I say, as I walk around to my suitcase and hastily shove stuff back inside.

Danny picks up the black lacy number that I was wearing earlier from where I'd thrown it off into the middle of the floor.

'Just here on your own,' he says, again, with the same smirk he used to have on his face when he was a teenage boy.

'Yes,' I say, snatching it away and gathering up the rest of my stuff quickly. 'My friend Lucy helped me pack for any eventuality.'

'I think I like your friend Lucy.'

I shake my head at him and hurry about, putting the rest of the things in the case.

'So,' he says. 'I feel really bad that I'm gatecrashing your holiday. I could head into town and book a hotel, or I could crash on the sofa for tonight, if you don't mind?'

'You can't go into town, you've only just got here. Of course you can have the sofa,' I say, wondering if I should offer him the bedroom as this is his family home. I look at the sofa, which doesn't look big enough for me to fit on, let alone Danny.

'Great. So have you eaten, or . . .?'

'Yes, I had some tapas.'

'Down at Los Toros?'

'Uh-huh,' I say, hanging my head in shame.

'Isn't Steve great, and Liza. Such a wonderful couple.'

'Hmm, yes, they're just great. Do you need to eat?' I ask, praying that he doesn't want me to go back there with him.

'No, I grabbed something at the airport. I was just planning on chilling out when I got here.'

We're still staring at each other.

'How about a cup of tea?' I ask, taking the totally British approach.

'Why not? I'll go and put the kettle on.'

He goes out of the room and I breathe deeply.

My head is spinning. For so long I haven't let myself see Danny alone and now here he is, in a tiny one-bedroom apartment where I'm half dressed. I pick up my fleecy pyjama bottoms and slip them on. Along with a hoodie to cover up my braless pyjama top.

I can hear him banging around and I hastily rearrange my hair in the mirror and manage to tame it into a messy top knot.

I walk out into the kitchen and take a deep breath as I watch the steam coming out of the kettle. I can do this. I can totally do this. I'm a fully grown woman. Just because I want to shove him up against the breakfast bar and kiss his face off does not mean to say I have to act on it. I'm blaming the sangria and Lucy putting dirty thoughts into my mind. I'm sure I can be here with a man who's a platonic friend without letting my imagination run away with itself.

'You know, I could murder a beer,' I say, as the kettle whistles loudly on the hob. I get the impression that tea isn't going to cut it. 'Shame I haven't been to the supermarket yet.'

'Didn't my mum leave you any? Usually she gets the cleaner to leave a six pack of beer and some milk.'

He pulls open the fridge and there are both. I feel like such an idiot, I'd never even thought to look and I hadn't really enjoyed my black tea earlier. He takes two bottles out and opens them with the bottle-opener magnet stuck on the fridge. I can't help glistening with a slight pride that it's one of the tacky ones I'd bought him from the Munich beer festival. I'd got a bit carried away and bought him a selection, each more tacky than the last.

'See, I keep them,' he says, as he notices me watching him. 'But there're only so many bottle opener fridge magnets I need at home. He hands me over a beer and I try not to react to the spark as our hands accidentally brush each other.

'Thanks,' I say, taking the longest sip.

'Do you want to drink them up on the roof? It's a bit chilly out, but there should be some rugs,' he says, ducking into the lounge and returning with his coat on.

'The roof?'

'Have you not been up there yet?'

I shake my head. 'I only arrived this afternoon.'

'Ah, well, obviously the view's better during the day, but there's enough of a moon for it to look good tonight.'

He opens a drawer and pulls out a box of matches, before he closes the kitchen door, which reveals another door behind it that's bolted shut. He unlocks it and it swings open.

'I would never have known this was here.'

'I take it you haven't read the welcome pack yet,' he says.

'Not yet, I got here and went for a little sleep before grabbing some food.'

'Not like you.' He has a small smile on his face. 'You're usually so conscientious.'

'Very funny,' I say, pulling a face.

When we were kids he was the one who would dive into a new board game, cracking open the pieces and setting them all up in the way he thought they'd go, and impatiently rolling the dice. Whereas I'd be the one carefully studying the instructions and all the rules and objectives of the game.

'You can shut the door, keep the heat in,' says Danny as he marches through and climbs the stairs. 'It doesn't lock from the outside.'

'Good to know,' I say, nodding to myself before I do as instructed.

I follow Danny up the steep outdoor staircase and we soon find ourselves on a terrace on top of the house. There's enough ambient light from the street lights below for us to see what we're doing.

I gasp as I take it all in. The roof terrace is positively huge – at least in comparison to the rooms downstairs. It must have the same footprint as the whole apartment but, without the dividing walls, it feels enormous. There's a large dining table at one end with eight chairs round it, a BBQ and what looks like a Tiki bar. Then at the other end, nearer to us, there's a set of two black rattan sofas facing each other.

Danny pulls cushions out of a box and starts passing them to me to put on the sofas. When we're done, I sit down and snuggle under a blanket he passes me before he lights the candles on the little glass-topped table.

'I can't believe I didn't find this place before; it's amazing.'

'I know, it makes the whole apartment. Downstairs is nice and all, but we usually all live up here when we're over.'

'Where do you all fit?'

He laughs.

'Sometimes I sleep up here in the summer on a camp bed. But Stuart's also got a little duplex in the same complex, so if we all come out as a family, then I'll often stay in one of his spare rooms. We still all hang out up here though.'

'Shame it's so dark.'

'You can still see the sea, though. Look,' he says, pointing.

I half stand up to look over the side of the wall and gasp again.

It's quite far away, but you can see where the buildings stop and the dappled moonlight is reflecting off the water.

'That's incredible,' I say, walking back over and sitting down.

'Yeah, I love it here. It's the kind of place I'd love to have a bolt hole, but seeing as most of the time I try and come when Mum and Dad or Stuart and his family aren't here, I just use this place.'

It feels so strange sitting here on a sofa opposite Danny, but normal at the same time. Like I haven't sat down with him for a beer for a couple of months, rather than years.

'I can't believe you're here,' I say. 'It's so weird to see you.'

'I know. It's like I know everything's that gone on with you with the letters and through Mum, but still I can't believe that I haven't had a chance to catch up with you properly since I moved back to England. Where's the time gone?'

'I don't know,' I say, shaking my head pretending it was a mystery. When I'd seen him a couple of years ago we said we'd meet up properly, but it didn't feel right seeing him alone when I was with Ross and so I never pushed it. When we broke up, I thought Danny was with Diana and I didn't fancy playing gooseberry.

'So, how's the events business? Have you had anything go wrong recently?' he says wincing. 'Sorry, but you make it sound so funny in your letters. That whole Dumb and Dumber thing with those people getting their tongues stuck on the ice.'

'Yeah,' I say smiling, 'that was an amusing one. The Willy Wonka-themed parties have been less dramatic. Although we did have to fire our original Willy Wonka as he kept touching up the Oompa-Loompas.'

'I always worried about that in the film,' says Danny smirking. 'Does it ever get exhausting just being at parties all the time?'

'It's not all the time. There's a lot of paper pushing involved too – event plans, risk assessments.'

For once I'm telling the truth as I'm responsible for the paperwork, rather than for the events themselves.

'The serious stuff,' says Danny, and I nod, pretending that my job is far more important than it actually is.

'But didn't you say you wanted less drama when you moved from your job in London?'

I close my eyes; I hate thinking about that job. One of the main reasons I'd gone for the job in the first place was so that I could be near Danny, only he'd gone to Tokyo before I'd even started it.

'It's certainly a lot calmer than that. It's just as busy, but a whole lot less stressful. My boss at Eventualities was something else.' I shudder at the thought.

'I always think it was a shame that you moved to London just as I left,' he says as if I moved there by coincidence.

Danny had arrived back from travelling and started his job in London just as I'd been offered a job at the company I'd been temping for in Newcastle, but a few months into it my dream job was advertised in London and I took it as a sign that I should be with Danny. I applied for it on a whim, got an interview and found out that I'd got the job just as I arrived at Danny's flat. I told him my good news only for him to tell me we were both celebrating as his company was sending him to Tokyo to complete his graduate programme. I was gutted, but not as gutted as I was when I nipped into the bathroom to get changed for our night out and I heard him telling his flatmate Gaz that our kiss was a mistake and that we'd only ever be friends.

If things had worked out for me in London then I could probably have looked back and laughed it all off, but it was the worst year of my life. The pay was terrible and all I could afford to rent was a shitty bedsit in Balham with non-existent heating, mouldy walls and a two-ring hob, so I lived off tinned spaghetti. Not even the job made up for it. My boss was a sadistic witch who shouted at me at every given opportunity and I ended up leaving London further into my overdraft than when I'd arrived.

'London's loss, but Tokyo's gain, huh?' I say trying not to sound too bitter. 'I was constantly jealous of you on your travels. Do you miss it? All those swanky cities you lived in.'

'Not really. It was exciting at first but, to be honest, I never really got a chance to enjoy it. Work was so intense and it was all consuming. We worked hard, played hard, but it was exhausting, and if I wasn't working or boozing I was sleeping. I could have been in any city – the people were always the same. Same type of bars. Same flats.'

'And there was me thinking you were living the high life.'

'I probably was to many. I mean, we used to go out some nights and we'd spend over a grand buying champagne and shots. I could buy anything I wanted when I wanted, but I wasn't happy. It was all too much pressure.'

'That's why you quit?'

He nods.

'It wasn't really that I had a burning desire to launch the video company, it's more that I was getting burnt out. Gaz had quit his job a few months before and wanted to set up the company and I decided to go in with him.'

Ten years we've been writing to each other and this is the first time we've talked properly about our lives. All those years I was jealous of his time in NYC and Tokyo and all the time he was hating it.

'It's great that your business is doing so well.'

'Yeah, it is. We mainly do corporate stuff, but we've just started to offer courses in video production for individuals wanting to start up YouTube channels. Teaching them the basics about equipment, lighting, editing and uploading, and how to embed it on their websites, how to think about content production.'

Even in the candlelight I can see his whole face lighting up, he's truly happy in what he does. It's funny as, when I first heard he was quitting his banking job and moving up north to set up a video production company with his mate, I thought he'd lost the plot. But he's got the sparkle that I'm so desperately craving.

'I think your mum loves having you close to her. I think she nearly had kittens when you said you wanted to work at hers.'

'Ha, yeah. Using their barn saves us a fortune in rent and she keeps us well stocked in tea and homemade shortbread. Not that we use it much anymore. We tend to film in client spaces and edit in our houses.'

'Oh, God, that shortbread. Mum still brings me home a tin whenever she goes up to visit Hazel.'

'She used to send some out to me monthly when I was working abroad.'

'I could just eat one, or ten of them, right now.'

Despite already having eaten my body weight in tapas, I could do with something sweet. I'd wanted to get out of the restaurant as quickly as possible and hadn't dared order dessert.

'Hold that thought,' Danny says.

When he's gone, I realise that my cheeks are aching from smiling, but I can't stop, even when he's not here.

He returns a few minutes later with a margarine tub.

'Please tell me that's not what I think it is.'

He nods and opens the lid and my stomach gurgles in anticipation.

'Mum gave me a big box over Christmas.'

I dive in and take out two biscuits before he even puts them down on the table.

He laughs. 'So where were we?'

'We were talking about you being incredibly brave quitting your well-paid job and moving miles away to work in your mum's barn with a mate.'

I bite into the shortbread as I wonder how it is that everyone else manages to create the life they want to live.

'I guess so – brave or stupid. We hadn't really planned to settle in the Lakes, but Gaz ended up meeting a woman a few months after moving up there and they moved in together pretty quickly. Now they're married with a baby on the way. Looking back we started the business with only an idea – we hadn't really researched whether we'd be able to build a client base and we didn't really have a clear idea whether we had a business model.'

'But you made it work,' I mumble between mouthfuls, trying to catch the crumbs with my hand.

'Yeah. We were lucky in a few ways. I'd had a good bonus from the bank so we could use that as start-up capital. Mum letting us use the barn for free was great, as pretty much all our meetings take place on our clients' premises. Then, we were there for the boom of the YouTube stars. Now, everyone wants to be the next Zoella.'

'I find it so weird that people hang out in their bedrooms and talk rubbish about their days to the Internet, but people find it so compelling.'

I'm totally pretending that I'm not addicted to Instagram Stories.

'I know, it's so weird. We had someone the other day as a guest speaker on a course and she literally uploads videos of herself painting her nails. She does a different style every day and she has over a million followers.'

'Wow. That's um . . .'

'I know, isn't it?' he says, shaking his head in disbelief.

'And that's her job?'

'Yeah, she earns all the money from the advertising on YouTube and brands pay her to create posts on Instagram, and she's got a talent manager and a book deal.'

'Blimey. Perhaps I'm in the wrong industry.' I look down at my nails; no one's going to want to see them. 'Although, to be honest, I can't imagine my life would be that exciting.'

'But that's the point. It's the fascination with an ordinary yet somehow extraordinary life.'

I laugh. 'My life is just ordinary – in fact, it's less than ordinary,' I say sipping my beer. 'But wow, YouTube, huh?'

'I know, but it's big business these days.'

'Luckily for you,' I say, raising my beer in a cheers motion.

'Luckily for me,' he says, laughing and sipping his beer. 'As jobs go, it's a pretty good one.'

'You say it's luck, but I know what you're like and I'm sure there would have been a whole heap of hard work involved.'

He shrugs his shoulders, confirming I'm right.

He was always going to be successful – he's a hard worker, but he's also a risk taker, and I guess that's what you need in business.

I drain my beer. 'Fancy another one?' I say, realising how awake I'm feeling.

'I should have brought some more up when I went down for the shortbread. I'll go.'

'No,' I say, going to stand up, but he's beaten me to it and is off down the stairs.

I get up anyway and go over to lean on the edge of the terrace, staring out into the darkness. I love how the streetlights all over the hill twinkle like a string of fairy lights. Although I live by the sea, this is so different. Instantly I know I'm somewhere abroad. Not to mention how quiet it is. There isn't the distant traffic noise or the sirens from emergency vehicles that you get back home.

I've only been here for a matter of hours and I'm already wondering if I'm going to be able to leave.

'Here,' says Danny, handing me a bottle.

I hadn't even heard him come up. He places his bottle down on the ledge and settles into the space next to me and stares out into the darkness too.

For a minute we lean on the wall, not talking. My mind's gone into a whirlwind with him being so close. If I just leaned a little to my right, I'd be brushing up against his body. All I want to do is kiss him again.

All those times when I've been feeling down about how my life's turned out or when I was worried that things with Ross weren't right, I always thought about that night with Danny; that kiss. I always try and tell myself that I've built it up to be more magical than it was. It was probably just my emotions running high on my sister's wedding day. But still, all I want to do is lean over and do it again. But I can't; not when I know he thought it was a mistake.

'What are you thinking about?' asks Danny.

'Oh, you know, how nice it is to smell the sea.' WTF? Not only does that sound really flipping weird – does anyone really like that fishy smell? – but we're also a couple of kilometres from the sea and can't really smell it.

'That's a shame,' says Danny. 'As I was thinking about the time I kissed you at Kerry and Jim's wedding.'

I snap my head round and we lock eyes. I can feel my stomach flipping, the electricity fizzing between us. He takes the beer bottle out of my hand and he puts it onto the ledge.

'I was thinking perhaps we should do it again,' he says, assertively.

I can't find any words, so instead I nod my head. He leans over to me and the anticipation is too much. His lips brush mine and I'm unsure if my legs are going to hold out. He's teasing me with his softly, softly approach, and it's killing me.

I can't take it any longer, and I find my hand flying up to the back of his neck and I pull him into me and then we're kissing. And oh boy, it's not like it was before; it's so much better.

Chapter Eight

I'm living in some sort of nightmare where people are lasso-ing in the street. Please tell me that you don't know the dance moves to 'Gangnam Style'? Even as I write that I know that you do. I bet you've been hovering over YouTube learning them – loser. Anyway, thought you'd get a kick out of this key ring I bought on the sidewalk – *cough* – I mean pavement, as you can tell I'm settling right into New York.

Parcel containing Psy key ring; Danny to Lydia,

August 2013

Oh boy. I'm lying here in bed with every muscle aching. It's the feeling you get after a punishing workout. Only the workout I had last night was far more pleasurable than anything that's ever happened to me at the gym. If they offered that at my old gym, it would have been worth every penny of the £39.99 monthly fee.

I'm almost glad that Danny and I didn't hook up properly the night of the wedding, as I get the impression that over the intervening years he's honed his skills and let's just say that he certainly knows what he's doing, probably a whole lot more than he would have done at twenty-two. There were butterflies, there were orgasms and there were fireworks – and this time they were between the sheets and not in the sky.

I've been awake for a while watching Danny – not in a creepy way, but rather trying to get my head round what's happening. His arm is resting over my belly and whilst I woke up thinking it was really cute, I'm now trying to work out how I can move it as I really need to pee. Trying not to focus on the likelihood of me wetting myself, I instead focus on the billion other thoughts running through my mind. Was it just a one-night thing? Is he going to regret it in the cold light of day? Should I go and put some make-up on before he wakes up?

The panic is starting to build up inside me as it really hits home what we've done. This isn't just a little kiss.

It's no good, I'm in danger of wetting myself if I stay here any longer. I've got no choice but to wriggle out from underneath his arm. I lift it up and he grunts a little and I freeze, wondering if I've woken him, but he simply moves his arm and rolls over.

I sigh with relief and tiptoe into the bathroom to relieve myself. After I've finished I can't help putting on some BB cream whilst I'm in there, just to give me a little bit of a glow, but when I look in the mirror I see that my cheeks already have one. I think back over the events of last night and have to steady my hands on the sink as I go weak at the knees.

I can't believe that for years I have fantasised about what it would be like to have sex with Danny, but even in my wildest imagination I couldn't have imagined it would have been *that* good.

I walk out of the bathroom and into the lounge where I spot Danny's discarded T-shirt on the floor from when we undressed each other on our way down from the roof terrace. I slip it on over my head, breathing in the smell of him as I do.

I wonder what time it is. There aren't any clocks in here and I look around for my phone, trying to remember when I last had it. I know I had it on the roof terrace. I walk over towards the kitchen to go up and see, and then I stop. It's December and I'm wearing a T-shirt. I spot my boots in the middle of the floor and slip them on, followed by my long coat. I'm looking a bit more like a hooker than I'd like, but I'm only going to be up there for a second.

I swing open the secret door in the kitchen and the cool air immediately hits me. I make sure I shut the door behind me after I walk through to keep the heat in. When I get to the top of the stairs I gasp. It might be cold, but it's a beautiful day. The sun is shining, the sky is blue and I'm sure somewhere in the distance I can hear birds tweeting.

I can now see down to the sea. It's pretty far away and somewhat hidden behind buildings, but it's still there and I officially feel as if I'm on holiday. I can't wait to go and explore. I look around the terrace and I spot Danny's phone on the table, but not mine. I poke about on the sofa where I was sitting, lifting the cushions and the blanket, but it's not there. It must be downstairs after all.

I slip Danny's phone into my pocket to give to him and then I head downstairs.

I turn the handle and pull the door, only it doesn't budge. Danny definitely said that you couldn't lock yourself out. I can't have turned the handle hard enough.

I try again and this time I turn the handle with all my might, and yet still nothing. I give it another go, and another, but it won't budge.

I'm going to have to wake Danny up and start to knock. I'm guessing that it'll be hard to hear as I closed both the bedroom door and the kitchen one.

I knock even louder.

'Come on, Danny,' I say, getting agitated. A cool breeze whips down the staircase and wraps itself around my bare legs. I'm starting to get cold.

And then I begin to panic. What if he wakes up and thinks that I've done a runner? What if he leaves thinking that's what I want? He was talking last night of getting a hotel.

I knock again with my fist. If only I had my phone. Then I remember I have his phone. I could use it to call my phone and hope that he picks it up, or at the very least that it wakes him up.

I press the home button, but of course it's locked. There's a message on the screen from a woman named Victoria, and I know that I shouldn't read it, but I can't help myself.

Hey where are you at midnight when I need you, huh? This mumma has needs. Had to do it alone ;)

I press the power off button to hide the screen and the message. I feel sick. He might have broken up with Diana but he's obviously not short of female admirers. Some things never change. I feel so stupid for thinking that I was special when clearly I'm one of many. I rest my head against the door, closing my eyes and I groan loudly.

I'm feeling very sorry for myself when I lurch forward as the door opens and I crash head first into Danny.

'Shit, Lydia, are you OK?' says Danny, as instinctively I put my hand up to my head. 'What were you doing so close to the door?'

'It was locked and I was stuck out here.'

'Locked? It's not locked. It gets a bit stiff in winter. You have to push the door frame as you turn the handle. Come in, your hands are freezing.'

He tugs me in and shuts the door behind him, shivering. He's only dressed in his boxers and I try not to perve over him.

'I was hoping you'd slipped out for breakfast. What were you doing up there anyway?'

'I was looking for my phone,' I say, feeling his in my pocket and remembering word for word what his message from Victoria said.

'You're shivering, let me warm you up,' he says, with a smile on his face as he walks towards me.

I'm desperate for him to wrap his arms around me, but at the same time I don't want to be just another notch on his bedpost.

'I found your phone,' I say, pulling it out of my pocket and handing it to him just as he pulls me close.

'Thanks,' he says, taking it and putting it on the side before he hugs me.

'You had a message,' I say, turning my head so that he can't kiss me on the lips. 'I didn't mean to read it, but it was just there.'

He picks it up and glances at the message before he looks up at me. Then he laughs.

'This is from Victoria.'

'I saw that,' I say, folding my arms.

'She's Gaz's wife.'

'Then what was she doing texting you in the middle of the night? Does Gaz know?'

'What? Oh shit, I can see why that looked dodgy. She's pregnant and for the last few weeks she's been having these cravings for Indian food late at night. Gaz isn't a massive fan and we don't have a takeaway near us so we have to drive to Windermere to get one, and so I've been going with her.'

I run it over in my mind. This mumma – *as in this pregnant woman* – has needs – *for Indian food* – had to do it alone – *drive to Windermere to go get food*. It all fits. I feel ridiculous. Again.

'Hey,' says Danny, pulling my hand. 'Were you jealous?'

'Of course not,' I say, all pitchy and squeaky. I know that I shouldn't be jealous when we've only just got together, and it's not even like we're really together, together, is it?

He pulls me forward and kisses me, just like he did last night, and suddenly none of my worries matter anymore – it's just him and me.

I'm vaguely aware of the sound of a phone ringing.

'Aren't you going to answer that? It could be Victoria,' I say with a laugh.

'It's not mine,' he says, turning round and pulling my phone off the side. It was here all along in the kitchen. Of course it was.

I don't recognise the ringtone and then see it's Facebook Messenger. I'm about to ignore it when I notice that Danny must have accidentally answered it as he handed it over.

'Hi Mum,' I say holding the phone up to my ear.

'Why's it all dark?' she says.

'Oh, are you video calling?' Great. That's just what I need. I pull the phone round to my face and nearly jump in horror at the split screen in front of me. I'm not just talking to my mother, but Danny's mother too.

'Oh, that's much better, love,' says Hazel, beaming away at me with much the same smile that her son is giving in the background behind the phone. Or at least he was until he heard his mum's voice and now he looks horrified. He's waving his hand and shaking his head and I get the impression that he doesn't want to let them know he's here. Not that I would have volunteered that information – I'd never get them off the bloody phone.

'Hazel and I were just having a chat and wondering how you were getting on. Your text last night seemed so rushed so we thought we'd call you.'

'Isn't technology amazing, we can all see each other,' says Hazel laughing.

'Oh, it's amazing all right.'

'Are you on your way out?' says Mum, which surprises me at first until I look down at my coat.

'You might want to do your hair first,' says Hazel. 'You've got a little bit sticking up.'

I'm tiny in my screen but I can still see what she's talking about quite clearly. I have the most spectacular bed hair.

'I'd just nipped out onto the roof to get something I'd left there last night.'

'Oh, it's lovely up there, isn't it, love? Such great views. You have to watch the door though, gets a bit sticky in winter. I left a note in the welcome book,' says Hazel.

'Oh, I bet reading that book was the first thing Lydia did when she got there,' says my mum laughing.

I can see Danny waving the welcome folder in my direction.

'Actually, I missed it,' I say, making sure that the camera's only showing my face when I flip him the bird with my free hand. 'But luckily I made it up and down in one piece.'

'Great, so you're settling in OK? Found everything you've been looking for?' asks Hazel.

I look over at Danny, who's leaning casually up against the worktop.

'Uh-huh, I think so. So far.'

'That's great. What did you do last night?'

I try to keep the smile off my face as I think about what Danny and I got up to. None of it's appropriate to be shared with our mothers.

I can't believe how much has happened in the last twenty-four hours. It feels like a lifetime since I had my not-a-real-date with Steve.

'I popped out for tapas.'

'At Los Toros?'

'Uh-huh.'

'Oh, is that that little restaurant we went to. The one with that waiter?' says Mum.

'Yes, that's the one – the *dishy* waiter,' says Hazel.

'Oh yes, he was certainly dishy.'

'And the food just continues to get better. The last time we went there we had these oysters and do you know, Linda, I never thought it was true what they said about them, but since then we've been making special trips to Whitehaven to get them in.'

Danny is cringing and shaking his head in shame.

I try and pat down my bed hair whilst our mums talk to each other. I'm bracing myself for when they turn their attention back to me.

'Did you meet Steve last night?' asks Hazel.

'Uh-huh.'

'I hope he behaved himself. He can be a big flirt.'

'Can he? I didn't notice.'

Even I can see my cheeks blushing red on the tiny screen as I lie.

'And Liza's a doll. So pretty. You know, before she got together with Steve, I tried to set her up with Daniel,' she says. 'I mean, you remember how beautiful that woman was, don't you, Linda? All dark hair and fiery personality.'

I try not to look directly at Danny, but I notice his cheeks are going red too.

'Of course, Daniel accused me of trying to get them together because of her cooking, which in fairness I probably was in part, but she's lovely, didn't you think?'

'Yes,' I say, barely getting a word in before my mum starts again.

'So what's on the agenda today? Are you going to get a feel for the place?' she asks.

'Oh, it's so important to do that. Now that I'm doing this reiki I'm so much more in touch with things and I can't stress how important getting a feel is.'

My mum is nodding sagely, and I open my mouth to reply, only Danny seems to have come alive with the word 'feel'.

'Um,' I say as Danny stretches his hand out to slide it under my coat, forcing me to bring the phone so close to me that the mums are treated to an extreme close-up of my nostrils.

I spin around trying to push him off.

'Lydia, I'm getting dizzy,' says Mum.

'Sorry, I'm just trying to show you the apartment.'

'It looks like you've had no trouble finding the beers,' says Hazel, as I manage to push Danny back before he retreats to the other side of the kitchen.

'Ah, yes, it was a long day yesterday,' I say, as I try to move the screen back to my face and away from the empty bottles on the side. 'Thanks for leaving those for me. It was a big help.'

'No problem. Now, you've got lots to do today so we should let you get back to it,' says Hazel.

'Yes, have a lovely time, darling, and enjoy whatever it is you decide to do later.'

Danny does an exaggerated wink and I try not to laugh. He starts to come towards me, his hands outstretched again.

'Thanks, Mum, I'll be in touch soon,' I say, squeaking as Danny's fingers comes in contact with my skin and he starts to stroke up my belly. 'Thanks for ringing.'

I just manage to turn the call off when Danny's hand reaches my boobs.

'I'm sorry,' he says, as I raise my eyebrow at him. 'I couldn't resist.'

'Those two. If they knew you were here.'

'I know, they'd be ringing us every five minutes for a status report,' he says, laughing.

'Although, a status report might be quite handy.'

He looks at me and then smiles. 'How about, we hooked up last night and we are going to do it again in a minute?'

'Are we now?' I say, quivering with excitement.

'Yep. I think I did something last night that you liked a lot.'

'I think you did.'

I slip off my coat and I can't help but be flattered by Danny's little whistle as he sees me in just his T-shirt and my boots.

'And then, afterwards, are we going out to explore the area?' I ask.

'Of course; I'll show you all the highlights. We've still got three days before I head to Ben's in Barcelona, plenty of time to see everything.'

It hits me square in the chest. Three days.

'Wow, that suddenly doesn't feel like a very long time,' I say, trying not to think about what's going to happen when he leaves.

'But imagine what we can do in that time,' he says, slipping his hands around my back. He bends down and kisses me gently.

I guess he's right, and my mind goes into overdrive imagining.

Chapter 9

I bloody hate New Year's Eve – all that pressure to make the perfect plans. Are you going to watch the ball drop in Times Square? I've never understood what the ball actually is but I bet it'll be amazing just like the rest of your life there if your Facebook photos are anything to go by! I wish I'd taken you up on your offer to come over for it – I'm not sure a night out at Tiger, Tiger in Portsmouth is going to be the same...

Email; Lydia to Danny, December 2013

'Fucking hell, Lydia. Are you trying to kill me?' asks Danny as he rolls over to look at me and props himself up on his elbow.

We've barely got out of bed in the past twenty-four hours and if I thought my muscles were in trouble yesterday, I was, quite literally, sorely mistaken.

'I'm thinking the same thing about you. I've been on some pretty gruelling hiking holidays, but I think this is the only time I've been in danger of walking home bow-legged. I mean, seriously. How could it even be that good?'

I nuzzle into the crook of his elbow and I fit perfectly. He drapes his hand over my stomach, swirling his finger around my belly button.

In the past I would have felt self-conscious lying here naked and would have pulled the sheet up around me, covering my modesty, or at the very least my bingo wings, but I feel completely at ease. Danny has explored every inch of my body over the last thirty-six hours, so there seems little point in covering up now.

'So do you want to head out or shall I do another run to the supermarket for lunch?'

I realise I'm starving and I have no idea what time of day it is. There's light poking through the edges of the shutters, which means it's day time, but I don't even know if it's morning or afternoon. It's all been a bit of a delicious blur of sex and sleep.

Unsurprisingly, we didn't make it out to see the sights yesterday. The only glimpse of the sea I've had since I got here was from the roof terrace yesterday morning. Danny did a quick run to the supermarket and bought the basics, and he went and got a takeaway pizza for tea. I guess I should be grateful that Danny isn't staying here for the whole week as I worry I'd be going home on a plane having only seen the inside of the apartment.

'I don't know if I can let you out of the bed again.'

'Oh really,' he says as he starts to climb over me so that his arms are propping him up above me. 'It's a pity we've only got two beers left. And no food.'

'Well, perhaps I can let you out, for good behaviour,' I say.

'What about if I'm bad?' he says, with a wink. He slides his hand underneath me and pulls me up towards him.

'How bad?' I purr in his ear.

He whips me round and I get the impression I'm about to find out.

We finally surface at just before midday. After a (not so) quick shower, we manage to put clothes on and keep them on. We have the most ridiculous grins plastered on our faces, and no matter how hard we try we don't seem to be able to wipe them off.

'So, what do you fancy doing. Lunch out? Picnic on the beach? Picnic in bed?'

'Down, boy. We cannot seriously do it again. I'm pretty sure that it should be anatomically impossible to have had this much sex. Isn't it? Do you think there's a finite number of times you can do it in a day?'

'I don't know, but we could test it, if you like?' he says, looking ever hopeful.

I give him a playful shove.

'No picnics in bed. Come on, let's get out of this apartment and get some food. I am ravenous and you are looking good enough to eat right now.'

He's still looking hopeful but I pull him out of the apartment and down the steps.

'Seriously, food. And maybe drink. Is it too early to have sangria? I love sangria.'

'Never too early when you're on holiday,' he says. We walk down the hill and he puts his hand into mine and I can't help but smile. 'Hmm, let's go to Los Toros, it's pretty hard to beat.'

'Um, or we could try somewhere else. I'm only here for a few days and I'm sure there must be loads of restaurants I should try.'

It might have been days ago, but the humiliation of my not-a-real-date experience is still a fresh memory.

'Yeah, but believe me, none are as good, or as close,' he says, pointing to it.

I'm having slight palpitations. What if Steve or Liza tell Danny what happened? I don't want Danny to think that I was trawling around for men on Thursday night in some desperate bid to get some action.

'We could—' but before I can finish my sentence Danny has pushed open the door and I can hear the sound of Steve's voice.

I take the deepest breath ever and walk in, trying to keep my head as high as I can.

'Ah, Lydia, back for more? Can't resist, huh?' he says with a cheeky wink.

Danny pulls me in to him and gives me a quick squeeze as if the thirty seconds I was away from him was hours.

Steve looks taken aback as he looks between us. He stutters for a second and his face wrinkles in confusion.

'Oh, so you two are together, are you?' He places his hands on his hips before dropping them again.

'We certainly are,' says Danny, grinning and squeezing me tighter.

'Lydia arrived early, did she?' asks Steve, raising an eyebrow. He's clearly wary about what's going on.

'Actually, I didn't know Danny was coming at all. It wasn't planned,' I say, pitching in.

'Oh, right,' he says. 'Like that, was it? Whilst the cat's away,' he mutters under his breath.

'No,' I say, getting flustered. 'Danny and I weren't together. I mean, we just got together on Thursday night – after I was here.'

'Busy Thursday,' he says, with a playful lilt to his voice. He seems to have relaxed now that he's realised I didn't go on what I thought was a date with him when I had a boyfriend.

'We've known each other for years,' I say, hoping it makes it sound better. 'Since we were kids.'

'Used to fumble around behind the bike sheds?' he says with a cheeky smile, the old Steve starting to resurface.

I feel my cheeks blushing as he leads us over to a table.

'We didn't go to the same school,' says Danny as he looks at me with the expression I've come to know means only one thing. 'But who knows, if we had . . .'

I'm about to reply when Liza walks up.

'Dan, it's so good to see you,' she says, wrapping him up in a big hug. She lets go of him and comes towards me, holds my hands and kisses me on both cheeks.

'Dan is with Lydia,' says Steve, 'like *with* her.'

Liza drops my hands like a hot potato and gives me a scornful look.

'To think I gave you extra *albondingas*,' she says pouting.

'It's not what you think. Danny and I aren't really together, together,' I say, trying to ignore the hurt look in his eyes. 'We just hooked up out here.'

She's looking at me sceptically.

'We've been friends all our lives and we once had this kiss. This really magical kiss and since then we haven't really been in the same country and single at the same time and then Danny turned up here the other night and, well, one thing led to another. And now we're . . .' I don't know why I'm explaining it all to her but I can't help myself. I want her to know that whatever is going on with Danny and me is something special.

'What's going on?' asks Danny looking between the three of us. My cheeks are burning hot and I'm starting to sweat worse than when I was walking around the complex looking for Hazel's apartment.

Liza plants a smile on her face and takes Danny's hand as she leads him over to a table. 'Nothing,' she says unconvincingly. 'It's just so good to see you; I hope you are looking out for yourself.'

'Thanks, Liza,' he says. 'I think you mean looking after myself. Which I am.'

Her English has been pretty faultless up until now so I'd be surprised if that was a slip rather than a dig at me.

'We're actually really hungry,' says Danny.

'Of course. Steve will take your order and I'll go and cook. I'll see you later on. It's so nice to see a Whittaker back.'

She smiles at us, without really looking at me, and heads back towards the kitchen.

We sit at the same table that I sat at the other night and the embarrassment comes flooding back.

'So, do you need some time to choose off the menu or did you want a platter?' asks Steve as he hovers over his pad.

'A platter sounds good to me, whatever I get here is always good,' says Danny.

'Yes, me too,' I say, careful to choose my words this time.

'Is that the only thing you want off the menu today?' says Steve, wickedly. I can tell he's trying not to laugh.

Danny gives me a look and I give him my best don't ask face.

'Let's have some sangria,' he says, handing the menu to Steve.

'Coming right up,' says Steve as he takes my menu and walks away.

'So what was all that about?' asks Danny.

'What was all what about?' I reply, fluttering my eyelashes as best I can.

'Come on. Something was definitely up with you three. What happened here on Thursday night? I've never seen Liza act like that with a guest. She was so cold and Steve, well, that was weird.'

I watch Steve preparing our pitcher at the bar. I get the impression that he's going to be making digs all night and after that cold shoulder from Liza . . .

'So, funny story,' I say, cringing before I've even started to tell it. 'I was lost when looking for the apartment and I bumped into Steve and he gave me directions. He then, well, I thought he invited me on a . . . on a . . .' It takes me three attempts to get the word out. 'A date.'

Danny isn't saying anything. His lips are pursed. Between that and the silky numbers in my case it makes it look like I was on a mission to get lucky in Spain.

'It was all so embarrassing,' I say, looking down at the table. 'I got here and I thought I was on a date but then realised he was, of course, with Liza. It's not like I arrived here *looking* for someone to go out with. I don't want you to think that I was meeting him and then I ended up in bed with you. I really did come here to soul search; not to, you know.'

I chance a look at Danny and he is trying hard not to laugh.

Steve comes over and brings us the jug of sangria.

'Lydia's just been telling me about the mix-up on Thursday.'

'Oh, that was funny. Can you imagine anyone paying me to take them out? I mean, me, an escort?'

Danny's head whips back to me.

'Oh, yes, thanks, Steve. I'd left that bit of the story out. I got an even wronger end of the stick.' I shield my head in my hand and wish for the second time when sitting in this restaurant that there was a black hole that I could sink into.

Steve chuckles before he walks away.

'And there was me thinking you getting caught singing out-of-tune Madonna in the most ginormous pair of pants was the most embarrassing thing that could have happened to you on Thursday.'

'Nothing was more embarrassing than being caught in those pants.'

We both start to giggle and Danny reaches his hands out to mine.

'Only you, Lydia Stoker, would get yourself into such a muddle. I can just imagine how you would have written about that in one of your letters.'

I smile and finally start to relax. Danny pours me a glass of sangria and I exhale deeply. I love that he isn't weird about it or jealous in the way that Ross used to be. He would even sulk when I got a letter from Danny, despite me telling him hundreds of times that we were only friends.

I soon find myself swaying to the gentle salsa music that's playing in the background. I haven't touched a drop of alcohol this morning, yet I feel giddy. I've never felt like this and I didn't think it was possible outside of the pages of a Mills and Boon book.

'What are you thinking?' asks Danny.

'Oh no, I'm not sharing these thoughts. I already can't walk,' I say, winking as I take a sip of sangria. Since when have I been this flirty?

'Now, now, that's not fair. You're making me want to run out of the restaurant and take you back to the apartment when we've just ordered the food. You're going to make me choose between meatballs and you.'

I'm about to say something smutty about having balls in my mouth but I think better of it. The less encouragement Danny has the better.

'I've tasted those meatballs and I can tell that would be a tough decision,' I say instead. We laugh and I look up at the kitchen not only wishing the food would come quickly as I'm starving but also because I want to be back at the apartment and have Danny all to myself again. What is wrong with me?

'So, how do you find it up in the Lake District? Do you miss city living?' We didn't really do a whole lot of talking yesterday and I'm trying to get sex off the brain.

'A bit,' he says as if mulling it over. 'I miss the convenience of it all. But in some ways it's similar.'

'Yes, I've heard that. New York is just like the Lakes.'

'I mean, the same things frustrate me. Tourists. Traffic. Congestion.'

'But it must be beautiful.'

'Oh, it is, without a shadow of a doubt. I love going hiking on the fells and going out on my mate's boat on the water. It's also handy as it's not far on the motorway to places like Liverpool and Manchester.'

I nod.

'And you, you're happy in Southsea?'

'Uh-huh, it's nice. I love the sea and there are coffee shops everywhere now. You'd notice a real difference from what it used to be like. Do you remember when we used to get the train in when we were younger?'

'It always seemed so huge then, didn't it? We'd get off in the town centre and our mums would grip our hands tightly until we got nearer the sea and then they'd forget and let us loose on the penny sliders,' he says, smiling at the memory. 'Please tell me they still have penny sliders?'

'Oh, they do. I think they're ten pence sliders now.'

'Inflation gets to the best things.'

'I know. I still think of you whenever I have a go on the horse racing. You know it still never pays out for the orange.'

I think of the amount of time and money we spent watching those tiny mechanical horses judder over the fake race course, our eyes pressed against the Perspex box that housed it, willing our riders to reach the end first.

'Come on, I wasn't the only creature of habit. You used to bet on Red Rum every time?'

'Yeah, but more often than not it won and I won ten pence.'

'But you paid ten pence to play. It was much better going for the big gamble. God, I'd forgotten all about that machine. Place your bets now,' he says, mimicking the robotic voice.

I can't help but laugh.

'We'll have to have a rematch,' he says.

I open my mouth to invite him to, but Steve places a steaming hot plate of food down in the middle of us.

'*Patatas bravas*,' he says triumphantly. 'And Manchego, and Andalusian chicken.'

'I am so hungry,' says Danny. 'Let's start, as the rest of the food will probably come out in dribs and drabs.'

'OK,' I say, stabbing some cheese with my fork and placing it on my little plate.

'So, how's your mum getting on? I almost didn't recognise her when I saw her in November. The Patsy's gone for good, then?' he says, as if he's just as sad as I am.

'I think so. She looks like a respectable middle-aged woman now, although of course she's still acting anything but respectably.'

'Is she still with that guy that she brought to mum's sixtieth?'

'Keith, yes. I'd forgotten she'd brought him. He so rarely comes to anything we do. She keeps him very separate, but he's nice enough.'

'And your dad?'

'Still a bit of a wanker, to be honest. But at least now he's with Frances I get a birthday card every year. It's not in his hand writing, but it has his name on it.'

Danny leans his hand over the table and strokes mine as I realise that the smile has fallen a little from my face. There's something so comforting in knowing that I don't have to explain anything about my family to Danny. When my dad left my mum, she whisked us away in the car the twenty-minute drive to Petersfield to stay with Danny's family. We went there most weekends after that. I used to sleep on a metal camp bed with springs that dug into me and squeaked whenever I moved.

'How are your folks, anyway?'

'Same as ever. Bickering, but I think they're happy. The move's been good for them. My dad's less stressed.'

'That's good.'

Steve brings over more dishes and the hunger of not having eaten and doing far too many bedroom workouts means that we devour the food. We keep the talking to a minimum whilst we stuff our faces.

'So,' says Liza as she walks past and stops at our table. 'Is everything OK?'

She's looking at me with the same warm smile she had on Thursday, thank goodness. All has apparently been forgiven.

'Great, thank you,' I say.

'And how is your mother and the family, are they well? And what was the name of the blonde you were with the last time?' she says, turning to Danny.

He coughs and dabs crumbs from the corner of his mouth with his napkin.

'My mum's fine; Stu, Iz and the kids are fine; and um, Victoria is too.'

'I'm so glad. And how long are you here for?'

'Just a couple of days. I'm heading to Barcelona for New Year's Eve and then on home from there.'

'Oh, then you've got time to eat here again before you go,' says Liza breezily, as if that's the only concern in the world and like my heart didn't just break a little at the thought that I've only just got Danny and I'm going to lose him again in a couple of days.

Liza and Danny chat a little about people they know, and I force myself to smile, picking at the last crumbs on the plate, trying not to think about what's going to happen the day after tomorrow. It's not as if the Lake District is just around the corner. Southsea's right in the middle of the south coast and the Lakes are almost as far north as Scotland. I'm sure it would take five or six hours to drive there, and on the train probably a whole day. I'm starting to feel a little down and that's before I even let myself think about what Liza said about Victoria being here with Danny.

'What's wrong?' he asks when Liza's gone.

'Nothing,' I say pretending that I'm fine. 'Did you come here with Gaz and Victoria?'

'Just Victoria, actually. Gaz was supposed to be coming, but he got sick at the last minute. Victoria had been going through a rough time so he still wanted her to get away.'

'You two are close, then?'

'Yeah, pretty close. I guess the three of us hang out a lot. Is that why you look so sad?'

'No,' I say shaking my head. I realise that I'm not going to be able to keep this from him. 'It's more that you talked about going in a couple of days' time. Two days. It's going so quickly.'

'I know.'

He looks at me as I blink back tears. I feel utterly ridiculous. How could I be thinking like this after we've only spent thirty-six hours together?

'I don't have to go. I don't expect Ben would miss me and I wouldn't miss crashing on a sofa. We could have an extra day and night together.'

I try to conceal my excitement.

'Are you sure? Of course I'd be totally fine with hanging out by myself in that apartment with no TV whilst you went to a party.'

'Well, in that case . . .' he says, laughing. 'No, I'd much rather spend New Year with you. We could always go to Barcelona anyway, get a hotel, make a proper night of it.'

'We could,' I say, but to be honest I reckon I'd be just as happy curled up on the roof terrace staring up at the stars. 'Or we could stay here.'

He grins at me. 'Are you sure you're going to be able to cope with me for an extra day?'

'I think so. If you can do that thing you did last night again.'

'Which thing?' he says, leaning over. 'The one with the kisses or the—'

'Dessert?' says Steve, thrusting menus in our faces.

'Um,' says Danny giving me a look.

I try and give him a down-boy look. 'Yes, dessert would be great,' I say, picking the almond cake before Danny reluctantly orders the chocolate fondant. 'And coffee. I think we're going to need some coffee. We've got a long day ahead of us.'

Steve nods and gives Danny a knowing look before he walks off with the menus.

'Are you sure you don't mind not going to see your friend?'

'No, he'll understand.'

'And you're flying out then on New Year's Day?'

He nods. 'And you?'

'The second. I start back at work on the third,' I say. It still doesn't give us much time together.

'Well, at least now we can look forward to seeing the New Year in together.'

'Ah, and a New Year's kiss,' I say, trying to ignore the symbolism I told Lucy about.

'And not only a kiss. There's quite a lot more I'd like to do on New Year's Eve, too.'

'Ohh, is that right?'

'Uh-huh. I could give you a little preview this afternoon, if you're interested.'

I look up towards Steve who's carrying the desserts, wondering if we'd have been better off not ordering any.

'I'm definitely interested,' I say with almost a wink as the plates are put down in front of us and we begin to wolf the desserts down. Not due to hunger this time, but to the desire to get out of the restaurant and back to the apartment as quickly as possible.

Chapter 10

Totally nailed this fridge magnet thing. I mean nothing says the Bahamas like two bare bottomed boys with sun hats, right? I've had a great few days down here. Managed to go diving, parasailing and kite surfing – I bet you'd have loved it ;)

Parcel containing fridge magnet;
Danny to Lydia, March 2014

'You know last night when I said that today I wanted to go further afield than Los Toros and that we should see more of the coastline? This isn't really what I had in mind.'

'I know, but it's a great idea, right?' says Danny with a big grin on his face.

I look down at the harness that's giving me a wedgie. I'm not entirely sure about that.

'We could just go for a hike.'

'Or we could sail into the sky. Trust me on this, it's an amazing feeling. You're going to love it.'

I don't agree, but I take a deep breath. All I can see from here is a cliff and the sea. It's not exactly inspiring me with confidence.

'You'll be fine,' says Paul, as he comes along to double check my harness. 'Have you decided what type of landing you want?'

'A good one,' I reply, nervously wondering what other type there might be.

'Very funny. No, I meant, did you want a normal descent or a rapid one? On the rapid one, we get up some speed and then we corkscrew down to the ground. You can pull five gs – same force as you get in a Formula One car.'

'That sounds awesome,' says Danny.

'I was going to say that it sounded terrifying. Perhaps I'll stick to the normal descent today, as it's my first go and all that.'

'Fair enough,' Paul says, as he clips his harness to mine. 'Now you remember what you need to do?'

I nod.

'OK, then, and don't forget, when we come into land you need to start running along before we hit the ground, OK?'

I bend at the knees and try to remember. 'Uh-huh,' I say with a wobble to my voice.

This is going to be fine, this is going to be fine, I chant to myself.

My trip away was supposed to be a break from my everyday life to think everything through and to put myself out of my comfort zone. Whilst I've been too busy with Danny to think about the big things that I was supposed to, this at least is challenging me. I'll be well and truly #LivingMyBestLife, if I don't wet myself or black out first.

'You're going to take a photo, right?' I say to Danny as I try and stop myself from hyperventilating.

'Yeah,' he says waving the camera. 'And my GoPro will record it on your helmet.'

He walks over and flicks a switch. Perfect, now my screaming will be recorded for posterity.

Danny leans over and I grab on to his neck and kiss him like this is going to be my last. Because, who knows, it might be. I signed the waiver for this; I know there are risks involved.

Paul the pilot coughs behind me. 'Do you guys need a room, or . . .'

'Just in case something goes wrong,' I say.

'OK,' he says whistling. 'I guess it's always good to say your last I love yous.'

I feel my cheeks flushing. We haven't even said our first yet. I can't look Danny in the eye. Even if it were true, I couldn't tell him for the first time with a stranger strapped to my back – it wouldn't really set the right mood.

'This wind is perfect,' says Paul. 'Let's get going. Ready?'

'As I'll ever be,' I mutter, looking up at Danny in desperation.

'OK, I'm dispatching the sail,' says Paul.

Danny gives me a thumbs-up and suddenly I've twisted round as the parachute juts out behind us.

Paul gives me a nudge as he gets the sail under control and I start to walk forward as instructed. It's all a bit jolty and chaotic and I'm beginning to panic until I realise that my legs are no longer in contact with the ground and I'm sort of hanging mid-air. My stomach lurches as we bob up and down catching the wind and I may or may not have screamed just a little, or should that be a lot.

I daren't look around at Danny behind me and instead I focus on the beautiful blue sky and the light twinkling off the sea. I'm still struggling to breathe. I've never been phased by heights, but it feels a bit weird having absolutely nothing beneath me. But oh my God is it beautiful, and I feel so free.

The next twenty minutes pass by in what feels like seconds and no sooner have I started to relax than it's time to descend. I can see Danny on the beach below and I feel my stomach flip, and it's nothing to do with the thermals we're flying through. He's waving and smiling and I can't wait to tell him how amazing this was.

We're coming ever closer to the ground and I'm trying to ignore the sea that seems pretty close on my right and the cliff face that's perilously close on the left. I keep focused on my shadow on the beach, which is growing ever larger, and all of a sudden we're within touching distance of the sand and I straighten my legs before bam. I fall over and feel the weight of Paul falling flat on top of me. I'm about to try and move before we're encased in the parachute.

'Did someone forget to run in the air as we landed?' says Paul, laughing.

'I think so,' I say wriggling around like a beetle trapped on its back.

The parachute blows up at the side and I see Danny poking his head underneath.

'Oh, like that, is it?' he says, laughing at our collapsed heap.

Paul unclips himself and shimmies off me before pushing the parachute off backwards while Danny helps me up to standing.

'Well?' he says, raising an eyebrow.

It takes a second or two for me to stand properly as my legs have turned to jelly.

'That was incredible,' I say, letting out the biggest breath. 'Absolutely incredible.'

'I heard screaming and I wasn't too sure . . .'

'Screams of joy,' I say and he gives me a dubious look. 'Well, maybe not at first, but when I finally got into it they were joyful.'

'My turn next,' he says giving me an even bigger grin. 'Can't wait.'

I can see Danny coming into view. It doesn't look quite as relaxing as I remember it being as now I can see just how tight the landing area is. It felt close from the air, but from here I can see it's even closer than I thought.

I edge forward on the rock I'm on, hoping that a big gust doesn't blow Danny and Paul off course. I hold my breath and cross my fingers, only to exhale with relief as they're nearly down and I giggle as Danny begins to run in the air. They hit the ground in a walk and remain standing. What a pro.

I walk over as Danny unclips himself from the harness and takes his helmet off. He sweeps me into a big kiss.

'Such a good flight.'

We chat to Paul for a while as he packs up, then we say our goodbyes. Danny takes my hand and we start to walk along the deserted beach. Paul offered to drive us back to the main town, but apparently it's only a forty-five minute walk over the headland to get back, and seeing as how this is the first time in three days we've made it off the apartment complex, we've decided to walk it.

The two of us cannot stop talking about our flights. Danny's gripping my hand and I can't remember when I last felt this alive. Today totally ticked numerous boxes on the Living the Best Life quiz – doing something that scared me, doing something new, doing something that will stay with me forever.

'Thanks, Danny,' I say, turning to kiss him.

'For what?' he says, confused.

'For this; I needed it.' I stop and look out at the waves crashing onto the rocks. It's stupid, as I live right next to the sea, but I so rarely take the time to look at it or to appreciate it. 'This last year, it's been . . .' I struggle to find the words.

'I guess it was rough breaking up with Ross.'

I shake my head. It's the first time that we've mentioned Ross. We've been too caught up in this delicious holiday bubble and neither of us have talked about our love lives and exes.

'It was and it wasn't. It's been an adjustment getting used to being single after so long, but I don't regret it for a second. It wasn't right for so long. It was like all of a sudden it clicked and I knew I had to end it.'

I hesitate because I don't want to tell Danny that he's the reason that I broke up with Ross. He'd said something in one of his letters about all his friends settling down and me and Ross getting engaged and it had made me realise how much I didn't want that.

'I think I just expected that after I broke up with him I'd revert back to who I used to be – you know, regain a bit of sparkle – but I didn't seem to be able to. But that, paragliding, that made me feel it. This whole holiday has. I've felt properly alive. So thank you.'

'Well, it's been pretty hard work,' he says, rolling his eyes.

'Ha, yes, it's seemed like it.'

'So you're all set and now all you have to do is keep that sparkle when you go back home.'

I turn and look at the beach we've come from, mainly because I don't want him to see the tears in my eyes at the thought that I'm going to have to go back to the real world without him.

'Yes,' I lie.

'You're off to a good start. The events you manage sound amazing and you like where you live.'

I bite my lip. Now would be the perfect time to tell him that I might have embellished things a little. Tell him I'm an events coordinator and not an events manager; that I live in the granny flat in my sister's basement.

'Yeah, work's great,' I say, bitterly disappointed with myself. 'It's just . . .' I feel embarrassed. Danny's always had a high-flying career and even when he'd given that all up he's launched his own business which is doing really well too. I don't know if he'd understand.

'It's just what?'

'I feel as if I can't go any higher at my company and that I'm ready to. I don't think my boss will promote me because she thinks I'm too good at what I do.'

'So quit,' he says, shrugging his shoulders as we start walking again.

'I can't. Well, I can, but I like where I am and I'm scared to move. The company I worked for in London was so awful and I had no life. I couldn't go back to that.'

'But you can't stay in a job you're unhappy in through fear of something worse.'

'Can't I? I'm not unhappy per se, I just want a promotion.'

'And if they're not going to give it to you, why don't you work for yourself? Go freelance or set up your own business.'

I sigh as I think about Roni and how happy she looked, but I know how much I'd hate it.

'I don't think it's really me.'

'Sorry,' says Danny grimacing, 'you were so happy, I didn't mean to bring you down.'

'You didn't,' I say, trying to get back to that feeling of soaring. 'But you're right, I need to think of making a change. That's what I was supposed to be doing on this holiday. Having a think about what I really want out of life.'

'Ah, and I've been distracting you.'

'You've been a very welcome distraction,' I say, as he helps me scramble over some rocks to get to the next cove.

'As have you,' he says. 'Wow, this beach is stunning.'

We've found ourselves in a tiny deserted cove with just a tiny strip of sand in front of the cliff face.

'It's beautiful,' I say, realising how much we've probably been missing out on while we were hauled up in the apartment for the last few days.

'You know, some of the beaches are naturist. How about it? When in Rome . . .'

I hastily wrap my coat further round myself.

'If you think I'm getting my baps out in this weather, you're severely mistaken.'

Danny laughs. 'Worth a try.'

'No, during this excursion we're keeping our clothes on. I'm sure we can do that for a few hours, right?' I say more to myself than to him. I seem to have zero willpower when it comes to Danny.

I see him wavering, but a man with a fishing rod walks down the cliff path in front of us. 'Right,' he says. 'It is pretty cold. How about we go and get hot chocolate and churros instead?'

'Sounds good to me.'

It doesn't take us long to climb up the cliff path and after another twenty minutes of walking we make it back to civilisation. We find a cute looking cafe just off the main drag and settle ourselves into a table by the window. The waiter takes our order and I rub my hands together relishing the warmth of being inside. It's not long before the waiter returns with our order. and I greedily rip a churro apart and dip it into my drink.

'You still look a bit down,' says Danny. 'Are you still thinking about your work?'

I don't tell him that I'm thinking about the fact that we've only got a short time left together.

'It's not just my work. I think it's just been a funny year. You know we're at that age, aren't we, where everyone is settling down and getting married? My best friend Lucy's wedding is in August and my friend Caroline recently had a baby. I guess it makes you think about your own life. I just expected to be settled by now, or at least to know what I wanted to do with my life.'

Danny stops dipping his churros and looks at me seriously.

'We don't have to have all the answers in life. You know my mum and dad were settled in Petersfield and then moved up to the lakes in their fifties, as they thought there had to be more to life. And look at me, I realised that I didn't want to be doing what I was doing and I moved continents.'

'And do you now think you're living your best life?'

'Oh, I hate that hashtag. What does it even mean?' he says screwing his face up.

'Ha, exactly! But are you?'

He shrugs his shoulders. 'I'm on holiday and I'm eating fried dough dipped in hot chocolate, and I've had more sex than I thought was humanly possible in three days, so I'm pretty sure if I could Instagram a photo of us right now, that would be the hashtag. I mean, I don't think life gets better than this, does it?'

I stare at the chocolate moustache he's got and I can't help but laugh at him.

'You've got a little something,' I say pointing at his face.

'Oh have I now,' he says grabbing a churro laced with hot chocolate and popping it on my nose.

'Hey,' I say, slapping at his hands.

He leans over and kisses my nose as he licks it off.

'I was wrong, it can get better,' he says.

I can feel my heart burning in my chest. He's right; at this moment in time, we are absolutely living our best lives.

'So, do you want to take a slow walk back to the apartment after these? Do you think you've done enough sightseeing for the day?'

I look up at the clock on the wall and see it's almost 3 p. m. We've been out of the apartment for at least six hours now. I think that's respectable.

'Let's head home.'

'And perhaps we could stop by one or two of those underwear shops to find out why everything in the window is red,' says Danny.

'Uh-huh, just out of curiosity, or to make a purchase?'

'Curiosity, of course, but I did think one or two things I saw would look rather good on you.'

He has the same glint in his eye that seems to have got us into so much trouble over the last few days. I realise that we've finished our drinks and Danny gets up to pay.

'I can't believe that tomorrow's New Year's Eve,' he says as we walk out. 'Are you absolutely sure you don't want to go to Barcelona?'

'Positive, unless you want to see your friend after all?'

'Nah, I've emailed him and said I'm not coming. Shall we just book a table at Los Toros?'

'Yeah, why not. That sounds great. Something low key and chilled.'

I don't want to think about tomorrow being our last night together before Danny flies home and I certainly don't want to think about New Year's kisses and what I think they mean. For once I'm not going to overthink things and I'm going to live in the moment, pretending that we're going to be in this holiday romance bubble forever.

Chapter 11

It was so lovely to see you last week! I'm so sorry we didn't get more of a chance to talk but I'm glad you got to meet Ross briefly and to see how nice he is. He asked me to move in with him last week and it seemed silly not to say yes. So here's my new address - I wouldn't want my Christmas decoration getting lost!

Email; Lydia to Danny, November 2014

Danny grabs my hand and tries to pull me into a run up the hill.

'I can't,' I say, my stomach like a lead weight anchoring me to the ground.

'Hurry up,' he says, laughing as he pulls me harder. 'We've got to get back and get ready before midnight.'

'We've got plenty of time,' I say, protesting. Although in truth I'd lost track of time somewhere after the restaurant had cleared away the tables to make way for the dancing.

'No, we haven't. If we want to see the new year in on the roof terrace, we've got to get a wriggle on.'

I don't know whether I'm drunk on all the cava or on love, but my head's in a lovely spin and I honestly don't care where we see the new year in, as long as I'm with Danny.

The plan had been to have a quick meal at Los Toros before heading back for the rest of the evening on the roof terrace. Only the sleepy tapas restaurant had woken up and the whole town seemed to have descended on to it, resulting in a party atmosphere. I would have been happy to have stayed for the whole party, but Danny's on a mission to get us back.

'Come on,' he says, scooping me up, and I scream as he starts to run up the hill with me.

'You'll put your back out,' I say, unable to stop myself from laughing. 'Are you sure you're all about New Year and not just wanting to see the red underwear on?'

We'd popped into one of the lingerie shops and it turns out that Spanish women wear red underwear on New Year's Eve if they want some good loving in the year to come. Of course Danny was fully in favour of supporting this tradition and bought me some and it's been driving him crazy that I haven't modelled it for him yet.

We finally make it to the stairs of number 76 and he plonks me down on the ground.

'Great. Eleven forty-five,' he says, looking at his watch. 'Made it just in time.'

'With plenty of time to spare,' I say waltzing in. I'm about to collapse onto the sofa in the living room, full from the food and knackered from the run up the hill.

'Oh no you don't,' says Danny grabbing my hand. 'Come on.'

He leads me up onto the terrace and I stop dead. There are loads of little tea lights lit around the terrace and a string of fairy lights down one side of the wall.

'When did you?'

'When you were salsa dancing with Steve's dad.'

'I thought you were in the loo,' I say, realising that I'd been having so much fun I hadn't noticed how long he'd been gone.

On the centre of the little table is a bottle of fizz in an ice bucket. Although it's cold enough for it to have stayed chilled without it.

'This is lovely,' I say, leaning into him and giving him a kiss.

'I wanted our last night to be special.'

'It's all been special,' I whisper.

I've loved our lazy days spent walking hand in hand around the little town of Roses, ambling along the beach and stopping off for churros, and our nights spent up here on the roof terrace, staring up at the stars and chatting about anything and everything.

My stomach turns into a sharp knot at the thought that it's our last night together. It seems to have gone by in an instant. I know it's a cliché and cheesy as hell, but these last few days with Danny have been the best of my life. I never knew I could be as comfortable, that I could laugh so much or that sex could be that good. I don't want it to end, but holiday romances always do, don't they?

'So, do we pop the cork now, or after midnight?' I ask, not that I need any more alcohol.

'I think we should wait,' he says, wrapping a blanket over us, and we snuggle up together. It feels perfect and it makes me want to cry.

'I wish we could stay here forever,' I say, wistfully.

'I know, me too.'

'Could we pull a ginormous sicky and stay here for another month?' I say.

'Wish I could.'

'Wow, when did you become Mr Responsible?' I think back to when he was trying to get me to quit my temp job and go travelling with him.

'When Gaz and I set up the company.'

He squeezes me that much tighter and he starts to trace patterns on my leg over the blanket.

Neither of us have said anything about what's going to happen when we get back. It's like the invisible elephant that's sitting in the room, only he seems to be growing bigger and bigger and he's starting to sit on us and suffocate us.

'So,' Danny says, checking his watch again. 'Ten minutes to midnight.'

'Have you thought about any New Year's resolutions?' I ask,

'I've been a bit distracted of late,' he says, grinning. 'Let's see: drink less, eat less crap, go to the gym. Isn't that what you're supposed to say?'

'I meant, what do you want from the new year? I always love making a plan in my head for what I want it to hold.'

'And what is it that *you* want the next year to hold?' he asks, turning to me with a serious look on his face.

I don't know if I'm brave enough to say what I'm really thinking, but I lost him once before and I can't do it again.

'I'm hoping it'll hold a future for you and me,' I say, hoping his feelings have changed over the last few years.

He smiles and takes hold of my hands. 'I'd like that too.'

'You would?'

'Lydia, why are you so surprised? We've been inseparable for the last four days.'

'It's just that you said you only ever wanted to be friends with me.'

'When did I say that?' he says, furrowing his brow.

'At your flat in London. When I came down for that interview at Eventualities and we were going to dinner. Remember the night you told me you were moving to Tokyo?'

I can still feel the pain in the pit of my stomach.

'But I never said—'

'You did, to Gaz. You were talking to him whilst I was changing and I heard you say that we'd kissed once but it was a mistake and that you only thought of me as a friend.'

Danny laughs and shakes his head. 'I told Gaz that because we'd noticed that he used to make a special effort to hit on women that the other guys in our group were after. It was as if it was a challenge or something. In fact, he still did until he got married – I went on a date with Victoria originally and then he met her and I guess the rest is history.'

My jaw drops open as I realise what this means. All this time I thought he wasn't interested. All this bloody wasted time.

'Is that why you were so weird that night? You barely stayed to eat dessert before you ran off for the train.'

'One of the main reasons I went for that job in London was so that I could be near you.'

'Really?'

I nod. 'I'd lied to you then when I said that the company in Newcastle had only given me a temporary contract. I quit the job to move to London, in part because of the job, but more because of you.'

'I had no idea. I never would have gone to Tokyo.' He wipes a tear away from my cheek. 'Hey, don't be sad. We can't change the past but we can change the future. When I get one of your letters . . .' he says, a smile creeping over his face.

'I know, it's . . .' I don't know how to express it. 'I feel it too.'

'Lydia, we can't go on pretending anymore, not after this week. We've got to give us a go.'

'How can we? You live in the Lakes and I live in Southsea. I know exactly what would happen. We'd see each other a couple of times and it would be great, but then it'd become too much effort. We'd use excuses – "I've got too much work" or "I'll come next week" – but we wouldn't and it would all fizzle out. No more emails. No more parcels.'

Danny takes my hands in his and he's got that look on his face. His pupils are wide and he's blinking rapidly.

You see, this is the problem with knowing someone forever. I know what that face used to mean when he was a child.

'Oh no. What's your crazy idea, Danny Whittaker?'

'How do you know that it's going to be crazy?'

'It's that twitch you get in your eye.'

Danny laughs as he starts scrunching his eyes up, only it makes him look more ridiculous.

'Better?' he says, now looking as if he's doing a zombie impression.

'Much,' I say, giggling. 'So what's your grand plan?'

'Well, remember when we made that pact – at Kerry's wedding?'

My mind starts to run away with itself. The candles. The fairy lights. Him racing to get us back here before midnight. The cava on ice. What if he's going to ask me to marry him? I'm being ridiculous. It's far too soon for anything like that. Isn't it?

'The "if we're not married by the time we're thirty",' I say, and he nods encouragingly and I can't stop myself from thinking that I was too quick to dismiss the idea. I mean it all fits – the setting, him bringing up the pact . . .

I get flashbacks as if we're in some movie of us when we're kids, when we were teenagers; that kiss at Kerry's wedding and then the parcels and letters, and then this week. Only the montage doesn't stop with us, it shows me the rest of my life – stuck on a loop and stuck in a job that hasn't changed and in loveless relationships. Danny's right. We should totally get married. 'YES!' I scream a little too loudly.

'Yes, what?' asks Danny, a bit confused. 'What was the question?'

'Didn't you just ask me to marry you? I mean, it wasn't the proposal of my dreams or anything. It didn't exactly knock me off my feet, but—'

'I didn't actually ask you, I was just asking if you remembered the pact? That's what I was going to lead with in relation to us trying long distance, but, hang on a second, you said yes? You'd say yes?'

'Well, no,' I say mortified that I got it so wrong.

'No? You shouted yes, I reckon everyone at Los Toros heard it too.'

'Yes, I said yes. But only because I thought that was what you wanted to do. I thought it was your idea. So if I wanted to get married to you, you'd marry me?' I ask. My mind's in a maelstrom. Does he want to marry me? Do I want to marry him?

He grins at me and takes my hands in his again. 'I'd marry you if you wanted to marry me. Lydia, it's not as if we haven't known each other forever. We get on great. You know I'm not an axe murderer or a con artist and I know that you're not deranged or a bunny boiler.'

'Important considerations,' I say, nodding mockingly.

'I mean, we know each other. We've got lots of shared memories. My mum loves you, and your mum loves me, or at least I think she does. We have amazing sex. We'd have cute-looking kids.'

'Woah there, hold your horses,' I say suddenly breaking out into hives as he plans our lives. 'One minute it's marriage, the next it's kids?'

My voice is all squeaky and my heart is beating rapidly. All I wanted was an extra week or two of blissful holiday romance and somehow I'm almost at the stage of coming away with a mortgage and 2.4 children.

'I'm sorry, kids was probably a little much. But seriously, I've dated a lot of women over the years.'

'I don't really want to know about them,' I say, feeling prickles of jealousy.

'Why is this so bloody hard? What I'm trying to say is that I never felt like this with any of them. Have you felt like this before? Honestly?'

I'm looking straight at him and I know I can't lie. 'No, I haven't,' I say, the jokes fading away. 'It feels like—'

I stop myself. I can't say that. No one says those words after four days together. Even if it is different with him.

'It feels like you're falling in love with me?' he says slowly, and I nod. He's a mind reader on top of everything else. He moves my hands gently up and down and stares me straight in the eyes. 'That's what I feel too.'

'You're falling in love with yourself,' I say, trying to lighten the mood, only there's too much tension in the air and it falls flat.

'I love you.'

Those three little words floor me.

'I love you too,' I say without hesitation. I've never been surer about anything in my life.

'Don't you think the timing of it all is perfect? Us here at the countdown to midnight. It feels like the right thing to do. The right way to see in the new year.'

'I thought you'd planned it all. Getting me back here, the tea lights, the fairy lights, the bubbles on ice.'

Danny laughs. 'I just wanted it to look nice. The fairy lights have been here all week; I just haven't switched them on, and as for getting you up here, I just wanted to have you all to myself at midnight and not to have to share you.'

'Trust me to jump to the wrong conclusion,' I say, feeling flushed.

'But why? I can't imagine that I could have planned anything better. This is our place and the start of a new year: the year of us.'

He lets go of my hands and gets up off the sofa and crouches down on one knee.

'Lydia Stoker, sexiest woman in the world, will you marry me?'

He slips a tiny ring off his little finger and holds it out to me.

For a second I'm speechless. I know I just said I'd marry him, but the whole proposal – him on one knee with a ring. Oh my God. This is actually happening.

'Yes, Danny Whittaker, nicest guy in the world, I will.'

I hold out my hand, wondering what the hell has come over me. I feel a rush of emotion and it feels good; it feels right. Only Danny pulls the ring back.

What is this man doing to me?

'Hang on a second. I tell you that you're the sexiest woman in the world and I get that I'm the nicest guy? The *nicest*?'

'Everyone wants to marry a nice guy,' I say, genuinely confused.

'Do they? Do they really? Don't they want a Stark in the street but a Wildling in the sheets?'

'What the hell does that mean?'

Danny looks shocked and I'm sensing this marriage might be off before it was ever on.

'Um, Lydia, please tell me you watch *Game of Thrones*.'

'Is that the thing with the dragons and all the shagging?'

'Um, there's a bit more to it than that,' he says, shaking his head. The ring's almost going back on his own finger.

'If I promise to watch it, will you give me the ring?'

'And you've also got to promise you'll call me anything but nice?'

'OK. Danny Whittaker, or should I say Adonis, as you're the hottest man on the planet . . .'

'That's a bit better. Although I don't know if Adonis is really me – I don't think my abs are really up to that.'

'Just put that bloody ring on my finger before I change my mind.'

Danny does as he's told. Obedience is a key requirement in marriage – I've seen Kerry and Jim in action over the years.

Getting the ring on is a bit of a squeeze but it just goes over my knuckle, even if it is in slight danger of cutting off my circulation.

We both stare at the tiny ring and take in the symbolism of it.

I'm getting married.

Scratch that.

We're getting married.

My heart could burst. The fact that I'm the sexiest woman on the planet might be up for dispute, but there's no question that I am the happiest. Danny kisses me and it only confirms this is the right thing to do.

'Holy shit,' I say, looking up at him.

'I know. Now we've just got to work out how to do it.'

'How to do what?' I say, absentmindedly wondering how quickly your finger can drop off through lack of blood supply.

'The wedding.'

'Oh, God. The wedding,' I say, thinking back to my sister's overly elaborate do. It was spectacular and wonderful but it isn't what I'd like. It cost thousands and that was over ten years ago. Things have moved on and are even more elaborate now.

'My mum's going to be a nightmare.'

She loved Kerry's wedding. The planning. The hen do. The run-up to the big day. It was as if she'd found her true vocation.

'Can you imagine mine?' he says, wincing.

Danny's mum Hazel is lovely, but she's bat-shit crazy. Goodness knows what ideas she'd have.

'She'd want to do a solo – do you know that she plays the ukulele?' he says.

'My mum's new year's resolution is to do the Paleo Diet,' I say, wincing.

'Mine's doing vegan and raw.'

I shake my head. They're best friends for a reason.

We both shudder and stare at the ring.

'It seemed like such a good idea,' I say, wistfully.

'It still could be. Why don't we elope?'

'What, go to Vegas?'

I start to imagine myself surrounded by Elvis impersonators and slot machines. That's not very me either.

'No, we could go to Gretna Green. It's not very far away from me at all.'

'OK,' I say, slowly thinking that that's more like it. 'But wouldn't our mums try and talk us out of it?'

'Not if we went before we told them. We could go tomorrow.'

'What?' I say, the heat creeping over me once more. 'What do you mean?'

'I've got an afternoon flight to Glasgow. You could book on it too. My car's there. I could drive us to Gretna. I'm sure we could be married by teatime.'

My head's spinning. My heart and my lady bits are telling me to go for it; that a lifetime of Danny would be the most amazing thing ever. My brain, however, is telling me to slow down, that there's no rush, especially when we haven't worked out the post-wedding logistics.

'But what about my flight? I'm supposed to fly into Bournemouth. I've got work on the third.'

'I can't drive you back as I've got meetings all week but there are trains that run from Oxenholme to London pretty regularly and it doesn't take that long.'

'I guess that could work.' Short-term logistics taken care of, but they're not really the important ones. 'But do you think we should wait? You live at one end of the country and I live at the other. Shouldn't we work out, you know, that little old thing like where we're going to live?'

'I can work anywhere with my business, but I think you'd love it up in the Lakes. I've got a beautiful little house in a pretty little town. You were only saying yesterday that you wanted a change. Perhaps it's time to move jobs. There's bound to be event-planning work up near me.'

I think of my life in Portsmouth, the one I used to love. It's definitely not the same anymore since everyone else's lives have moved on. I've been feeling as if something's missing and that I needed a change and perhaps this is it. Perhaps marrying Danny and moving up north is the fresh start I need. Perhaps that's what's been holding me back over the years that I haven't been more impulsive. Just because it didn't work out when I moved to London on a whim doesn't mean to say I shouldn't take more risks.

'OK,' I say nodding. 'I'll move up to the Lakes with you.'

'What? Really? Don't you want to think about it? Will you not miss your flat?'

I think of my funny little studio under Kerry and Jim's house – it's not as if it's my forever home.

'No,' I say shaking my head. My mind is made up. 'Sod it, I know this is right, Danny. Sometimes you've got to take a leap of faith, right?'

'Absolutely,' he says, kissing me and then leaning his forehead on mine. 'So we're getting married tomorrow.'

'Do you really not think we should wait?'

'If we wait, then our mums will hijack it. You know what they'd be like.'

'They'll also be devastated that we did it without them.'

'They might be, but don't you think they'll just be pleased that we got together?'

'I guess they would.'

I can imagine what they'd be saying right now if they knew that we'd been here all this week. They'd probably have had the knitting needles out making cardigans for our firstborn.

'We're actually doing this,' I say giggling.

'We actually are,' he says. His whole face lights up and he kisses me as the fireworks and firecrackers crackle loudly around us.

'Happy New Year, soon-to-be-Mrs-Whittaker.'

'Oh my God. That sounds so weird. I'm going to be a wife.'

'Uh-huh, my wife,' he says, kissing me gently again before picking up the bottle of cava.

He pops the cork and I put the glasses underneath the stream of fizzy wine.

'To us. Here's to the start of an incredible new year,' he says.

'To us,' I say chinking back. 'And to tomorrow.'

'Today,' he says as he sips his drink. 'Here's to getting married today.'

I lean over again and kiss him. It's certainly going to be one hell of a start to the year.

Chapter 12

It was really nice seeing you last month. And finally meeting Ross; good to put a face to a name and all that. I'm guessing that it must be serious now that you've moved in together. I'm really happy everything's going so well for you. I just hope that he shares your love of tacky decorations – as here's another one.

Parcel; Danny to Lydia, December 2014

'This is so exciting,' I say, gripping Danny's hand even tighter as the plane starts to drop down on its descent.

I can't believe we are actually doing this. We're landing in Glasgow in a matter of minutes and we're getting married.

'Yes, it is,' he says through gritted teeth. 'Any chance I could keep some feeling in my fingers? I might need to sign a marriage certificate or a register, or whatever else it is you do.'

'Oh yes, totally,' I say, letting his hand go and practically elbowing him off the arm rest so that I can grip that instead.

'Are you always this scared of flying?' he asks. 'I mean, it's pretty calm out, there's not even any wind.'

'Hush,' I say, momentarily lifting my hand up to put a finger to his mouth before grabbing hold of the armrest again as if I'm on a white-knuckle ride. 'I don't want to think about us hurtling towards the earth in this baked-bean tin at God knows what speed.'

I'm not the world's worst flyer, but I'm certainly not the best either. I seem to be OK on take-off, optimistic that if we can make it into the air, that's where we'll stay, but as soon as we start descending again I feel the fear overwhelming me. All those sudden bumps. And all those other planes. What if someone points a laser in the captain's eye? Or there's a rogue drone? Or a bird strike? Or the wheels don't come out? What if . . .

'What do you think we should do after the wedding? Stay in a hotel in Gretna or head back to my cottage?' asks Danny, trying to distract me. He's obviously seen my rapid blinking, indicating that my mind was running away with itself again.

I breathe out and try to focus on his question.

'I'm not sure. It is our wedding night, so perhaps we should stay in the hotel. What time's your meeting in the morning?'

'It's at ten. Might be cutting it a bit fine. Perhaps we should stay at mine.'

'I guess we hadn't really thought this through very well. It would have been nice to have a proper honeymoon.'

'Why don't we go somewhere after you've worked your notice? A proper honeymoon? Maldives, Mauritius, the Caribbean, somewhere where you won't be wearing many clothes,' he purrs into my ear and I push him away, hoping the little old lady sitting next to me has dodgy hearing.

'That sounds pretty much like the holiday we've just had; we could just go back there. It was perfect.'

'Yeah, I'm missing it already.'

I rub my head, which is all fuzzy from the drinks last night. Luckily, this morning has been such a whirlwind – booking me a seat on the flight, packing and tidying the apartment, getting to Barcelona, not to mention wedding-dress shopping – that I haven't been able to dwell on my hangover.

'It's lucky that Zara was open at the airport,' I say, thinking of the dress.

'I'm glad it was. We're going to be at risk of looking like hipsters, but I'm thinking that's preferable to you wearing that reindeer onesie.'

'There's still time; I could dig it out of the case.'

Danny gives me a look.

'I'm hoping our wedding will be memorable in other ways, not for being dressed in novelty outfits.'

'OK,' I say nodding, 'so the idea of you hiring a kilt from the venue as we're getting married in Scotland is—'

'Out. Most definitely. I wore a kilt for a fancy-dress party once and it did nothing for my knobbly knees.'

'Ah, but I love your knobbly knees.'

I run my hand over them gently before the plane bumps suddenly and I hold my breath as I look out of the window, only to notice the drab grey buildings to the side of us that must be Glasgow airport.

'Phew, we made it,' I say, genuinely relieved.

'You do know that something like eight million people fly every day? That's hundreds of thousands of planes in the sky every day, millions of flights a year.'

'Uh-huh,' I say, 'and doesn't it scare you that all those planes are hovering precariously close to one another?'

Danny pats me on the knee as if to subdue me and we taxi round to our gate. When the plane finally stops and everyone does a mad rush for the door, we stay sitting, grinning at each other.

'Not long now, kiddo.'

I'm getting excited. There's such a lovely feeling bubbling away in my stomach, I grip Danny's hand, yet not as tight now that we're back on the ground.

'It's going to be great,' he says.

I nod. It is, I can just tell.

I look at myself in the mirror of the dimly lit toilets at some random motorway service station. If I'm totally honest, this isn't where I pictured myself getting ready for my big day. But, as I stare back at my reflection, I do look almost bridal with my hair pinned to one side, loose curls cascading down my face, dressed in a silky cream dress with pearl detail at the top, and I've applied almost flawless make-up. I'm pretty impressed.

'Ooh, I know where you're off to, lovie,' says a woman with a wink as she washes her hands.

I feel my cheeks flush as it feels as if we're doing something illicit.

I smile back and totter out awkwardly.

I catch sight of Danny shuffling around in his skinny-trousered suit, his hands in his pockets. He looks so handsome; I can't quite believe that he's going to be my husband.

He turns around and does an embarrassingly loud wolf whistle as I walk up to him, and I do a little curtsey.

'You look amazing,' he says, kissing me on the cheek.

'It's not too short, is it?' I say, as I awkwardly pull the hem down as it's barely covering my bum.

'The answer to that question is always going to be no. Things are never too short in my book.'

He grabs my hand and I slip my thick coat on as we hurry to the car through the light drizzle.

'Right, next junction down and we're there,' says Danny.

I almost yelp with excitement. I try and block out thoughts of my mum and Danny's mum, my sister and Olivia – all of them are going to be so peeved at us. Instead I keep trying to focus on the big picture. I'm sure they'll all be happy in the long run.

In a matter of minutes Danny's pulling off the motorway and I almost wet myself as we see the little road sign that's so synonymous with elopers. This is it. We're here and we're really doing this.

'So, how does this work, do you think? Do we just turn up and book in, then wait in a queue?'

'I have no idea. I've only seen Vegas weddings in movies and they just rock up.'

Gretna looks like your average town with houses and shops and people going about their everyday business. I don't know if I'd expected to see couples running down the road in puffy wedding dresses and kilts, but it seems surprisingly normal.

'What about that place?' he says, driving slowly past and pointing to a black-and-white building that's got a big sign out in front of it declaring it *the* venue to get married in Gretna.

'It says that it's world famous.'

'I guess that's what we're after,' I say, as Danny turns into the car park.

We look at each other as he pulls up the handbrake. There's no turning back now.

My heart is racing as we walk into the reception. Danny grabs at my hand but it's so sweaty that it slides around and, in the end, I have to take it back and wipe it on my coat.

'Hello, there,' says the cheery receptionist as we walk up to her, hand in hand.

'Hi,' says Danny, flashing a winning smile. 'We're here to get married.'

'OK, then,' says the woman. 'You've come to the right place. Our marriage planners are based next door in the hotel. I'll see if one of them is free to have a wee chat with you. Did you have a date in mind?' She's picked up her phone and is covering the mouthpiece as she chats to us and dials at the same time.

'Yes, we want to do it now. Well, today,' I say, all high pitched and squeaky. It just seems so weird to say that out loud.

'Right,' says the woman, sliding the phone away from her ear and hanging it up. She looks over the counter at our outfits with a mild look of horror on her face. 'You do know that you can't get married today, legally?'

She's wrinkling her face up and looking at us with a mixture of pity and exasperation at the fact that we haven't researched this before coming.

'Can't we?' says Danny, raising an eyebrow.

'No, we're not Las Vegas,' she chirps back. 'But the good news is that you only have to wait twenty-nine days from when you hand your forms to the registrar. So, do you think you'd want to come back then? We're obviously full around Valentine's Day, as you can imagine, but early February is freer and we've got good availability for most of March. I can get one of our wedding planners to talk you through your requirements and they'll even help you fill out the M10 form.'

'The M10?' I ask, feeling deflated.

'The form you need to submit legally to the Gretna registry office. Have you got your birth certificates on you?'

'Um, just our passports,' says Danny wearily.

'Oh no, you'll need to give the registrars your birth certificates too. No matter, the registry office is closed today anyway. But you'll need them when you come back, along with proof of address – like a utility or council tax bill.'

'Oh,' I say, thinking that we should have stopped running around this morning to do a bit of research. 'So much for eloping.'

I feel Danny squeeze my hand.

'Do you still want to see the marriage planner?' asks the receptionist.

Danny turns to look at me and I stare back at him.

'Do we? I mean, if we've got to plan a wedding in advance is this where we want to do it?' I ask.

Danny shrugs. 'It'd still save all the hassle. We could sort everything out today, I guess. If you post me your birth certificate, I could come back up on Friday with the forms for the registrar. Do we both need to be here?'

'No, just one of you.'

'OK, then we could have the wedding in early February. We could either keep it a secret or we could tell everyone about it and then they'd be here, but there'd be no room for interference from them.'

I guess this way our mothers won't disown us when they find out we got married without telling them.

'Yes, that's a great idea. And twenty-nine days isn't a long time, is it? It'll fly by.'

'And you'll be well on your way through your notice period, too.'

'So you'd like to go ahead?' asks the receptionist. 'I'll call Grace to come and chat to you.'

She talks to her colleague on the phone and I turn to Danny. 'Twenty-nine days,' I say. 'What date would that be in February?'

Danny pulls out his iPhone. 'Hmm, if I can get the forms up to the registrar on Friday, twenty-nine days from then will be. . . ' he says counting out loud, 'will be Saturday the second of February.'

'OK, I guess that would work, if they've got availability. I wonder what we'd do afterwards?' I say more to myself than to Danny. I see his eyebrows raise. 'Yes, I know what we would do afterwards, I just mean with everyone coming. Will we go for a meal after or have a proper reception?'

'We just do the ceremonies here, but we have a choice of three hotels to have a reception in, if you want one. If you've only got a small number attending, there's bound to be something free,' says the receptionist helpfully.

'Yes, perhaps we can just have a small dinner. No first dance. Or photo booth, or big thing.'

'Exactly,' says Danny nodding as if we're completely on the same wavelength.

'Great, that's entirely doable. We have private dining at our hotels. Ah, here's Grace, she can tell you more about it,' says the receptionist as another woman walks over. She has the biggest smile on her face.

'Hello. I hear you want to get married quickly?' She ushers us out of the reception and into a hallway that has some chairs outside, and she sits down for a chat.

Danny and I smile. 'Yes, we do. I'm going to drop the paperwork in to the registrar on Friday, so twenty-nine days from then.'

'Yes, at least. So let's look at this. That brings us to Saturday the second. Hmm,' she says wincing as she flicks through her book. 'What sort of numbers are you talking?' She looks up at our blank faces.

'We just know we want small,' I say shrugging.

'How many people other than you are coming? Just family or close friends as well?'

Danny and I look at each other.

'I guess there's our mums and dads,' says Danny.

'Yes, and Frances, Dad's wife. And Kerry and Jim and Olivia.'

'Stuart and his wife, their two kids.'

'I'll have to invite my best friend Lucy and she'll probably bring her fiancé Ed.'

'And Gaz and his wife Victoria.'

We look away from each other and back at Grace.

'So you're looking at around twenty people, then? If a few of them are children, then we can just about squeeze you into one of the private dining areas of our main hotel, if you wanted something quite small and intimate. That's more of a dinner than a reception. If you wanted something with dancing, then we could do one of our bigger reception suites.' She whistles through her teeth as she looks at the availability. 'But we probably couldn't do that at a weekend for a while, but mid-week might be an option.'

'No, a private dining area would be fine.'

'OK, I can show you that after I've shown you the venue, if you like. You've got two options size wise – our more traditional room is the most popular and it has two time slots available.'

'Great,' I say, my head spinning at the thought that I'm shopping for wedding venues.

This time last week I was excited about shopping for mini toiletries for my holiday. How times have changed.

'Well, I think I should show you around now, as there's a wedding in an hour and guests will be arriving soon, and then we can go round to the hotel and I can talk you through the prices. Then I can give you your forms and make sure you're happy filling them out. And with your wedding being so soon, you'll probably have to pay the full balance. Is that going to be OK?'

I go a bit pale. I've got some savings, but I hadn't really budgeted for a wedding.

'That's fine,' says Danny, as if she's just asked him to pick up a round of drinks.

'Is it?' I whisper, looking at Danny, and he squeezes my hand and nods.

'Great. Come on, then,' says Grace.

She clip-clops along in her heels and I think how cool her job must be. It must be lovely seeing so many people in love. I have to admit that I get the warm and fuzzy feeling in the pit of my belly when we're running a work party and two work colleagues hook up when they're drunk. I like to think I can tell the difference between those who will regret it the next day and those who have been staring longingly at the other over the photocopier for a long time.

'You two are adorable,' she says turning her head and catching us mid-swoon at each other. I've found we do that a lot. 'Have you been together long?'

I look at Danny and raise an eyebrow.

'Five days,' he says, completely dead pan.

I see the look of horror creep over Grace's face.

'Five *days*?' she says slowly, as if he's made a mistake.

'But, when you know, you know, right?' says Danny.

'Besides, we've known each other since we were about six months old. We practically grew up together,' I say. 'He's like a brother to me.'

Grace is looking even more horrified.

'But not like that. I mean, I don't think of him as a brother. I wouldn't fancy my brother, not that I have a brother.'

'She just means that we've known each other for a long time,' says Danny, rescuing me.

'Right, well, I've seen it all here. Really. I've seen couples that get married after thirty years of being together, and ones like you that have been together days or weeks. Marriage is a bit of a gamble and who's to say which one's more likely to succeed?'

'Or end in divorce,' says Danny, quite unhelpfully.

'Er, yes,' says Grace, awkwardly. 'That too. So on that happy note, here's the room.'

'Oh, wow,' I say gasping. It's not how I imagined it at all. It's definitely got an 'olde worlde' feel to it. It's really old fashioned and everything's crooked: the ceiling, the whitewashed walls, the black timber beams. It's got horse brasses and bellows and a massive bit of wood in the centre, with two chairs either side.

'So this is where most couples get married. It's been a venue for marriages since 1784. You can feel the romance in the room, can't you?'

I look over at Danny who's grinning back at me and I wish we still lived in the 1780s. I know the sanitation and the bathing wouldn't have been so good, and, of course, there'd be no telly, but at least I'd be able to marry him right here, right now. There'd be none of this twenty-nine days malarkey and I'm sure they didn't have to provide birth certificates and utility bills.

'I love it,' I say honestly.

Grace beams at me.

'The ceremony itself takes around fifteen minutes, although maybe a little more if you have some readings or songs or anything special. So we tend to allow for an hour for the room. People often arrive half an hour or so beforehand and then it gives you time to be late and for people to take photos afterwards.'

'Right,' I say, trying to take it all in.

'So, let's walk over to the hotel and I can show you the dining options, and then I can answer any questions.'

'Perfect,' says Danny. 'You OK?' he asks, whispering in my ear.

'Fine,' I say, nodding.

'You sure this is what you want to do?'

'One hundred per cent,' I say. 'Twenty-nine bloody days from Friday can't come soon enough.'

He kisses me on the lips and pats my bum affectionately before we hurry out of the room to catch up with Grace.

'What do you want to do now, then?' says Danny as we get back into the car after finishing our meeting with Grace.

'I don't know. What do you do when you've just booked your wedding?'

I still can't believe that we've done it.

I lean over and kiss Danny. It's all so simple and so right. Nothing has ever clicked like this.

'So, do you fancy grabbing dinner on the way home, or getting a takeaway back at my house?'

'In the Lake District?' I say.

'That's where I live.'

'Uh-huh, and that's where your mum lives.'

There's been a sort of magic in our relationship that it's just been about us. It feels weird for us to go back to his house and to our everyday lives where we're going to have to tell people about us.

'Yes, but she lives in Hawkshead and I live in Ambleside. She doesn't have to see us.'

'OK,' I say nodding.

'Are you nervous about telling people?' he says, putting the keys into the ignition.

'Are you not?'

He turns and looks at me. 'Not really. I think everyone's going to be really happy for us.'

'Are they? I hope so,' I say. I've got a rumbly feeling in my belly.

'Let's just go to my house and we'll take it one step at a time, OK?'

'OK,' I say nodding, letting my breathing even out. 'So what's your house like, then?'

'Don't you mean what's *our* house like?'

I feel a bit faint all of a sudden. I hadn't thought of it like that. I've agreed to live somewhere that I haven't seen. What if I hate it?

'I can't imagine what it's going to be like,' I say, 'I never had you down for a cottage. I imagined you living somewhere super swanky. Sort of penthouse. Shiny wooden floors. Steel kitchen. Awesome view of the water.'

Danny laughs.

'What, am I close?'

'You were. That's the type of flat I had in New York. Couldn't swing a cat in it, but it was swanky.'

'So this is a bit more rustic?'

'Not rustic,' he says, his brow furrowed, as if he's searching for the right words. 'I love it and I hope you will too. I mean if it's got to compete with the flat you're living in now. That sounded pretty amazing in your letters.'

'Hmm,' I say, glancing out the window. Somehow I don't think my tiny studio flat in my sister's basement is going to rival a cosy cottage in the Lakes. I may have over exaggerated it slightly.

We start to drive towards the motorway to a house I'm going to be living in very soon.

I try and push away the fear and instead concentrate on us, taking one step at a time.

Chapter 13

*I saw your mum at the weekend – I bloody love that woman.
She really is mad as a box of frogs and I love the fact that
she never changes. She said that you're getting all American.
Come on, Whittaker, let me remind you that an ass is a donkey not an arse, there is no may in tomato and dressing is
never to be taken on the side. Seriously, though, sounds like
you're having the time of your life . . .*

Email; Lydia to Danny, February 2015

The last time I came to the Lakes I was blown away by their
beauty, and this time, as we drive down the little lanes that annoy
Danny so much during the tourist season, it's no different. It
might be a blustery, wet winter's day, but somehow this place
suits that type of weather, with the grass all different shades of
green and the little stone walls dotted across the fells.

I get all excited as Danny drives us through Windermere,
giving me a bit of a tour. I love the fact that the Christmas lights
are still up, which give everything a warm glow as it gets dark.
I marvel at the restaurants and shops and I feel as if I could get
lost for hours here.

I love how busy it is and the chaotic nature of it all. There's a busload of Chinese tourists that have stopped not far from the centre and it's causing chaos as the passengers are ambling across the road, seemingly unaware of the drivers fighting to get down the packed high street.

Once we're out of the town we start driving around Lake Windermere and I can't believe the size of it.

'You can get a ferry from here to my mum's over in Hawkshead. I say ferry, it's a small boat that takes a few minutes. Handy in the summer when the roads are bunged up.'

'So where's your place in relation to your parents'?'

'About halfway between them and Windermere, if you drive round.'

I nod. I love the changing scenery as the road winds around. Sometimes I catch a glimpse of the lake and of the hills that surround it. It's stunning.

Danny points out Ambleside as we drive through. It's obviously not as touristy as Windermere, but it has a charm about it. It seems to have functional shops and a few cafés, and I'm looking forward to exploring.

We pull up into the courtyard of a large building that's covered with a myriad of grey slate and stone. For a second I'm overwhelmed. Is Danny super rich? Was he being a bit coy about his little house? It makes me feel even more pathetic that I live in my sister's basement. I try to calm myself down and look at it properly. I spot a number of doors dotted along it and I realise that it's not one great building but a number of properties and suddenly it's not so intimidating.

Danny gets out of the car and stretches as he walks over to the front door. It's been a long day.

'So, this is where you live?' I ask excitedly, as he approaches a cream-coloured front door with a panel of opaque glass divided into quarters.

'It is indeed. This is my little cottage. Wait,' he says, blocking the doorway with his arm. 'Am I supposed to carry you over the threshold?'

'No, you idiot,' I say, bashing his arm away and walking straight in. 'That's for when we're married.'

'Oh, good. I've got four weeks to pump my arms up a bit at the gym, then.'

'Are you saying that I'm heavy?' I ask indignantly, wondering if all that tapas is starting to show.

'Well, you did eat all that food last night.'

I give him a playful shove as he starts laughing. I know he's only joking.

I walk into the cream hallway, which has a light grey marl-tiled floor. I slip my shoes off, despite Danny's protestations, and I expect the tiles to be cold underfoot, but they're surprisingly warm.

'Underfloor heating,' says Danny, as he taps his phone. 'I set it to come on when we were in Gretna.'

'It's lovely,' I say. 'Makes it nice and toasty.'

I'm looking at the coat hooks and the framed photos on the wall. There's Danny and a mixed group of friends, all dressed in thick jumpers with beers in their hands, smiling for the camera. Then in the next photo they're all in salopettes and bulky ski jackets, their goggles perched on their heads. The final one is of Danny and another guy, their arms around each other's shoulders.

'There's Gaz,' says Danny, walking up behind me. 'We went to Val d'Isère the year before last. Great trip.'

I look over at the other faces. All of a sudden it seems funny that he has a whole life that I don't know about. Friends. New family members – a sister-in-law I've only met in passing, a niece, a nephew. It didn't seem weird when we were in Spain. We talked of our lives back home, but only in an abstract way, as if they didn't really exist. But here we are home, or at least in Danny's home – his world – and it's as if I'm getting to know him for the first time.

'Do you want a tour? I bet you're itching to have a nosey round.'

I nod, suddenly apprehensive. What if I don't like it?

He opens a door off the hallway and reveals a bedroom. It's a typical man's bedroom. The duvet is dark grey, the walls off white and there's not a decorative cushion in sight. It's pretty though. There's a warm-looking fluffy cream carpet on the floor and heavy cream curtains at the window. There's also a wooden blind to give an element of privacy.

'This is nice,' I say, nodding around. He takes my hand and leads me to the next floor, which hosts a lovely pale wooden kitchen with black granite worktops, a family bathroom with an old-fashioned roll-top bath, a shower that looks as if it's big enough for two, and a tiny box room bedroom that Danny uses as an office.

'Now this,' says Danny, as we climb the final staircase to the third floor, 'is my favourite room.'

He opens the door and there at the top of the house is a beautiful lounge. It's spacious enough, but it slopes into the roof, which gives it a cosy feel. There's a large L-shaped fabric sofa that looks as if you could snuggle comfortably into it, and a huge TV mounted on the wall.

'It's a shame it's dark,' he says, 'as the views are cracking.'

He goes over to the log burner, and loads it with logs before lighting it.

'So, what do you think?'

I finish looking around the room and I grin at him.

'It's lovely, it really is. It's not what I would have expected of you, but it actually suits you.'

Danny's laughs. 'Thank you. But will it suit you?'

I look over at the sofa where I imagine Danny and I curled up together.

'Yes, I think it will.'

He pulls out his phone and after a few clicks music fills the room. The unmistakeable sound of The XX fills the room and it sets the mood perfectly.

'Do you have an app for everything?'

'Pretty much.'

He leans down and gives me a kiss, and at first I think it's going to be a quick peck, but he soon reaches his hand around my neck and I know that it's going to be more.

'You know, we've gone almost a whole day without me jumping on you.'

'Really?' I say, thinking about how long the day has been. He's right though. We left the apartment at ten this morning in a taxi and there was no time for any funny business before.

'Uh-huh.'

'Well, we'll have to do something about that,' I say, gently kissing him back. Suddenly, the bedroom seems a very long way away.

I slip off his tie first, before slowly unbuttoning his shirt, all the while keeping my eyes firmly on his. He slips my mini dress off over my head and before I know it my bra is off and he's bent down to remove my tights.

He rolls them down and lifts my legs as he pulls them off, before he kisses around my thighs and I start to lose myself as I watch the flames dance in the wood burner. He's teasing me, getting ever closer to my lace knickers, and I'm starting to stroke his head, trying to guide him so that he puts me out of my misery.

He reaches round and is pulling at the lace of my thong when the door to the room flies open.

'Cooey!' shouts a voice.

Both of us freeze as if we're playing a game of musical statues. I daren't look round at the woman who's just walked in.

'Shit, shit, shit,' whispers Danny as he tries to leap up, only his hands are tangled in my knickers and he sort of pulls me along with him.

I clutch at my boobs, trying to preserve what little modesty I can, and attempt to turn towards the window figuring I'd rather the woman saw bum than boob.

I'm slightly in denial about whose that voice was. I try and pretend that perhaps Danny has a cleaner he hasn't mentioned, or maybe even a girlfriend, either would be preferable. But that shrill was unmistakeable and I can't kid who it belonged to. I close my eyes, wishing I could curl up right here and die.

'Mum, could you give us a second,' says Danny as he finally gets his hands free of my knickers. He retrieves his shirt off the floor and wraps me up in it. It might be covering me up, but it's white and I have a horrible feeling that it's see-through and Hazel probably has a pretty good view of my bum still.

'Well, Daniel, if you give me a bloody key you should warn me that you're going to be performing cunnilingus in your front room for all and sundry to see.'

Oh dear God. Did Hazel just say the word cunnilingus? I'm closing my eyes really tight just like Olivia used to do when she was a toddler playing hide and seek. I'm going by the same logic that if I can't see her, then maybe she can't see me.

'We're three stories up and we face a lake. No one can see us. And cunnilingus, Mum, really? Are we in a Jilly Cooper novel? Look, can you give us a second so that Lydia can get dressed.'

'Of course I can. Hang on. Lydia? Our Lydia?'

She pulls at my shoulder and turns me round as if this is perfectly normal and she hasn't just walked in on a very intimate situation.

I hastily fold my arms over my chest and wince.

'Lydia,' she says, seemingly delighted to see me.

I try and push my lips into a smile, shaking my hair back and pretending that everything is A-OK.

'Hazel,' I say, as she's leans forward and gives me a hug.

'What an earth are you doing here?' she says looking at me as if I'm a big shiny Christmas present that's arrived a little late. 'You're supposed to be at my apartment in Spain. I spoke to you there.'

'Yes, well, I was, but Danny was there too.'

'Was he now?' she says, turning to him and raising her eyebrows.

'I was going to see Ben in Barcelona for New Year and I thought I'd have a bit of peace and quiet beforehand. I hadn't realised that Lydia would be there too.'

'What a happy coincidence. So you two,' she says, pointing between us.

My cheeks are still burning. It's quite clear that us two are an *us two*.

'Hang on,' she says digging in her handbag.

I look over at Danny and wiggle my eyebrows at him. 'Blanket?' I whisper.

He shakes his head.

'Cushions?'

He gives me a don't-be-stupid look.

Why don't men have blankets or bloody cushions? Men always seem to question what use they are, but clearly this situation totally justifies them. When your soon-to-be mother-in-law turns up when you're getting down and dirty and you need to cover your private parts.

I turn back to Hazel who has now got her phone out and is calling someone. Oh God. I know instantly who she's ringing.

'Linda. Linda, you're not going to believe this. I'm only in Daniel's house and guess who's here?'

The phone spins round to me and I'm suddenly face to face with my mother on FaceTime.

I can see her scrunching her eyes up. The light's quite dim in here – you know mood lighting and all that – and I can see she hasn't got her glasses on.

'Lydia. Is that you?'

'Hi, Mum,' I say with a pathetic wave.

Hazel snaps the phone round.

'You'll never believe what they were up to when I walked in.'

'No, no,' I say, practically leaping on the phone and snatching it away. 'That's enough of that. Mum, I'll call you back in a bit and explain.'

'But darling . . .'

'I'll speak to you soon,' I say, hanging up.

I hand the phone back to Hazel.

'You can't do that, Lydia, she'll be dying. Look, she's ringing again,' she says as the phone starts to vibrate noisily. 'Yes, Linda. I think she's embarrassed. She's wearing some cheese-wire knickers.'

Danny takes control of the situation. He marches his mother, who's now filling my mother in on what state of undress we were in, and ushers her out of the door, stopping just short of pushing her down the stairs.

'Go and make us a cup of tea. We'll be down in a minute.'

Hazel waves as she carries on talking to my mum. There's all sorts of shrieking going on and I bet they're planning the wedding already. Ha ha ha – little do they know it's already all done.

'I need something stronger than a bloody cup of tea,' I say, as I desperately scramble around picking up my clothes.

'Me too. God, I'm so sorry. She only has a key for emergencies, she's not actually supposed to use it,' he says, slipping my bra back on and kissing me gently on the nose. 'It was always going to be a big thing for them when they found out.'

'But did it have to be when I was wearing next to nothing? And cunnilingus? What type of a word is that?' I say. 'There are certain things that parents should never say. It reminds me of the time we were playing Scrabble with my mum and she got a triple-word score with the word fellatio and as if it wasn't bad enough that she put it on the board, she then proceeded to read the dictionary definition in case Kerry and I didn't know what it meant.' I shiver at the memory.

'Well, it could have been worse,' he says. I can tell that he's trying not to laugh.

'How? How could it have been worse?'

'You could have been naked.'

'Yes, because that lace thong did a great job of covering up my arse.'

'OK, well, I could have been naked or we could have been doing some of the things we were doing in Spain.'

I slip my dress back over my head as my cheeks start to burn at the memory of some of our steamier sessions. 'You're right, but it doesn't make it any better.'

'So now we just have to work out what we're going to tell her. Are we just going to say we're going to see what happens, or are we going to tell her that we're getting married next month?'

'Oh my God. Are you serious? I just came up to see if you took sugar.'

'Mother, will you learn to knock? Seriously.'

'You're getting married? I've got to phone Linda back. She's never going to bloody believe it. She wouldn't have believed that you were here at all, if she hadn't seen you with her own eyes.'

'Please, don't,' I say, holding my hand up. 'I wanted to tell her in person. You understand, don't you? We wanted to tell you in person, too,' I add, as it sounds like the right thing to say. 'We were building up to it.'

'So, let me get this straight. You're together, like actually together. And you're getting married? Next month?'

'Uh-huh,' says Danny slipping his fingers through mine and holding my hand. 'Isn't that great?'

Hazel, for the first time since I've known her, is speechless and for a second I think that she's going to have a heart attack. She's gone all pale and is slightly shaking.

'What's wrong with her?' I hiss out of the corner of my mouth at Danny.

'I have no idea. Mum? Mum,' he says, walking forward as she leaps up and throws her arms out with a shriek.

'You're getting married. Ah, my darling Lydia,' she says, wrapping her arms round me and dancing me around the living room. 'Do you know Linda and I used to joke about you two tying the knot when you were little. And now you are! I can't wait. I'd always hoped that I'd get on well with Daniel's wife's mother, but now I know it's going to be Linda, it's perfect. So many of my other friends have trouble with the other mothers – all that competitive grandparenting – but Linda and I will love it. We can all go on holidays together. Babysit together. I can't wait.'

'You do know that we're getting married, not having a baby,' says Danny.

'Details, schmetails. The two go hand in hand. Besides, carry on like you were doing when I walked in and there'll be one in no time. So, when are you going to tell Linda? We've got so much to sort out. Besides, I tell her everything and this is quite possibly the biggest news I've had this year, or even this decade.'

'We hadn't decided when we're going to tell her,' says Danny, and I watch his mum's face fall.

'Perhaps we should tell her now.'

'What?' says Danny. 'I thought you wanted to tell her in person?'

'I did, but can you imagine going through this again?'

He shakes his head.

'Right, Hazel. Call Mum again.'

It's no surprise that my mum answers almost immediately. 'So,' she says, 'I hope you've got clothes on now.'

'Hush, Linda,' says Hazel. 'They've got news.'

'Oh my God, I'm going to be a grandmother,' she shrieks.

'No, they're getting married,' says Hazel, before clapping her hand over her mouth. 'Sorry, you were supposed to say that.'

I shrug. I know we hadn't planned it and this would have been about as far away as anything we would have ever thought of but there's a tiny little bit of me that's relieved that it's all out in the open.

'You're what?' She takes a sharp breath and there's a pause and I'm wondering if the phone's frozen. 'That's so wonderful,' she says eventually. 'Tell me all the details. Is it going to be a long engagement? There'll be so much to sort out.'

'Won't there? I think they should have the reception in the barn, don't you?'

'Oh yes, Hazel, it's so beautiful out there in the summer. That light.'

'Yes, only it's next month that they're doing it. Of course, it doesn't give us much time to practise, but I think I can get the other band members together.'

'Band members?' I ask, as Danny shakes his head at me as if to say don't ask.

'Oh yes, hasn't Daniel mentioned that I'm in a ukulele band?' she says proudly. 'Have you still got that one I got you a couple of Christmases ago, Danny? I could give Lydia a little demo. I'm sure she'd be impressed.'

'Ah, Mum, I'm not sure where I left it.'

She eyes him suspiciously. Like her, I know that look of his. It's the one he used to use as a child when he'd broken something and hidden it. I imagine the ukulele has either winged its way to the dump or to a charity shop.

'Pity, pity. Right, now, I was getting tea. But I feel as if we should have some champagne or something.'

'There's a probably a bottle of Prosecco lurking in the fridge, I'll go and get you some,' says Danny, leaving me alone with Hazel and my mother. Both have already forgotten that it's our wedding and are debating the pros and cons of sit-down meals over hog roasts and barbecues.

I shake my head. This is exactly why eloping would have been the best idea.

'Listen, Mum,' I say, stealing away the phone. 'How about you pop round at the weekend and we can chat about it then?'

'I wish I was with you all. I feel as if I'm missing out on a party.'

'Ooh, an engagement party, we should have one of those.'

'Yes, that's a cracking idea. You phone me when you're back at yours, Hazel, and we'll get something sorted.'

'No,' I say waving my hand. 'It's a small wedding. We don't want a big engagement party. No hen dos. No stag dos,' I say, trying to lay down some ground rules.

Both mums look heartbroken. 'I promise, you'll be involved though.'

My mum nods as if pleased with the olive branch.

'I'll speak to you soon,' I say, as we say our goodbyes.

I hand back the phone to Hazel and she takes it, before she grabs my hand and yanks me over to the sofa. 'Now, Lydia, you have to tell me how this all happened. Do not leave out any details. In fact, yes, leave out details. I feel as if I know too much about your sex life already. Just tell me what happened the times when your clothes have been on.'

I pause as, to be honest, that's not been that much.

'Well, Danny came into the apartment in Spain and it was all a bit of a misunderstanding. He didn't know I was there and we both got a bit of a shock, but then we started chatting and then we kissed,' I say dreamily, closing my eyes and seeing us back up on that roof terrace under the stars.

'I'm so pleased for you,' she says, patting my hand. 'So pleased for both of you.'

She's beaming and I'm beaming. It's not every day that you could be caught in almost your birthday suit by your future mother-in-law and within five minutes be sitting next to each other on the sofa chatting away.

Yet more proof that this is meant to be.

Danny comes back into the room carrying a tray with a bottle and three champagne flutes.

He pops it down on the coffee table and opens the bottle. The cork goes flying across the room and we scramble, laughing, to get the drink into the glass.

'To you two. My lovely son and my new daughter-in-law. I can't believe that Linda and I are going to be related.'

Danny and I exchange a look, but we're both still smiling.

'I probably shouldn't drink this as I drove over. Unless I call your father.'

She picks up her phone and walks across the room.

'Brian, you'll never guess what I just caught our son doing. Uh-huh, uh-huh. Yes, with Lydia. Lydia Stoker. Uh-huh, uh-huh. And they're getting married. Next month. Uh-huh. Uh-huh. Yes, love. And bring a bottle of fizz,' she says, hanging up the phone and downing her glass. 'Your dad's on his way.

'So, let's start this wedding planning, then. How are we going to get it all done in a month?'

'Actually, Mum, we're eloping to Gretna Green. You're invited, but it's a really small affair. We don't want a big fuss.'

Hazel laughs out loud.

'You're not joking,' she says when, visibly shocked, she sees our faces. 'But you'll still have me and the band, won't you?'

'The thing is, Mum, it's going to be really small. Just immediate family and best friends.'

'Right,' she says nodding. 'So, just me on the ukulele, then. I can do a nice little song whilst you sign the register or something. How about that?'

'Perfect,' I say, smiling, and she beams back at me. It seems like a small concession to make.

'I'll pick the song,' she says with a little wink. 'It'll be my present to you.'

'Super,' I say.

She looks between the two of us, before taking both of our hands in hers.

'You two,' she says, as if she couldn't be any happier.

I don't know why I was worrying about how they were going to take this. The mums have given us their blessing. If I had any fears that we'd made an impulsive decision in our holiday romance bubble, they've well and truly been laid to rest. It seems everyone's as excited as we are.

Chapter 14

I've gone all old skool and made you a mix tape. Or a mix CD, to be more accurate. I was inspired by hearing 'Let Loose' on the radio the other day. It might be Kerry and Jim's song, but it always reminds me of you at their wedding when we changed the lyrics – FYI I'm still lazy like you. Still the best wedding I've ever been to.

Parcel containing a CD; Lydia to Danny,

September 2015

My head's a bit fuzzy when I wake up and it takes a few attempts to sit upright. I blink through a haze, trying to work out where I am, before I take in the grey duvet and realise that I'm in Danny's bed.

I roll over to his side and it's all warm and cosy, but decidedly empty. I'm a little disappointed that he's already gone to work and that he left without saying goodbye. It's the first day in almost a week that I've woken up without him, and it's just a teaser of what it's going to be like whilst we do long distance for the next few months.

Just as I'm holding a private pity party, the bedroom door swings open and Danny walks in carrying a large tray. He's already dressed in smart jeans and a dark checked shirt.

'So, I made you some breakfast and some tea. I wasn't too sure what you had on your toast so I've brought some marmite, raspberry jam and marmalade.'

I can't believe that he eats not one but two of the spreads I hate – marmalade and marmite. I'm actually more of a Nutella girl myself, but he still gets bonus points for bringing me breakfast in bed in the first place.

'Thanks, that's really sweet of you. Raspberry jam is just fine,' I say, ignoring the others.

'Great. So I'll be home about half two and then I'll run you to the station later in the afternoon. If you want to go for a walk into town this morning, you just hang left at the bottom of the hill and follow the shops. Here's a key.'

'Thanks, don't look so worried. I'll be fine. My sense of direction isn't that bad and I've got my phone.'

'OK, and you can always ring me. Or my mum. She's got to pop round at some point to pick up her car anyway, I'm sure she'd be happy to go for a coffee.'

'At least this time I'd have my clothes on,' I say, cringing at the memory of last night. I wonder how long it's going to take me to be able to think about it without doing a full-on body shudder of embarrassment.

Danny leans over, laughing, and gives me a big fat kiss on the lips. 'I'd better run, Gaz is picking me up from the end of the road.

Be good, and try not to do too much snooping,' he says as he walks out of the door.

'Ooh, there are things for me to find, are there?' I say, raising a cheeky eyebrow. His whole face falls. 'See you later on.'

He hesitates before he gives me a wave and disappears out the door. I hear the car pull away and I look around the room realising how content I feel.

I spread jam on my toast and munch away, flicking on the telly and watching the news.

There's an interesting story about gut bacteria that reminds me of a funny story from an event we'd had at work, and I turn to tell Danny only to realise he's gone. It's so strange as, for six days, we've been inseparable and I suddenly feel lonely without him.

'Pull yourself together, Stoker. You're being ridiculous,' I say, giving myself a pep talk. Besides, he's left me home alone. It would be a bit wrong to waste the opportunity to have a teeny tiny poke around his house whilst he's not here.

I need to get washed and dressed first. I'm wearing one of the skimpy nighties that Lucy gave me and I don't want Hazel to pop in with wedding magazines and see more than she bargained for again.

I go in search of the bathroom, pleased that Danny doesn't have an aversion to bath towels like he does cushions, and see he's left some out for me. I have a quick shower using his toiletries (my mini bottles didn't make it back from Spain) and come out smelling decidedly like a man. I smell like Danny and I rather like it.

Dressed and ready to go, I wander into the kitchen and open up the cupboards, putting on my best Loyd Grossman voice to do a *Look Through the Keyhole* impression. 'Here we have some chickpeas and harissa paste. This person clearly likes their North African dishes. And over here are lemongrass and fish sauce – definitely some South-East Asian influences to his cooking,' I say, pushing my mouth around to give my accent a twang.

I'm secretly pleased that Danny's got a good mix of aromatic herbs and spices. Clearly, he knows his way around the kitchen. In Spain, we lived on tapas and takeaways, and I haven't had the chance to see his culinary skills in action yet. I'm one of those people who thinks I'm cooking if I use fresh pasta and sauce from the chilled aisle.

Hastily, I pull open the other doors and I'm relieved to see one bulging at the seams with carbs – pasta, couscous and bulgar wheat. And there doesn't appear to be a tub of protein powder or supplements like there would have been in Ross's house.

It's funny getting to know Danny this way as I feel as if I already know so much about him, yet, in other ways, I know nothing at all. Up until half an hour ago I wouldn't have been able to tell you if he was a marmite lover or hater. And we all know that's a big thing. There's literally nothing worse in my mind than giving your other half a kiss when they've been eating the vile stuff – I'm almost retching at the thought.

I'm just about to leave the kitchen when I see his fridge is chock-a-block full of the garish fridge magnets I've sent him over the years. I look over all of them, laughing at the memories of me skulking round tourist shops trying to find the worst ones and checking out tacky seaside shops along the coast near me. I thought he was joking when he'd said he'd kept them.

Happy that there's a little part of me in the house already, and that I've discovered that Danny's more competent in the kitchen than I am, I head towards his office. If I was going to have anything personal or incriminating, that's where I'd keep it. But as I touch the door handle it feels wrong. I'm trying to get a feel for his life rather than snooping to catch him out. Instead, I head upstairs to check out the lounge.

Along the wall of the lounge is a built-in bookcase and it's filled with all manner of books, CDs and DVDs. I quickly scan the books. There're the usual ones that find themselves on people's shelves – classics like *The Catcher and the Rye*, *The Great Gatsby*, *War and Peace*. Then there's a whole section of Ian Rankin, John Grisham and Lee Child novels. Followed by a whole shelf of what look like fantasy novels. Most surprisingly of all there's a shelf of 'how to' books. *How to Draw!*, *Car mechanics 101*, *Flamenco for Fun*: books that I'm surprised he owns. I try and imagine Danny dressed in a little mariachi-style jacket clapping his hands and stamping his feet. I know that he's always liked to try new things, but Flamenco?

The DVDs are a similar eclectic mix. There's a box set of *Frasier*, no surprise there, but also *Scrubs*, *The West Wing*, *The Blacklist*, *House of Cards*. All things that I'd happily watch. There's also *Game of Thrones* so I guess I'm not going to be able to wriggle out of watching it.

I start to relax. Just because someone doesn't share my hate of Marmite doesn't mean to say that we'd be incompatible in other ways.

I'm just about to turn and head downstairs when I catch sight of a mix CD I sent him years ago perched at the end of the shelf. It's as if he didn't know where to put it in the rest of his alphabetised collection.

I flip it over and instantly laugh at the random nature of the mix. I find the stereo and slip it in and 'Crazy' by Let Loose starts playing out.

Content that I'm all alone and still deliriously happy, I pick up the remote control and start dancing around pretending it's my microphone.

I'm strutting around and I do a big jump round to face the door when I freeze as I realise I have an audience.

'Does every woman in this town have a bloody key?' I mutter under my breath.

The woman in the doorway looks as shocked as I do and as I fumble with the remote control to turn off the CD, I see her trying to compose herself. She pats down her hair as if she was the one playing the air guitar and leaping around the room. I can only imagine what a mess my hair is in, seeing as I hadn't got round to styling it after washing it.

The immaculate woman is staring at me and I glare back at her, only it makes me feel worse about myself. Her hair's super sleek and straight and it's cut in a trendy angular bob with a block fringe. Her make-up is as you would expect, classic and flawless, and she's wearing a white wool coat that is just as white as it would have been in the shop.

I wonder who she is. She doesn't look like Diana as she'd had fierce blonde ringlets, and I can't imagine Danny has another girlfriend as, surely, Hazel would have known and reacted differently last night.

'Sorry about that, I wasn't expecting anyone,' I say finally.

'Evidently,' she says, pouting.

'I'm Lydia,' I say, planting a smile on my face to counteract her pout.

She still doesn't smile and doesn't bother to introduce herself. 'So Dan's not here?'

'No, he's left for work already. He's got a meeting in Keswick.'

'Oh,' says the woman nodding, as if she should have known, and it causes my muscles to tense. 'Have you finished?'

'Um,' I say, unsure what she's implying. 'Yes, I was just having a little dance, I couldn't believe the CD I'd found.'

'No, I mean here. Are you finished here? Or are you just slacking?'

'Excuse me?' I'm lost.

She looks me up and down again. 'Are you not Dan's cleaner?'

I can feel my cheeks flush. 'Um, no,' I say irritated. 'I'm Danny's fiancée, actually. And you are?'

I instantly regret saying it out loud. I have no idea who this woman is and what her relationship is to Danny. We promised we wouldn't tell people until our families knew and here I am blabbing it to just anyone. The only consolation is that she does have a key, so she must at least be close to him – or does that technically make it worse that I was the one to tell her?

'His what?' she asks. I can tell she's taken aback by the information.

'Fiancé,' I repeat, in a less confident voice. 'Lydia.'

'Right,' she says, smoothing down her hair, even though it's not out of place. 'I'm Victoria, Gaz's wife. Dan might not have mentioned you to us, but I guess he'll have mentioned us to you.'

Ah, this is the famous Victoria. She looks different from the skiing photo on the wall. Her hair was longer then, and lighter.

'He has, Victoria,' I say, holding out my hand, 'it's so nice to meet you. Danny's always talking about you two.'

'Danny? He lets you call him Danny?' she laughs.

I'm confused. Danny's his name. It's always been his name.

'Why wouldn't he?'

'Oh, well, everyone else calls him Dan.'

I think about it, but our family's only ever called him Danny. We don't have any friends in common so I've never heard what anyone else uses.

'Right.'

'You must be special,' she says. 'But I guess we know that since you're his fiancée and all.'

I can feel a chill in the air and I don't think that even the fancy wood burner would fix it.

'Did you want to stay for a cup of tea?' I ask, feeling the need to act as the lady of the house and stake my claim.

'I am in a bit of a hurry.'

'But you had time to talk to Danny? That's why you came, wasn't it?'

She looks agitated but nods.

'A quick cup of tea, then,' she says, turning abruptly and heading down the stairs.

I follow her into the kitchen and I sense her watching me as I subtly look around for the kettle. I triumphantly find it and fill it up a little from the tap.

I switch it on and it rattles away as I try to remember which cupboard I saw the cups in and if I saw any tea during my cupboard snooping.

I open a cupboard of plates and hastily close it again. Then I peer into another one and I catch sight of Victoria's smug smile.

She strides over to another cupboard and finds two white mugs, before pulling what looks like a thin cupboard open, and it comes out like a drawer.

'Normal tea for you?'

I nod as I watch her put a tea bag in for me, before she undoes a packet of herbal tea for herself.

'I take it you can find the milk in the fridge. Well, as long as you can find it under all those ghastly fridge magnets.'

The fridge!

I glide over to it.

'You know, I'm the one who bought him all these ghastly magnets,' I say, with a who's-got-a-smug-look-on-their-face-now-then look.

'You gave them to him?' she asks, backing up towards the sideboard as if she needs to steady herself. 'You're Lydia? His mum's friend's daughter? The Lydia who sends him things?'

She gives me another look up and down and I really wish that I'd done some washing in Spain so that I wasn't standing here in jeans with tomato sauce stains.

'So you have heard of me,' I say.

The kettle boils and clicks off, which helps to break the tension.

'Yes, I have, but I seem to have missed the bit where you got engaged.'

'We had a pact to get married if we were both single at thirty And, well, we are. So . . .'

Victoria looks at me with disdain.

'A pact? You're getting married because you made a pact when you were teenagers?'

'It's not only the pact, obviously,' I say, pouring water into the cups.

'Obviously,' she says, not even attempting to hide her eye roll as I hand her a mug with the tea bag left in it.

I'm doing my best to be friendly as I know she and Danny are close, but I haven't warmed to her in the slightest.

'So, I take it you're from around here?'

'I'm originally from York, but we've got a family holiday home here in Ambleside. I was living in it when I met Dan and Gaz.'

'Do you want a biscuit?' I offer, before trying to rack my brains as to where I'd seen the Jaffa Cakes.

'No,' says Victoria as she slips her white coat off and hangs it over the chair at the tiny table at the end of the room.

'I'd thought we could sit upstairs,' I say, not relishing the thought of having to sit too close to her.

She turns and I see the big baby bump that I'd failed to notice before. 'I'd rather perch here. If I sit down on that sofa I probably won't be able to get up again.'

I see a fleeting hint of a genuine smile, as if she was actually sharing a joke with me.

'Oh, of course,' I say, remembering her midnight text to Danny. 'When's the baby due?'

'April,' she says, stroking her belly and smiling.

I'm starting to think that I judged her too harshly and perhaps we just got off to a bad start. Perhaps we could be new BFFs after all. But no sooner has she smiled then it's gone again and the frosty expression is back.

'So how exactly did you and Dan get together? We saw him on Christmas Eve and he said nothing about you.'

She's clearly not a woman who does small talk.

'I was in Spain, at his mum's house, and he didn't realise. He'd gone over to spend New Year in Barcelona with his friend Ben and had stopped off at his mum's for a few days beforehand and ran into me. One thing led to another, and . . .' I say, drifting off, desperately wishing I was back there with him.

Unlike Hazel, who was transfixed – hanging on every word with an expectant smile on her face – Victoria is frowning as though I'm telling her a story about drowning puppies.

'And that was when?' she asks, as she picks up her tea and starts to sip it.

'Last week.'

'Last week? And you're engaged already?'

'Uh-huh.'

'Why so soon? You can't be pregnant or, at least, you can't know you are.'

'There are other reasons people get married quickly.'

She sips again and stares hard at me.

'I do know that, but usually it's because someone wants something. Residency. Money.'

'How about love?'

She almost spits out her tea. 'Right, as it only takes a week to fall in love?'

'What is it you do?' I ask Victoria.

'I'm a solicitor.'

I smile. Of course she is.

'I've decreased my hours recently, though, for my pregnancy.' She stops speaking and shakes her head. 'Look, Dan's a good guy. I don't want to see him get hurt by anyone.'

'I know that Danny's a great guy. I've known him all my life.'

'But you haven't really spent much time with him over the last few years, have you?'

'Well, no, but we've written.'

'You send each other crappy Christmas decorations and fridge magnets. It's hardly love letters you've been trading, is it? All I'm trying to say is that you don't really know each other. Not anymore.'

'I know enough about him to know how I feel.'

She nods, giving me a look as if to say that I'm naive. 'And what is it that you do, Lydia?'

'I'm an events co-ordinator,' I say, not missing the look she gives me.

'You're a party planner. Nice. Well, I specialise in family law,' she says coldly. 'I hear stories of love that are swiftly followed by divorce.'

How cheery.

'And you're planning to move up here?' she says.

'Yes,' I say, not relishing the thought of being neighbours with her.

'You're moving from the other end of the country, just like that?'

'Yes. It seems logical, Danny works with Gaz.'

'Of course he does. This is so typical of Dan. Always impulsive and ever the optimist.'

There's a bitter tone to her voice and I'm starting to wonder why she's so down on the whole thing. I can understand her being protective of him, I would be too, but there's an edge to her voice that doesn't belong to a friend.

She looks at her watch and drains the rest of her tea.

'It was nice to meet you briefly. Perhaps if you're up this way again, then you can come to dinner with me and Gaz. We can talk properly.'

'I'd like that,' I say, lying heavily, but hopefully I make it seem convincing. 'I'll let Danny know you came over, shall I? Do you want me to give him a message?'

'No, no. It'll keep. I'm sure I'll see him soon enough.'

I go to stand up.

'Sit back down, I'll see myself out. I wouldn't want you getting lost trying to find the front door,' she says with a sly smile.

I'm too stunned to even say goodbye and she mutters an insincere one as she struts out of the kitchen.

I get up anyway, opening all the cupboards looking for that big packet of Jaffa Cakes. I've got some serious comfort eating to do to recover from her visit.

I think back to what Danny said about how great it was going to be moving up here and how Victoria and I would become the best of friends. He was wrong about that, but I hope that doesn't mean to say he's going to be wrong about everything else too.

Chapter 15

Today for dinner I ate grasshoppers and black ants. No, I haven't been sent on some god-awful reality TV show to the back and beyond, I went to a quirky Mexican restaurant in the Village. I was going to send you some, but I wasn't too sure how long ants kept for before being past their sell-by-date or whether they'd get through customs.

Email; Danny to Lydia, November 2015

Bloody hell it's cold. I pull my coat tighter around me and start walking more quickly towards Danny's house. I'd packed for a slightly chilly Spain, not the Lakes in the middle of winter. I keep spotting fells in the distance, which have an icing sugar-like dusting of snow and make me feel even colder. I haven't even got my old faithful scarf or any gloves, and my coat has those useless fake pockets that have a flap at the top and nothing underneath so that I can't even slip my hands inside it.

I nearly bought myself a down jacket and ski gloves from one of the outdoor shops during my walk around Ambleside. I figured that they might come in handy when I move up here, but I couldn't bring myself to do it as it made everything seem so real. In fact, it all did. I was pottering round the eclectic mix of shops and restaurants thinking how lovely they were and feeling like I was on holiday. Only then it hit me that in a few weeks' time I'd be living here – permanently.

It seemed like such an easy decision to make when we were in Spain, drunk on love (and probably sangria), but now that we're here and reality is starting to sink in, it suddenly seems incredibly daunting. I'm not at the stage of changing my mind, but it's going to be a huge adjustment.

Danny should be back from his meeting soon and I can't wait to see him. Whenever I start to have a wobble about moving, I just think of him and I can't bear the thought of us being apart. It's only been five hours since he left for his meeting, but it feels as if it's been five days. I walk into his courtyard and feel my stomach flip as I see his car before I remember that he didn't take it. I hurry to the door to check he's home only to be disappointed when I see Hazel peering through the frosted window of the front door.

'Hello,' I call, as I walk up behind her and she jumps almost a mile.

'Oh, Lydia, love. I'd knocked and I was trying to see if I could see any signs of life. I didn't want to use my key after last time.'

I can feel my cheeks warming. If only I'd thought about last night's events when I was walking around town, I would have been toasty.

'Can we not talk about that,' I say, as I slip the key into the door and open it.

'Ah, there's nothing to be embarrassed about. I'd be strutting around naked if I had a body like yours. Not that not having a body like yours stops me. Last year I did a twelve-week burlesque course. Hey, now, there's an idea, perhaps I could do a performance combining that with the ukulele for the wedding. A ukulele burlesque act – that would be different, wouldn't it?'

She's shimmying and she starts to peel her driving gloves off slowly and seductively.

'That's one word for it,' I say. 'I think it might be better just to stick to the ukulele, though.' It's bad enough that I've got a mental image of my mother-in-law-to-be with nipple tassels, let alone seeing it in real life. 'There are going to be children present too.'

'Oh yes,' she says, as she stops the shimmying and pulls off the rest of her glove with one sharp tug. 'I'll stick to my song. I've already narrowed it down to three. Exciting, huh?'

'It is indeed. Did you want a cup of tea?'

'Yes, please. If I'm not intruding. I came to pick up my car and to drop something off for Daniel.'

I look at the large bag hanging off her wrist and I wonder what's in it.

'You're not intruding at all, come on up.'

This time I make the cup of tea without any problems, having memorised exactly where everything is.

'I was speaking to Stuart this morning and he said that he and Isabelle and the kids have booked into the hotel already for the wedding.'

'Wow, they didn't hang around.'

'I think they're excited. We all are.'

I smile and hope that my family are going to share their enthusiasm. It's not so much telling them about the wedding that I'm dreading; it's the whole moving to Cumbria part.

'Are you sure there's nothing that needs to be done? What about making little wedding favours?'

'It's just going to be low key, so I doubt we'll do favours, and if we do, it'll be something already thrown together, like bags of chocolate coins.'

Hazel's pulling a face.

'I just don't know if you and Danny are thinking about this properly. You only have one first wedding.'

'Um, I'm hoping to only have one wedding,' I say as I pour the tea.

'When you get to my age, you get a bit more pragmatic about things like that. I've been to so many second and third weddings that I'm getting a bit blasé about it. But what I'm trying to say is don't sell yourself short. Especially if this is the real deal. I am happy to help you. Perhaps we should make our own photo booth? I've got a selfie stick and I'm sure we could make props.'

I'm about to suggest that we have loads of props in the cupboard at work but I don't want to add any more fuel to this fire.

'We don't want a fuss,' I say.

'Well, if you change your mind, I've got a great fancy-dress box. I've got everything from wigs to whips.'

'Should I be worried?' asks Danny, as he walks into the kitchen.

My stomach does an involuntary flip at the sight of him.

'We're just talking about the wedding,' says Hazel, waving a hand.

He walks over and gives me a quick kiss and drapes his arm around my shoulders.

'Like I said, should I be worried?'

'Not at all. Lydia's not having any of my ideas.'

'Good,' he says, giving me a little squeeze. 'That's what I like to hear.'

'How was your meeting?' I ask him.

'Good. Long, but good. Now, are you all set to go, as I thought I'd drive you the scenic way round to the train station.'

'Oh,' I say, confused that we're going to have to rush off, 'I didn't think there was any hurry.'

I can't believe I'm leaving already and I'm not going to see him for two days. OK, that doesn't sound like a long time, but I feel as if our relationship so far has been in dog years. Ten minutes apart feels like ten hours.

'I just want to show you some of the countryside views before you go.'

'Lovely,' says Hazel clapping her hands together. 'It's so beautiful around here.'

I try and plant a smile on my face, I'd much rather look at the views in here but Danny's got a determined look on his face.

'I haven't unpacked much but I've got to pack away my clothes from last night.'

'Do you want to get your stuff together and then we'll leave?'

'OK,' I say, uncurling myself out of his arms and heading downstairs.

I'd been hoping we'd at least have had time for a quickie before I went – it's going to be two long nights without him after I've been so used to having him at my beck and call. I'm surprised that he hasn't suggested it himself as I've been having to drag him out of bed most of the rest of the week.

I quickly pack the few bits I'd unpacked and I look around Danny's bedroom in case I've forgotten anything. I feel so sad to be leaving and I feel like I want to leave something of me behind, so I decide to write him a little note.

I dig a pen and paper out from my handbag and begin to write.

Or at least I try to. I've written Danny gazillions of letters and emails over the years, but now I can't think of anything to say.

Hey Sexy,
   Can't wait until I'm back up here sharing your bed again. Sweet dreams (Preferably of me).
   Love L x x x

I cringe a little, but I think it does the job, and I slip it under his pillow.

Hazel and Danny's voices grow louder and I realise they're talking outside the bedroom door so I get up to meet them.

'Hey, all set?' asks Danny.

'Yes, I think so.'

'Great, Mum's just going, so we could probably go too.'

'When you said now, you meant right now?'

I flash Danny a look to suggest a quickie; I can't exactly spell it out as I don't want his mum to think I'm totally sex obsessed.

'Have you got something in your eye?' he asks, furrowing his brow.

'No, no. Everything's fine.'

'Great. I'll get your case,' he says, leaning over and taking it out of my hands before he practically pushes me out the front door that Hazel's just opened.

'I'll see you when you're next up, Lydia,' says Hazel, squeezing my hands as if she can barely contain herself.

'See you soon.'

'Come on, tick tock,' says Danny. 'You've got a train to catch.'

'It doesn't matter, there's one an hour.'

'You don't want to get home too late,' he says. 'Bye, Mum.'

Hazel waves as she goes off to her car and Danny holds the passenger door of his open for me.

I look back up at the house, wondering if I could pretend I left something inside in a ruse to get him to come back in with me.

'Let's go, it's freezing.'

I climb into the car. Danny's already started the engine and is clearly not in the mood to do anything but get on the road. I wonder what's happened to him. I'm getting hot under the collar just being in such close proximity to him. He places his hand on my seat as he reverses back and for some reason I find it incredibly sexy and almost instruct him to pull over immediately so that I can take care of business. But I don't. Instead, I sit on my hands and try to enjoy the changing views out of the window that Danny was so desperate for me to see.

'So, I hear you met Victoria this morning,' he says after a few minutes of silence.

'Yes,' I say, playing with the hem on my coat. I'm trying to choose my words carefully as I know the two of them are close. 'How did you find that out?'

I wonder if she'd been straight on the phone to him when she left me. I could just imagine: *I met your fiancée, how can you marry someone who has terrible taste in music and doesn't know where you keep your tea bags?*

'She phoned Gaz on her way home and of course I was with him. Luckily, I'd told him about us on the way to the meeting.'

'Yeah, sorry about that. I know it wasn't my place to say anything, but it just slipped out.'

'Oh, I don't mind, if you hadn't told her Gaz would have done.'

'Was he as shocked as she was?'

'I think he was more than a little surprised,' he says tactfully.

'So, does she do that a lot? You know, turn up unannounced and let herself in?' I say, looking out of the window, trying to pretend that it's perfectly normal behaviour from his best friend's wife.

The roads are quieter and narrower over this side of Lake Windermere and it feels as if we're in the middle of the woods.

'Not usually. She's going through some stuff at the moment . . . it's complicated.'

I nod as if it doesn't bother me and Danny pats my leg.

'If I could tell you, I would, it's just . . .'

'Complicated?' I offer.

'Yes, complicated,' he says, as if he knows it's a cop out.

'She's not much of a talker, is she?'

'She has her moments. She's just got a lot on at the moment. What with the baby and other things.'

'Complicated ones,' I say mockingly. 'Ooh, by the way, am I the only person who calls you Danny?'

He braves a look at me with a small smile on his face before he snaps his head back to the road.

'Did you not know that?'

'No; I thought everyone called you that. You've never corrected me.'

'That's because I've always liked you calling me it.'

'You have?'

'Uh-huh. It made me feel a bit special.'

'Danny Whittaker, you're very soppy, you know that? Ooh, this place is pretty,' I say as we skirt around a little village.

'This is Hawkshead, where my mum lives.'

Speaking of whom, Hazel beeps and waves frantically as she turns off into the main village.

'Have we got time to pop in to have a look around the town?'

'Um, no. I'm sure we'll go there next time.'

I've given up telling Danny that I'll catch a later train. I'm trying to delay my trip home and he seems desperate to get me there. A wave of panic floods over me. What if he's changed his mind? What if Gaz convinced him that he was making a huge mistake and he's trying to get rid of me?

He pulls off the main road and goes down a smaller one, presumably a short cut. We head down the road for a minute or two and then we come out at a lake.

'Is this part of Windermere?' I ask, not knowing the area well enough to have got my bearings.

'No, this is Esthwaite. It's much smaller and, in my opinion, prettier.'

He pulls up into a little car park and turns the engine off.

'Have we got time in the schedule to get out of the car?' I ask, lifting an eyebrow.

He gives me a look and opens his door.

'I take that as a yes, then.'

He's right about it being much smaller than Windermere. We come out of the clearing and onto the edge of the lake and, bar a few fishermen dotted further down to our left, we've got the place to ourselves.

There's a bench down at the edge and Danny walks over and sits down. The view is incredible and it takes me a few moments to catch my breath before I walk over and sit next to him. I can't put into words how beautiful it is with the green hills that roll right into the lake. It feels like our own secret place.

'This is beautiful.'

'It's my favourite lake. It's much less touristy than the others and it's mainly only fishermen who come here.'

I listen to the sound of the water lapping at the rowing boats nearby. It's instantly calming.

'So this is why you wanted to rush? You wanted to show me your favourite place up here?'

'No, this is why I wanted to rush,' he says as he holds out a ring box.

I look down at it and freeze. I know he's already asked me to marry him, but that was born out of a misunderstanding. Now he's holding an actual ring box. He slips the lid open and there is the ring glistening away at me.

He holds it closer and I gasp at how the diamonds, which are set on either side of a blue sapphire, catch the light. It looks familiar, but I can't work out from where.

'I don't know if it's going to fit, but we can have it resized. It was my nan's.'

'I remember,' I say, realising that's where I'd seen it before. His nan died when we were in our late teens. Danny had been close to her and it had hit him hard.

'You do?'

I squeeze his hand. 'I do.'

'It doesn't have to be this ring. If you think it's too weird, I can buy you another one, it's not me being tight. She'd left it to me in her will and I've always treasured it. But it's not just that it's special to me, I've always thought the sapphire was pretty and those are real diamonds, too – tiny, but real.'

'It's gorgeous. I love it.'

Danny's whole face lights up and he slips the ring out of the box and onto my finger. It fits as if it had been made for me.

'Well, how about that,' I say. 'It's as if it was meant to be.'

'She would have loved to have known you had this. She was always saying how you were such a nice girl and how I ought to make a move before you got snapped up.'

'Ha, that's so funny.'

I look down at my hand. It's never looked so good. I'm probably going to start having manicures now to show it off properly.

'Is this what your mum came to drop off?'

'Uh-huh.'

'And why you practically threw me out of your house?'

'Yep, I needed to get here before the sun started to go down.'

'Thank you,' I say, looking between him and the ring; marvelling at both. 'This is a lovely thing to do. I mean the other ring was nice and all,' I say, handing the tiny ring I'd been wearing back to him.

He takes hold of both of my hands.

'I wanted you to have a proper ring before you went home because I want you to know that this is serious. Victoria made Gaz put her on speakerphone and she kept going on about me marrying my back-up plan, and I wanted you to know before you see your friends that you're not my back-up plan. You're my first choice, Lydia, you always have been. It's just we took a roundabout path to get here.'

I can feel tears forming in my eyes.

'Are you OK?' he asks, wiping my eyes for me.

'Yes, it's just . . .' Uh-oh. Actual tears are rolling down my face. I don't know whether it's because five minutes ago I was worried about him changing his mind or whether it's because this is the most romantic moment of my life – but I am full on blubbing happy tears now.

I sniff loudly as I try and get myself under control.

'I'll ask you again, are you OK?'

'I'm fine,' I say wiping my eyes and laughing. 'I'm fine. You're pretty incredible, Danny Whittaker. Do you know that?'

'I know,' he says laughing and slipping his arm around me.

I lean into him and almost purr like a contented kitten.

'Can we stay here for a minute? We're not in a rush, are we?'

'Nope, we've got all the time in the world,' he says, squeezing me tighter.

I look down at my ring and catch it in the light. I'm not saying that the ring has changed everything, but something's shifted and it's helped to ease my nerves at going home and telling everyone. This time tomorrow, me and my sparkly ring will have handed in my notice at work and I'll be one step closer to moving up here and starting my new life with Danny.

Chapter 16

OMG, I had a day off and watched a boxset of Frasier and now I totally get why you used to bang on about it. I don't know if it knocks Friends off the top spot, but it's pretty close. The writing and the timing of the lines – genius! You realise that now you've got to watch Friends, right? I've looked it up and it's on Netflix – so there's no excuse!

Email; Lydia to Danny, January 2016

I run around the basement frantically looking for my keys. How can I have lost them in my studio flat? It really isn't big enough to lose anything in.

I rifle through the pile of washing that I pulled out of my suitcase when I arrived home last night. I'd been so optimistic to think that I'd put a wash on when in reality I'd phoned Danny instead. I shove the clothes into the washing machine, quickly feeling for the keys as I go.

I can't be late for work today, not when I'm handing in my notice. I've got my game plan all worked out: arrive early with doughnuts for everyone, slip in the news that I got engaged and hand over my letter of resignation to my boss. With any luck I'll have it all over by 9.30 a.m.

I start to retrace my steps, pulling up sofa cushions and opening the fridge. I've always found the little studio to be cosy, but since I've got back I've realised how small it actually is. The little apartment in Spain, with its separate rooms and its roof terrace, had the illusion of space, and Danny's house, whilst small, is still split over three stories. I put my hands on my hips and look around the room. I can't imagine what Danny's going to make of it.

I've really got to tell him where I live or else when he arrives in thirty-six hours it's going to be one hell of a shock. I should have been honest with him from the start and then I wouldn't be in this mess.

I hear a *thud, thud, thud*, on the floor above and realise it's Olivia heading towards the kitchen. I've got to get out of here quickly. If she catches me, she won't let me leave until she's got her present from Spain, and then I really will be late for work. Plus, I've got to nip to the post office to send my birth certificate special delivery to Danny so he can give it to the registrar tomorrow. Where are my bloody keys?

I suddenly remember that I was desperate for the loo when I got back last night and I'm relieved when I see my keys on the floor in the corner of the bathroom.

I scoop them up, grab my bag and hurry out the door before Olivia's present radar starts going wild.

'Happy New Year,' I say walking into the little office at the back of the large hangar where we hold our events. I put a tray of Krispy Kreme doughnuts onto the table that we use for meetings and open the box. Almost immediately my colleagues head over like bees to honey.

'Bloody hell, Lydia, I started my diet this morning,' moans Helen as she gets up like a rocket and practically barges me out of the way to get a doughnut.

'I really shouldn't,' says Lyn, our finance manager, 'but I'll just have one.'

Soon the whole office, aka all eleven of them, are hovering round the table and stuffing their faces.

'It's not your birthday, is it, Lydia? Surely it would have pinged up on Outlook.'

'No,' I say, taking a deep breath. I was sort of hoping that someone would have noticed the ring sparkling away on my finger, but everyone's too busy getting their sugar rush on. 'I, um, got engaged.'

I push my hand out in front of me in embarrassment and people start to pull it this way and that as they coo over the ring.

Helen stares at me in disbelief. 'Who, Ross?' she practically whispers.

'No, an old friend. Danny. I ended up in Spain between Christmas and New Year and one thing led to another that led to – well, um, Gretna Green, actually. And now we're getting married next month.'

'Next month! Bloody hell, that's not leaving you much time to plan it, is it?'

'Well, it's only going to be small. Just immediate family.'

'How lovely,' says Tracey. 'Congratulations.'

'Thank you,' I say, beaming.

'Ohh, now this really calls for a glass or two of fizz,' she says, going over to the fridge. I expect she won't be thinking that when I give her my resignation in a few minutes.

'Um, as much as I'd love that, I don't know if I could handle a glass at 9 a.m., it's been hard enough to try and get back into a work frame of mind as it is,' I say, giggling a little.

'Of course. How about we have a little tipple at lunchtime, then,' she says, with a wink.

Everyone perks up a bit before drifting back to their desks.

'Um, Tracey, is it possible to have a little chat with you?' I ask, my heart pounding.

'Of course. I was hoping to have a word with you this morning, too.'

'Oh, right,' I say, wondering what that's about.

'Do you want to come over now?'

I haven't even had time to take my coat off, but I nod. I guess the sooner I get it over with the better.

She walks over to her office and I follow, my hands starting to shake.

I need to go first. I need to go in quick like I'm pulling off a plaster. Short and sweet.

'So,' she says as she indicates with her hand for me to sit down as she takes her chair. 'I've been thinking a lot about our conversation at the Christmas party. About the proms.'

'Oh, right, well about that,' I say, thinking that I want to pre-empt her before she tells me again why I would be wrong for the job.

'I think I was a bit hasty and have been re-evaluating the situation. Yesterday I went through the figures and spoke with Christian. We've been looking at the schedule for the year ahead and think promoting you to event manager might solve a few of our issues.'

'Oh right,' I say, dropping my handbag with the resignation letter in it to the floor.

'Obviously you've occasionally run our small events for us, so we thought we'd give you a test run to see how you get on. Helen's been taking on a lot of new business lately so I'm going to get her to reassign a couple of her events that have already been planned for this month to you. Think of it as a one-month trial period and in the mean time we'll also be assigning you new events to plan from scratch.'

My jaw is practically on the floor. This is what I have wanted for years. I'm positively ecstatic. Until I catch sight of the engagement ring on my hand which seems to be flashing at me as a reminder of what I'm supposed to be doing.

'So, how does that sound?' she asks, looking at me expectantly.

'I, er,' I stutter, as I reach for my handbag. 'I'm lost for words. Thank you, Tracey, it's a wonderful opportunity and I'm so flattered.' I go to pull the letter out of my bag, but my hand won't move. 'And I'd be delighted to accept.'

'Fantastic. Now I'll speak to HR and get them to send over the Ts and Cs for the trial period and obviously there'll be an adjustment in salary.'

'Thank you,' I say, not quite believing that this is happening.

'So, what was it you wanted to talk to me about?'

'Oh, I er,' I stutter, pulling my bag close into my chest. I don't want the letter to accidentally fall on the floor. Not when I've got my dream job offered to me on a plate. 'I can't remember now . . . No, it's gone.' I shrug my shoulders and shake my head a little.

'Well, if you remember, just pop back in.'

'I will do. Thank you for this opportunity, Tracey, you won't regret it.'

She smiles and I take that as my cue to leave.

I walk out of the office and do a little fist pump.

I sit down, my cheeks flushed and my hands still shaking as it takes me a minute to compose myself.

'Are you all right?' asks Helen.

'I just got a promotion. I'm going to be an events manager, too.'

'Congratulations,' she says, grinning.

'You knew?'

'I was in yesterday and Tracey had a word with me. I'm really happy and relieved – there's just too much new business for me to do all of the events. And I'm so happy for you, too, you deserve it.'

'Thanks, Helen.'

I'm just about to turn my attention to my overflowing inbox when my phone beeps.

DANNY WHITTAKER

Morning, Beautiful, I hated waking up without you this morning. Hope your first day back at work's going well. Thinking about you and our new life. Did you talk to your boss yet? x x

I love the fact that he texts me when he feels like it. There're no games or having to schedule when we're going to speak to each other, as he just picks up the phone when he's thinking of me. What I don't love is the fact that I'm going to have to tell him that I didn't quit my job.

> **I miss you too. First day back is going rather well and there's a slight change of plan. I got a promotion! Yay! But that means I'm not moving as I've worked too hard for my dream job so you'll have to move instead. OK? Love you xxx**

Of course I don't write that. Instead I text:

> **I miss you, too. Yes, spoke to my boss. It went well x x x**

I instantly feel awful for lying, but in my defence it's only a month's probation. It might all go horribly wrong and then I can quit knowing that I'd make a crap events manager. And if it goes well, then it will look so much better on my CV, even if I do only have the job for a month, or two or three . . . I'm sure that Danny and I could live apart for a few months. It's not like we'd be the first couple ever to do long distance. People in the Armed Forces do it all the time. They up and leave and don't see each other for months on end. We're only talking about not seeing each other midweek. It would be totally worth it in the long run. Better career prospects, more money for both of us etc., etc. I'm sure Danny will be well on board when I tell him tonight on the phone. As obviously I'm going to tell him tonight. Right after I've told him where I live.

DANNY WHITTAKER

   Well done!! I'm off out with Gaz and Victoria tonight and won't be back until late. I'll text before I ring to check you're still up. Although it's nice to say I'll be down to see you tomorrow night x x

ME

   I know, sounds so much better. Even if you're not going to make it down until after 11 p.m. x x

DANNY WHITTAKER

   I'll try and get there as quickly as I can. Better do some work, speak soon x x

I can't stop grinning as I put my phone down and I've momentarily forgotten that I'm in the office.

'Lover boy?' asks Helen, as she sits down at her desk opposite me.

'How can you tell?' I say laughing.

'So, what the bloody hell happened? And, more importantly, do you need ice?'

'Oh yes. When Danny's around, all the ice is needed.'

'So he's an old friend.'

'Uh-huh, I've known him forever.'

'I guess that explains why it's a little on the quick side.'

'We almost got together ten years ago, but the timing wasn't right.'

'And now it is?' she says, as she flicks through her diary at the same time as talking to me.

'Yes,' I say resolutely. 'It is.'

'Then I'm super dooper happy for you. Does he live in Portsmouth, too?'

'Not exactly. He lives in the Lake District.'

She flips her diary shut and looks up, giving me her full attention.

'He lives where? What are you going to do when you're married? Are you . . .?' she says, checking over her shoulder to make sure that Tracey isn't in earshot – 'leaving?' she mouths.

'No, of course not. Not now that I've got the promotion. We're just going to do long distance and he can work from home down here,' I say, hoping that might be true.

'Oh, thank God for that. I thought for a moment you were going to say that you were giving up your whole life to be with him,' she says laughing.

'Ha, ha, ha,' I say, doing an over-the-top laugh back, as if it's the funniest thing in the world and not exactly what I'd been planning to do up until ten minutes ago.

'Yeah, it's a bit of a stretch to think you'd move up there, what with all your friends and family down here. You're so close to your family, aren't you?'

I think of my mum popping in when she's passing and of Kerry and Olivia. As much as I'm embarrassed that at the ripe old age of thirty I'm still living with my family, I'm going to miss them terribly when I move out. I've got so used to the thud, thud, thud of Olivia doing her fairy elephant dancing and her shrieking as she comes down the stairs to see me. I know that I'm going to miss seeing her every day and watching her grow up. And then there's Lucy. The older you get the harder it is to make friends.

If I'm only going to be here for another few months, then I'll have to make sure that I appreciate them more.

I realise that I've been staring into space for a long time and I turn back to Helen. She's looking at me carefully and gives me a little smile.

'I'm so glad you're staying though,' she says, smiling. 'Who else am I going to have to cover my arse when I get myself into trouble?' she says lowering her voice. 'Thanks for that. I'd just found—'

'Crisis meeting, everyone,' says Tracey, walking up to us.

My cheeks immediately flush and I wonder if she's about to tell us that the company's gone into a sudden financial crisis and my promotion is no longer on the table.

'Helen, Lydia, Jasmine, Matt to the table,' says Tracey, calling the operations team over. 'I've just had a phone call from Henry's House about their black-tie Valentine's Event. They're concerned about the theme of the masquerade ball as it turns out that there's a Help for Heroes charity ball with the same theme the week before.'

'Does it matter?' asks Helen. 'Surely they'll have different audiences. One's a military charity and the other's a children's hospice.'

'They're worried enough to want a different theme, and the trouble is that we've ordered everything already. It's all black and white, so we need to think of another idea that will work with the props and staging.'

There's silence at the table – our brains all still fuzzy from the break. Instinctively, we all look at Helen. Tracey was spot on before Christmas when she said that she was the fun one. She always comes up with creative ideas.

'What about the 1920s? We could do a speakeasy. We've got the props from the Christmas parties we did a few years ago,' she says.

'That was the first thing I mentioned to them and they didn't think that a speakeasy was in keeping with the charity.'

I'm a little gutted as I have the best flapper dress that I wear to those events. It's got gorgeous black tassels and a tiny black headband that matches.

'There must be something else,' says Tracey, looking desperately at our blank faces.

I stare at my ring, which seems to have been flashing at me ever since I accepted the promotion. I think of the wedding and everything it stands for and I try to stop feeling so guilty by imagining me and Danny on our wedding day. By the time this ball that we're talking about comes around, I'll be married. I'll have worn a lovely dress (I'm going to replace the Zara one) and I'll have a shiny wedding band to go with the engagement ring.

But it's the dress I can't stop thinking about. I can't wait to find something quite a bit longer with a lot of swish.

'I've got it,' I say, surprising myself. It's as if the promotion has turned me into a creative genius. 'Why don't we do a wedding-dress ball? You know, women wear their wedding dresses or bridesmaid dresses. Men can wear suits, I guess. Maybe, as Henry's House is so well known locally, some of the suit-hire shops will do a special discount for people hiring for the night.'

Everyone's quiet for a second before Tracey's face lights up.

'I love it,' she says. 'But I'm a bit worried that people might not be able to fit into their dresses.'

'Then we'll put on the flyers that you can come as a wedding guest if you want to,' I say. 'It could be the ultimate wedding reception.'

'Is it a DJ or a band that night?' asks Matt.

'It's a band. The Wizards – we used them last year for the event and I have a feeling they do weddings, too,' says Tracey, nodding. 'Then Dave is DJing during the breaks.'

'Ooh, we could get people who buy tickets to say what their wedding song is and Dave could do one of his mash-ups using the different songs,' suggests Jasmine.

'I love that,' says Tracey, clapping her hands together with delight. 'This is perfect. I know that Henry's House are going to love it. Well done, Lydia. Great idea.'

I feel my cheeks flush with pride. Helen gives me a thumbs-up.

'Right, so, Lydia, you'll be managing the event. So start by looking into how these wedding-dress balls work and let's make a list of any extra props or theming we could use from the stores to tie it all in a little better.'

'OK,' I say, scribbling on my notepad.

'Great, thanks everyone,' she says, getting up and we all follow her lead.

'Well done, Lydia. Awesome idea. I'll have to dig out my wedding dress from my loft and maybe I'll buy a ticket,' says Jasmine as I walk back over to our desks. 'I've been dying to wear it again.'

'It's a great idea,' says Helen. 'Everyone loves a good wedding and this way it's without all the expense of having to fork out for the present and the hen do.'

I smile back, pleased at myself. Not that I have time to dwell on it. My inbox is calling to me. December's always such a blur in the office as we spend most of our time in the events space and we only react to the most urgent of emails, which means that today, when I open my inbox, I have 900+ emails to sort through.

'Coffee?' asks Jasmine.

'Yes, please,' I say, nodding, as I'm about to dive in. I'm just clicking on the first email when a new email notification pops up in the corner of my screen and I realise it's from Tracey.

FROM: TRACEY WOOD (TWOOD@BLANKCANVAS. CO.UK)

TO: PETRA THOMSON (PTHOMSON@BLANKCAN- VAS.CO.UK)

CC: LYDIA STOKER (LSTOKER@BLANKCANVAS. CO.UK)

SUBJECT: Promotion LYDIA STOKER

Petra,

Further to the informal chat yesterday I am delighted to write and tell you that Lydia will be accepting the promotion, provisionally for a one-month period. Please can you follow up with a revised contract and salary details.

Yours,

Tracey

I have to reread the email a number of times for it to really sink in. I am actually getting this promotion.

I look down at my ring and I think of Danny. I've never felt so torn. I want to be with him, only I want my promotion too. What am I going to do?

Chapter 17

I'm sorry I didn't make it over for your mum's big birthday bash. I hear from Mum it was a good one. I hear there was minimal pants flashing too so I guess that's a bonus? I would have actually loved to have come to Portsmouth, I don't think I've been since I was at uni. Perhaps next time I'm over I'll come and visit.

Email; Danny to Lydia, July 2016

Despite me actually only having two days back at work, it still feels as if it's been a long week as I pull up outside my house. I'm looking forward to having a long hot soak in the tub, and having a bit of a rest before Danny arrives later tonight. I don't even have to cook as I'm grabbing a curry with Kerry and Jim upstairs.

I groan as I think about Danny. Not at the thought of seeing him, I'm ridiculously excited about that, but because I still haven't told him where I live. I got home from work quite late last night and I was so exhausted from the holiday and travelling back down from the Lake District that I fell asleep not long after I got home. I made the fatal mistake of slipping into bed to read whilst I waited for Danny to text and the next thing I knew it was morning already.

I step out of my car, trying to psyche myself up to ring Danny and explain when I hear him shouting my name. I really must be more tired than I thought, as I'm starting to hallucinate.

'Lydia!' he shouts again and I turn and see him standing by his car, which is parked three ahead of mine.

I run up to him and plough straight into him, banging my head into his.

'Aw, fuck,' says Danny, as we both rub at our heads.

Why is it things like that always look super romantic in films and on the telly? I bet we're going to have matching bruises tomorrow.

'Sorry for being so clumsy.' I lean up to him slowly and kiss him gently, making sure that I cause no further injury. 'What are you doing here so early? I wasn't expecting you for hours.'

'I know, but my meeting this afternoon got cancelled, so after I delivered the certificates to the registry office, I thought I'd come and surprise you.'

'I'm glad you did,' I say, wrapping my arms around him and kissing him again.

'Get a room,' shout some passing teenage boys, sniggering.

We pull away and Danny raises an eyebrow, 'They've got a point, shall we?'

He leans over to his boot and takes a rucksack out before he looks at me expectantly. 'I'm intrigued to see your place.'

'Hmm, yes, I can't wait to show it to you.' *All ten square metres of it.*

'You know I'll have to have a proper tour of it. Preferably starting with the bedroom.'

'Oh,' I say pulling him along. 'That's no problem.' *Seeing as you see that as you walk in.*

I take his hand in mine and walk over to the house. We're about to walk down the side to the entrance to my flat when I see a woman waving down the road. I try to drag Danny in more quickly, but he's seen her.

'Isn't that Kerry?'

I bite my tongue, wishing that I'd made more of an effort to tell him about my housing situation before.

'Oh, so it is. Kerry and Olivia,' I say, pretending that it's a total shocker that they'd be on this road.

'Aunty Lydia,' says Olivia, practically bowling me over with a hug. She's so excited to see me that I feel bad that I haven't made more of an effort to see her since I got back. But I've snuck off for work early the last two mornings, and last night I came in from work late and fell straight to sleep.

'I guess she's missed me,' I say to my sister as she reaches us. She's all bundled up in a winter coat and her cheeks are red from a walk in the sea breeze. 'Can't blame her, I suppose. I'm her cool auntie.'

'Did you bring me a present back from Spain?' she asks the second she pulls away.

'Ah,' I say, feeling a lot less loved. 'Of course I did, just don't get your hopes up too much.'

Kerry gives me a quick hug hello. 'Happy New Year, Sis. And you, Daniel Whittaker, it's been a while.' She gives him a hug, too, mouthing over his shoulder at me that he's looking pretty hot. I give her a quick nod to say I know. 'Are you coming up for a cup of tea?'

'Um,' I say, looking at Danny, who's rightly confused.

'Yes, we'll dump our stuff and be right up,' I say.

'With the present?' asks Olivia.

'With the present.' I nod.

'OK, see you in a little bit, then,' says Kerry with a wink.

She heads up the front stairs and I walk around the side of the house to the little staircase.

'So,' I say, turning to Danny. 'Perhaps I should have mentioned I live under Kerry's house.'

'Um, might have been an idea.'

I push open the door to my little granny flat and I look at it through Danny's eyes, wondering what he's going to think.

'Ta da,' I say, wincing a little as I walk over to the lounge curtains and open them up. 'I know, it's nothing like your comfy cottage in the Lakes.'

I look around my little flat. I've grown to love it over the last few months. It might have been a little bare when I first arrived, with its whitewashed walls and wooden floors, but when I was going through my hygge phase, I added the white furry rug, comfy cushions, candles and throws and have made it feel like home.

'It's very you,' Danny says eventually. 'And it's cosy. Why didn't you tell me you lived with Kerry? All this time I've been writing to you here.'

'I know,' I say, perching on the arm of the sofa. 'It's just I felt a bit pathetic. When I broke up with Ross, I just couldn't face doing another house share; I can't really afford to buy, and if I rented by myself, then I'd only just be breaking even every month and I'd have no chance to save. I was toying with the idea of moving back in with mum, but then Kerry suggested this place. The people who had lived here before had converted the basement into a granny flat for their mother and Kerry and Jim had always thought they'd do it up one day and perhaps pop it on Airbnb. So we all worked on it for a week and put new flooring down and painted the walls. I sanded down the kitchen units and repainted them.'

'You've done a great job,' he says, looking over and nodding his head in approval.

'Plus, I have the bonus of getting to see people's feet as they go past,' I say, pointing at the window at the front, which is made of frosted glass.

'Bonus,' he says.

'It's not quite a view of a lake.'

Danny's about to reply when we hear Olivia shrieking.

'Auntie Lydia,' she shouts, running down the stairs and causing us to spring apart.

'I guess I've got to start locking the top door now. Yes, Olivia?'

'Mum says the kettle's boiled.'

'Thanks, sweetie. We'll be right up.'

Olivia doesn't move. And I realise that Danny and I are going to have to finish our conversation later. He doesn't seem too angry with me, which bodes well for when I tell him later that I'm not moving up to the Lake District as quickly as we'd planned.

Olivia is impatiently tapping her toe and I reach over to my half-unpacked suitcase and pull out a paper bag that's been taped together with red and yellow ribbons.

Her whole face lights up just like it had on Christmas Day and she rips the paper off in seconds.

She shakes the tambourine noisily then looks puzzled at the wooden toy in her hand.

'They're castanets,' I say, taking them off her and showing her how to clack them together. 'They're a Spanish musical instrument.'

She starts to bash them together clumsily.

'Lovely,' I say.

'Don't forget the tea,' she says over her clacking. 'Come on.'

She's staring hard at Danny and I get the impression that she's going nowhere unless we follow her.

'Right, then, tea,' I say, with an apologetic look at Danny.

'Tea,' he says, nodding, and Olivia takes us both by the hand and pulls us upstairs.

Kerry's in the kitchen pouring it out when we get there.

'Ah, my sister and my soon-to-be brother-in-law,' she says, patting Danny on the back and pushing him down into a kitchen chair. 'Come and tell me how it all happened, then.'

Olivia is exhibiting great skill playing the castanets with one hand and the tambourine with the other as she dances around the kitchen. I'm already regretting my present choices.

'Have you said thank you for those, Olivia? Let me say thank you for those too,' says Kerry, pulling a face at me.

'Thank you,' says Olivia.

'You're both very welcome,' I reply.

'Liv, why don't you play that in your room?' shouts Kerry over the noise.

'But I'm doing it for Uncle Danny,' she says, grinning at him.

'Oh, that's lovely of you,' he says. 'Uncle, huh, already?'

'Well, it's only four weeks until it's official,' says Kerry with a sly wink.

'I want to impress him,' says Olivia proudly.

'Perhaps he can impress you,' I say. 'Danny knows how to flamenco.'

'What?' he says, looking at me as if he's misheard me.

'What's flamenco?' asks Olivia, her eyes wide.

'It's a type of Spanish dancing,' says Kerry. She perches down on the end of the sofa. 'Come on, then, Danny, let's see it.'

'Yes, yes,' says Olivia, jumping up and down on the spot. 'I can play the music for you. Is it like this?'

She shakes the tambourine to almost breaking point and Danny gives me a look, before he gently takes it off her.

We all stare wide eyed as he takes to the middle of the floor, seemingly unbothered by the audience.

'It's more like this,' he says, taking the tambourine up to the side of his head and rhythmically clapping along whilst doing a funny stompy walk around the kitchen.

Whilst it wouldn't be a ten from Len for his efforts, he's not half bad. Yes, he's out of time and he's a little stiff in his movements (that car journey's probably done him no favours) but there's something about it that's still quite masterful and sexy.

I suddenly wish I had one of those swishy dresses that I could whip around me and strut about in.

'*Olé!*' he shouts as he lands on his knees.

Olivia claps and shouts, 'Again, again!'

Kerry and I look at each other trying not to laugh, but clapping all the same.

'It was a bit like the passey dobble,' says Olivia taking back the tambourine.

'The Paso doble,' says Kerry, correcting her.

'That's the one. From *Strictly*,' she tells me as she looks us in the eyes.

'Where did you think I learnt that from?' Danny says back with a broad grin.

'Did you not learn it from your *Fun Flamenco* book?'

Danny looks confused for a second.

'Oh, God. My mum bought that for me for Christmas one year. We all went to a flamenco show in Spain, one that was really cheesy and touristy and I got dragged up on stage. I'd had way too much rioja and thought I was some sort of Ricky Martin and my mum thought I was a natural.'

'Oh,' I say.

'Yes, pretty much all the books on that shelf are Christmas presents from Mum. Just to save any future embarrassment when we're at a jazz club and you commandeer the stage or we're in Vegas and you see a high-stake poker table – I can't play the piano, and I'm pretty hopeless at Poker.'

'Good to know,' I say, secretly sad about the piano thing. I'd had all sorts of fantasies of me lying on the piano *á la Pretty Woman*.

'I'm going to practise. There'll be a show tonight,' says Olivia to Kerry.

'OK, then, we will clear a place in tonight's schedule for it,' she says, mock saluting.

'And you,' she says pointing to Danny, 'you'll have to come and practise too.'

'Don't you think it'd be better on your own? I hear you're a wonderful dancer,' he says.

'Oh no. Everyone knows that you need two people for the passey dobble.'

I try and stop myself from laughing.

'Uncle Danny,' says Olivia stamping her foot like a diva at the kitchen door. 'Uncle Danny.'

'You might as well go and get it over with. She'll keep calling you until you go.'

He looks at me as if I've got some magic pass to get him out of it.

'Don't look at me. You started it with your groovy moves.'

'Didn't you start it when you told her that I did flamenco, and when you bought her the instruments?'

'Hush now, none of that logic applies when dealing with an almost seven-year-old.'

'Just you wait until you meet Stuart's kids; you think you're feeding me to a lion here,' he says with a slightly evil-sounding cackle. He leans over and gives me a kiss before heading upstairs, clapping to an invisible flamenco beat as he goes.

I watch him go and I'm still grinning as I hear him stomp noisily around the lounge. I realise that Kerry is staring at me.

'You have to tell me everything. I mean, what the bloody hell happened? You went on a holiday to get some space and you've practically come back with a husband,' says Kerry.

'I know. Can you believe it?'

'No, I bloody can't. I'm happy for you. I am, truly. I think that Danny's a great guy. I just worry that you're rushing things a little. I mean, you're getting married in a month. What's the hurry?'

'Why wouldn't we hurry? I love him, Kerry. I think I always have.'

'I know you were close when you were younger, but people change.'

'But we've been writing to each other for all these years.'

'I thought you just sent each other silly presents. Do you talk about real things in your letters too?' She's got that superior older-sister look on her face.

'No, but we got together once. At your wedding, actually,' I say a little sheepishly. I've never told anyone in the family that. 'It didn't work out then, the timing was all wrong. But I've always wondered what would have happened if we'd tried harder.'

'At my wedding? So that's why you were looking so weird during breakfast the next day. Keep you up all night, did he?'

'No,' I say shaking my head. 'We only kissed.'

'That's good to hear. I would have been peeved if you'd got action on my wedding night when I didn't. God, Jim and I were so drunk I don't think I even got out of my wedding dress.'

'Classy.'

'It's funny, though, as I thought that if you were going to get together with one of the Whittaker boys at the wedding it would have been Stuart. I thought I saw you flirting outrageously with each other over the meal. But I guess I got that wrong.'

I scald my mouth as I try and drink my too-hot tea.

'I just don't understand. Why couldn't you have got together then?' she asks.

'I had that job up in Newcastle and Danny went off travelling before he went back to London. But by the time I moved to London, he'd been sent to work in Tokyo,' I say, giving her the edited highlights (or lowlights) as they really were.

'Hang on, is that why you moved from Newcastle to London?' asks Kerry, as if it's all suddenly fallen into place.

'Part of it.' I shudder at the thought of that job, that cold, dank bedsit by the tube station. 'I thought the job in London was better for my career and it was just a bonus that he was there too. He told me he was moving to Tokyo the night I went to tell him I was moving to London.'

There's a bang from the lounge and instinctively we both look up the hallway as if to see the walking wounded appear.

'Do you think he's OK?'

'I think he's just fine,' says Kerry. 'She's probably roping him into doing some sort of elaborate lift. She's obsessed with *Strictly*. She's devastated that it's not on again until the autumn.'

I try and imagine what chaos is going on and I can't help smiling to myself.

'So, you think the timing is right now, with Danny?'

'Yes,' I say nodding my head. 'I'm not letting him go again.'

'So, we really are losing you from the basement?'

I shift a bit uncomfortably in my seat. We'd already told our families that I was moving up to the Lakes; it's not only Danny that I've got to break the news to that I haven't given up my job just yet. But I can't tell anyone until I've told him. 'I've really loved living here. I honestly can't thank you and Jim enough for letting me.'

'Don't be daft, if it wasn't for you we never would have pulled our fingers out and got renovating. Plus, now we can put it on Airbnb in plenty of time for the summer.'

'Summer,' I say nodding, thinking that gives me at least six months. That should be enough time to get into my promotion, shouldn't it? And I'm sure Danny would understand if we had to do long distance until then. It'll go by in the blink of an eye.

'We're really going to miss you,' says Kerry. 'It's not even like you're moving just around the corner.'

'Tell me about it,' I say, the long train journey fresh in my mind, and now that we'll be doing long distance for months, I'm going to be doing it a whole lot more. 'I bet you're going to miss your on-tap babysitter more.'

She laughs. 'I certainly am. That and the impromptu girlie nights when Jim's pissing me off. I've loved having somewhere I could storm off to.'

She comes over and gives me a hug and I can feel tears glistening in my eyes.

'I'm pleased for you, Lydia, I really am. The only thing that worries is me is that Danny's so impulsive and he's always chopping and changing what he's doing. Are you sure this is for real?'

I think of him over the last ten years. Yes, he's lived in London, Tokyo, Singapore, New York and the Lakes, but he's settled now, isn't he? He's got a house and a business.

I nod.

'What Danny and I have, it's so hard to explain. It just feels like the right thing to do. I've got all these butterflies in my stomach.'

There's a pause and Kerry stares hard at me.

'You know marriage is about more than butterflies?'

'I know.'

'It's hard work,' says Kerry. 'You have to love someone despite them at times seeming like the most irritating person on the planet. Like when they continuously leave their dirty socks next to the washing basket as if it's too much effort to lift the lid. Or when they put bottles of beer in the freezer to chill and then forget and they explode, leaving beery-smelling ice all over the inside.'

'Or when they pee on your rhubarb,' I say grinning.

'Exactly. Believe me, husbands can be pretty damn annoying. But you've still got to love them despite all of that and they've got to love you when all the mystery has gone. When you've let your bikini line go au naturel or you've had food poisoning at the same time as each other with only one toilet in the house.'

I wrinkle my nose up.

'What I'm trying to say is that it's great that you feel so strongly for Danny and I really hope that it lasts, but make sure that it's not just an infatuation. Jim and I have been married for almost ten years now and not all our friends who got married at the same time have lasted as long as us. Those who have gone the distance seem to be the ones who accept that it's not perfect.'

I think back over all the Sunday dinners that I've been to in this house and the way that I've watched Kerry and Jim. There's no denying that they love each other, but she's right, I've seen them niggling at each other and the dagger looks that they've thrown.

'Don't forget we practically grew up together. I know Danny inside out.'

'You knew each other when you were kids. You're both grown-ups now,' says Kerry, sternly.

'Am I? I still don't feel like one.'

'I know, but people can change over time. Jim's not the man I married. He's not grown up at all, which means I sometimes feel like I'm a parent of two children. He's much more stubborn than he used to be, and he's definitely more risk averse.'

'We just spent a week together in a tiny apartment in Spain,' I say. 'I don't think there was much there that we could hide from each other.'

'But that wasn't real life, was it? Look, I'm happy for you, I really am,' she says, getting up and retrieving a cake tin off the sideboard. She opens it up and offers me a homemade mince pie. 'It's just that I think you should make sure that this is really what you want. And if I'm honest, I think you should give it a bit more time. It's not that long since you broke up with Ross.'

'It was five months ago.'

'Have you told Ross?'

'Told him what? That I've met someone else?'

'That you're getting married,' she says.

'No. We're all going to do the pub quiz next week, I'll tell him then, not that he's going to mind.'

'I think you'd be surprised. You were together for five years.'

'I know, but it was a mutual break up. We've both moved on.' I try and put the thought of the mistletoe kiss out of my mind. It was nothing like the kisses I've had with Danny over the last few weeks. 'I should have been honest with myself a long time ago and ended things years before. It was broken for a long time.'

'Was it? Or was it just not as exciting as things are now with Danny?'

I don't get to answer the question as we hear footsteps down the hallway.

'Flipping heck, she's in training to be the next Arlene Philips. Talk about a bossy little choreographer.'

Kerry smiles. 'She gets that from me. Sorry, I should have brought your tea in to you. You must be desperate for one after that long drive. I'll make you a fresh cup.'

'Don't worry, I'll just get a glass of water. That was quite the workout.'

Kerry walks over to the cupboard with the glasses in and she's going over to the tap to fill one up when she hears Olivia thundering down the hallway. She leaps into the kitchen and Danny looks nervous, wondering if she's going to drag him back to the lounge.

'So, can we talk about my bridesmaid dress now? Mum told me that I wasn't supposed to ask until after you'd officially asked me. But you're going to, aren't you? I'm going to be bridesmaid?'

I look between Danny and Olivia. We'd said we'd only have a small wedding. But those big puppy dog eyes of hers . . .

'Of course you're going to be bridesmaid,' I say, planting a smile on my face.

Olivia starts screaming and running around the kitchen and only stops when the doorbell rings.

'Grandma! Grandma's here,' shouts Olivia, as she tears down the hall to get her.

We hear the door open and the voice of my mother drifts down to us.

'I invited her over for curry,' says Kerry as she hands Danny his water. 'I guess you'll be joining us for that now, too?'

'Sounds good to me,' says Danny, and I give him a small smile. It's not quite the romantic reunion we'd wanted, but at least we've still got the rest of the weekend together.

We hear my mum's footsteps clip-clopping along the floor and I see Danny tense as she gets closer. 'You've seen my mother a gazillion times before,' I whisper.

'It's not the same,' he whispers back. 'She's the monster-in-law now.'

'Well,' she says theatrically as she opens the door. She's looking at me and Danny with the most intense gaze and it reminds me of the time she found us raiding her booze cabinet when we were in our early teens. 'It's about bloody time.'

Chapter 18

Kerry and Jim are moving next weekend and I went over to entertain Olivia whilst they were packing and they found their wedding DVD. Man alive I still can't believe she made me wear that monstrosity of a dress, it was even more hideous than I remembered. You seemed to do well dodging most of the video footage, but there is one bit that caught you dancing to Single Ladies. Oh, Danny Whittaker, you've got moves I never knew you had!

Email; Lydia to Danny, June 2016

What was supposed to be me grabbing a quiet takeaway with Kerry and Jim has now turned into an impromptu celebration. Here we are sitting in the lounge with not only Kerry and Jim, but also my mum, and the lesser spotted Keith – *'well, it's not every day my daughter gets engaged, darling'*.

The doorbell goes, 'Oh God, don't tell me you invited Hazel too,' I say to Kerry, wondering if she would have had enough time to get down from the Lakes.

'That'll be the delivery driver,' says Jim, jumping up.

I breathe a sigh of relief.

Olivia's treating us to her Spanish concert, which is an assault on the ears, and I think everyone wishes they'd offered to get the door instead.

'Right, Olivia, darling,' says Mum, 'we'll have to finish the show off later.'

'Or, actually, it might be bed time after the meal,' says Kerry, looking at the clock. 'It's swimming tomorrow morning.'

Olivia rolls her eyes like a pro. Heaven help Kerry and Jim when she's a teenager.

'Grub's up,' shouts Jim as he passes the doorway en route to the kitchen.

'I'm starving,' I say getting to my feet. Danny grabs my hand and I do a little swoon.

The doorbell rings again.

'Lydia, why don't you get that?' says Kerry.

Perhaps I wasn't wrong and Mum has called Hazel after all.

I open the door and shriek with delight at the sight of Lucy.

'Hello, you,' I say, flinging my arms around my best mate.

'I want to know everything,' says Lucy, pulling straight out of the hug. '*Everything*.'

'And hello, Ed,' I say, as I stand back to let them in.

'Lydia,' he says, kissing me on the cheek. 'I hear congratulations are in order.'

'Ah, thank you. I can't believe Kerry invited you, too – it's like a proper party all of a sudden. I'm so happy you could come last minute.'

'You won't be,' says Lucy in a mutter. She's got a look in her eye and I suddenly realise as I shut the door that the chill in the air wasn't only coming from outside.

'So where is he, then?' says Lucy, snapping a smile back on her face.

'Well, yes, come on through and meet him.'

She grabs hold of my hand and is practically jumping up and down as we walk into the kitchen.

'Danny, this is my best friend, Lucy. Lucy, this is Danny, my fiancé,' I say, taking the word for a little test drive.

'Ah, Lucy of the great taste in underwear,' says Danny, leaning over to give her a kiss on the cheek.

He pulls back and notices Ed's face is like thunder.

'Ah, you must be her fiancé. Ed, is it? God, sorry, that sounded terrible. It's just that Lucy bought Lydia some cracking under-wear for her trip to Spain and . . .'

Danny turns round and sees that the rest of the guests round the table are staring at him.

'Oh, um,' he says, his cheeks going pink, and he sits down at an empty seat.

'You carry on, Daniel. I always like to hear about my daughter's knickers,' says my mum raising a playful eyebrow.

'I got Paw Patrol pants for Christmas,' says Olivia, thinking that's a perfectly normal addition to the conversation.

Jim pats her on the head affectionately. 'Right, so I just ordered a selection of different curries and bits, so dig in.'

'This looks amazing.'

'Doesn't it? Makes a nice change from all the Christmas food,' says Lucy, sitting down next to Danny and leaving Ed and I to sit next to each other, opposite them. It's not all bad. I reckon I can play footsie with Danny from here.

'It's not doing much for my diet, though, and to think I've only got four weeks until I'm going to have to be in the mother-of-the bride outfit.'

'I thought you were doing your Paleo Diet?' I say as I watch her take a huge spoonful of lamb rogan josh.

'I couldn't get on with it. Too restrictive.'

'Haven't you only been doing it for three days?'

'I know, but I missed bread too much.'

'Right.' So typical of my mother. 'At least that makes it easier for the wedding dinner. Now we just need Hazel to stop being a vegan.'

'I think she's cracked too. She sent me a picture of her eating a huge chunk of brie at lunchtime,' she says.

'Perfect,' says Danny. 'See, nothing to worry about.'

'What about my dress?' asks Olivia. 'When are we going shopping for it. Tomorrow?'

'Danny and I are going out tomorrow, but I guess we'll have to get it soon,' I say, thinking about all the things that still need doing.

'What about your dress?' asks Lucy. 'You've got to get that too.'

'Yes, I keep daydreaming about it and forget that I need to actually buy it.'

'I liked your other dress,' says Danny with a wink.

'I'm not wearing that again,' I say thinking of the effect it had on Danny in his living room and how I ended up naked in front of his mum.

'I'll buy your wedding dress, darling. We can go shopping together.'

'OK, great.'

'Yes, I'll look for an outfit too whilst I'm at it. I've got to find something utterly fabulous to wear as mother-of-the-bride. '

'I love a good wedding,' says Lucy, clapping her hands together.

'Just not your own,' mutters Ed.

I don't think he meant for everyone to hear, but we all seem to be mid-mouthful and quiet.

'So, Keith, are all your children married now?' asks Kerry as she shoves the bag of naan breads in his direction in a bid to ease the tension between Ed and Lucy.

He looks so formal compared to the rest of us. He's wearing chinos and a neatly pressed jumper over a checked shirt. It's not only the clothes he's wearing but also the way that he's carrying himself. He's so upright and he holds his knife and fork the polite way. Before he speaks he dabs at the corners of his mouth with his napkin.

'Almost. Suzanne, the middle one, is getting married in September,' he says, as he takes a naan and puts it on the side of his plate next to the neat little piles of curry, rice and saag aloo.

'Ah, that's nice. Two weddings to look forward to then, Mum,' I say.

Mum's fork clatters to the table. 'Yes, well, I don't know if I'll make that. Might be a bit awkward.' We all look at her, waiting for her to elaborate. 'You know, with Keith's ex.'

I don't really know much about Keith's divorce, but I do know that that kind of thing can be complicated at weddings. I look over at Lucy, who's nodding sagely.

'I know exactly what you mean, Linda,' says Lucy. 'Weddings can be so awkward when you've got people who hate each other having to be in the same room. My mum's already told me that she won't come if my step-mum comes, and my dad says that he's not coming unless she does.'

I give Lucy a sympathetic smile.

'But weddings, right. Everyone's supposed to love a wedding.' She lunges towards a bottle of red wine and almost knocks it over.

'Here,' says Danny. 'I'll do it.'

He pours her a large glass and she practically downs it.

'At least there'll be free-flowing alcohol. That's always the answer, isn't it?' says Ed.

'Anyone else want some wine?' asks Danny.

'Yes, please,' mutters everyone at the table, except Olivia, who's oblivious to what's going on with the adults.

'So, I FaceTimed Hazel this morning and she played me the ukulele solo that she's working on for the wedding. Now, I know you wanted things low key, but I had this idea that I could accompany her.'

Instinctively I pick up my glass and start to drink the wine Danny's just poured me. I really hope that Kerry and Jim have enough bottles to cope with all this.

'With what? The triangle? Olivia's tambourine?' I ask. My mother is not known for her musical ability.

'No, darling, I could sing.'

'Ah,' I say, struggling to think of a diplomatic answer. I think it would be easier to find more tuneful stray cats to sing for us. 'Well, actually, Mum, we thought you might want to do a reading instead.'

I catch Danny pulling a surprised face.

'Oh, but I had this dance all worked out,' says Mum, looking hurt.

'Dance?' pipes up Olivia. 'I could do a dance. Oh, Auntie Lydia, I could do an awesome dance.'

'To the ukulele music?'

'Oh no,' she says shaking her head. 'I could dance to Beyoncé and I can floss.'

'I don't think now's the time to brag about dental hygiene,' says Mum.

'No, Grandma,' she says rolling her eyes. 'The floss. Watch.'

Before Kerry can stop her, Olivia's jumped up and started to dance around the table nearly knocking everyone out as she flings her arms around.

'Grandma, you can do this with me.'

'Of course I can, darling,' my mother says, pushing her chair back. I watch in horror as she starts dancing what can only be described as seductively round the table. She's missed the point of the dance, her arms being too fluid and her hips more wiggly, and now she's doing a shimmy at the back of Keith's chair.

Kerry grabs at her wrist and guides her back to her seat. I'm sure she was about to whip her leg over to straddle Keith.

'Naan breads are nice, aren't they, Keith?' I say to him.

'Yes, lovely. This curry's really rather good. Much better than my local takeaway.'

There's not a hint of embarrassment on his face. It's as if he's blind to the crazy antics of my mother. Maybe that's the secret to them still being together after all these years.

'We have made an extensive effort to try out all the ones that deliver for free in a five-mile radius,' says Jim.

Keith nods as if that's a very wise thing to do. He doesn't carry on the subject but that doesn't surprise me. He's very much the type of person who speaks when spoken to and only then.

My mum and he are like polar opposites and I'm sure that she doesn't bring him to many family functions as we all find it so fascinating that they're a couple that we study them as if we're watching a nature documentary.

'So can we?' says Olivia, looking expectantly at me.

'Can you what?' I say, bringing myself back into the conversation.

'Can Grandma and I do a dance for you at your wedding?'

'Um, how about you could do the reading with her instead? It's a really small room that we're getting married in.'

'I can dance small and do something other than the floss,' she says, putting her hands over her head like little waves.

'I don't think the venue would let you as there are lots of things that you could break,' says Danny.

'I could do it at the meal afterwards. We could do the Passey Dobble that we've been working on,' she says to Danny.

'Um,' I say, 'I think he's going to be busy on the day. But how about we just buy you an awesome dress instead?'

'And some sparkly trainers too?'

'Um, yes, I guess so. And we could give you a pretty bouquet,' I'm hoping to distract her from the dancing.

'A bouquet?'

'Of flowers.'

'Oh, I'd rather have a magic wand.'

'OK, then. Magic wand, sparkly shoes, bridesmaid dress. Anything else on your wedding rider?'

'What's a rider?' asks Olivia. 'Am I going to get to come in on a horse?'

'No, sweetie,' says Kerry through a mouthful of curry. 'It just means your list of demands for you being bridesmaid.'

'I get to make demands?' she says, her eyes lighting up.

'You've created a monster,' says Jim, rolling his eyes. 'I think shoes, a dress and a wand are enough.'

'So, is Olivia going to be the only bridesmaid, then?' says Lucy putting her fork down and giving me the same puppy-dog look that I got from my niece earlier this afternoon. 'You are my bridesmaid and I always thought you'd return the favour.'

'Oh, so you've decided on your bridesmaids, then,' says Ed. 'Must be about all you've decided on.'

Lucy ignores him and flutters her eyelashes at me.

'Well, we weren't really going to have bridesmaids and then Olivia said that she wanted to and –' I look between Lucy and Danny and he gives me a little nod. 'But I guess it wouldn't be the same if you weren't a bridesmaid too.'

My sister does a loud cough and I wonder if she's got something stuck in her throat. Jim gives her a playful pat on the back as he laughs.

'You all right there, wife?'

'Fine, thanks, just um, reminding my sister that I'm here. I'm also fully available for bridesmaid duty.'

'I can't have you as a bridesmaid as well, at this rate twenty per cent of the guests will be fulfilling that function.'

'Well, if you will have a small wedding,' she says stroppily. 'I thought it would be fitting, seeing as you two did kiss at my wedding, where you were my bridesmaid.'

'I was and you made me wear that hideous dress. Yes, perhaps I should have you as one and then I can get my own back. The bridesmaid dresses I'll choose will be meringue like and corseted and quite horrid.'

'Uh, well, you can count me out of that,' says Lucy, laughing.

'Oh, that sounds more like it,' says Ed.

'This reading that I'm doing,' pipes up Olivia. 'Do I just read the book I'm reading now? I'm reading a Horrible Histories about Egyptians. Did you know they used poo in their medicine?'

All the adults at the table try not to smirk.

'I'll choose you a nice poem. And before you ask, Mum, we don't want you to read an extract of what you're reading at the time either,' I say.

My mum reads romance books on the other end of the scale to the ones I read, less cupcakes and bunting and more whips and handcuffs.

'Don't worry, I've got something in mind,' says my mum. 'We read this great book of poetry at our book club.'

'At your erotic book club?' says Jim, his ears perking right up.

'We'll give you a poem, too, Mum,' I say shutting this conversation down before it can get started.

She sighs heavily. 'There was a time when you used to appreciate the arts,' she says sniffily.

'I still do. That's why I'm giving you a poem.'

'I'm sure the one I would have chosen would have been a lot more entertaining and probably quite informative too, you know, for the honeymoon.'

I shut my eyes in horror as I hear Jim sniggering.

'At least you won't be able to censor my speech. You'll have at least one surprise,' she continues.

'What speech?' I say, almost choking on a bit of naan bread.

'The speech – you know, the father-of-the-bride one? I doubt your father will actually do one, so I'll have to step in.'

'Actually, we weren't going to do speeches.'

'Oh, come on, you have to do speeches, it's like the law,' says Kerry. 'And you can't get Dad to do one; he'd probably forget your name.'

'Kerry's right, you can't not have them,' says Mum, ignoring the jibe about dad. 'I've been saving up stories about you for years specially. And I've got so many about you and Danny from when you were younger. You know you got married when you were four?'

'We did?'

'You did,' says Kerry, clapping her hands together. 'I remember that. I married Stuart and you married Danny. You had Mum's old white flouncy shirt on.'

I shake my head. 'Do you remember that?' I ask Danny.

'No,' he says laughing.

'Yes,' says Kerry, her eyes lighting up. 'I hadn't thought about this. There are so many stories to choose from. Like when you used to go around lifting up her skirt playing knicker chase.'

I close my eyes and smile at the memory. 'That was so wrong as games go.'

'Yeah,' says Danny. 'I don't think kids would be able to do that now. Going around lifting girls' skirts up.'

'We didn't play anything like that at our school, just kiss chase,' says Lucy.

'Also wrong, when you think about it,' I say and we both nod.

'I thought I could talk about seeing Danny naked,' says Mum, and we all stare at her open mouthed.

'When?'

'Oh, when he was little. When he was in the bath with you.'

'That makes it sound so much better,' I say, realising how the case against speeches is mounting.

'I wouldn't worry,' says Mum. 'I've seen Jim naked too. Only he was fully grown.'

Kerry bangs her cutlery noisily on the plate.

'Mum, I thought we weren't going to talk about that ever again.'

'But, darling, it's so funny.'

Jim has gone bright purple.

'Don't worry, darling,' she purrs to Keith, who's quietly eating his curry. 'He was very drunk and mistook me for Kerry.'

'Not making it any better, Mum,' says Kerry, her head in her hands.

'It was after Kerry's thirtieth birthday,' I say, to clarify for those at our end of the table who haven't heard the story before. 'We had this cottage in Devon.'

'Pre-Olivia,' says Kerry. 'It was boozy. Can we change the subject? How about we talk about when Hazel saw you naked the night before last?' she says to me.

'What?' says Lucy.

'No, we're not talking about that,' I say.

'What happened?' says Lucy, turning to Kerry.

'Well, Hazel walked in on them when Danny was about to . . .'

'Seriously, stop,' I say mortified. 'So, Keith, did you have a nice Christmas? You were with your daughters, weren't you?'

'Yes, that's right. It was perfectly satisfactory.'

I wait in case there's any more to come, but he adds nothing further.

'So, wait, did we agree I'm doing a speech? It's either me or your father,' says Mum.

'Oh, God, that *would* be worse,' I say.

'See, everyone hates speeches,' says Lucy to Ed.

'Well, I for one don't hate them, I think they're a great idea,' says Mum.

'I agree,' says Ed. 'Nice and traditional.'

'Bloody traditional,' mutters Lucy under her breath.

'If you do a speech, though, my mum's going to want to do one,' says Danny.

'Oh God, your mum,' says Jim laughing. He stares at me and Danny. 'Are you sure you've thought this whole wedding thing through? I somehow think eloping would have been the better strategy.'

'Been there, done that,' I mutter with a smirk.

The table goes silent and all eyes fall on me.

'That's what you were talking about when you mentioned the other dress. You tried to elope, didn't you?' says Kerry. 'That's what the rush is. You're married already, aren't you, and this is some sort of blessing. No wonder you want it low key.'

'What? You eloped,' says Mum, a hint of hurt in her voice. 'Without us?'

I look nervously at Danny and he holds my hand across the table as there's an uncomfortable silence.

'We tried to elope but then we found out that you have to wait twenty-nine days and, to be honest, we were relieved,' he says. 'I don't think we would have been able to go through with it without you all there.'

I know that you shouldn't love someone when they lie, but in this case, I do. And it's not that much of a lie – there's an element of truth in it.

'But you were thinking about it,' says Kerry. There's an audible hint of hurt.

'We just didn't want a fuss. We didn't want a big wedding and we were worried that it would spiral out of control,' I say.

'Amen to that,' says Lucy, finishing another glass of wine.

'You were the one who wanted to invite your great-aunt Dora,' says Ed.

'She practically raised me as my mum was always working. It's a bit different to you asking your old boss,' she screams.

Lucy's eyes are almost glowing red. Whatever tension has been bubbling beneath the surface suddenly comes out in a huge explosion. It might have taken the heat off the whole eloping revelation but I can't help feeling for my bestie.

'Sometimes it's useful to network,' says Ed, exhaling loudly afterwards.

'Not on your wedding day, it's not,' Lucy stands up and throws her napkin down. 'Thank you, Kerry and Jim for your hospitality. And Danny, it was so good to meet you. I look forward to seeing lots more of you.'

She gets up from the table and leaves the kitchen. I look around the table, stunned at what just happened, before I push my chair out and hurry off after her.

'What's going on? Are you OK?' I ask, grabbing at her arm to stop her from leaving.

'I'm fine, it's just wedding stuff. It's getting to us a bit at the moment. I think hearing his mum's plans for our big day over Christmas didn't help. Do you mind me going?' she says, grabbing her coat off the hook and slipping it on. 'I just don't want to bring you guys down. It's such an exciting time for you and I think we're ruining it.'

'Don't be silly. You're not at all,' I say. 'Making sure you're OK, that's what's important.'

I see tears welling up in Lucy's eyes.

'I think I'm better off alone. I'll talk to you tomorrow,' she says.

'Are you going to be OK getting home?'

'Yes, fine. I'll see you later,' she says, giving me a hug and wiping away her tears before she hurries off out of the house.

I'm just about to shut the door behind her when Ed walks up to me.

'Sorry, Lydia. For ruining your night and being a dick. I do love her, you know.'

'I know,' I say, feeling sorry for him. He looks heartbroken.

'It's just weddings. I get the impression that she wants to be married to me but it's like she's lost sight that that's what the wedding is actually about and all she can see is stress.'

'You're going to work it out,' I say, confident that they will. There was no one more excited than Lucy when they got engaged.

'I hope so. I'd better go,' he says, leaning over and giving me a kiss. 'I've got to catch up with her before she goes too far.'

'Night, Ed.'

I close the door and wonder if I could sneak back downstairs to my flat. I think it's too much to hope that people will have forgotten about the whole eloping thing. But I know I can't leave Danny there alone.

'So,' I say sitting down at the table in Lucy's seat. I look at Keith, wondering what inane question I can ask him this time.

'Can we do the passe dobble now?' asks Olivia, interrupting me.

'Actually, I'm kind of stuffed,' says Danny, rubbing his belly.

'Do the dance,' I whisper.

'Yes, do the dance,' says Kerry. 'I think we all need cheering up after that revelation.'

'I'm sorry, Kerry, but you've got to remember that we didn't actually do it and you're going to be bridesmaid,' I say cheerily.

'With no meringue or corset?'

'No,' I say. 'You can choose your own dress.'

'Excellent.'

'So, am I forgiven?'

'Hmm, maybe a couple of nights of babysitting might help it along.'

I smile.

'So come on, then, Michael Flatley, let's see those moves,' says Jim.

'Is that like Flat Stanley? Hay is for horses?' says Olivia giggling.

'No Michael Flatley was a dancer in the olden days,' says Kerry and I'm about to correct her when I realise how long ago it must have been when *Riverdance* came out. 'We're waiting, Danny.'

He looks at me pleadingly and I give him a wink of encouragement.

'Come on, then, Miss Olivia,' he says standing up. 'Let's get this show on the road.

'He's definitely a keeper,' says Kerry, whispering to me.

'I know,' I say, 'I know.'

Chapter 19

Happy New Year! Hope you had a good one. I finally got to watch the ball drop in Times Square. The ball was a bit weird and disappointing but the atmosphere was electric. Very sore head today. BTW if you could understand the answerphone message ignore my drunk ramblings. It might have sounded like I didn't like Ross, but I was talking about my Boss who is such a dick. I obviously do really like Ross and think he's a great guy.

Email; Danny to Lydia, January 2017

'So this is nice,' says Danny. We're lying snuggled up in bed staring up at the ceiling. It's not quite like it was in Spain. For starters it sounds like there's a herd of elephants in the room above us, who seem to be watching *Frozen* on a loop.

'Hmm. I wish we were at your house or back in Spain,' I say, realising how much of a problem my living arrangements are.

'It's not that bad,' he says as 'Let it Go' comes back on and the noise increases tenfold as Kerry joins in with Olivia in murdering the song.

It really is that bad. Last night Danny had to gag me when we were having sex, not because we were doing something kinky but because Kerry and Jim were having some kind of heated argument and we didn't want them to overhear us.

'I am going to miss this place,' I say.

I don't know why I'm so sad, it's tiny and slightly damp smelling when I do my laundry and it has nowhere near enough light. And that's before I start on the noise from my family above. But despite all that, this place is special to me. It's felt like home to me at a time when I needed a refuge.

'We can always come and visit. We can stay here when we come back; if Jim and Kerry are going to do Airbnb anyway we can just book it out. And you've still got a few weeks to make the most of it before you leave.'

This is probably the perfect time to tell him about my promotion and adjusted timescale for the move. I take a deep breath, but Danny beats me to it.

'Don't be too sad about moving. I know that it might be convenient here, I mean you've got the city on your doorstep and you barely have to get out of bed to make a cup of tea,' he says, laughing.

I poke him in the ribs for taking the piss. He might have misread the apprehension on my face, but he's right, I'm going to miss living in a city.

Moving down to Portsmouth was the easy option after I quit the job in London. It was a city I knew well having grown up on the outskirts, but there was also a lot going for it: there were lots of flat shares available, Kerry and Jim had just bought a flat here and despite the economic downturn there were still jobs. I hadn't really expected to fall in love with it as much as I did. Living in Southsea feels more like living in a village than a city, and I love being right next to the sea.

'Ambleside has a lot going for it,' he says. 'I'm sure you'll settle in quickly.'

'I'm sure I will,' I say, ignoring the pang in my heart at leaving.

'And next weekend I'll give you a proper tour of the area so you can imagine it. So, what's on the agenda for us today?'

He's looking like an excited puppy and I decide now's not the right time to tell him about the promotion.

'I thought we could go the Dockyard to see all the ships.'

'Sounds great. I haven't been since I went with school.'

'I'll jump in the shower, then,' I say, going to get out of bed, but Danny pulls me back in. 'Before you go, I reckon that no one can hear us down here above the *Frozen* racket,' he whispers in my ear, before he runs his hands down my body.

'Won't they now?' I say, yelping a little as his fingers start to trace patterns on my inner thighs.

'Not a thing. We can sightsee later, I promise.'

Maybe things aren't too different to being in Spain after all.

'Wow,' says Danny. 'I know I came here on a school trip but I don't remember it being quite that interesting.'

We walk off the gangway from HMS *Victory* where we've just done an audio guide tour.

'I know; there's something so weird when you think you're standing where actual history took place. I mean, seeing the spot where Nelson was shot.'

'I know, and seeing how tiny his little cot bed was.'

'Yes, it was so funny to think how small everyone would have been. You would have been like a giant.'

'I know. I wouldn't have fancied that. I've got bruises all over my head from hitting all those beams and we were only on there for an hour.'

'Ah, poor Danny,' I say, rubbing it for him. I'll take any excuse to touch him.

We wander back into the main area of the Dockyard and weave through the crowds of people.

'So, what should we see next?' he asks, pulling his ticket out from his pocket. 'I quite fancy seeing the Mary Rose Museum. Or we could go to the Naval Museum?'

I stop and look around. There are so many options. The Dockyard is a large site that contains different historical ships and museums and one ticket covers entry for all of them, which makes it tricky to know what to do first.

I haven't been here for years and I've forgotten how interesting it is. I feel a bit bad as Ross has an annual pass and he used to always try and get me to come with him, only I used to fob him off.

'We could go and see HMS *Warrior*,' I say, as I'm enjoying walking around the ships. 'I remember liking that one.'

We start walking towards it, Danny talking about the time when he came on a school trip and what he and his friends got up to, only I've stopped listening. There on the deck of HMS *Warrior* is Jules aka Wonder Girl – Ross's girlfriend.

I immediately drop Danny's hand and turn away from her, pretending that I'm looking for something in my bag.

'You OK?' asks Danny.

'Yes, yes. I'm fine. I just fancied some Polos.'

'Pretty frantic Polo hunting.'

'Uh-huh,' I say, finally finding some and bringing them out.

Danny's at the gang plank to get on the ship and I'm desperately looking for Jules. I can't imagine that she's here alone. Ross has to be here somewhere.

'Actually, I've changed my mind,' I say, tugging at his sleeve and looking over my shoulder as I go. 'I think we should go on one of the harbour tours. Look.' I point at a board, detailing the tours you can take.

'We'd get to see the naval base. That sounds good, doesn't it? And we'll get to go on a boat that actually moves. Come on.'

I tug at Danny's sleeve and give him no choice. I spot a guy on *Warrior* dressed in a red down jacket. He's got his back to me and he's bending over a sign, but the jacket looks just like the one Ross wears.

I slip round the other side of Danny so that I'm hidden behind him and I quicken my pace.

'Slow down,' says Danny. 'It says that it doesn't go for another ten minutes. What's the rush?'

'I just want to make sure we get on. I'm sure there'll be a queue and I want to get good seats.'

We walk on board after getting our tickets signed and it's practically empty. We go over to take some seats inside near the front.

'Ha, look, great seats,' I say starting to relax. I'm sure by the time we're back on dry land Ross will have finished on *Warrior*. He never used to spend the whole day here, so hopefully he and Jules have only popped in for a little bit.

Danny goes back to telling me the story about his school trip and I try and laugh in the appropriate places. It's hard, though, as I can't help thinking about Ross. I was going to wait to tell him about Danny until I saw him at our Tuesday-night pub quiz, but really I should have made an effort to tell him earlier. I've already told Lucy and Caroline, effectively half of our social group.

'Everything OK?' asks Danny. 'You're not suddenly remembering that you're actually scared of boats, are you? Am I going to lose feeling in my hands again like I did on the plane?'

'Ha ha, no. I don't mind boats quite as much as planes. But really, when you think about it, boats are probably more dangerous, aren't they? There's probably more that could go wrong. We could bump into one of the ferries or it could get overcrowded and sink. Or we could hit something and puncture a hole and take on water. And what if there aren't enough lifeboats and we have to jump overboard? Then we'll be in the freezing sea and the lifeboats won't come and save us and . . .'

'Um, are you just telling me the plot of *Titanic*? I think we're going to be OK. We're right next to shore in a small boat and,' says Danny, looking around at the people coming in, 'whilst it's getting busy I don't think there's any issue with overcrowding.'

I nod. I wish we'd never started this conversation.

'You know, when I was working in Asia, I went on holiday to Bali and you should see how they overcrowd the boats there. It felt like we were skimming the bottom of the river as we went along.'

'Not helping,' I say, looking around at everyone coming aboard and wondering how many people is too many. It's then that I hear Jules's tinkling laugh and I turn and spot her walking on holding Ross's hand.

My heart sinks.

'You know,' I say, wondering if we could somehow sneak off without them seeing us, 'I think it might help me if we got some fresh air. Why don't we go onto the top deck? It would make me less nervous. I'd feel less trapped.'

Danny gives me a WTF look. 'Are you sure, don't you think it'll be a bit windy?'

'No, I reckon we'll be fine.'

I tuck my hair into my scarf and hurry up the stairs just in front of us.

'See, this is great,' I say, trying not to recoil at the biting wind as I slide open the door.

'Yeah, that rain cloud looks especially enticing.'

'Hush now, I'm sure it won't come to anything.'

It's one of those deep dark clouds that will almost certainly turn to rain. I just hope that the tour isn't that long and it holds off.

Danny's phone beeps and he pulls it out of his pocket. He swipes around and taps out a reply.

I try to pretend I'm not desperate to know who it is.

'Just Victoria,' says Danny as he puts his phone back in his coat pocket.

'Again?' I mutter under my breath, wondering what part of her complicated problem this is about. She texted a few times last night and they've already had a text conversation this morning.

The boat jolts and starts to move and the commentary begins. The tour guide is pointing out the different things we can see as we move around the harbour. I'm sure what he's saying is fascinating but I don't really hear a word of it as I'm too busy wondering how we're going to get back onto dry land without Ross and Jules seeing us.

Danny's marvelling at an impressive-looking modern Navy ship when I feel a big splodge of rain hit my jeans. I look up at the cloud and see that it's not alone.

'Come on, let's go downstairs,' says Danny.

'I think we'll be OK,' I say pulling up the hood on my jacket, which isn't known for its waterproof qualities. 'It's just spitting.'

It's as if the rain heard me and it starts to hammer down. I can hear the raindrops hitting the deck of the boat and there's absolutely no way we can stay here any longer without getting soaked to the skin.

Danny grabs my hand and pulls me towards the stairs. We follow the exodus of the other brave, but stupid people who were outside.

I try to hang back behind the other people, but they soon thin out looking for seats.

'Do you fancy something from the bar? Hot chocolate?' asks Danny, as he shakes the water off his head like a shaggy dog.

'That would be great, thanks.'

'You go and see if you can get us some seats.'

I'm still hiding behind the last group from upstairs and when they start to move I move with them, panning to see if I can find Ross or Jules in order to avoid them.

'Lydia,' says Jules from behind me. 'I thought that was you. I said to myself as you came down the stairs that looks like Lydia, and there, when you spun around, it was you. Are you OK? Did you have a nice Christmas? What are you doing here?'

She's holding two hot drinks and she's sneakily come from the bar, where I wasn't looking.

'I'm showing a friend the Dockyard,' I say, choosing my words carefully. 'He's from out of town.'

'Oh, lovely. I always do that when I've got visitors too. We're just here playing tourists. Ross and I come here all the time, ever since we discovered on our first date we both loved it here. It's like our special place. We're going on the M-33 next; it's one that I've not done before. It's from the First World War. Should be so interesting. Have you been on it? Have you done the *Victory* yet? The *Warrior*? Where else have you been this morning?'

I'm blinking to keep up with her rapid talking, but also to keep an eye out to see where Ross is.

'We've done *Victory*, then we're going to do the *Mary Rose* after lunch.'

'Oh, perfect. Are you sitting down? There're some free seats next to us.'

'Oh, no, I think we'll probably stand.'

The boat jolts a little and I feel myself wobble and can't help but cling onto a rail.

'Come and sit with us,' says Jules. 'I'm sure Ross will be pleased to see you.'

Danny did want us to get a seat . . . Besides, the tour is going and no one – apart from me and Jules – is really talking. Everyone's listening. Ross takes this stuff so seriously, so he won't want to make idle chit chat. All I need to do is make him think that Danny and I are still only just friends until I can get him alone and tell him the truth.

I follow Jules over and sit down on the plastic chair next to her.

Ross leans forward and gives me a look. 'Lydia, I didn't expect to see you here,' he says, raising an eyebrow.

'Yes, well, just seeing the sights,' I mumble. 'Good Christmas?'

'Yes, it was nice, thanks, and you?'

'Uh-huh, it was fine,' I say, glossing over the monumental life-changing decision I made.

'Oh, Ross, look at that view,' says Jules, as she points out of the window.

I breathe a sigh of relief but then Danny comes over and sits down, presenting me with my drink.

'That should warm you up a little bit. And if it doesn't . . .' he says, playfully rubbing his hands on my thighs.

'Ha ha,' I say, trying to beat his hand away with the back of mine so that my engagement ring isn't visible.

'Ooh, hello,' says Jules leaning over and waving at Danny. 'I'm Jules, it's lovely to meet you. Lydia says you're from out of town. Are you enjoying your visit? I love it here at the Dockyard. It's so interesting. Don't you find it interesting?'

Danny's mouth has flown open. 'Um, yes,' he says, unsure which question he should be answering.

Ross snaps his head round and his eyes almost pop out of his head when he spots that Jules is talking to Danny.

'Danny,' says Ross holding his hand out awkwardly.

Danny looks equally surprised to see him, but he takes his hand and shakes it.

'So, how do you two know each other?' asks Jules.

'Lydia and Danny have been old friends for years,' says Ross.

'Well, actually,' pipes up Danny, but before he can finish a man leans forward from the row behind.

'Excuse me, sorry to be rude, but do you mind talking when the tour's over? I'm having trouble hearing.'

'Of course, of course,' we all mutter.

I try and distract myself by drinking the hot chocolate, only Danny puts his arm around me and I try and wriggle myself free a little. 'I haven't told Ross yet,' I whisper. I can't fail to miss the hurt look in his eye.

I turn my head to look at the thing the captain is referring to, and I see that Ross was watching us. He turns away and I feel awful. I wonder if he has already guessed. Kerry was right, I should have told him.

After twenty agonising minutes the tour eventually comes to an end.

'Right, we'd better get going,' I say, wondering if I can drag Danny away without the inevitable awkward conversation with Ross and Jules. I leap up, only to see that there's a big slow-moving queue to get off the boat. We're never going to be able to sneak off.

'So how long are you down for, Danny?' asks Ross.

'Just until tomorrow night. Lydia's doing her best to show me all the sights.'

'Is she now? It's funny, as I could never get her to come here with me.'

I slowly close my eyes. This is going to be every bit as awkward as I imagined it would be.

'Well, I thought I couldn't show Danny the city without bringing him here. Besides, I haven't seen the new *Mary Rose* museum.'

'I've got quite low expectations since I last saw the *Mary Rose* – it looked like a lump of wood being sprayed with oil.'

'Oh, it's not like that at all now. We went not so long ago, didn't we, Ross? I found it fascinating. All those artefacts that they got from the wreck, too. Those weapons and the cutlery. And they had these tiny shoes. It was all amazing,' says Jules. 'You're going to have such a super time. I'm almost tempted to tag along. It's that good that you can see it again and again.'

I'm about to object when she carries on.

'But I really want to concentrate on the more modern history today.'

'Shame,' I say, nodding in relief.

'Of course the *Mary Rose* isn't the best example of a warship raised from the seabed,' says Ross, looking directly at Danny. 'That's arguably the *Vasa*.'

If we weren't in front of Danny, I'd probably take the piss out of Ross for saying 'arguably' in a sentence, but seeing as things are already a bit awkward, I let it slide.

'I've actually been there and it is pretty impressive. I was over for a conference in Stockholm for a few days.'

Ross's nostrils actually start to flare. He'd suggested we go a few years back, but I'd put him off when I'd told him that we'd have to go to the ABBA museum.

'Did you go to the ABBA museum, too?' I say, hopefully.

'I did, and I sang "Waterloo" in the studio karaoke bit.'

See – Meant. To. Be.

'You know that always reminds me of the time I made you watch *Muriel's Wedding*,' I say.

'Oh, don't even go there. Those are two hours of my life I'm never getting back,' he says, shaking his head.

'I love *Muriel's Wedding*,' says Jules, clutching her hand to her chest. 'It's so funny, but at the same time it's so gritty and raw. Those looks that the swimmer gives her, it's all so heartbreaking. Don't you think it's so heartbreaking? I actually cried the first time I watched it.'

'Did you cry, Danny?' I ask, raising a cheeky eyebrow.

'I think I cried in pain. It's not really my cup of tea.'

We start to shuffle towards the door and I'm hopeful as we've almost made it onto dry land and Ross hasn't asked about Danny and I.

Someone pushes Jules from behind and she falls forward. I slip my hands out of my pockets to catch her.

'Oh, Jules. Are you OK?' I say.

'Yes, fine,' she says, steadying herself.

I take my hands away and she grabs the one with my ring on.

'Oh, Lydia, that ring is beautiful. Are those real diamonds?'

She's pulled it right up to have a good look.

'It's beautiful the way they catch in the light, and that sapphire too. Did you get it for Christmas?' she says looking at me.

I'm staring at the ring wondering how I'm going to explain this one away.

'Isn't it on your ring finger?' says Jules. 'Oh my God, are you engaged? Ross, have you seen that Lydia's engaged? You're engaged?'

'I think we've confirmed she's engaged,' says Ross, as he puts a hand on Jules's shoulder to stop her talking.

A few people turn and smile at us and a few of them mutter congratulations and I can't look Ross in the eye. No one says anything and I'm almost willing Jules to start firing off her rapid machine-gun questions to break the silence.

'Lydia and I had one of those, if-we're-not-married-by-the-time-we're-thirty pacts,' says Danny eventually, 'back when we thought that thirty was old and that if we were still unmarried then it would be the end of the world. Anyway, we had this great holiday together between Christmas and New Year and the pact got mentioned and we ended up engaged. Not that I needed the pact, I'd have married her anyway after that trip.'

I chance a look at Ross and wish I hadn't. He looks so wounded.

'Congratulations,' he says after a long pause. 'I'm sure you'll be really happy with each other.' He's only looking at Danny. 'Does that mean you're moving down here?'

'Actually, Lydia's moving up to be with me. I've got a house in the Lake District and I've got my own business, so it makes more sense for her to move.'

Ross snaps his head round to look at me and tilts it as if he's studying me.

'I was going to tell you, but I wanted to do it face to face. I was waiting until I saw you next week at the pub quiz.'

'Right. You're giving up your job too?'

I feel my cheeks flushing.

'After my long notice period,' I say vaguely. 'I'm hoping it won't be too difficult to find something suitable up there. There are loads of hotels and I'm sure there must be something in events.'

I don't actually know if that's the case. It's all been such a whirlwind and I haven't had time to check. Perhaps I would have been crazy to have handed in my notice without lining something up first. This way I can get the event manager experience and look for a new job. The more I think about it, the more Danny's going to absolutely agree with me that taking the promotion was the right thing to do.

'Well, that's just wonderful news. I love the Lake District,' says Jules. What a surprise from the woman who loves everything! 'All those little stone walls and the lakes and the little quirky shops. We'd love to come and visit up there, wouldn't we, Ross? We'd be able to go hiking in the fells and row boats across the lakes. Ooh, it sounds wonderful.'

'Hmm,' says Ross noncommittally.

We finally follow the crowd out into the fresh air, but we're not free yet. We all walk towards the main thoroughfare of the Dockyard.

'I want to hear all about the proposal. I love hearing about proposals. Did you get down on one knee? Did you say yes straight away? It's all so exciting,' says Jules.

Ross is gritting his teeth.

'It was all very low key,' I say, waving my hand before I realise I'm waving the engagement ring practically in Ross's face. 'Bit of a misunderstanding at first.'

I trail off and I try not to look at either Ross or Danny – neither look impressed.

'Right, well, we're going to go and see the *Mary Rose*,' I say, with relief as we reach the path that leads to it.

'Lovely to meet you, Jules,' says Danny. 'Ross.'

'Yes, see you again, I guess. And Lydia, I'll see you at the pub quiz on Tuesday,' he says.

Jules leans over and gives us each a quick hug, but Ross doesn't move at first and eventually she has to tug him away.

'A bit of a misunderstanding?' says Danny raising an eyebrow when they're gone.

'Well, there was, but I felt a bit funny telling my ex about how romantic it all was.'

'I didn't realise that you were still friends with him,' says Danny as he takes hold of my hand. 'Like hang-out-and-go-to-pub-quizzes-type friends.'

'Our break-up was mutual and there were no hard feelings, and he's moved on, I've moved on,' I say, pretending that we'd all just had a lovely conversation when in reality there was more tension than there is in the Golden Gate Bridge.

Danny nods. 'I've just never been friends with any of my exes.'

'That's because you've probably been a heartbreaker, Danny Whittaker. Now, come on, let's go and see this old ship.'

'Ah, yes, we've got to go and see the lump of old wood. You know we could just go back to yours,' he says, grabbing my hand and pulling me in closer.

'And what, see another type of wood?' I say, knowing what he has on his mind – what he always has on his mind. 'No, come on, I promised you I'd show you my city and that's what I'm going to do.'

'OK,' he says, pulling his coat further round him as if to brace himself for the strong winds that are accompanying the drizzle.

'And then we'll definitely go home after that.'

'Deal,' says Danny, leaning over and giving me a kiss.

We walk towards the entrance of the museum and I turn to look over my shoulder. I see Ross and Jules behind us. I see him turn his head away. I feel my stomach sink. I know what I said to Danny was true – that we've both moved on – but that doesn't mean to say that news of our engagement didn't hurt him; I'm sure that if it was the other way round I'd have been a bit thrown by the news.

The only consolation is that now pretty much everyone knows that we're getting married and that I'm moving. All I've got to do now is tell Danny about the amended timescale and then I'll have no more secrets from anyone.

Chapter 20

Um – I think your mum has played some April Fools joke on me. She told me that you were trading NYC for the Lakes? What are you thinking you crazy, crazy man. Just in case it's really true I'm sending you a present, as you've probably forgotten how to be British after all your jet setting.

Parcel containing *Very British Problems*;

Lydia to Danny, April 2017

I usually love January as it's quiet in the office. Most of us take time off in lieu of the extra time worked at the Christmas parties and there are very few events to organise, but now that I'm on my trial promotion I'm working harder than ever. I'm currently knee deep in researching proms and wedding-dress balls.

'Morning, Lydia,' says Tracey, as she swans past. 'I've got your new job description hot off the press from HR. I've had a look through it and it seems OK to me, but can you just give it a once over and check it's all there?'

I take the piece of paper.

'Thanks, Tracey. I'll give it a look and get it straight back to you.'

I start to scan the job description, not quite able to believe I've waited for so long to do this role, and here it all is in black and white. I can't help but thinking it would be much more of an entertaining, and realistic, read if it was annotated with real life examples.

Problem Solving in high-stress situations – E.g. Must be able to think on your feet when you catch the local Mayor in a compromising position with a guest whilst touring with a press photographer around the building.

Excellent customer service skills and ability to liaise with VIPs – E.g. Must not turn into fangirl when Claudia Winkleman turns up to host an event. You must absolutely not ask her to do your eye make-up.

Ability to deliver projects on time and to budget – E.g. Must be able to have a thick enough skin to stand up to clients who try and bully you into having actual gold statues as props.

I'm starting to get excited as I read through what my new job will entail. It's similar to what I've been doing up until now, but on a much bigger scale, and with more responsibility. It's more client facing and far more creative.

'Have you seen Helen?' asks Fred, who works in our estates team. 'I sent her an email this morning about sending through the layout plan for the event tomorrow as we need to start set up this afternoon. It's not like her to send it over so late.'

'I'm sure she'll send it over soon. She's just nipped to the loo, so when she's back I'll get her to email it to you.'

'Great, thanks, Lydia. Congratulations on the promotion, it's about time.'

'Thanks, Fred,' I say, beaming.

I look over at Helen's computer. It's on the screensaver, meaning she must have been gone for over twenty minutes – that's a pretty long bathroom break and I figure I should go and find her.

I scan the open-plan office as I leave, but there's no sign of her. I poke my head into the little kitchenette, which is empty.

I walk into the toilets and push the doors of the stalls to see if they're vacant and see that the last one is occupied.

'Helen,' I whisper as I knock.

I hear a sniff like she's been crying before the toilet flushes. I feel a little awkward as I wait for her to come out.

She opens the door and pats her hair as she walks past me. I try to pretend that I haven't noticed her red, puffy eyes.

'Is everything OK? Do you need to go home?' I say, walking up to her and resting my hand on her back.

'No, no,' she says, forcing a smile as she washes her hands. 'I'm fine. Absolutely fine. Fine, fine, fine.'

'Don't forget that I'm supposed to be taking some of your workload, so if you're feeling overwhelmed with too much you can always pass some of your events to me.'

She smiles warmly. 'Thanks, Lydia. I might need to take you up on that. It's all got so busy.'

'That's why Tracey promoted me. And Helen, you know I'm here for you if you need to talk about anything else, don't you?'

'Yeah, but totally not needed. I'm just coming down with a cold or something. I'm all snuffly and it's playing havoc with my eyes.'

'Sounds more like an allergy,' I say, despite the fact that we both know it isn't.

She rummages through her make-up bag that she's been carrying and puts some Touché Eclat under her eyes.

'Yes, perhaps. Maybe I'm allergic to Ben's new aftershave.'

'It is pretty overpowering,' I say, giggling. 'Fred's been looking for you. He wants the layout plan for tomorrow's event.'

'Crap, I meant to send that last night. I totally forgot. Thanks for finding me, I'd better go and do it.'

'Are you sure you don't need me to get involved?'

'No, I'm fine. I just need to get my head back into it after the holidays, that's all. Besides, you must have a million things to do, what with your new responsibilities.'

'Tell me about it. Plus, I've got to start training Jenny up to take over parts of my old job.'

'She'll do a super job. She's so organised. Oh God, not that you're not,' she says quickly.

'I know what you mean, I think she'll do a cracking job too.'

'As will you.'

'Thanks.'

I feel myself blushing. Everyone's been so lovely about my promotion. It's really getting to me, especially as I can't share the news with anyone at home. I can feel myself welling up. I'm worried that Helen's not going to be the only one leaving here with puffy eyes at this rate.

'I guess we'd better get back to it then,' says Helen, giving herself one last look in the mirror.

I give her a sympathetic arm rub, wondering what's really going on, before we head back into the office.

I left work late today which meant that when I parked my car at home, I was left with a dilemma, I could either go straight to the pub quiz and be early or I could pop into my flat for a little bit and inevitably be late. In the end, I plumped for being early as I figured that if I went home, I would have a) collapsed on the sofa and not managed to get up again or b) faffed around getting changed.

I push open the door to The Dog and I scan our usual table just on the off-chance anyone else is here already and spot Ross nursing a half-drunk pint. Bugger. He's the last person I want to be alone with.

I give him a quick wave and head on over to the bar. I'm hoping that if I take enough time, Lucy, Caroline or Rob will have arrived to rescue me.

'What can I get you?' asks the barmen.

'Oh, um, I'll have a large Malbec, please, and a pint of Stowford Press.'

'Coming right up,' he says.

He's overly cheery and obviously new. The rest of the bar staff are slumped at the end of the bar enjoying the calm before the storm. The Dog has a late licence so most of its business is late at night. Not that I know much about that these days. The quiz finishes at 10 p.m. and I'm usually tucked up in bed by eleven.

The drinks are handed to me and I string out paying for them as long as possible by counting out coins, whilst watching the door. No one else has arrived by the time I'm finished and I'm forced to take the drinks over to the table.

'Here you go,' I say to Ross, sliding the pint across the table to him.

'Thanks,' he says, taking it and giving me a small smile.

We sit for a moment in painful silence. It's so weird to think that we were once boyfriend and girlfriend. We weren't lovers like Danny and I are. There was never that kind of passion, and the sex was more of a B+ than an A* like it is with Danny, but there was something there that worked. Once upon a time I was happy; we both were.

I try and shut out the good memories that are now playing like a film montage in my mind. I don't know what's wrong with me, it was me that suggested we break up and I'm super loved up with Danny – why am I now sad remembering our 'best bits'?

'So, you're here alone tonight, then?' he says, sipping his new pint.

'Hmm, yes, Danny's up in the Lakes. Look,' I say, swirling the wine round in the oversized glass, 'I should have told you. I meant to tell you, or at least I wanted to tell you before you saw him.'

Ross shrugs his shoulders and keeps quiet causing me to get flashbacks of when we used to argue.

'I didn't think that you would be that bothered since you're with Jules.'

Ross sighs and takes a deep breath before he folds his arms.

'That's not the same thing at all. First, Jules and I are dating, we're nowhere near getting married. And second, I didn't spend the whole time that we were together telling you that Jules and I were just friends and that you had nothing to worry about. Even when you were sending each other Christmas baubles of naked Santas.'

I guess when he puts it like that . . .

'Every time one of those bloody packages arrived you told me that there was nothing between you and there never would be, and I believed you. Then, a few months after we break up, suddenly you're getting married to him, and so quickly. It's as if you don't need any time for the engagement as you've been building up to the marriage for years.'

'Ross, it wasn't like that. We were just friends. I promise you that when we were together it was just letters and nothing more. Honestly.'

Ross spins his pint slowly round on the table. It's his trademark move when he's thinking.

'I'm happy that you found Jules and I guess I was hoping that you could be pleased for me too.'

'You're happy for me that I'm with "Wonder Girl".'

I bite my lip.

'I know that you girls don't like her. You think that she's annoying and over the top, but she's nice, Lydia. She's really nice.'

'I know she is, and I do like her. It's just weird seeing you with someone else,' I say, and this surprises me as much as it does him.

He drinks his drink before slamming the glass down on the table.

'Then imagine that in reverse – but worse, like if I was with someone you were jealous of the whole time we were dating. And you went with him to see the *Mary Rose*,' he says throwing his hands up in the air incredulously as if that was the worst bit. 'You never wanted to go and see that with me. You always said it was boring. And then suddenly you go with *him*.'

I feel awful as I knew that Danny would get a kick out of it and that's why I took him. I never even stopped to think that it wasn't what I would have picked to do for an afternoon; I wanted to please Danny. And yet, Ross is right, I'd never gone with him.

'But that was different. We lived together and we were always doing things without each other. We never really did the whole going-on dates thing, did we, because we just ended up together.' I shake my head. 'That came out all wrong. I just meant . . .'

'I know what you meant. It was different with us. We drifted together and what started out of convenience turned into a habit.'

'No, that's not what I was saying.'

'But it boils down to the same thing. You're in a whirlwind with him, I get it, but have you stopped to think about what you're doing? Have you asked yourself why he's in such a hurry to get married? What's he hiding?'

'He's not hiding anything. We're in love.'

He blows through his teeth. 'Sure, *love*.'

He laughs bitterly and slips on his coat as he stands up to leave.

'Are you not staying for the quiz?'

'I'm not in the mood.'

'Ross, please don't go. I want us to be friends. Can't we work this out?' I say pleadingly. I hope that I haven't finally broken up the friendship group like everyone feared we would.

'I don't know, Lydia, I don't know at all.'

He gets up and walks out of the pub in a hurry and I'm left looking at my glass, wondering if I should go after him. I hesitate for a while, not knowing what I'd say to him, but I guess I should at least try to talk to him. I stand up to go just as Rob and Lucy walk into the pub their arms linked.

They make a beeline for the table and I sink back down into my chair.

'So where is this ring, then?' says Rob, yanking at my hand. 'Bloody hell. Even I'm jealous of that one. If Gavin and I ever get married, then I want a mengagement ring. Why is it women get all the fun?'

'Dunno,' says Lucy, 'but with the ring comes great responsibility. Like embroidering one hundred napkins according to Ed's mum. That was her actual idea for a wedding favour, me embroidering the initials of every wedding guest. The last time I sewed it was under duress during Home Ec. I need a drink.

'Same again? Kronenbourg?' she says, turning first to me and then Rob before she goes off to the bar.

'I see Ross has been and gone,' says Rob, sliding the empty pints to the edge of the table as he takes his seat. 'I take it he didn't take your news well?'

'Not exactly. But it's a bit hypocritical. He's been dating Wonder Girl for weeks and brought her out with us on a number of occasions and I've been nice to her.' Rob gives me a look. 'I've been mainly nice to her – to her face, anyway. He's moved on, why can't I?'

'I think perhaps because you're getting married. Didn't you always poo-poo his ideas of you two getting married?'

'Yeah, but I didn't want to get married then.'

'And now you do. It's a bit of a kick in the balls. Plus, you *have* been writing to Danny all these years.'

'You've spoken to him already, I take it?' I say, sipping my drink.

'We went out for a drink last night. He'll come round, just give him some time. Break-ups can be complicated.'

I give Rob a look.

'I was watching a phone-in on *This Morning* the other day about this type of thing.'

'Working from home's going well, then?'

'Most of the time.'

Lucy returns with the drinks, just as Caroline runs in. She unravels her coat to reveal a jumper with a small splodge of baby sick on her shoulder and her hair is half hanging out of its bun. She's far from the Caroline of old who used to iron her underwear and bedclothes and would never go out with a strand of hair out of place. Not that any of us care, we're just happy she's here.

'It's been one of those days. Where's Ross? Not like him to be late,' she says, as she sits down next to me.

'Been and gone,' I say.

'Oh, OK. Well, let's just hope there's no sports round this week. Oh God, Lydia, I forgot. Baby brain. Let me see the ring. That's gorgeous,' she says as I obligingly show her my hand. 'I can't believe you're getting married so soon.'

'I know, are you sure you're OK about not coming?' I say to her and Rob. I feel awful that they're not invited but we had to make the cut-off somewhere.

'Well, of course I'm pissed off. But I can't really talk as Gavin and I always said we'd marry in Vegas and fuck everyone else off. So I'm with you, Lyds,' says Rob, chinking my glass.

'And I'm gutted, I really am, but at the same time I couldn't imagine how we'd manage it logistically. Ethan doesn't do more than about two hours in his car seat before he screams the car down, and he doesn't sleep at home, so I can't imagine he'd sleep in a hotel room. And I couldn't come on my own as I can't express that much milk, and he's stopped taking the bottle and, bloody hell, my head's going to explode just thinking about it.'

I hold her hand and give it a squeeze.

'And breathe. We'll have a meal out here one night afterwards to celebrate.'

'Yes,' she says. 'An evening out, that might just work. And I'll try to make it to the hen do.'

'Um, I'm not having a hen do.'

'What?' snap Lucy and Caroline.

'You have to have a hen do,' says Lucy. 'How else will I take revenge for mine?'

'You haven't had yours yet, how do you know that I'm not going to do something really nice?' I say, remembering that I was supposed to contact her uni friend to start organising it.

'Well, I need to be prepared, just in case.'

'There's no hen do,' I say again. 'Just a tiny wedding and a tiny meal down here afterwards. OK?' I say, raising my sternest eyebrow at Lucy.

'OK,' she says, nodding, and I almost do a fist bump with myself under the table. I'd expected more resistance. And with that, I feel as if I can change the topic of conversation. 'So, did everyone have a nice Christmas?'

'Ethan had a growth spurt and fed for seven hours straight so I got pinned to the couch,' says Caroline.

We all pull a sympathetic face.

'No, it was a Christmas miracle. I got to sit and watch TV for seven hours without having to lift a finger. Matt had to keep bringing me food and drinks and I ate a whole tub of Quality Street – it was amazing.'

'Gavin and I had a massive fight. Do you know, he actually wanted to watch the Queen's speech at Christmas. I mean, who actually watches that?'

'My mum,' say Lucy and I together, laughing.

'Exactly.'

'Right,' booms a voice out of the speakers. 'Question one of the quiz is coming up, come and get your quiz sheets.'

'I'd better nip to the loo. Anyone want another drink?' asks Rob.

'No, thanks,' I say.

'I'll get the drinks,' says Lucy. 'Gin, Caroline?'

'Lovely, thank you,' she says as Lucy disappears off to the bar, then she turns to me and lowers her voice. 'Whilst they've gone I've got something I've been meaning to ask you, but there hasn't been the right time. We're having Ethan christened next month and we wondered if you'd be godmother.'

'Me?' I say, totally bowled over.

'Yes, I've watched you over the years with Olivia and you're such a wonderful aunt and I know that you'd make a wonderful godmother too.'

'I'm so touched. I'd be honoured,' I say, as she throws her arms around me. I haven't told Caroline that I'm moving up to the Lake District yet, but I can't imagine that it's going to change things, is it? I'm sure it isn't a prerequisite of being a godparent that you live nearby.

'Matt's going to be thrilled. We did toy with asking his cousin Gemma, but she lives all the way down in Cornwall and we wanted someone who's actually going to be involved in his life, you know.'

Oh, crap. Now's the time to tell her, but as she squeezes my hand she looks so pleased and I'm so happy that she asked. Besides, everyone knows that in this day and age godparents don't do much other than buy an extra birthday present, do they?

Lucy comes back from the bar and immediately launches into telling us about her day at work and a couple of minutes later Rob comes back over with the quiz sheet in his hands.

'This is the winning paper right here, guys. I can feel it,' he says, sitting back down.

I'm really going to miss our regular Tuesday pub quiz. I can't help but feel a little down at the thought that I'm not going to be here every week.

But it's not only finding another quiz, it's my friends. As they take the piss out of each other and laugh, in that easy-going way that comes from long friendships, I feel sad that I'm going to have to start from scratch all over again.

It's funny, as it's only a night out in what used to be our local pub, but it's only dawning on me now how much of life I've taken for granted. Danny's got a tough job at the weekend to convince me that where he lives is better than here.

Chapter 21

Start spreading the news, I'm leaving today. Oh wait, that's what I should have written when I was going to New York, not when I was leaving it. Sorry I haven't been able to email with more details about the move but I can finally reveal I'm going into business with my mate Gaz. (Think you met him when you visited me in London that time?) I can't believe that I'm going off the advice of a $10 psychic but the future she told me of sounded pretty good. Also, she sold key rings with fake rabbit's feet, which I thought would be right up your street. Hope it brings you luck!

Parcel containing fake rabbit's foot;
Danny to Lydia, May 2017

I step out of the car after six and a half hours and I'm walking like I've run the London marathon. I stopped briefly three times – once to buy a jumbo coffee to keep me alert and the other two times to pee as a result of it. But I've made it. It's 10.30 p.m. but I'm actually here. I'm seconds from seeing my Danny, or maybe minutes, depending how long it takes my aching muscles to get to the front door.

The door flies open and he comes to me, which is even better. If he suggests this time that he needs to carry me over the threshold I'm all for it.

'Hey, you,' he says wrapping his arms around me.

'Hey,' I say, burying myself in his chest. I want us to stay like this forever, but it's bloody cold and I can see the bright lights of his house calling to me. He must have read my mind as he pulls my hand and leads me inside.

'I'll get your bag for you. Go on upstairs, the fire's on in the lounge.'

I slowly walk up the two flights, my muscles loosening with every step. I push open the door and it feels like I've come home. The fire is blasting and the heat hits me immediately. The lights are down low and it's more hygge than I've ever managed to achieve.

Danny follows me in and he's carrying a large tray of nibbles.

'I know you said you'd eat at lunch, but I thought you might be hungry now.'

I stare at the crackers and cheese, olives, sun-dried tomatoes and charcuterie meat and I feel as if I'm in heaven.

'I was going to say I'm not hungry, but my stomach is saying otherwise.' As if on cue it growls angrily at me.

'Drink?' he says, holding up a bottle of red, and I nod. 'So was the traffic bad?'

'No, it was OK. I took the M6 toll so that saved me a bit of time. It is a long drive though.'

'Yeah,' he says nodding. 'It would be tough if we had to do it forever, but at least we know it's only going to be a few weeks, right?' he says leaning over and giving me a kiss.

'Just a few weeks.'

Twenty-five weeks can count as a few, can't they? But even twenty-five weeks seems too few as, over the last few days, it's continued to dawn on me what I'm giving up. It's not just my job but Kerry, Jim and Olivia, Mum, Lucy, Rob, Caroline and Ross.

I keep trying to tell myself that I'm being ridiculous. People move around all the time. There's always FaceTime. Besides, how often do you fall in love? I mean properly earth-shatteringly in love. This is once in a lifetime. I can't ignore it.

'You OK?' asks Danny, stroking my leg.

'Just tired.'

He pulls me in for a hug.

'We'll eat this and have an early night, if you like?'

'That sounds lovely. Although I'm guessing it's not going to be that early is it?' I say, my fingertips creeping under his belt line.

'I'm guessing not,' he says, leaning over to kiss me gently.

'I don't even think I'm that hungry after all,' I say between kisses. 'But I am ready for bed.'

'OK, then,' he purrs. 'I'll just put the sausage in the fridge.'

'Well, that's romantic,' I say, thinking I've never heard it called that before.

'I just don't want it to go off,' he says picking it up, 'it was from a fancy deli in town.'

'Oh, you meant the meat,' I say, laughing at myself.

'What did you think I meant? Lydia, that filthy mind of yours. One of the many reasons why I love you,' he says, pulling me to standing as he takes the tray downstairs.

'One of them. And what are the other reasons?'

'I can't tell you that now. What would I say in our vows?'

'Don't tell me we're going off book?'

He has a twinkle in his eye and he cackles as he walks down into the kitchen.

'I thought the whole point of having a quickie wedding was to take away the stress. Writing our own vows is definitely a stress.'

He's still laughing as he deposits everything in the fridge.

'Come on,' he says, grabbing my hand. 'Let's get the other sausage in the fridge.'

I laugh and follow him downstairs.

Danny gets out of bed early the next morning to make us a cup of tea. It's a serious downside of not living in a tiny studio flat, as in mine I can lean out and pretty much make a cup without having to get my feet out of the cosy warm bed. But it's Danny rather than me who's up, so I make the most of having the bed to myself and make starfish bed angels as I snuggle in. Man, this bed is comfy. This is reason enough for moving up here alone. It's definitely not the budget IKEA model that mine is.

'What are you doing?' he says, looking at me as if I'm nuts.

'Bed angels. You know, like snow angels, but in the sheets. You should try it. But not now,' I say, as he snuggles in, 'when you're on your own, or else you'd tip me out.'

'You're weird, Lydia Stoker, you know that?'

'I do. And luckily you do, too,' I say sitting up and taking my cup of tea. We sit there in companionable silence for a moment and I wonder if we could stay like this all day – it's perfect – but

I know Danny's probably got the whole day planned. 'I'm looking forward to doing some sightseeing.'

I'm picturing a tour of all the little tearooms in the area, sampling the cakes, pottering around the touristy shops. I've got tingles just thinking about how perfect that sounds.

'Yeah, we'd better get a wriggle on, or else we'll be late.'

I blow on my tea to cool it down more quickly so that I can drink it. 'I can't wait. So what's first up, breakfast somewhere?'

'Um, we'll probably have to grab something here. I'll make us bacon sandwiches whilst you shower.'

'Oh, OK. So where's up first?' I ask, noticing that he's acting a bit shifty.

'You'll see.'

'Am I going to like it?' I ask. He's not usually so cagey and it makes me think I'm going to hate it.

'Um, I think so.'

That doesn't sound convincing.

'Am I going to be sailing through the air again?' That doesn't hold the same appeal in this weather.

'No, definitely not airborne.'

'Any other clues?'

He shakes his head, downs his tea (and probably burns his throat).

'I'm going to grab a quick shower. And then you can have a quick one. No need to wash your hair today.'

I run my hand through my curls. I wash my hair almost every day to get rid of the halo of frizz that builds up. Danny knows that and now I'm worried about where we're going.

I look out of the window and up over at the fells, wondering if I'm going to be spending the day hiking. I look at the rain running down the window pane and I hope that I've got it all wrong.

After my shower I'm handed a plate with a bacon sarnie dripping with ketchup. Danny then steers me into the bedroom where he's replaced the jeans and jumper on the bed that I'd laid out to wear with thick walking trousers and a fleece.

I look up at him for an explanation.

'You wanted to see the best of the Lake District. Unfortunately, there's more to it than tea shops.'

'Are you sure about that, as I've heard otherwise,' I say, as I bite into my sandwich. He's good, distracting me with food when he's dropping a bomb shell.

'Don't worry, you're not going to be in these all day,' he says with a wink, and I start to relax. I guess a little bit of hiking followed by a tearoom would be OK. It's not like I have an aversion to the great outdoors, and I'm not going to melt in the rain, am I? It's only a little bit of drizzle. I'm sure it'll be fine.

An hour and a half later, when I'm standing in a tiny cold dressing room on the edge of a lake, I start to re-evaluate my whole I'm-sure-it'll-be-fine frame of mind. When Danny said that I wasn't going to be in my hiking gear all day, I'd assumed he'd meant we'd come home and change or at the very least that he had something a little smutty planned. I did not think that I'd be stripping off and getting into a wetsuit.

I'm climbing into the no-nonsense swimming costume that Danny has bought me to put on underneath. At least he didn't buy some sexy dental-floss bikini which not only would have been uncomfortable but also would have missed an opportunity to provide me with much-needed extra layers.

I look down at the wetsuit, which everyone knows is the least flattering outfit known to man. I'm swearing like a trooper as I climb into it, and I know that the other women in the group are giving me a wide berth. I watch the way they jump expertly into their suits. I bet they do this all the time. I finally wrestle mine on and slip on the shoes I've been given, which are wet and slimy.

I'm going to kill Danny. And to think I spent three hours last week in a museum for him. I would have taken him for a three-hour shop around the designer outlet if I'd known that we were supposed to be providing the other person with their idea of cruel and unusual punishment.

I slip the life jacket on over the top of my wetsuit and waddle out to meet Danny.

He looks hot in a wetsuit. Of course he does. He's got a Keanu Reeves in *Point Break* thing going on.

'You look good,' he says, kissing me on the cheek and playfully slapping my bum. Right now I want to slap him back, but not in an affectionate way. 'You'll be needing this.'

He passes me a helmet as he straps one on his own head.

'Thanks so much,' I say sarcastically, but after listening to the safety briefing I take it gladly and make sure that I secure it firmly to my head.

Our guide passes us bright red waterproof clothing to go over the top of the wetsuits, and I'm at least thankful that people won't be able to see so many of my lumps and bumps.

'Right then, everyone ready to go Ghyll scrambling?' says John our over-enthusiastic guide. 'Let's go.'

'If everyone's going, then the little wooden huts will be free. You could peel me out of this wetsuit,' I say.

Danny cackles. 'Nice try, Stoker, but peeling a wetsuit off isn't every man's fantasy, you know. Come on.'

He takes my hand and I sigh as he pulls me to the path and we follow in single file up the side of a hill.

'I can't believe we're actually going to do this,' I say as we start walking to our first ascent. 'I mean, how is this even safe? How can we walk up a waterfall?'

Danny gives me a wide eyed grin and it only makes me panic more.

'Ok, so we're going to start climbing up here,' says John. 'Just trust the path we show you.'

I'm relieved to see that the slope up is more of a diagonal angle rather than a vertical drop. I think when he'd said waterfalls I'd been imagining Niagara Falls. Not that it makes it any easier; it still looks impossible. I watch in disbelief as the guide scrambles over some boulders and pulls himself up between a tiny gorge.

'My bum is never going to fit between that,' I say, completely seriously to Danny.

He just laughs at me and scurries up it like Spiderman and I have no choice but to follow him.

I grit my teeth as I feel the water soaking through my neoprene shoes. Bloody hell it's cold.

It takes a few stumbles and slips for me to start to relax, and a few more before I get the hang of it. After a while I start to learn where to put my feet on the slippery rocks and heave myself up like a pro. I may actually be enjoying it too – but I'm not going to tell Danny that just yet. I don't want him to be bringing me here every week.

'Right, so now we get to the fun stuff,' says John when we reach a vertical cliff face. 'We're going to descend. I'll go first and Chris will be at the rear.'

'He's not serious,' I say to Danny as I look down at the path he's pointing at. 'That's way too steep and narrow. And what if I hit my head and knock myself unconscious. Or my bum gets stuck. Or I—'

'—Or you have a good time,' says Danny, squeezing my hand. 'Relax, it's going to be fine.'

It does nothing to ease my apprehension. I'm suddenly terrified. I don't mind heights and I don't mind water, but I do I mind throwing myself into rapids that are whooshing down a gorge.

Danny gives me a quick kiss. 'I'll be right behind you,' he says, pushing me forward.

A few people start to scream excitedly as they jump down, and I try to take comfort in the fact that they don't sound too scared.

'You did say that you wanted to do adrenaline-fuelled things,' Danny says as we edge ever closer. 'Remember that letter that you wrote to me after I came back from the Bahamas.'

I curse myself, wondering what the bloody hell I put in all those letters and hoping that he won't be throwing me out of a plane next weekend.

'Three, two, one, go,' shouts Chris as he puts his thumb up.

I stare blankly back at him. He can't be serious. I look down at the waterfall again and see the little helmets bobbing along.

'Go on, the longer you stay here the harder it'll be.'

I turn and see Danny grinning at me.

'You'll only have to walk back down the side of the hill if you don't,' says Chris again.

He seems to be full of motivation.

I look back at Danny once more and then I push myself off. It's weird as I expect to get flung down, but it's sort of fast then slow as I bump along between the rocks and all the while the water is rushing around my ears and trying to force me along. My heart is racing and I get a rush of adrenaline, and suddenly I want to do it again. When I see that everyone else is going headfirst down the next one, I don't think of the worst case scenarios, I just copy them.

I can hear Danny woohooing behind me and I catch myself laughing. I'm actually enjoying this. And I whoop back a couple of times as John scoops me up by the shoulders and makes me scramble over a narrow rocky ledge and down a tiny gorge. It's unlike anything I've ever done and I'm loving it.

The morning passes in a blur and we're back heading to the wooden huts before I know it. My teeth start to chatter now that we've stopped and are out of the water.

'That was amazing,' I say, realising how much I enjoyed myself.

'If you liked that, then you're going to love the afternoon I've got lined up for you potholing.'

'You are kidding, aren't you?'

He gives me a wink. 'Let's just say you're going to get your money's worth out of your swimsuit.'

I groan and skulk off towards the wooden hut muttering under my breath the whole way. I know that it's nice to go out of your comfort zone occasionally, but I couldn't be doing this all the time.

'I haven't bothered to do my hair,' I say as I climb into the car, after we've changed back into dry clothes. I wring out the worst of the water from my ponytail outside before I shut the door.

Danny's almost pissing himself laughing. He's loving this.

'You know, when I said in my letter that I wanted to do more adrenaline-type things, I was only trying to make myself sound good. I don't really want to be the next Lara Croft.'

'You don't? Shit, perhaps I got this wedding all wrong.'

I pull a face.

'Don't worry,' he says. 'I knew that that wouldn't have been your first choice of things to do round here. I will make you do stuff like that if you move up here though. Not every week, but you can't live up here and not make the most of it.'

'As long as I will get to see some tearooms whilst I'm here, I'll be happy.'

'Of course. Your wish is my command,' he says, a little cheesily, as we pull up into a car park. 'Now don't eat anything too huge as I've got a big dinner planned.'

'OK, but I feel as if I could eat a horse after that. I definitely worked up an appetite.'

'Me too,' says Danny as we get out of the car.

We manage to get seated in the busy tearoom in the corner by a window which is steamed up with condensation.

'This is cute,' I say picking up the menu and instantly deciding on the chilli con carne jacket potato. I need something warming after this morning.

'Yeah, I've not been here before, but Victoria raves about it.'

Instantly I tense at her name. She and Ross are the only two people who aren't happy about our wedding and at least I can make sense of why Ross is so against it.

'How is Victoria? Still complicated?'

Danny nods. 'At the moment, yes. But Gaz wants us to go over and see him tomorrow.'

'Oh, that'll be something to look forward to,' I say, trying not to sound sarcastic. 'I liked him when I met him before.'

I think of that brief time in London, the time that I overheard Danny telling him he didn't want me. It's funny to think that Gaz is possibly the reason that we didn't get together all those years ago.

'Yes, he's looking forward to meeting you properly too. So what are you going for?'

'Jacket potato with chilli.'

He looks around at what other people are eating.

The waitress walks up to take our order.

'So what would you recommend?' asks Danny. 'What's your best seller?'

The young waitress looks a bit dumbfounded by the question and she fluffs a bit as if she doesn't want to give the wrong answer.

'I guess our winter-warmer soup is the most popular this time of year. It's got pasta and winter veg and it comes with crusty bed.'

'Great. Is that what that is?' he says pointing to the next table.

She looks over and nods.

'Then that's perfect,' he says again, as I order my jacket potato.

'Is that what you always do?' I ask, realising that I know so much about Danny but in some ways I know so little.

'If I'm somewhere new, then yes. It's the best way. I learnt to do it in New York when this woman walked straight up to me when I was eating in a restaurant and asked me what I had and if it was any good. As I'm all reserved and British, I was a bit embarrassed at first, but actually it makes sense. If something's popular, then that's usually a good sign. Most of the time it works out OK.'

'Perhaps I'll have to try it. So, what are we doing for dinner tonight, then?'

'Well, like the rest of today, that's a surprise too.'

I smile. This whole day is giving me the same rumbles in my belly of anticipation and excitement that I used to get when I received one of his packages.

Our afternoon also involved swimsuits, but it couldn't have been further from our morning. Danny took me to a hotel not far from him, where we spent the afternoon in the spa, hanging out in a heated pool and hopping between the sauna and the Jacuzzi. We even sat in fluffy towelling robes eating scones.

But now it's time for dinner, and Danny is apparently cooking for me.

'So, I hope you're prepared to be sous-chef,' says Danny as he flattens a printed recipe out on the sideboard and starts emptying his cupboards of ingredients.

'Um, if it's chopping onions, I'm your girl, but to be honest, I don't know how to do much else. I'm a hopeless cook. Good job you know what you're doing.'

Danny slams the door of his saucepan cupboard shut as he stands up with a wok in his hands.

'You can't cook either?' he says, a look of horror on his face.

'What do you mean either? Your cupboards are full of ingredients.'

'Yeah, well, I buy them every time I cook something and am always left with loads of things I never use again. I usually eat ready meals from Booths. What do you eat?'

'When I lived with Ross, he cooked and nowadays I mostly eat leftovers, which Jim brings down and leaves in my fridge whilst I'm at work. He thinks the kitchen is too small for me to cook in, so he takes pity on me and feeds me. Why can't you cook?'

'I never had the time when I was a banker. I always ate on the run and when I moved here I guess I never learnt.'

We look down at all the herbs and spices on the counter assembled and ready for him to make a Thai curry and suddenly they look a bit scary.

'Shit, we're going to starve when we get married,' I say.

'We've always got Booths. It's a bit like the northern version of Waitrose,' he says.

'That doesn't help us tonight, though, does it?'

'We could always get a takeaway,' he says wincing.

'No, come on,' I say, picking up the piece of paper. 'How hard can this be?'

I roll up my sleeves and Danny does the same. We're two professional, degree-educated people. Surely we can follow a recipe.

We try our best to follow the instructions and after a fraught thirty minutes over a hot stove comes the moment of truth.

'You taste it,' I say, scooping a little bit of sauce onto my spoon and offering it up to him.

'Ladies first,' he says, pushing it back to me.

We both stare at the spoon. It smells bloody awful. To be fair to us, we did nearly everything right; it's just not my fault that the fish sauce came out rather too quickly and we may have used at least triple the amount. And it totally wasn't Danny's fault that he didn't know that TSP stood for teaspoon rather than tablespoon. I'm sure it won't make that much difference to how much chilli he put in, right?

I decide to be brave and eat a spoonful. It tastes all right initially. 'That's good,' I say.

'Really?' he says, taking the spoon and going in for the taste. But all of a sudden my mouth starts to burn, like really burn.

I stumble over to the fridge and pull out a pint of milk and drink straight out of the bottle.

'I'm so sorry,' I say. 'That's bloody hot.'

'Tell me about it,' he says fanning his mouth before grabbing the milk and finishing it off. 'That's so gross.'

'Agreed.'

'Inedible.'

'Probably salvageable, if we knew how.'

'But we don't,' says Danny and I nod.

'We're going to starve,' I say sighing. 'At least one of us should be able to cook.'

What if this is proof that we're not meant to be together? I start to feel a bit dizzy.

'Look, we'll take cooking lessons,' says Danny wrapping his arms around me. 'It's no big deal. We can't be the only people in their thirties who can't cook. Don't take this as some sort of cosmic sign.'

That man knows me too well.

'We'll do one of those subscription services where they send you all the food or we'll go to one of the hotels and do a residential cooking course. We could even cook along with one of those YouTubers.'

'Oh God, I tried that once, they never give you enough time and then your iPad gets smeary from all the times you put your dirty fingers on it to press pause.'

I'm starting to feel a little teary and I don't think it's anything to do with the fact that we can't cook but more that there's so much that's so unknown between us.

'Hey, Lydia, come on, it's no big deal. Grab your coat. Let's head out and get a takeaway.'

'But doesn't this worry you?'

'What, that you're not a natural Nigella?'

'No, that we didn't know this about each other. I've known you for as long as I can remember and I've been writing to you all my adult life and I had no clue that you can't cook. It just scares me a little that we're going to get married and we don't know everything about each other.'

Danny's scrunching his eyes up as if he's trying to work out where this has come from.

'Of course we're not going to know everything about each other. You won't know, for example, that I once ate raw squid and it made me vomit on my boss's shoes and you won't know that I once had to go down to a hotel lobby naked as I got lost looking for the bathroom and locked myself out of my room in the middle of the night.'

I splutter with laughter.

'And I'm sure there are loads of things that I don't know about you.'

My heart sinks, thinking about how true that is, mainly as I still haven't been honest with him.

'But I know the important things. I know that you're kind and that you think of everyone else before you think of yourself. I know that you're always scared to try new things but when you do, you embrace whatever it is and you give it your all – like today. I knew you'd be terrified of the ghyll scrambling, but that you'd plunge yourself into that freezing water anyway. I know that you worry that your mum's nuts and that you're going to turn into her. And, most importantly, I know that I'm constantly surprised by you. And love that I'm going to be constantly surprised by you for as long as I live.'

A full-on tear runs down my face.

'You're pretty good with words, Danny Whittaker.'

'Thanks, aside from cooking I'm pretty good at a lot of things. And in the months and years you'll get to know what they are.'

I dry my tears and smile at him.

'Don't be scared,' he says. 'Or, if you are, remember just to give it your all.'

I nod. He knows me almost better than I know myself and as I lean into him I think that he's right. I might be scared but I'm going to give it my all anyway. It could be the key to me actually #LivingMyBestLife. Not to mention that the thought of not being with him is far scarier.

Chapter 22

What is this madness that we're now living in the same country. It seems a little surreal, especially that you've bought a house, in Cumbira. It's the last place I'd ever imagined you'd settle down. But congratulations on your move! Maybe I'll have to get in the car and drive up and see you sometime, especially as I know your mum will keep you well stocked in shortbread. Hope the business with Gaz is working out well and you like the housewarming present!

Parcel containing cleaning products;
Lydia to Danny, August 2017

Danny parks the car and turns to smile at me.

'Why do you look so nervous?' he says as he pulls the keys out of the ignition and takes off his seatbelt.

'I'm not nervous,' I say, in a tone of voice that suggests otherwise.

Danny raises his eyebrow.

'OK, so Victoria and I didn't get off to the best start and she and Gaz are your best friends. I just want them to like me.'

'Of course they're going to like you,' he says, patting my thigh as if to reassure me. 'Just relax. This is going to be a fun lunch, OK?'

'OK,' I say taking a deep breath. It's just lunch, I can do this. 'You're right. And it's not going to be as awkward as when you met Lucy and Ed.'

I think back to the curry night and realise that even the nicest of people can have off days.

'Yes, there definitely won't be that kind of tension in the air.'

We get out of the car and Danny takes my hand as we walk up to the front door but Gaz opens it before we get there.

'Hello, hello,' he says, as he ushers us inside. 'Lydia, it's lovely to see you again.'

He leans over and wraps me up in a bear hug as if we're long-lost friends. I'd tensed all my muscles ready to see Victoria again, but this hug makes me relax them slowly.

'It's nice to see you too,' I say offering a bottle of wine. 'Thanks for having us over.'

'No, thank you for coming,' he says. 'We couldn't wait to get to know you properly. By the way, congratulations! I cannot believe you're actually making this man settle down.'

'Thanks,' I say.

'He's just pleased as he's finally getting rid of the third wheel,' says Danny, as he slips off his coat and hangs it on a hook.

'I've been trying for years,' says Gaz, taking my coat for me.

'Or maybe you've gained a fourth wheel,' says Danny.

I really can't imagine that after the other day, but I smile. I really hope that Victoria was having a bad day when we met and that we can all be BFFs. It would make it a lot less scary moving up here and away from all my friends.

'I certainly hope so,' says Gaz, with a wide smile as he opens his arm to usher me into the adjacent room.

I walk into one of the most beautiful lounges that I've ever seen in real life. It's like stepping into a photoshoot for a glossy home mag. There are delicate cream sofas and plump red velvet cushions in the centre with dark wood furniture lining the walls. My eyes are drawn to the tall thin bookshelf in the corner full of terribly serious-looking books with not a lot of colour on the spines and an ornate mirror hanging over the period fireplace. It's not cosy like Danny's, but what it lacks in comfort it makes up for in taste.

'What can I get you both to drink? Wine, aperitif?' asks Gaz, almost theatrically playing the host. He's rocking a little bit and I get the impression that he started drinking without us. He goes through to the dining room and picks up an already open bottle of wine.

'Actually, I'm not drinking,' I say. 'I've got to drive home tonight.'

'And I drove us over so I'm not drinking,' says Danny.

'And Victoria's not drinking,' says Gaz. 'So I guess that's all the more for me, then.'

He pours himself a glass, which is mainly the dregs as he drains the bottle.

I look over at Danny, wondering if this is normal behaviour, but I'm guessing from the way he's staring, open mouthed, that it's not.

'Where's Victoria? Ah, speak of the devil.'

She walks into the room and despite the smells wafting from the kitchen, which seem to indicate that she's preparing a culinary feast, she's dressed immaculately again. Not like on the rare occasions when I attempt to cook and I get half the ingredients down my clothes and in my hair. She, however, is dressed in a sparkly cowl-neck maternity dress and tights with neat little pointy boots. I feel positively underdressed in my jeans and baggy jumper.

'Dan,' she says, a warm smile falling over her face as she gives him a kiss on the cheek.

'Look at you and that bump,' he says, rubbing his hand over it as if he's expecting a genie to appear. 'You look radiant.'

'That's the sweat from cooking,' she almost purrs back at him and laughs. 'And Lydia, hello again.'

She's still smiling but I can almost see the strain in her muscles. It's not natural, like when she saw Danny.

'Has Gaz offered you drinks? Or has he just been helping himself?' There's a coolness to her voice, but that's nothing compared to the look Gaz has just given her. So much for no tension.

'He has, and we're not drinking. We're both driving.'

'Ah, join the club. I'll make us a pitcher of elderflower cordial.'

'Do you need any help? It all smells delicious,' I ask.

'Thank you, it's only beef,' she says, waving her hand dismissively as if that means it's less work. 'It's all under control. You stay here and talk to Gaz.'

She retreats back to the kitchen, and Gaz stares after her.

For a moment none of us says anything. Then Gaz plants his host-with-the-most smile back on his face.

'So, Lydia,' says Gaz as he sits down on the sofa, 'are you all ready for the big move?'

I sit down opposite and practically bounce up again off the rock-hard couch.

'More or less,' I say, not wanting to think too much about it. 'I can't wait to be up here with Danny all the time.'

'Lov-e-ly. Lov-e-ly.'

'What's going on?' says Danny as he folds his arms over his chest. 'Why have you necked the best part of a bottle of wine before lunch?'

The smile falls from Gaz's face. 'Just fancied a drink, that's all. There's no crime in that, is there?'

'No, but you wouldn't usually.'

Gaz folds his arms defensively.

For a minute or two we stay silent and I'm contemplating how unlucky we are to have found ourselves again in the middle of another couple's dramas.

'Do you think Victoria's acting strangely?' he asks suddenly, as if it's just occurred to him.

'I think you're acting a little strangely,' says Danny diplomatically.

I want to add that I think she is, but then she was the last time I met her too, and I'm worried that's what she's like all the time.

Gaz sighs and Danny sits down on the sofa beside him.

'How is she acting?'

'Shifty. She always seems to be lost in her own thoughts and when I ask her what's up she snaps at me.'

'It's probably just pregnancy hormones. My sister was a right nightmare when she was pregnant,' I say.

He starts to sniff and I realise that he's got a tear in his eye. He's gone pale and he's ever so slightly shaking and I don't think it's got anything to do with the wine.

'Are you OK?' I ask, wishing I could sneak off to the kitchen to help Victoria.

He blinks rapidly as if he's trying to blink away the tears. 'I'm fine,' he says a little squeakily. 'I'm fine,' he says again, a bit too gruff this time. And then he coughs and tries a third time, 'I'm fine.'

None of them convince me that he is.

He groans and looks up at the door as if he's worried that Victoria's going to come bursting through at any second.

'I think she's having an affair,' he says quietly. 'And I'm wondering if it's even my baby.'

Shit. This is deep. I look over at Danny for reassurance as to whether I stay or go but he's looking down at Gaz's feet.

'I mean, she always used to work such long hours and she wasn't contactable by phone.'

'She's a solicitor, though, so surely that's part and parcel of the job,' I say wondering why Danny's not jumping in to save me here. He's his best friend, not me. 'And I thought she said she'd reduced her hours.'

'She has now, but it's more than that. She's always on the phone and she hangs up when I get near.'

I think back to what Danny was saying about Victoria and it being complicated and I wonder if he knows something. His silence is definitely speaking volumes.

'Maybe she's organising a surprise for you,' I say, clutching at straws.

'For almost a year?' he sighs.

'I don't think you've got anything to worry about, mate,' says Danny eventually. 'You're probably just reading too much into it. Lydia's right, it's probably just pregnancy hormones.'

Danny's started to act jumpy and weird and I wonder what his excuse is. Definitely not pregnancy hormones.

'But why would she be making all those secret phone calls?' asks Gaz. 'If she didn't have anything to hide.'

I think of all the times that Victoria rang the weekend before last when Danny was visiting me. I think of the fact that she has a key to his house. The fact that she hates me. That she texted him that message when I was in Spain with him. That they were alone in Spain together.

My brain is working overtime. What if Danny's the one having an affair with Victoria? But no, he wouldn't do that to his best friend, would he? I watch him looking at Gaz and instantly I know I've jumped to the wrong conclusion. I can see he really cares about Gaz.

'Trust me,' says Danny, slapping his arm around him. 'You've got nothing to worry about. Absolutely nothing. Lydia's right, there's bound to be logical explanations for everything. He gets up and sits down next to me, taking my hand. Look at us being the couple who councils other couples. He strokes my hand and I know that my suspicions are ridiculous. It's much more likely there's some other explanation.

'Dinner's ready,' says Victoria walking into the room with a big beef Wellington on a wooden board.

'Oh my God, that smells amazing,' I say jumping up to be the first at the table and away from the awkward conversation with Gaz.

'You've excelled yourself as always, Victoria,' Danny says as he walks over and sits down.

'Gaz, come on,' she commands as she passes.

He looks at her as if he's about to say something, but he bows his head and comes over to the table.

'I'll just get the veg,' she says.

'Do you need help?'

'No,' she calls. 'Dan, you can carve up the Wellington, Gaz looks as if he'd carve up the table if he was left in charge.'

'How big do I cut it?' he asks, looking at me.

I shrug my shoulders. It's like the blind leading the blind.

'I think it's usually like this,' I say, pinching my fingers together to show him and he gives it a go. It cuts beautifully, probably more to do with Victoria's cooking than Danny's carving skills, but he looks pleased none the less.

Victoria arrives back and places the veg on the table.

'Dig in, dig in,' she says, 'before it gets cold.'

'I can't believe you cooked this,' I say as I bite into my slice of beef Wellington. It tastes so good and all the better after my and Danny's abysmal attempt at cooking yesterday.

'It's nothing really. It's just following a recipe. Anyone can do that.' She shrugs.

Danny gives me a small smile. Anyone except us.

For a while we're all quiet as we're too busy eating but it soon turns into an awkward silence and all I can hear is people chewing and their cutlery as it scrapes along the plates.

I look over at Gaz, who is slowly shovelling the food into his mouth. At least that should soak up some of the alcohol.

'Your house is beautiful, did you do it yourselves?' I say.

'Um,' says Victoria, 'you mean decorate it? We had professional decorators in.'

'Of course, I meant the interior design. Did you have someone in to do that too or . . .?'

'No, I did that.'

'Well, it's lovely, you've obviously got good taste,' I say, wondering how many more compliments I need to give her before she initiates a conversation.

Gaz clatters his fork around the plate and I can see it grating on Victoria. I think he's realised and is doing it on purpose. It was bad enough being amongst my family when Lucy and Ed were arguing last week; I don't want to be ringside at another fight without any back-up.

'So, how long have you got at work before you go off on maternity leave?' I ask, instantly regretting the question when I see Gaz is looking at his wife's bump.

'About another six weeks.'

'Wow, that's soon. You must be excited.'

'Oh, we are so excited. Aren't we, Victoria? I can't wait to meet *my* son or daughter,' says Gaz.

Victoria coughs as if some food's gone down the wrong way and she picks up her drink to clear her throat. 'Excuse me,' she says.

I can't help noticing she looks a little sheepish.

'Have I said that the food is excellent?' I say again, feeling awkward. 'Danny and I have been so spoilt with food lately.

What with all those delicious meals we had in Spain. There's the most marvellous tapas restaurant near Danny's mum's house.

'Los Toros,' says Victoria.

'Oh, I forgot, you went there so you know.'

'Yes, their food was out of this world. I seem to remember ordering most of their menu. And their wine, huh, Dan?' she says with a small smile on her face.

'The wine was pretty good too,' I say, looking at Danny, only now it seems to be his turn to look sheepish and I'm beginning to get suspicious again.

'So my mum's been practising her ukulele solo for the wedding. Apparently she's got her band to record a backing track and everything,' says Danny, quickly changing the subject. 'And Lydia's mum wants to do some sort of a dance.'

'Sounds lively,' says Victoria, nodding.

'Hmm, should be interesting,' I say, nodding, but really wondering why Danny didn't want to talk about his trip to Spain with Victoria.

'So Lydia, tell me about your job. What was it you said you do, you're an event manager?'

'Event co-ordinator,' says Danny, making me feel guilty that he's correcting her with my old job title as I still haven't told him about the promotion.

'Oh, my mistake. Event co-ordinator,' she says, narrowing her eyes at me and giving me a small smile. 'And how long have you been in that role?'

'I've been with the company for seven years,' I say, which is at least true.

'It must be a nice company to have worked there for so long.'

'Yes, it's pretty good. I had a stressful job in London before that and I've learnt that sometimes it's more important to be happy in a job than constantly climbing up the career ladder.'

'Well said, Lydia,' says Gaz, nodding.

'It seems such a shame for you to give it all up and move up here.'

'Things we do for love, hey?' says Danny, laughing.

'Yes,' says Victoria. 'It is amazing. I know I'd do anything for love.'

I notice the way that she's looking at Danny and not Gaz and it makes me shudder.

Gaz is oblivious and he starts to sing the classic Meatloaf song. Danny joins in and I start to giggle at the scene, trying to brush off the niggle that Victoria seemed to linger over my job title, as if she knew the truth.

'Perhaps we should do a duet of this at the wedding,' says Gaz hopefully.

'Now you're sounding like our mothers,' I say groaning.

'You're missing out, but still, we're really looking forward to the big day,' says Gaz. 'It's so nice to think that Danny's going to be as happily married as we are.'

'Let's propose a toast,' I say, ignoring the sarcasm in his voice. 'To the wedding.'

'To the wedding,' everyone chants and I don't fail to see the daggers in Victoria's eyes.

We climb into the car after what was one of the most delicious but equally one of the most excruciating lunches of my life.

'Well,' says Danny.

'Well, indeed.'

'Do you think we should just never go out to eat with other couples?'

'I think that's our only option,' I say, laughing. 'Seriously.'

'But, having watched Victoria with you I'd say that she likes you.'

'You got that from that lunch? I felt like I was in danger of being served up for dessert.'

'Believe me, she liked you. If she hadn't we wouldn't have had the cheese course. And she asked you questions about your job, she was taking an interest.'

'An interest? It was more like a cross-examination.'

'Well, at least it took the heat off Gaz.'

'Now that was weird. Do you think Victoria is having an affair?'

He starts up the car.

'You know, don't you? That's what you meant about it being complicated.'

He stops reversing out of the drive and turns to me. 'If I could tell you I would,' he says.

'I don't think it's me you've got to tell, I think it's Gaz. He's going to be crushed if he finds out that you knew before him.'

Danny finishes reversing and drives down the road and lets out a deep breath.

'Gaz can't find out, it'd kill him.'

I see the weight that Danny's carrying on his shoulders and I rest my hand on his thigh to comfort him.

I'm just hoping the reason Danny thinks it's complicated is because he knows what's going on, rather than that it's complicated as it's him she's having an affair with. I hope that my overactive mind is just playing tricks on me again, but I saw the way Victoria was looking at us over lunch and I can't help worrying that there's more to it than my overactive imagination.

Chapter 23

I seem to be getting wedding invitations every week at the moment; it seems like the whole world is getting engaged. Even Gaz, the eternal bachelor, is getting married to his far-too-good-for-him girlfriend Victoria. I guess it's only a matter of time until I get an email from you telling me you and Ross are engaged, right? We've got to that age where everyone settles down, haven't we – we're officially old. I shouldn't complain though, I've got to remember that where there's a wedding there's a stag do, and Gaz's is going to be epic.

Email; Danny to Lydia, January 2018

'And then, I'm going to go like this,' says Olivia as she does a high kick, nearly knocking a mannequin over.

'OK, sweetie,' says Kerry, steadying the child mannequin. 'Perhaps you can practise that when we get home. Why don't we concentrate on finding something sparkly to wear.'

It seems that Olivia wasn't listening when I said there'd be no dancing at the wedding as she seems to have put her heart and soul into choreographing something. She's even been getting up twenty minutes early in the morning to stomp around the living room. Which, of course, means that I've been getting up then too, as no one could sleep through that noise coming through their bedroom ceiling.

'Fine,' she says stamping her foot and walking round to the other side of the gondola to look at dresses.

'What was that?' I ask.

'A preview of her teenage years. You're lucky you're moving away before all that happens.'

'I guess I am,' I say, pulling a face. My little niece is growing up so quickly.

'What about this one?' I say, picking up a sequin number.

'I think that would chafe under the arms,' says Kerry rubbing it and wrinkling her nose. She puts it back.

'Did I tell you that we've got our first Airbnb booking? It's for a whole week at May half-term. Isn't that great?'

'Yes, great,' I say with a bit of a gulp. I'd still planned to be living there then. 'I thought that you were putting it on for summer.'

'We were, but then we thought, what's the point of having it empty, you'll be gone in a few weeks and it won't take that long to get it ready to rent out.'

I nod, knowing that I can't confide in her until I've told Danny. It makes me more determined to get it all out in the open. I'll have to do it when I see him this weekend.

'What about this one? Olivia?'

My niece rolls her eyes at me.

'What's wrong with it?' I say, thinking to myself that it's really cute.

'It's too pink,' says Kerry.

'But she's always wearing pink.'

'It has to be hot pink.'

'Right,' I say. Seven-year-olds are so much more demanding than they were when I was little. I didn't get any choice in what I wore. I mostly just had Kerry's cast-offs and the only criterion was that there weren't any holes.

'How's the wind down going at work?' Kerry asks, as she rakes through more dresses.

'Um, well, it's busy. You know what handovers are like,' I say. It's not a total lie. This week I have been handing over to Jenny.

'And how were the Lakes at the weekend?'

'Really good. It's so beautiful up there.'

'I can imagine. You're so lucky. I sometimes wonder if Jim and I should move out of the city. You know, so that Olivia grows up somewhere a bit greener.'

'Really? I've always thought you loved living where you had everything on your doorstop and that you could walk Olivia to school and to the shops if you wanted.'

'Yeah, I do love the convenience of it all, and I love living by the sea, but sometimes the city gets you down. I hate the fact that we don't have a driveway and I sometimes have to walk miles with the shopping. And I hate that we have to walk half an hour to the common to reach some greenery to have a kick about with a ball or to fly a kite.'

'But there are so many opportunities that she can have here that she wouldn't get there. Look at all the after-school clubs she does and there's always some event going on.'

'I know, I know. I think I'm just a bit jealous that you're having a big change, that's all.'

'Really? I've spent most of my adult life being jealous of you and Jim and your cosy life.'

'What? You've wanted a husband who pees on rhubarb and then serves you up crumble from it?'

I laugh. 'You know what I mean.'

'I know and I know that I'm lucky that we've got such a lovely life here, it's just sometimes I wonder if we wouldn't be happier somewhere else, if we should take a risk and move somewhere new. I guess you're lucky in a way that you've met Danny and it's just happening for you.'

I fold my arms defensively over my chest. 'It's still not an easy decision to make. I've got to give up my whole life.'

'Of course,' says Kerry pulling a face as she knows she's put her foot in it. 'Ooh look at this dress, it's perfect. Olivia, what do you think?' she says brandishing a hot-pink bridesmaid dress with a glittery band around the middle.

Olivia gives it a look up and down. 'Not bad. That's almost my style.'

'Almost,' I say, raising an eyebrow and trying not to laugh.

'How about we get you to try it on and perhaps we'll buy it anyway just in case?'

Olivia stares hard at it again.

'OK. But I've found the shoes.'

She shows us a pair of bright turquoise trainers with diamantes on them and Kerry and I look at each other and laugh.

'Deal.'

'Now all we need to find is the wand and a tiara.'

'A tiara? I don't remember that being part of the deal.'

She shoots me a look.

'Tiara, right, OK.'

My phone buzzes in my pocket and I see that it's Lucy and answer it.

'Hey, I'm here, finally, sorry. Where are you?' she says, audibly flustered.

'We're in the kids department.'

'Great, be there in a jiffy.'

'See you soon,' I say, hanging up.

'Lucy on her way?' asks Kerry, picking up tights to go with the dress.

'Yes, so now we can go and look at our dresses.'

'This is so exciting. I wonder if Mum's found anything yet?'

'I've found a wand,' she says as she appears.

'Wow,' says Olivia. 'That's the best wand ever.'

She starts flinging it round and we all get it jabbed into us in at least two places before Kerry takes it off her.

'It'll be all the more special if we just keep it for the day, sweetie.'

She looks disappointed but nods.

'Hey,' says Lucy as she bounds up.

'Look at my dress,' says Olivia pulling it out of Kerry's hands.

'Wow, looks great,' Lucy says, giving Olivia a big thumbs-up, which is met with smiles.

'We're just ready to go upstairs and try on some big girl dresses now,' says Kerry with a grin.

I clap my hands together. It's a whole lot more exciting shopping with the girls than it was doing a supermarket sweep in Zara at Barcelona airport.

We glide up the escalator into women's wear and I can't believe how empty it is. I'm used to doing battle at the weekend, but here we are at 5 p.m. on a Tuesday evening in January and there's hardly anyone about. Tracey's always banging on at us to use our time off in lieu and whilst I've been trying to work extra hard of late in my new role, I figured that leaving a bit earlier tonight wouldn't hurt. Especially as it saves me having to do this at a weekend which means I can see Danny instead.

Focused by the fact that we only have an hour before the store closes we spot the dresses and immediately split up. Mum and Olivia park themselves outside the changing room on the comfy chairs and they do some puzzle book that seems to be more puzzling to Mum than to Olivia.

I pick up everything in my size that is remotely bridal. If I've learnt anything from *Don't Tell the Bride* it's that it's often the plainest ones on the hangers that surprise the brides the most.

I am feeling optimistic. With less than three weeks to go until the big day I have pretty low expectations. I know that I don't have time to order a bespoke bridal dress and my options are limited to off the peg. Not that that matters, it's all in keeping with our low-fuss, low-key approach to the wedding. I've already briefed the girls.

'Oh, my God,' says Lucy. 'Look at this on the sale rail.'

She pulls out a dress and I gasp and practically drop the rest of the ones in my arms. There is a beautiful long ivory dress with tiny silver beaded flowers sewn onto netting over the top half and a swishy skirt at the bottom. I never expected to fall in love. Forget Danny, I wonder if I could marry the dress.

'That's beautiful,' I say, looking at the size-ten label and starting to weep. I haven't been a ten since somewhere around puberty. 'Have they got any bigger sizes?'

'Um, there's an eighteen,' says Lucy.

I look at the size-ten dress and down at my hips and back at the dress again. I'm pretty much a size twelve in most shops, but the skirt looks quite generous. It's not a brand I recognise and maybe, just maybe, it could be one of those labels that has a liberal approach to sizing.

'I'll try it,' I say snatching the dress from her hands in the nicest possible way.

'Great, and I found us some dresses,' says Kerry, handing one to Lucy.

'What are we? The ageing aunts?' she says. 'Where's the cleavage or the leg?'

'I thought they might be flattering.'

'Hmm,' says Lucy. 'What about these?'

'We're not providing the evening's entertainment for the stag do,' says Kerry, folding her arms over her chest.

'What about these?' I say, finding a compromise: a short turquoise dress with a lace top and a hot-pink one that's calf length.

'I guess one of those might work?' says Lucy.

Kerry gives the dresses a suspicious look.

We all go into our little cubicles and I pretend in my head that we're in a movie. The loud music that's pumping in the speakers is just perfect. I can't wait until we do the big reveal where we all swish back our curtains and whoop with joy.

I strip off quickly and undo the little zip at the side of the dress and try and climb into it, only it's a lot narrower at the thighs than I thought it was going to be. It's pretty deceptive. I try to breathe in before I realise that that makes absolutely no difference. How an earth do I make my thighs breathe in? I try and stagger my stance to accommodate it but it's not going to budge and I let it drop to my feet.

I look at my tree-trunk thighs and wonder if I'm going about this the wrong way. Maybe I should slip it on over my head.

'Oh wow. This is hideous,' says Kerry.

'Which one?' asks Lucy.

'The pink one. The pink is a no go.'

'OK, I've got the turquoise one on. Could be a goer.'

I pick up the dress again and take a deep breath as I pull it on over the top of my head.

The good news is that I've got it on over my chest. Never have I been so thankful to only be more of a B than a C cup. The bad news is that I've got it stuck on my hips, but I reckon with a little wiggle . . .

'Ooh,' shouts Kerry. 'Winner, winner, chicken dinner. I think this is our one.'

I hear the sound of the rings scraping along the curtain rail at the top from both sides of me and there are excited squeals from the two of them as they've found their dress. But hang on, in the movie in my head, I'm supposed to be there too.

I'm eager to join them and show them mine and I wiggle again and this time I get my thighs in. Hurrah!

I look at the zip on the side and there's absolutely no way that that's going anywhere. But it's not as if the dress is going to fall down with it open, is it? I bet I could get a floaty bit of fabric to cover it and it would blend right in with the rest of the dress.

'How are you getting on, Lydia?'

'Well, I'm in,' I say, wondering if it matters that I'm not going to be able to eat or maybe even breathe during my wedding.

Lucy yanks open the curtain and gasps.

'Oh my God, Lydia, you look beautiful,' she says, pulling me out of the cubicle.

'Oh,' says Kerry clapping her hand to her mouth. 'It's gorgeous, it's just . . .' She spins me round on the spot and I shuffle round like a broken ballerina in a music box as the two of them exchange glances.

'It's a little tight,' I say, trying to place my hand strategically over the gap.

'Just a little,' says Kerry.

My mum walks in at this point with Olivia.

'Aunty Lydia, why are your pants see-through?'

'Darling, that would look lovely on you if it was the right size. I'll go and see if they have one.'

'They don't, I checked,' I say.

'Then I'll get them to phone other stores or order it online. Take it off,' she says, shaking her head as if I'm being utterly ridiculous.

Lucy helps me shuffle back into the changing room.

'Do you want a hand?' she asks.

'I might need one.'

'I think you need more than one,' says Kerry.

'Everything all right?' asks the sales person.

'Fine,' we all say.

I've gone bright purple with the exertion.

'Ooooookay,' she says with a roll of her eyes. 'I've got some scissors if you need them. Of course, if I cut you out, you'll have to buy the dress.'

'No, it's fine, it's nearly off.'

'Whatever,' she says, skulking off.

'Oh God, what if I have to buy this dress *and* another dress. I'll have bought three wedding dresses,' I say, sighing.

'At least it would be third time lucky,' says Lucy.

'And we could always make something out of the material,' says Kerry. 'Olivia loves playing brides; we could make her a wedding dress from it.'

'Oh great, a two-hundred-pound bespoke dressing-up dress,' I say.

'I bet it would really be the best present ever though,' says Kerry laughing.

I sigh and suck in every ounce of flesh until eventually Lucy pulls the dress clear of my hips and from there it's a quick pass over my head. It turns out Kerry was right; I definitely needed an extra hand – six to be exact.

I pass it to my mum to take to the counter to see if she can track down a bigger size, and I slip my normal clothes back on. I'm relieved to be able to move every muscle without restriction.

'So your dresses looked lovely,' I say as Kerry and Lucy emerge with them draped over their arms.

'Well, at least we got ours sorted,' says Kerry. 'It was probably too much to hope for that we'd get all of them done and dusted today. If Mum can't track yours down, perhaps we can go to Southampton at the weekend. They've got a big John Lewis there.'

'Yes, maybe. Danny's coming down at the weekend, though, and time seems to go so quickly, what with all the travelling,' I say, sighing. 'Plus, I really should make an effort to take him to see Dad and Frances.'

Kerry rolls her eyes. 'I wouldn't worry about Dad, it's not like he'd even speak to you when you were there anyway. He seems to have 'Ultimate Trucks' on loop.'

'I guess, and then I'd have more time to spend with Danny.'

'If you're so short on time together, why don't you meet halfway?' says Kerry.

'What, like a mini-break? Why didn't I think of that?' I say, thinking that I'd get an extra few hours with him, I'd get to have him all to myself and there'd be no fear of running into Ross.

'Yes, that way neither of you would have that long drive. I guess Worcester would be halfway, wouldn't it? You'd have to check, but we stayed in a lovely cottage in the Malvern Hills a few years ago when Olivia was little. I could give you the details. I bet it would be dead cheap this time of year.'

'Kerry, you are a genius.'

'I know,' she says, beaming.

'I'll talk to Danny about it tonight.'

'And I'll dig out the link to that place. In fact, I got on really well with the woman who owned it, I bet I could phone up and cheekily get a discount.'

'Now that would be great.'

It sounds like the answer to my prayers. By the time I made it home on Sunday night at nearly midnight, I was knackered and felt as if I'd blinked and the weekend had gone by. At least this way we'd get to have a Friday night together and a bit of Sunday evening too.

'Right, they have this in size twelve in Winchester,' says my mum. 'I've put it on hold and I'll pick it up tomorrow.'

'That's amazing. Thanks, Mum,' I say, wrapping my arms around her and giving her a big hug. 'Well, I guess that's everything sorted. I don't know why people get so stressed about weddings,' I say jokingly before I realise that Lucy's face is falling. 'Ah, Lucy, I didn't mean it like that.'

She smiles.

'No offence taken. I think it's great what you're doing. I wish we'd done the same,' she says.

'But your wedding's going to be great.'

'I know it will be, but I don't know if it's what I want anymore.'

There are tears in her eyes and Mum and Kerry give me a look.

'Why don't I go and buy these dresses?' says Mum, taking them off Lucy and Kerry, 'and you girls go and get a cup of tea or a glass of wine. I'll give you a ring tomorrow.'

'We won't stay, I'll get Olivia home for her tea,' says Kerry, and after quick goodbyes they all hurry off and I put my arm through Lucy's and take her upstairs to the cafe.

'Is Ed's mum putting too much pressure on you?'

'No,' she says, shaking her head. 'It's everything. I just thought that if I threw myself into the planning that I'd get swept away by it all, but the more it goes on the more I'm still terrified and Ed's so upset. He keeps thinking that I don't want to marry him, and I do.'

'You just don't want to have a wedding.'

'Exactly,' she says. 'Or not the type of wedding that Ed's mum wants.'

We order hot chocolates and sit down on the comfy sofa to wait for them.

'But surely Ed can understand that?'

She shakes her head. 'He can't. He thinks that we're only going to do it once so we should make it a big one. God, you're so lucky that you and Danny are on the same page.'

'I think it was just the circumstances. Who knows what would have happened if we hadn't tried to elope. Why don't you talk to Ed again? Like *really* talk to him, and I'm sure you'll sort things out. Maybe scale it back a bit.'

'Like cancel the harpist for the wedding breakfast. And the doves.'

'Yes, like that,' I say, pulling a sympathetic face. I couldn't think of anything worse. 'Why don't you make a list of the things you want from the wedding and get Ed to do the same and then go from there.'

She nods. 'That's not a bad idea. Thanks, hon. What am I going to do with you up in the Lakes? Who's going to calm me down?'

'I'll be at the end of my phone. You can FaceTime me anytime, well, anytime within reason.'

'It's not going to be the same though, is it?' she says, stirring the cup the waitress plonked down in front of her.

Now it's my turn to blink back the tears.

'It's going to be fine. We'll see each other all the time and we'll phone. Plus, I'm not going yet, I've still got my long notice to work.'

She nods but neither of us look at each other. I know that I'm not going to lose touch with her and she'll still be my best friend, but both of us know this is the end of an era. I try and keep the tears at bay and I focus all my thoughts on Danny as I tell myself for the billionth time that I'm doing the right thing.

Chapter 24

I'm officially broken and part of me is left in Riga. Whilst I organised what can only be described as an epic stag do, I can't actually tell you a lot about it. Not because of the law of the stag, but because I can barely remember a thing. Our hotel seemed nice and it was cold outside. I'm sure the city was beautiful?! I did, however, find this in my pocket when I got home so I presume I must have bought it for you. Or possibly an ageing aunt.

Parcel containing doll dressed in Latvian national dress;
Danny to Lydia, March 2018

I scrunch my nose up at the satnav, wondering exactly where she wants me to turn now.

Arriving at destination, on right. She says again.

I slow right down and look at the hedgerows, trying to see where the cottage is, but there's nothing here. The road is getting windier and I'm wondering if I should turn back to the main road when I see two oak trees flanking a driveway.

'Eureka,' I shout, as I turn down it. I pull up into a courtyard and my stomach flips when I see Danny's car already parked outside. There are what look like three little cottages all dotted around the courtyard, but only one has lights peaking out the side of curtains and smoke billowing out of the chimney at the top. It must be ours. It looks lovely and romantic and I can't wait to get inside and snuggle into him.

I hurry round to the boot to get my bag when the front door opens and Danny comes out.

'Hey, you,' I say as I fling my arms around him and give him a smooch.

'Hey, yourself. Did you have a good drive?'

'Yes, not bad at all considering it's a Friday night. I made it in two and a half hours.'

'Mine was pretty much the same. Makes a difference, doesn't it, meeting halfway?'

'I know, Kerry's a genius. And this place looks amazing,' I say as I pull my weekend bag out.

Danny takes it off me and takes my hand to lead me over to the front door.

'Wait until you see inside.'

We walk straight into the lounge and the warmth of the fire instantly hits me. The bleached wooden floors are full of furry rugs and the leather sofas are filled with cushions. Danny's already got a bottle of red wine open with two glasses next to it, Michael Bublé's playing and the lights are down low.

'So this is pretty romantic,' I say, turning to him and playing with the collar on his shirt.

God, I've missed him. It's been a bloody long week. I'm not looking forward to doing this for the next few months. We've only been doing it two and a half weeks and even that seems like two and a half weeks too long.

He puts his arm around my waist and pulls me in towards him.

'So, are you going to show me the bedrooms?' I purr.

'I could,' he says, slipping off my oversized cardigan. 'Or I could show you afterwards.'

He starts kissing down my neck and I think he's right; we're never going to make it upstairs. I unbutton his shirt and push him towards the sofa.

'Definitely afterwards,' I say as I pull my dress over my head. 'We've got plenty of time. After all, we've got the whole weekend.'

'Um, and this time we don't have to worry about mothers walking in on us or how loud we're being.'

'It's so nice that it's just you and me,' I say as he unhooks my bra.

Just me and him, exactly as it should be.

There's something so naughty and decadent about lying on the sofa naked with only a hint of a the sofa throw covering me. Danny tops up my wine glass and I throw my head back against the sofa and purr with contentment.

'I wish we could stay like this forever,' I say.

'Well, it won't be long until you'll be living with me all the time.'

'Hmm,' I say, thinking this is my perfect in to telling him about my job. The more I think about it, the more I'm convinced he'll think it's the right thing to do. It's good experience for my CV and will make the transition between jobs easier. 'About that,' I start, when there's a knock at the door. We turn and look at each other before Danny stands up to answer it.

'You can't get it, I'm naked,' I say, wrapping the sofa throw firmly around me.

'But it's obvious we're in,' whispers Danny. 'I'm sure it's probably someone telling us we've left the car lights on or something.' He shoves his shirt back on and quickly buttons it up before he pulls another throw off an arm chair and wraps it round his waist. 'Head into the kitchen and I'll let you know when they've gone.'

Reluctantly, I pull myself up just as whoever is at the door knocks again. How bloody rude, knocking twice. They're the ones interrupting our evening.

'Hey, Danny,' I hear my sister say as he opens the door.

I freeze in my tracks. What the hell is she doing here?

'Danny boy,' shrills Lucy.

'What's going on?' I say making sure the sofa throw is covering as much of me as possible as I walk back into the lounge.

'Aw, you two, matching outfits,' laughs Lucy as she strolls in, bottle of Prosecco in her hand.

Danny's about to shut the door when it gets pushed open again.

'Bloody hell, Dan, put some clothes on,' says his brother Stuart. He's closely followed by Gaz.

I suddenly feel exposed, even with the throw.

'Leave them alone, they're still in that honeymoon phase,' says Kerry, 'remember that time when you couldn't keep your clothes on? Oh how things change.'

The four of them snigger wearing smug we-know-what-it's-really-like looks on their faces. How do they know that Danny and I won't be at it like rabbits when we're old and grey?

Danny looks out into the courtyard as if waiting to see who else pops up, but with no one else lurking out there he shuts the door.

'What the hell is going on?' he says, looking between them all.

'Well, you know how you said that you didn't want a hen or a stag do,' says Lucy, grinning.

'Oh no,' I say, shaking my head. I've been looking forward to a cosy, romantic weekend all week. I don't want it ruined by penis straws and condom veils.

'Well, you didn't really think we'd let you get away without having one, did you?' says Kerry, giggling.

'You can't not have a stag,' says Gaz, slapping Danny on the back. 'Where's the fun in that? You've both got to be ritually humiliated as we were on ours.'

I'm slightly relieved that he seems a lot happier than he was at his house last week. Hopefully, he sobered up and realised that he'd let his imagination run away with itself, just like I had.

'Now, go get dressed, we've got lots planned for this evening,' says Kerry as she plonks a box down on the coffee table and starts pulling out champagne flutes.

I'm too shocked to move.

'You're throwing us a joint hen and stag do?' I say, looking over at Stuart. I haven't seen him since Kerry's wedding and I wish I was wearing more clothes.

'That's the plan. We've got a couple of things lined up for tomorrow and then we're going to have a big night here tomorrow evening.'

'Go on,' says Lucy, throwing our clothes at us. 'We'll get the bubbles flowing ready for you when you get back.'

Danny picks our clothes up off the floor where they landed and walks towards me. He has to bundle me out of the door as, whilst it's sweet of them to have gone to so much trouble to surprise us, I can't help mourning the loss of the lazy, romantic evening I had planned.

'I can't believe they've done this,' I say as Danny leads me upstairs into the bedroom. 'Kerry was so bloody sneaky suggesting we meet halfway and then helping me to find this place. She planned it all along.'

'I wouldn't be surprised if Stuart's been involved since the start too, it's the kind of thing he'd do.'

'Do you think we could just stay here?' I say, looking longingly at the super king-size bed that's covered in a thick white duvet with a silky turquoise throw over the top – it looks ridiculously comfortable.

'You know they'd knock the door down. Come on, it might be fun; there are only the four of them, it's not as if they've invited everyone we know.'

I start to put my underwear on.

'That's true, and it's nice that we're all able to spend some time together so everyone can get to know each other before the wedding.'

'Exactly. Plus, with it being a joint sten do, it's not like it's going to be wild with strippers and . . .'

'You don't know Lucy,' I say thinking back to Caroline's twenty-fifth birthday kissagram who did a little bit more than kissing.

'I think it's nice of them though, to have all got together and organised this,' he says.

I groan as I put the dress over my head. 'I know, I'm sounding ungrateful. It's just our time together is precious at the moment and I wanted you all to myself.'

Danny buttons up his shirt, leans over and gives me a kiss.

'We're going to have the rest of our lives together; I guess one weekend apart isn't going to hurt. Besides, we've still got this cottage and we'll be sleeping here.'

'Oh, yes,' I say, slipping my hands under his shirt. 'I guess that's true. And didn't they say tomorrow night's the big night? Maybe we can get everyone to have an early night tonight.'

'Knock, knock, knock,' shouts Lucy as she taps on the door. 'I hope you're putting on clothes.'

'We're decent,' we say, pulling apart.

She opens the door and strolls in handing us each a flute of bubbles.

'Time to get the party started,' she says.

'Right, now that we've all had a little something to eat, I think we should play a game,' says Kerry clapping her hands together. She's loving this whole sten do thing far too much and it's making me nervous.

'What type of game?' says Danny. 'Is this what women do on hen dos?'

'Go with it,' says Gaz. 'I'd been angling for us to do a stag thing – you know, stick the pubes on your face to make a beard-type thing.'

'I vetoed that,' says Lucy, 'as FYI that is officially the grossest thing that I have ever heard of. Why are stag dos so evil?'

'You've got to humiliate the stag, that's the whole point. Come on, I've seen enough hen dos, you do the same with the tacky L-plates and the like,' says Stuart.

'Yeah, why do we do that?' says Kerry. 'Fear not, there will be none of that here, well, not tonight anyway, but there will be games. So first up is Mr and Mrs. Now all we need to do is get you two to sit back to back.'

We get passed a whiteboard and a pen each.

I look at Danny nervously before I let Lucy drag me into position. If I'd known that they were going to do this, I would have let them organise an all-singing and dancing hen do somewhere far, far away from my fiancé. Having some slimy male stripper gyrating on me would have been preferable to this. What if I get none of the answers right? I've known Danny all my life, but I've only known him as a lover for a few weeks. What if everyone realises how little we know about each other and they try and stop the wedding?

'OK,' says Kerry, 'so first question.'

'Hold up,' says Danny. 'What is this, can you at least tell me the rules?'

'Oh, I just assumed you'd have watched the TV show. OK, so I ask a question like 'What's Lydia's favourite drink?' and you have to write down what you think it is and Lydia has to write down what her actual favourite is.'

'OK, that doesn't sound too bad,' he says. 'Beer.'

'Yes, but obviously we won't make it that easy. So, first question. What is the name of Danny's celebrity crush?'

Oh God. I know this. I actually know this. I scribble furiously on my white board, even drawing a picture. Please don't let it have changed. Please don't let it have changed.

'OK, so Lydia.'

'I've got Kylie Minogue.'

'What the fuck's that drawing?' says Lucy almost dying with laughter.

'It's Kylie in her gold hot pants.'

'Danny,' says Kerry and there's a low whistle as he reveals that it's Kylie.

'In her gold hot pants,' she says, reading it off the board. 'Really? Isn't she old enough to be your mum?'

'Woah,' says Stuart holding his hands up. 'You can't diss Kylie.'

'No, no, no,' says Gaz shaking his head.

'Move on,' I whisper. 'Move on quickly.'

'OK, then, Danny, who would play Lydia in the movie of her life?'

I scribble down my answer, not having a clue who Danny would pick. This hasn't exactly come up in passing.

'So Danny . . .' says Kerry leaning forward, clearly on ten-terhooks.

'Anne Hathaway.'

'What?' I say rolling over my board to reveal Jennifer Lawrence. Kerry and Lucy nod in approval. 'You think Anne Hathaway would play me?'

'What? She's pretty and she'd play the girl-next-door role perfectly.'

Lucy and Kerry tut and shake their heads.

'What's wrong with Anne Hathaway?' asks Danny, genuinely sounding hurt. 'I thought you loved her in that movie, what was it, the Princess thing? You made me watch it.'

Gaz rolls his eyes.

'No, it was when we were teenagers,' he says for clarification. 'Julie Andrews was in it.'

'Oh, that's doing your street cred so many more favours,' says Gaz.

'*The Princess Diaries*,' I say. 'She was all right in that. I mean she's a really good actress, it's just she's not Jennifer Lawrence.'

'She is not,' says Kerry shaking her head. 'Next up, Lydia, what's Danny's favourite part of your body?'

I don't even hesitate before writing boobs, and, of course, I'm right. I am so winning this game.

'Danny, what food would Lydia most want to lick off your body?'

I think back to his selection of spreads – if he writes sodding marmalade, the wedding's off.

'Nutella,' he says and I give him a little congratulatory pat on the arm.

We breeze through the rest of the questions and it turns out we know each other surprisingly well, although it did highlight that we should maybe be a bit more adventurous as we both put doggy style for our favourite position, and the strangest place we'd had sex was in my room whilst *Frozen* was playing in the living room above.

'So,' I say yawning theatrically, 'have you got much more planned for us? It's been rather a long day.'

'No, that's it for tonight,' says Lucy. 'We're saving the best for tomorrow.'

'Can't wait,' I say sarcastically. 'So, we'll see you all for breakfast, then.'

I expect them to get the hint and drink up, and I'm relieved when Lucy and Kerry jump up.

'Right, let's go,' says Lucy, trying to pull me up too.

'Uh, what do you mean? I'm staying here.'

'Oh no, we might have given you a joint hen and stag do, but we're separating you overnight.'

I look at Danny in horror.

'Come on,' says Lucy picking up my bag from the corner of the lounge. 'We've got a nice bed for you next door.'

I can't believe we're going to be separated all weekend. At this rate Danny and I will be sneaking off to the woodshed – but I guess at least that would help us with our need to be more adventurous with our sex life.

'You know this is our only chance to see each other?' I say pleading on behalf of my libido. 'We've not seen each other all week.'

'Well, it's lucky you got a little bit of time together before we arrived, then, wasn't it?' says Kerry grinning. 'Chop, chop.'

I lean down and kiss Danny on the lips.

'Get a room,' says Gaz, throwing crisps at our heads.

'I'll see you tomorrow,' I say longingly, as if I'm never going to see him again.

He doesn't let go of my hand and instead pulls me in for another kiss before he whispers he'll miss me.

I notice as we leave that Stuart has put another three tins of beer on the table. I'm guessing they're not turning in any time soon.

This so wasn't what we'd planned for our weekend away.

'Come on, you'll need your sleep,' says Lucy, giggling. 'You'll need all your energy for what we've got in store for you tomorrow.'

No, not what I'd planned at all.

Chapter 25

I see your stag do and I raise it tenfold with the hen do from hell for my friend, Caroline. I thought it was going to be a tame affair as she's pregnant and we'd chosen Paris to be cultural. Only the rest of us ended up drinking Champagne like it was water, which turned out to be no bad thing as the Moulin Rouge cabaret evening that they'd planned was a bit less can-can, a bit more fan-fan, if you get what I mean. Needless to say, I don't have any souvenirs to send you other than the mental scars I have on my brain.

Email; Lydia to Danny, April 2018

'Right, so what's on the agenda today then?' I say skulking downstairs in a pair of oversized pyjamas. Lucy and Kerry very astutely guessed that I wouldn't have packed anything to wear in bed, or at least anything that was suitable to wear in front of the girls, and they'd picked me up some pyjamas. And after the changing-room incident they'd erred on the side of caution and gone bigger just in case.

The stairs in the cottage lead straight into the open-plan lounge-diner and I notice that they've laid the table like it's a B&B. Kerry pulls a tray of hot croissants out of the oven and gingerly picks each of them out and throws them down onto the plate, all the while blowing her fingers as they're so hot.

'Yum,' I say feeling spoilt. 'This looks amazing.'

'I thought we'd start with these,' she says handing me a cup of hot coffee.

'Eat a lot,' says Lucy sitting down at the table. 'You need to keep your strength up.'

'Oh God, please tell me that we're not going ghyll scrambling. I don't think I could do that again, and I've washed my hair this morning.'

'No, your hair will be fine,' says Kerry and I notice that Lucy wrinkles her eyebrows. 'Oh yes, your hair might not be fine – but it won't get wet.'

She smiles and nods as if this is a bonus but that just makes me fear that it's going to get messy from bungee jumping. I keep reminding myself that a few weeks ago I told myself I was going to make more of an effort to #LiveMyBestLife and I should be embracing all these new adventures and spontaneity. Clearly, I should be careful what I wish for.

'What time are we leaving?' I say, reaching over and taking another croissant.

'Nine o'clock,' says Kerry.

I look up at the big clock in the living room; we've got an hour. I reach over for my phone to text Danny. Maybe he's got some clue as to what we're doing today and maybe we've got time to rendezvous at the wood pile.

I've got as far as typing *Hey Sexy* when the phone is snatched out of my hands.

'What the—?' I say looking up at Lucy, who's turning it off and slipping it into her pocket.

'I don't think so,' she says shaking her head. 'Not on the hen do.'

'No, no, no,' says Kerry joining in.

I finish eating my second croissant in a bit of a sulk.

'Right, we better get you ready,' says Lucy, standing up.

'But I haven't finished my coffee.'

'You can bring it with you,' says Lucy.

Her eyes are dancing and I haven't seen a smile on her face like this since she discovered that nutella had brought out a chocolate bar.

I slowly stand up and walk upstairs, wondering what horror is going to face me. For Kerry we went out with her dressed in a floral bridesmaid dress circa 1980. I can't even hope that Lucy will go easy on me for fear of retaliation on her hen do, as, to be honest, she is up for anything when it comes to fancy dress, and she can pull anything off too.

I open the door and there, neatly laid out on the bed, are a pair of white yoga pants and a white camisole.

'Um, is this it?' I ask, cautiously. Despite the trousers looking a little MC Hammer I seem to be getting out of this lightly.

Lucy cackles with laughter. 'There are more clothes, but pop these on first and then your dressing gown and we'll dress you downstairs.'

I give my best scowl but Lucy winks at me before disappearing out of the door.

Ten minutes later, and I'm in the living room. I'm not the only one in odd clothing. Kerry's in a red T-shirt and Lucy's in a green one and both are wearing black leggings. I have no idea what is going on.

'Do you think it's time?' asks Lucy.

'I think so,' says Kerry and she hands me a suit bag.

I don't know if I really want to look, but I take it and hang it on one of the wooden beams and slowly unzip it.

There's a purple waistcoat with gold trim inside.

'Aladdin? You want me to be Aladdin,' I say, slipping it on.

Lucy comes over and fastens the waistcoat together with a safety pin.

'You need the hat.'

I look in the bag and there at the bottom is what looks like a puffy shower cap that's got white and red spots on it.

'Um . . .' I say, looking at it.

'We warned you your hair might get messed up,' says Kerry laughing.

I look at them and then back down at the shower cap before I slip it on. 'What the hell am I supposed to be?' I ask, as I look at myself in the mirror.

Kerry and Lucy go over to the other side of the room and slip on dungarees and suddenly it all seems to fit into place. Especially when they attach oversized moustaches to their faces and put on their hats.

'Mario and Luigi,' I say giggling. They actually look pretty good. 'So that makes me?'

'Toad,' says Kerry enthusiastically. 'The mushroom from Mario Kart. We thought you'd like it because we used to play it with Danny all the time when we were kids.'

I nod. We did. We also used to play a lot of Donkey Kong too, so I guess it could have been worse.

'We should go and see if the boys are ready,' says Kerry, laughing.

'Do we have to? I thought we were doing a girls thing today?' I say, suddenly embarrassed. I'd been secretly hoping that I'd get to see Danny, but not dressed like this. Neither the waistcoat nor the trousers are flattering, and my mushroom head is doing nothing for me. I look like a prepubescent boy.

'We are. It's girls versus boys. Come on,' says Lucy bundling me out.

All sense of embarrassment is eroded when I see Danny standing in front of me dressed as Princess Peach in a pink dress, blonde wig and complete with blue clip-on earrings that would give Pat Butcher a run for her money.

'Hey you,' he says, walking over and giving me a quick kiss. 'Do you think it suits me?'

I look at his hairy legs sticking out of the bottom of the dress.

'You've never looked sexier,' I say, deciding that I definitely got out of this more easily than he did.

He laughs and pats me on the head.

'My little mushroom. Imagine if we'd given them more time to plan this,' he whispers.

'The mind boggles.'

'Right then, you two. That's quite enough of that,' says Gaz as he walks over. He's dressed as evil Luigi in yellow dungarees. 'Boys versus girls, remember. No fraternising with the enemy.'

'Any idea?' I ask Danny.

'None,' he says.

And with that I'm pulled away into Kerry's car and I wave as Peach is put into Gaz's.

Half an hour later, we're standing at the side of an indoor go-kart arena. The staff gave us that not-another-stag-slash-hen-do-fancy-dress-group look then issued us with boiler suits to wear. I don't look half bad in mine, or at least I look a whole lot better in it than in the outfit I arrived in. I'm guessing that's not often the case.

Danny is looking particularly interesting in a boiler suit and a full face of make-up.

'Now then, no one's been drinking this morning, have they?' says the guy in charge of putting us in the cars when we get trackside.

'No,' we all say shaking our heads.

Although I could have done with a glass of something half an hour ago when I was full mushroom. I see a nun walk out of the changing room and it makes my costume seem half decent. Surley she must be on a hen do. I do a double take, though, as her full-length robes are very convincing, but then I see the condoms stapled to the bottom of her costume. Yep, it definitely could have been worse.

'As you're doing girls versus boys, I've put the girls in red helmets and the boys in blue. You've got half an hour to see what time you get and the only twist is that you are racing like Mario Kart, so if you get close enough to the back of someone, you can shoot them with a laser.'

'What, an actual laser?' I ask, worried that this is sounding a little dangerous.

Danny winks at me as Kerry gives me a gentle shove.

'They are real lasers, but not the kind that could slice you in half. Essentially, it's the same as when you used to throw a shell to hit someone in the computer game. It'll just slow them down.'

'OK,' I say, thinking that it sounds a little less scary.

'Just remember that this isn't dodgems, and you'll be laughing. Now, did Simon already do the safety brief with you?'

We nod. Simon was very comprehensive with his safety briefing.

'And you've signed your waivers?'

We all nod again.

'Great, then get in your cars. The lights will flash overhead for a countdown and when they disappear, you go.'

'That's it?' I mutter. 'No practice laps?'

'Not on a Saturday, we're chock-a. You'll be fine,' says the guy as I double check my helmet's safely fixed on my head.

'Come on, Toad,' says Kerry, 'don't let the girls down.'

We climb into our cars and Danny blows a kiss at me, which is a little disturbing as he has bright pink lipstick plastered on his face.

I look down at my pedals and try to remind myself which one is stop and which go, when all of a sudden the engines are revving and I look up to see the lights overhead disappearing and everyone is off but me. Bloody hell. I floor the accelerator and jerk off the starting line, desperately trying to catch everyone up.

Luckily for me it doesn't take long to catch up, thanks to the lasers that everyone's firing. It's hilarious as, for a few seconds, the lasers make you slow right down as if you're driving through treacle. I give a little wave as I weave and dodge between those who have been hit, until I'm in the lead. Woohoo. Or at least I am until I crash into a pile of tyres.

Stuart gives me a little sarcastic wave as I try and manoeuvre back onto the track, which only spurs me on.

I draw level with Lucy, who gives me a little thumbs-up as we're not that far behind Danny and Stuart. Remembering that we're girls versus boys, I shoot Danny with my laser and nip on round, letting out a cackle as I zoom past. I always remembered Mario Kart being fun when we were kids, but this takes it to a whole new level.

I'm just adjusting my mushroom hat ready for my podium entrance when Danny walks up to me. He slips his hand onto my back and pulls me towards him, bashing into me with his fake boobs.

'I don't remember the princess being quite so voluptuous.'

'I think this is all from Stuart's imagination.'

He leans over to give me a quick kiss.

'I've missed you,' he whispers into my ear.

'I've missed you too,' I purr back, and I'm about to give him another kiss when Stuart shows up.

'Now, now, you two. You know the rules,' he says, gently dragging Danny away.

I look around hoping to see one of the girls, when I see Gaz standing in the corner looking at his phone, his brow furrowed.

'Hey there,' I say, smiling as I walk over to him.

'Hey,' he says, putting his phone in his pocket.

He looks up at me and I can't help thinking how ridiculous he looks with his giant moustache.

'Listen, I'm sorry about lunch at our place last week. It got a little out of hand. I shouldn't have had all that wine on an empty stomach.'

'It's fine. Really.'

'It's not. The lunch was supposed to be meeting you properly and getting to know you and I start telling you that I suspect my wife's having an affair.'

'It's fine, really,' I say again, hoping that someone will come and rescue me soon. Despite Danny not telling me everything before, it's still making me feel awkward that I know that Gaz isn't totally making it up.

'Well, thanks for being so understanding, anyway.'

'It's no problem. We've all been there – it's easy for our thoughts to run away with themselves.'

He nods. His eyes look tired and I get the impression that he's been losing sleep over it.

'The thing is, I keep calling her today. I even called her in the middle of last night on our home phone. I was so convinced that she was going to be with someone else.'

'And?'

'She gave me a bollocking for waking her up. I don't know what's wrong with me. I just convinced myself that she was having an affair and I was going to catch her out.'

Unless the person she's having an affair with is here too I think, looking over at Danny, before instantly getting cross with myself. Ross has put all sorts of doubts into my head with his questions about Danny's motivations and what he's hiding.

I pat Gaz's arm sympathetically. It's all I can do, I don't really feel I know him well enough to give him a proper hug.

'Hey,' says Lucy bounding up, and I sigh with relief. 'I hope you're not fraternising with the enemy.'

'Not at all,' I say, smiling and remembering that I'm on my hen do.

'Good, because they're doing the podium now. Get ready to take your place.'

I smile back and try to tell myself that I'm wrong about Danny and Victoria.

'I guess we're not going to live it down that we got beaten by the girls,' says Gaz.

'I don't think so,' I say, just as we get called up to take our place.

I climb up and the boys stand in front of us bowing their heads that they've lost out to us.

Kerry pops the cork of a bottle of Prosecco and pours me a glass, which I practically inhale as we start to sing 'We Are the Champions'.

I feel uneasy after the conversation with Gaz and I need to take the edge off it.

'Blimey, there was no hanging about with that Prosecco, was there?' says Lucy as she tops me up. 'You'll have to pace yourself – we've got a whole day and evening still planned for you two. Besides, we've got a better use for this.'

She puts her thumb over the bottle top and starts spraying us all.

'Let's get this party started,' she says with a whoop.

Danny scoops me up and starts to run away with me as Lucy chases after us.

'What have we let ourselves in for?' he says, giving me a sneaky kiss.

He couldn't be more right.

Chapter 26

I am never drinking again. Never. Ever. I thought that the stag do got out of hand. It turns out it was only the preamble to the wedding. Man did that get rough. The wedding went off without a hitch. The best man remembered the rings and presented them to the vicar with the utmost professionalism, and his speech was the right balance between embarrassment and sentimentality. And I was so relieved that I'd finished my duties that I felt like I then drank everyone's allocation of wine. Never ever again.

Email; Danny to Lydia, May 2018

'I just love you guys so much,' I say practically decapitating Kerry and Lucy as I get them both in a crook of an elbow and squeeze them into me. 'Thank you so much for organising this.'

'Despite you not wanting us to,' says Kerry. 'I knew that you would secretly want one.'

She wrestles herself free and smooths down her hair.

'We'd better get some food on, the boys will be here any minute.'

I actually sigh, the kind of contented sigh that only Disney heroines make when the main man appears.

'You are so sickeningly in love,' says Lucy as she shakes her head. 'I mean, I can't believe it. All those years with Ross I never realised what a hopeless romantic you were.'

'That's because what Ross and I had,' I say shaking my head, 'was so different. I wonder if we should have only been friends.'

'Really?' says Kerry. 'You were together five years, the whole thing couldn't have been a mistake?'

I feel a bit bad as I still think of him as one of my best friends and in not wanting him in that way I feel as if I'm slighting him, especially when we did have some really good times. Only there was never the passion that there is with Danny.

'I guess "mistake" is a bit harsh, but I think I knew for a long time that he wasn't the one.'

'Do you think he'll marry Wonder Girl?' asks Lucy as she goes in search of more Prosecco in the fridge – which is not a particularly good idea given how much we've already consumed.

'I don't know. I can never tell if he's serious about her or not but sometimes I see him smiling at her as if he's enchanted. He was never enchanted by me.'

'Oh, that's not true, is it?' says Lucy. 'He must have loved you.'

I wonder if that's not fair, maybe he was once but he certainly didn't look at me in the same way at the end – neither of us did.

'I think he loved me, but I don't think he was *in* love with me. Not really. We had that kind of sex that scratched an itch, you know?'

'What, as opposed to the sex that gives you an itch, as I'm pretty sure that's what you want to avoid,' says Kerry. 'Seriously, though, you know I think that's what most relationships grow into in the end. Don't be disappointed if Danny's not copping a feel every time he walks past you in a few years.'

'Come on, I've seen Jim, that's what he does.'

Kerry laughs.

There's a knock at the door and my stomach flips. I feel as if I'm a teenager again getting all excited that the boys are coming over.

I open the door, still dressed as Toad the mushroom, only it's not Danny in front of me, it's Victoria.

'Oh, hi,' she says, as she looks me up and down. 'I almost didn't recognise you.'

'How nice to see you. Do come in,' I say, as I step back for her. 'This is Gaz's wife, Victoria. Victoria, this is my sister Kerry and my best friend Lucy.'

'Ooh it's so great to meet you finally in person,' says Kerry. 'Victoria helped to arrange all this.'

I watch in amazement as Kerry and Victoria hug like long-lost friends.

'It's so lovely to meet you too. I'm so glad that I made it for at least some of it.'

'Let's get you some bubbles to catch up,' says Lucy, just as Victoria takes her coat off and reveals her baby bump.

'Better not,' she says, smiling widely at them. 'I brought some tonic water with me. So tell me all about what you've been up to.'

She sits down at the table and I can't believe what I'm seeing. She's like a different person.

'Well, the girls won the go kart racing,' says Kerry proudly.

'Excellent, I can imagine that went down badly with the boys.'

'Yeah, I don't think they've got over it yet.'

'And the Mr and Mrs game went well.'

'Yes, Danny and I got most of them right,' I say as I sit down. She looks at me as if that's hard to believe before she smiles again.

There's another knock at the door and I get up to answer, thinking that it really must be the boys this time, only to see that it's Caroline and Rob.

'Oh my God, you made it,' I say flinging my arms around them. 'I'm so touched. Where's Ethan?'

'With Matt at his mum's in Stourbridge. Rob gave me a lift and Matt's coming to pick me up in a couple of hours.'

'That's amazing,' I say, hugging them again. 'Let's get you drinks.'

I don't even notice when the boys come in, until Danny walks past and gives me a quick kiss before he makes a beeline for Victoria.

'I didn't know you were coming,' he says.

'I couldn't let you have a stag do without me, could I?'

Gaz walks over to her and gives her a kiss and rubs the bump affectionately, but she barely looks at him as she's still grinning at Danny.

I gently pull him away and introduce him to Rob and Caroline.

'I'm so thrilled to meet you,' says Caroline giving him a big bear hug. 'You're one lucky man bagging our Lydia.'

'Don't I know it. Every morning I wake up and I can't believe my luck.'

'Ah,' I say, letting him give me a hug.

Caroline's wrinkling her nose up and smiling.

'So let's get this celebration started,' says Kerry popping open another bottle of fizz from the seemingly never-ending supply.

Everyone picks up a flute as she tops up the glasses and I notice Victoria has stood up and is pawing away at Danny again.

'There's so much to celebrate,' says Caroline to me as she sips the drink. 'The sten do *and* your new promotion,' says Caroline.

The smile instantly falls off my face and I hope that Danny didn't hear.

'I went into work to arrange my keeping in touch days and I heard the great news.'

Caroline's on maternity leave from the design agency that we outsource our marketing to, with her not working there at the moment I hadn't even thought of her finding out that way. I risk a look at Danny, who seems to be listening intently to Victoria.

Caroline chinks her glass with mine.

'Looks like this is going to be your year.'

'Looks like it,' I say, wishing that it was all going to be that simple.

There's another knock at the door. Kerry's the closest and she opens it and the sound of 'The Stripper' starts to fill the room and my stomach sinks. Have the boys organised for Danny to have a stripper? Am I going to have to watch my husband-to-be get someone's boobs thrust in his face whilst I pretend not to be bothered?

Lucy drags me forward, and Stuart pushes Danny towards the door. Danny takes my hand for moral support. He doesn't seem crazy about the prospect either. We're just reaching the doorstep when a leg kicks out across the doorway, causing Danny and I to take a step backwards. Another leg kicks from the other side, then the two legs clad in tights and high heels take turns to high kick to the beat. Before I can worry who the legs belong to, giant feathered fans shake down the side of the doorway, before two women pop out; they're holding two fans each which are obscuring their faces and bodies.

The fans are shaking as the song builds up to its climax and presumably the great reveal. I'm not entirely sure I want to know what's behind it – burlesque isn't really my thing. Uh-oh. Alarm bells ring in my head – I know whose thing it is. I look closer at the heeled shoes and those legs and I don't know whether to be more or less scared of the reveal now that I know who these two women are. Please God let them be wearing clothes underneath those fans.

'Ta-daa,' shout my mother and Hazel as they drop the fans down to the side. I'm relieved that they're at least covered up – I just hope that I'm brave enough when I'm their age to pull off a sparkly leotard like the ones they're wearing.

'Had you going there, didn't we, love? Your faces are pictures,' says Hazel pulling at Danny's cheeks.

She gives me a quick hug hello and waltzes into the kitchen.

'Hazel's been teaching me burlesque. I think I'm a natural,' says Mum as she drifts in after her.

I don't say anything for fear of encouraging her. One day she's crashing a hen do in a leotard, the next she's crashing the wedding in nipple pasties.

'You look so surprised, Lydia. But you didn't think we'd miss your hen do now, did you?' She gives me a hug and cackles wildly. 'Did we miss all the drinking fun?'

'No, you're right on time,' says Lucy, looping her arm through my mum's and leading her to the booze.

I'm left staring in her wake wondering how many more surprises tonight has in store for us.

'I don't think this is such a good idea,' I say to Lucy, who's now pushed her moustache up to the top of her head so that it looks like a bow on an Alice band.

The party is in full swing and I feel as if I've spoken to everyone and no one. I've been trying to talk to Danny to double check he didn't hear what Caroline said, but I haven't been able to get near him.

'Of course it's a good idea. We need some kind of drinking game to keep it interesting. Everyone, make a circle,' says Lucy clapping her hands.

She gently guides me to the sofa as she encourages everyone into the lounge area from the kitchen. She makes sure Danny sits down on the opposite side from me. I don't like playing 'never have I ever' at the best of times, but do I really want to find out what the worst things Danny has done are?

'Don't worry,' says Victoria with a sly smile. 'It's not as if you or Danny have got any big secrets from each other, is it?'

My blood runs cold as I worry about what will come up.

I make a last-ditch attempt to change everyone's minds. 'I don't know if it's appropriate in front of the mothers.'

'Please, Lydia,' says Hazel. 'I'm sure your mum and I understand that you're not an angel. I mean, I did walk in on you . . .'

'Yes, yes, we don't want you to say *that* word again.'

'What Hazel's trying to say is it's just a bit of fun. And to be honest, I'm sure there isn't much that you've done that we haven't.'

Hazel and my mum laugh in exactly the same way and a ripple of dread rolls over me. I realise it's not what Danny has or hasn't done that I should be worried about, but more what my mum has or hasn't. At least the two of them have changed out of their burlesque outfits and are now semi-respectable – well at least until we play a game.

'Right, does everyone have enough drink?' asks Kerry as she goes round with a pitcher of cocktails that she's made, topping everyone up anyway.

'OK, I'll start,' says Lucy. 'I have never flown in an aeroplane.'

There's a collective groan as we all drink, well, all of us except Hazel.

'Mum, you've been on a plane,' says Stuart, tutting.

'What, I drink if I *have* done it?' she says, wrinkling her eyes up.

'That's how the game works,' says Lucy nodding. 'If you agree with the statement and you have never done whatever it is, you don't drink, but you do if you have.'

'Right, gotcha,' says Hazel. 'This is rather fun, isn't it?'

'Ssh, Hazel, time to concentrate,' says Mum. 'I'm confused enough as it is without missing bits.'

'I have never had a threesome,' says Kerry.

I look nervously over at Danny but to my relief he doesn't drink, but there are gasps around the room as someone is drinking. I almost drop my drink in shock when I see it's my mum.

'Oh Jesus, Kerry, of all the questions to ask,' I mutter.

'I didn't expect her to have done that. Mum, are you sure that you understand the game?'

'Or the question? Perhaps threesome meant something different when you were young.'

Hazel snorts with laughter.

'I know how the game works and girls, don't forget, my teenage years were in the Sixties. They didn't call it the Swinging Sixties for nothing.'

Kerry and I look at each other in horror before drinking. We need something to numb us after that revelation.

'I have never played Never Have I Ever,' says Caroline sailing us back into safer territory and insuring that we all drink.

'I have never flashed anyone,' says Stuart.

We all drink again and I start to relax a little, mainly as I think I'm getting very drunk very quickly.

'I've never been skinny dipping,' says Victoria as Danny laughs before he drinks. She picks up her glass too and smiles. I flash a look at Gaz to see if he's noticed, but he's laughing along as Rob and Caroline drink too.

Perhaps I'm reading too much into it; it's not as if it's uncommon to go skinny dipping, perhaps the in joke is that they both talked once about doing it. Or perhaps it's further proof that she knows things about Danny that I don't. Or even worse that they did it together in Spain?

'Hey, you need to drink too,' say Caroline nudging me. 'You came skinny dipping with us that time in Greece.'

'Oh shit, yeah,' I say drinking.

'My turn?' asks Danny. 'I have never gone commando.'

All the boys, Hazel and Lucy drink.

'What? It makes going to work a whole lot more interesting,' says Lucy.

'Eww,' I say pulling a face. My big knickers are firmly staying put during work hours, in fact, most hours if Danny isn't around.

'Mum,' groan Danny and Stuart.

'What? There's no way I'm wearing a thong at my age and just because I'm old does not mean I want a VPL.'

My mum nods and chinks Hazel's glass and they both drink.

'I have never kissed anyone of the same sex,' says Rob with a twinkle in his eye.

He and Caroline drink, and Lucy and I raise eyebrows in her direction.

'At uni, no closet confessions from me, I'm afraid,' she says, blushing.

'I have never done the walk of shame,' says Gaz.

All of us but Kerry drink.

'Come on, Kerry, you must have done,' says Lucy. 'How have you missed out on that?'

'That's what happens when you marry your childhood sweetheart.'

'Ah, that's so sweet,' says Victoria, cocking her head. 'Your turn, Lydia.'

'I have never locked myself out of a hotel room naked,' I say, grinning at Danny.

'That's mean,' he says drinking.

Stuart drinks too and we all laugh.

'I couldn't find the loo,' he says shrugging.

'That's what happened to me,' says Danny.

'Family trait,' say Kerry and Lucy laughing.

'I have never fallen on my arse whilst pole dancing,' says Lucy.

Lucy, Caroline and I all drink.

'Caroline's hen do,' I say to the raised eyebrows.

'That's a shame, I thought you might have had a hidden talent,' says Danny.

'I have a feeling that my pole dancing is on a par with your flamenco.'

'Shame,' he says, shaking his head.

'OK, let's see if I've got this right. I have never performed burlesque,' says my mum. And her and Hazel drink between their giggles.

'I have never been to G-A-Y,' says Hazel, and only her and mum drink again.

We all look at them.

'What? We were up in London for a night out and we met these lovely young men who were going and we went with them. It was such fun,' says Mum.

'And everyone thought we were in fancy dress, they thought we were doing Edwina and Patsy in *Ab Fab*.'

I really hope that Lucy and I act like them when we're in our sixties.

'I have never been to Harrods,' says Kerry.

'I have never been to Tescos,' says Caroline.

'I have never been to the Malvern Hills,' says Stuart.

We all drink to all of them and I can feel the room starting to spin slightly as the cocktail starts to go to my head.

'I have never lied to someone I love,' says Victoria looking at me.

I don't know how she found out about my job, but I'm sure she knows.

'Oh, that's not in the spirit of the game,' says Kerry. 'Everyone's lied to someone they love at some point.'

'Then we should all drink,' says Victoria, putting her nice voice on. We all drink a little uneasily.

'I have never crossed a road,' says Danny, choosing us a safe topic.

'I have never eaten chocolate,' says Gaz.

'I have never drunk alcohol,' I say.

'I have never kissed either the bride or groom,' says Lucy.

I look over at Danny and I smile as I drink, before I notice that Danny and I aren't the only ones to raise our glasses. Both Victoria and Stuart drink too, and I suddenly feel nauseous.

I stare at Gaz and he's laughing. 'I still find it funny that I stole Victoria off you,' he says.

'You didn't steal me off him,' says Victoria, putting down her tonic water. 'I chose you.'

I notice there's a hint of bitterness in her voice, and I can't help thinking that she wishes she'd chosen differently.

Gaz shrugs and drinks anyway.

I'm not overly happy to hear that Victoria and Danny locked lips once before, but I'm hoping that with everyone looking at them they didn't notice Stuart's admission. All I need is for Kerry to come out with something quick so that we can forget about it.

'Hang on,' says Victoria. 'Stuart drank too.'

Everyone turns to look at him and I watch as Danny's face begins to fall as he realises that means he's kissed me.

'Don't look so worried, bro, it was years ago,' says Stuart. 'Back at Kerry's wedding.'

I close my eyes. Why couldn't he have just said that it was years ago and I could have pretended it was long before Danny and I had our kiss?

'You kissed each other at Kerry's wedding?' he says slowly.

'I didn't know that,' says Kerry, trying to laugh it off. 'Right, I have never played Monopoly.'

Everyone drinks but Danny.

'Come on, Dan, you've played Monopoly,' says Gaz, but he still doesn't drink.

'I want to know when you kissed Lydia,' he says.

'I told you,' says Stuart. 'At Kerry and Jim's wedding.'

'Before or after you kissed me?' he says, looking at me for the first time. 'Before or after you made the pact to marry me?'

Stuart looks between us.

'You kissed at the wedding too? Is that where you disappeared to? We were outside and I went to get us a drink from the bar and then when I came back you'd gone.'

My heart sinks as I watch as the hurt creeps into Danny's eyes.

'I can explain,' I say weakly.

Danny gets up and storms towards the door of the cottage. If it was any other time I would have laughed at how ridiculous he looked storming off dressed like a princess. But now's not the time for laughter.

'Dan, it was years ago,' says Stuart.

'Dan,' calls Gaz as he walks out.

'Oh Lydia,' says Hazel in a way so sympathetic that it makes me want to cry. Everyone else turns to look at me. I know they want an explanation, but I have to go.

'Danny,' I call, as I run after him.

'How could you, Lydia? He's my brother,' he says, yanking off his wig.

'It was a drunken kiss that didn't mean anything.'

'You were waiting for him when I found you. He was your first choice.'

'What? No, no. I didn't know what was going to happen with us. I didn't know we were going to get together, I never expected you to kiss me.'

'Oh, right. That makes me feel so much better. I was second best,' he says, shaking his head. 'Do you have any idea what that feels like?'

'Actually, I think I do. I mean, isn't that what I am? Isn't that why you've picked now to get together with me?'

'What are you talking about?'

'Victoria. You're in love with her. It's all started to make sense. All those jokes about you being the third wheel in their marriage. Not to mention the way she is with you. Those in jokes. Your little trip to Spain together. She has a key to your house and she phones you all the time. Gaz was right, wasn't he? She's having an affair – and it's with you.'

Danny holds his hands up by his face as he shakes his head.

'Is that what you think I'm capable of? You think I could do that to my best friend? That I could ruin his marriage? Things with Victoria, it's . . .'

'Complicated. Yes, you've told me, but I'm not imagining the way that Victoria is with you.'

He sighs loudly.

'Victoria's having doubts about her marriage. She and Gaz have been having problems and she's pregnant and full of hormones, she doesn't know what she's thinking.'

'But she thinks she's in love with you? Doesn't she? That's why it's so complicated?'

Danny nods slowly.

'And something happened between you.'

'There was a kiss,' he says eventually.

'Oh, so a minute ago you were shouting at me that I'd think that of you and now you're saying that I'm right.'

'No, you're twisting things. Victoria kissed me, it was a mistake and I never kissed her back. I told her then what I'm telling you now: that we're friends, nothing more. She doesn't even love me, not really. Maybe as a friend, but that's it. It's just that I'm a shoulder to cry on, and she's confused. You know, Lydia, I just can't believe you'd think that I think you're second best after everything that's happened between us,' he says. 'Our time in Spain, the proposal. All of it, it was all real.'

'Exactly,' I say, 'and that's why Stuart is so irrelevant.'

His face clouds like thunder again.

'Don't you get it, Lydia? You never told me. You were never honest with me about that night. You weren't honest with me about where you lived and it makes me wonder what else you've been lying to me about.'

I shift uncomfortably on the spot.

'How about your promotion at work?' he says, staring right into my eyes.

I let out a pathetic whimper.

'I was going to tell you about that.'

'When exactly were you going to tell me that you'd accepted a promotion rather than handed in your notice? When we got married in a couple of weeks and I expected to carry you over the threshold, only for you to turn around and say, "sorry, I've got to get back home to Portsmouth as I'm not actually moving in with you"?'

'It's not as if I'm not going to leave. I'm going to move up to be with you. I'm giving up my whole life to be with you – just not yet. I've waited and waited for this promotion and it's so good for my career. I just wanted to do it for a few months to get the experience on my CV, and I thought it would be easier to get another job if I was in a job already.'

'Then why didn't you just tell me that?'

'Because you were so excited about me moving and because I was worried that you'd be mad or that you wouldn't want to do long distance for all those months.'

'Fucking hell, Lydia. We were getting married. If I couldn't have waited a few months for you then we really shouldn't have been bothering at all.'

'We *were* getting married?' I say, the words sticking in my throat, a pain burning in my chest.

'We were, Lydia. We're not now. How can I possibly marry you when I don't trust you?'

'You're making it sound as if I've got some massive problem with lying. I didn't tell you about Stuart at the time as I'd been relieved when you'd found me and you stopped me from doing anything silly. And our kiss we had then was so unexpected. I'd fancied you for years and I never in my wildest dreams thought that you might possibly kiss me. And as to why I didn't mention that since we've been together, it's not really the kind of thing you want to bring up, is it? "By the way, I once drunkenly snogged your brother."'

'And then there's where I live. I was embarrassed, OK? You have always been successful with your swanky flats and your high-flying career and now your business. I could only imagine what my place in Kerry's basement would look like to you. How at thirty I'd found myself living in that situation.

'And as for my job, I honestly have never been so torn in all my life. I want to give up everything to be with you, I do, but I just need to do this for myself first. For my future, for *our* future.'

He takes a deep breath and I'm wondering if I've got through to him.

'We're not going to have a future,' he says, the hurt audible in his voice. 'If you knew me at all, you'd know how ridiculous all that just sounded.'

He storms off down the road and I do nothing but watch him go. I keep hoping that he'll come to his senses and will come back and tell me that he doesn't mean any of it. But he doesn't.

I don't know how long it is before Lucy slips her arm around me. 'Are you OK? Where's Danny?'

'He's gone. The wedding's off,' I say, as the tears start to fall.

'Come on, he's just drunk. It'll all blow over,' she says, turning me back towards the cottage. I don't have the mental energy to correct her.

Naturally everyone's talking about us when I walk back in with Lucy and the voices immediately go quiet.

Lucy guides me back to the sofa and Kerry thrusts a glass of water into my hand as she sits down next to me.

'Lydia, I'm so sorry,' says Stuart. 'I'd never have admitted to it if I'd realised it was such a big deal.'

'It's not your fault,' I say shaking my head.

'I'm sure Daniel just needs to sleep it off,' says Hazel.

I nod, but I know that he doesn't. He looks devastated.

'Where's he now?' asks Victoria.

'He stormed off towards the main road.'

'I'll go after him in the car,' she says picking up the keys. 'He's far too drunk to be walking out there alone.'

'Of course you will,' I mutter under my breath, but she ignores me and carries on walking.

'I'll come with you,' says Gaz.

'And me,' says Hazel. 'I can't help worrying about him.'

Stuart looks at us nervously.

'I'll go and wait in our cottage in case he comes back,' he says, excusing himself and leaving me with my friends and mum.

'I've fucked everything up,' I say, shaking my head.

I don't often swear in front of my mum, but then again I don't often break up with a man I'm about to marry.

'He was the best thing to have happened to me in a long time and I fucked it all up.'

'It was over ten years ago,' says Kerry. 'He'll get over it.'

'It wasn't just that, I accused him of having an affair with Victoria.'

'What?' they all gasp.

'It all seemed to make sense. They'd gone to Spain alone together. She has a key to his flat. And Gaz thought she was having an affair with someone. Ross made me think the other day that it was weird that we were getting married so quickly and that Danny had to have a reason. This seemed to fit.'

'And what did Danny say?'

'He said', I say, looking up at the door to make sure that it's properly closed, 'that they kissed and that Victoria thinks she's in love with him.'

'Shit,' says Lucy. 'I take it Gaz doesn't know.'

'No, apparently Danny's been trying to convince her otherwise. He thinks she's just unhappy in her marriage and it's not really about him.'

'Blimey, that's big.'

'Yep.'

'But still, it's hardly reason to call off the wedding,' says Lucy.

'There's more. I didn't actually hand in my notice at work. In fact, I accepted a promotion.'

'What?' says Kerry.

'You were going to leave?' says Caroline.

I turn to her. 'I was supposed to move up to the Lake District after the wedding, and after I got the promotion I was going to postpone the move for a few months. I haven't told you yet as I was so honoured that you'd asked me to be godmother and I was worried you'd be mad that I was moving.'

'I'm pretty sure that you can still be a godparent if you live outside the county boundary, you know,' she says.

I smile at her. 'That's good to know. Not that it matters now. Danny's mad at me for lying to him about quitting and he said it shows that we don't know each other well enough to get married.'

'So did he actually say the wedding was off?' asks my mum, who's perched on the sofa behind me.

'Yep,' I say nodding. 'I knew there was a reason that I didn't want to have a hen do.'

I start to do proper, ugly crying – all snot and wails – and Kerry pulls me in for a hug.

'There, there. It all seems worse as we've drunk our body weight in booze. I'm sure when Danny sobers up tomorrow morning it will be fine.'

'You think?' I say, not daring to believe her. The look he gave me will forever haunt me.

'Yes,' says Kerry. 'Trust me, this will all be forgotten along with the hangover.'

I start to wipe my tears away desperately hoping that she's right.

Chapter 27

Thank you for my birthday card and the big 3-0 badge just in case I forgot how old I was. So I've got some news in that I've moved again, in case you didn't see the full page ad that Facebook seemed to have taken, Ross and I split up. It was all very amicable and we're still friends and I've found myself my very own lovely flat close to the beach.

Email; Lydia to Danny, August 2018

The past couple of days have been a blur. After my fight with Danny on Saturday night, I fell asleep in the very early hours. I woke hoping we'd sort it out, but then found out that Victoria had driven him home the night before, leaving Gaz to drive Danny's car back the next day. I don't know what hurt me more – the fact that he'd left, or that he'd left with her. It's what she probably wanted all along. Since then I've been going through the motions on half-hearted autopilot barely eating, sleeping or working. Which is not ideal when I'm supposed to be impressing my boss.

I've just got to make it through this afternoon and this evening's event, and then I've got tomorrow off. I had been planning to sort out the final wedding tasks with Mum, but all I'm planning to do now is to lie in bed feeling sorry for myself.

I start drifting off again when I look down at my hand and my ring catches the light. I can't believe that I'd forgotten to take it off. I slip it over my knuckle and zip it protectively into a pocket in my handbag. I'll give it back to Hazel when she comes down to see Mum later in the month.

Despite only having had it for a few weeks, my finger suddenly feels naked without it, and I bite down on my lip hard to stop myself from crying.

'Lydia, the set-up is finished downstairs, can you come and approve it?' asks Fred.

'Sure, I'll come now,' I say, picking up the folder for Helen's event that was reassigned to me. I should be excited, as it's my first big event that I'm managing by myself – an awards cere-mony for two hundred guests – but I've barely glanced at the folder. Luckily, Helen confirmed all the suppliers last week before she handed it over and her event plans are always flawless. All I'm hoping is that I get an early night. The awards are being run by *Family First*, which is quite a twee magazine, so I can't imagine that it's going to be a lively affair.

To be honest, I can't think of anything I want to do less than work an event where I have to be nice to people and pretend that I'm in the party spirit, but now more than ever I need to prove myself. I no longer have the option of quitting as I don't have Danny to run to and I need a job to be able to afford the place I'm going to have to rent now that Kerry's got bookings on my current flat.

I walk into the small conference suite and boy it's dark. Everything's black and there's soft purple lighting, which gives it a kinky Halloween feel.

'Are you sure this is the right colour scheme?' I say, flicking through the folder.

'That's what it says in the event plan.'

I pull out my copy and see it's all there in black and white, or at least black and purple.

'Right, then. I thought it was a group of mummy bloggers coming for an award ceremony and that it was being hosted by a kids TV presenter,' I say, looking round at something that's all together more adult than I was expecting.

'It all seems to be there, we've used all the props mentioned,' says Fred.

I look at the plumes of purple feathers that we last used for a burlesque-themed event and I try and ignore the feeling in my gut that something is wrong.

Helen's an amazing event planner and she always knows what she's doing. I've just got to trust her on this.

'It looks great, Fred,' I say – it isn't a lie, it does look great. Just not what I expected. 'Well done for all your hard work.'

'Thanks, Lydia. I hope it's a great party,' he says as he walks off.

I watch Fred go before I head into the kitchen to see the event caterer.

'Hi, Ben, everything OK?' I ask, as I try to resist the temptation to eat one of the giant langoustines that he's arranging on a platter.

'Yes, fine. We're all sorted.'

'Good, are the waiting staff here? I didn't see them setting up.'

'We're not using our waiting staff tonight. Helen's booked Allbrite.'

Before I can question Helen's choice of wait staff, the radio crackles in my ear.

'Lydia,' says Jenny, one of our junior events staff. 'Marie from Family First is here at reception.'

'Great, I'll come and meet her. Ben, are you sure it's Allbrite staff coming?'

'Oh yeah,' he says with a twinkle in his eye. 'I always love working events with them.'

My heart is starting to pound now as I try and piece this all together. Maybe I've googled the wrong company, maybe Family First aren't as conservative as I fear they're going to be. After all, they need to be pretty open minded if they're going to cope with the Allbrite waitresses. It's a company that specialises in scantily clad (if clad at all) waiting staff. We usually only use them at the client's request if they're trying to be a bit risqué or edgy. Which is mainly for our more liberal clients: media companies or large male-dominated, high-testosterone industries such as city bankers. Not family friendly organisations like this.

I wonder what the waitresses are going to be wearing tonight – I'm hoping they are at least dressed. The last time I was at an event with them they were naked apart from body paint.

I walk through the venue hoping that I'm fearing the worst and that Allbrite have branched out into pastures new.

'Hello, you must be Marie,' I say, planting an overly large smile on my face and holding out my hand. 'I'm Lydia. I think that Helen might have mentioned on the phone that I'm taking over tonight? She was very sorry not to be here in person, but she has planned you a fantastic event and you are in for a real treat.'

Whether you like it or not.

'Thanks, Lydia. We're so excited about tonight. I've got a couple of last-minute adjustments to the table plans. People who can't make it.'

'OK, well, we've set it up as per the last instruction from you so we can go ahead now and make the changes if you like?'

'Great. I can't wait to see the room. Wow,' gasps Marie as we walk in. 'It looks so different to how I imagined it would. Are those purple feathers?'

'Uh-huh,' I say, trying to work out if that's a good thing or not.

'I like it,' she says finally, and I sigh with relief. 'It looks classy. I thought that we were going for something a bit more vibrant, but this could work. I guess it's hard as we were a bit vague with what we asked for.'

I can sense that she's not so much disappointed as under-whelmed, and that's not really what we aim for with our events.

'Well,' I say, thinking off the top of my head, my heart pounding with the fear that I could mess this event up, 'we have yet to put in the giant lollypops and the candy canes that we thought would work with the brief.'

'Oh great,' she says, her eyes lighting up.

'If you're OK, I'll leave you to change the seating plan. There are some additional name tags here that you can write on if you need to change people. And if we can go over what you've done afterwards, then I can make sure that the caterers are up to date. And I'll chase up our estates team to sort out the additional props.'

'Perfect.'

I hurry away out of earshot and pick up the walkie-talkie, switching it to the channel that the estates team uses.

'Lydia to Fred.'

'Go ahead, Lydia.'

'Um, I've just had a last-minute addition from the client and they want some of the Willy Wonka props.'

There's a crackle and a pause at the end of the radio.

'The ones we've just bubble wrapped and put into storage?'

'Um, yes, those would be the ones. Not many,' I say, wincing. 'Say half a dozen lollies and four or so candy canes.'

I'm met with silence again and I see the door opening and a number of women dressed in black tracksuits walk in. Allbrite staff.

'I'll get Matt to give me a hand. We'll have them up within the next half an hour.'

'Fred, you're a star.'

'You'd better be buying another box of those doughnuts at some point soon.'

'Deal,' I say, thinking that that will be a small price to pay.

I don't have time to dwell on this crisis as I have another unfolding.

'Hi, there, ladies, are you from Allbrite?'

'That's right,' says a tall blonde woman who has her hair tied messily in a top knot. 'If you can let us know where we can do our hair and make-up, and what the timings are.'

'OK,' I say, wondering what the suit covers they're carrying are holding. 'I can show you to the changing room. Just one quick question, when you say hair and make-up, what theme have you got down for tonight?'

'Dominatrix.'

My heart sinks. Tight skimpy leather isn't really going to go with the giant lollypops.

'Right,' I say nodding. 'You see, the thing is, I'm pretty sure there's been a bit of a mix-up. The event tonight is a family friendly bloggers award ceremony. There's a kids TV presenter compering. We can't have you walking out dressed as dominatrixes.'

The woman in front of me unzips her bag and it's even worse than I could ever have imagined.

'There's no way we can have you wearing that.'

'But what are we supposed to wear instead?'

I look at the black tracksuits that they have on and I shake my head.

'I don't know. I really don't.'

I take a deep breath and have a think. I haven't been giving my work a lot of head space today as it's all foggy with thoughts of Danny and how royally I've fucked everything up with him. I should have looked at the event plan before now and then this would never have happened. I've got to sort out this mess or I'll lose this promotion as well as Danny.

The top-knot woman and her crew have now all either got their hands on their hips or their arms folded in exasperation.

'OK,' I say taking another deep breath. 'We've got to make you look more family friendly. I know, we've got the Oompa-Loompa costumes left over from our Willy Wonka-themed Christmas parties. They've been laundered ready to go back to the costume-hire place, but we can deal with that again tomorrow.'

'You want us to dress as Oompa-Loompas? Do you know our hourly rate?'

'Unfortunately I do,' I say, remembering the premium you pay for wanting less from your waiting staff. It's all going to eat out of the profits from tonight's event, but it will have been paid for already.

'Come on,' I say, 'I'll show you the costumes.'

Half an hour later and I'm looking at fifteen Oompa-Loompaesque waitresses. I've just about managed to persuade them to put the brown tops underneath the white braces that hold up the skirts, and, despite the skirts seeming a whole lot shorter than before, seeing as most of these women have legs that go all the way up to their armpits, at least they are decent.

I walk back into the venue as the waitresses start to sort out their welcome-drink stations and I see that Marie is smiling at one of the giant lollipops.

'This looks fabulous. And I love the waitress uniforms like candy canes, too. Great idea.'

I nod and smile. Candy cane, let's go with that. I guess without the green wigs and orange faces they look less like characters from *Charlie and the Chocolate Factory*.

'Yes, they look pretty good,' I say, nodding.

'Now, all we need is the presenter to turn up,' she says, looking at her watch.

I glance at mine and realise that it's almost 5 p.m. When did it get so late? The ceremony kicks off at 6.30, which means people will be walking the mini red carpet and having welcome drinks at 6.00. That gives us an hour until everything kicks off.

'I'm sure he'll be here in plenty of time,' I say crossing my fingers, as nothing else seems to be going my way tonight. It's so unlike Helen to mess up this badly.

'Lydia,' says Jenny, 'the ice luge is here.'

'Oh great, the ice luge is here,' I repeat for Marie's benefit as she doesn't have an earpiece in. I'm just hoping that she actually ordered one.

'Oh fantastic. That seemed like such a great idea. A perfect icebreaker – so to speak,' she says, laughing at her own joke. 'Especially as a lot of these bloggers have never met before and will be here on their own. I can't wait to see it.'

'Jenny, can you have them set up the block at the entrance lobby where the welcome drinks will be held and we'll meet you there.'

'Absolutely,' she replies.

'Shall we?' I say to Marie, holding my hand out to show her the way, and we walk out into the reception where there's a guy wheeling out a giant vodka luge made of ice in the shape of a pair of boobs. I stop and wonder if it's too late to bundle the client out of the way, but she's already pointing at them.

'Are those breasts?' she says, squinting, before she walks up to them.

We get closer and we can see that the luge is indeed cut into a very realistic pair of giant boobs. The kind that I'm sure would be at home at a stag party.

'Oh my God, they're brilliant. They fit in so perfectly with the campaign we've been running on social media to support breastfeeding. Wow, Helen really did her research,' she says, clapping her hands in delight.

I breathe a sigh of relief, just as my radio crackles again.

'Don't say anything to the client, but the kids presenter is here and you've got to see him.'

'Don't tell me, sauce for table three,' thinking that all we need is a drunk presenter.

'More like Mary Poppins has arrived.'

Great, a presenter that's high as a flipping kite.

'Everything OK?' asks Marie when she sees my face.

'All A-OK,' I say, as I leave her with the ice block and run off round the back to the staging area. I spot Jenny trying to calm down the man in front of her.

'Hey, I'm Giles!' he says with a big beaming smile. He's giggling maniacally and I can see why Jenny thought he was on something – he's positively wired.

'Hi, there, I'm Lydia, the event manager. I'm going to show you to your dressing room now. Can I get you anything on the way? A coffee perhaps, or a soft drink?'

A stomach pump?

'I'm fine, really. I don't do caffeine. I've got some water.'

'Good, good.'

I hope between now and when he gets on stage that he drinks a gallon of it.

'I am so excited to be here,' he says, hopping as he follows me. 'I don't often get asked to do these types of events. In fact, I'll let you into a little secret.'

He leans into me and I'm dreading what he's going to say.

'This is my first one. Can you believe it? I'm a little nervous,' he says, giggling again.

'So nervous that you had some Dutch courage?'

Or Colombian courage.

'Oh no, I don't drink. I actually don't do toxins. I'm vegan.'

'OK, then.'

'You think I'm on something, is that what you mean?'

He looks hurt, as if I've just drowned his puppy.

'No, not at all.'

'You do. I've had this before. Have you not seen my show? This is what I'm like,' he says. 'I'm naturally this happy.'

'Oh thank God,' I say with a sigh of relief. I could almost cry. 'Then let's get you ready and I can introduce you to Marie who runs the magazine.'

'Perfect! Let's get this show on the road,' he says, doing finger guns in my direction.

I bundle him into the changing room and shut the door, leaning against it and breathing out.

My phone buzzes and I see that it's Hazel. I can't face talking to her. Not while I'm at work. I put the call through to voicemail and my heart sinks. I'd got used to having her back in my life and I'd been looking forward to having her as a mother-in-law.

'Let's do this,' shouts Giles, as he comes out of the room and it snaps me back to where I am. With everything going so wrong tonight I need to be as focused as I possibly can. There'll be plenty of time to sort out the mess that is my life after tonight's event is over. But right now, I've got to make sure everything goes smoothly as now the promotion is more important than ever.

Chapter 28

Did your mum tell you what my mum did at my dad's birthday party? She only went and jumped out of a giant cake like some stripper. Thankfully, for everyone, she was fully clothed (or clothed at least) but she nearly gave my Great-aunt Hilda a heart attack. The party went a bit downhill from there; I found your mum holding my mum's hair back as she vomited into a flowerpot. Our mums huh? What a shining example of how to live.

Email; Danny to Lydia, September 2018

I put a pillow over my head and try to ignore the banging on my front door. I don't want to see anyone today.

After what turned out to be a successful awards ceremony last night I crawled into bed exhausted and I thought I'd reward myself with staying in bed all day and moping about the mess my life is in.

The knocking on the door stops and I feel relieved as the tears are prickling behind my eyes. I'm just about to indulge them and let them flow freely when the door at the top of the stairs to Kerry's house opens.

'Lydia, darling,' calls Mum as she walks down the stairs.

I groan.

'Come on, love,' she says as she sits on my bed. 'Get in the shower and let's get going.'

'I don't need to go shopping anymore. The wedding's off, remember?'

My mum strokes my hair and gives me a sad smile.

'I know, sweetie, and I'm sorry. But that's all the more reason to get out of bed. Wallowing about in self-pity isn't going to do you any good.'

'Wanna bet?'

'Come on, when your father left me, did you see me hanging around the lounge in my pyjamas all day?'

'No,' I say casting my mind back.

'Of course you didn't. We used to go out and about and keep busy, which is exactly what we're going to do with you. Let's go shopping. A little bit of retail therapy never hurt anyone.'

'I don't know, I'd rather just binge-watch Netflix and eat ice cream. It works for people in the movies.'

'Come on, let's go out for ice cream in real life instead.'

'You're not going to leave me in peace, are you?'

'No,' she says shaking her head.

'Fine, then,' I say, stomping out of bed and towards the shower.

'I don't understand why you drove us all the way to Southampton.'

'I just thought we needed a bit of a change of scene,' she says.

We walk out of the car park and into the giant John Lewis and the bright lights startle my eyes.

'Where shall we go first?'

'Well, not the evening-dress section,' I say, looking over at the long dresses and being reminded of our shopping expedition a week ago, when I was still looking forward to my wedding.

My mum links her arm through mine and starts walking with purpose into the ladies-wear section, but I can't feign interest in any of the clothes that she points out to me. This was a terrible idea.

'How about home-wears? You could buy a new duvet set; it's amazing how a new set of bed sheets can change your outlook.'

'Great idea, I can buy a duvet to go on the new bed I'm going to have to buy when I have to move house next month.'

'OK, so home-wear is out. What about going to look for something for Olivia for her birthday? We could check out the toy department.'

'Her birthday's not for another month.'

'Never too early to start shopping for that girl.'

I nod, guessing that there's a lot to depress me up there.

'Oh, look at this,' says Mum as she looks at the dogs that walk along and flip over. I used to have one when I was younger, but this one is a little less rigid in its movements. 'You used to have one of these.'

'I did. I don't think Olivia would like it, though, I don't think it would do enough for her.'

'No, probably not.'

I sigh loudly and stop at the Sylvanian Families wedding scene.

'Oh love. Come on, let's go and find some ice cream.'

My mum practically has to drag me out of the shop before I start to break down.

'Perhaps you were right, this was a terrible idea. Would you rather go to the cinema and cry into your popcorn?' she says as we leave the store and go into the busy shopping centre.

'No, I think if I'm going to start crying I'd get myself chucked out for making too much noise,' I say trying to laugh a little.

'Then ice cream it is, there's a nice little shop out on the old high street,' she says.

'That sounds great. Oh look,' I say, pointing at a man who's standing outside a shop with a young woman. He's holding lots of shopping bags. 'Is that Keith and his daughter?'

'Oh,' says my mum. 'I won't bother them; they look as if they're on a mission.'

'They're just standing there. Keith, hi,' I say as I walk up to him. 'And you must be one of his daughters. Are you Suzanne, Keeley or Nadia?'

'Suzanne,' says the woman looking at me as if I'm mad. 'And you are?'

'Oh, I'm Lydia, Linda's daughter.'

I turn to point to my mum, thinking she'll have followed me over, but she's standing stock still where I left her, her face ashen.

'Dad, who is this woman and who's Linda?'

Keith looks as pale as Mum and I'm desperately trying to work out what's going on, when an older woman walks up and takes Keith's hand and it all suddenly fits into place.

'There, got it,' she says to Keith and Suzanne, before she turns to me. 'Hello.'

'Hi,' is about all I can manage. I turn around and look at my mum again and she's still frozen to the spot.

Keith coughs. 'Let's be going, then,' he says, taking his daughter by the elbow.

'Dad, who was she?'

'Just the daughter of an old work colleague,' he says as he walks away with his family.

I turn and walk back over to Mum.

'Keith's married,' I say.

She nods and now it's her who's blinking back the tears.

'Do you want to come home and binge-watch Netflix and eat ice cream?'

She nods again and this time it's me that's leading her away before she bursts into tears.

An hour later and we're sitting on my sofa clutching a bowl of cold ice cream each. Neither of us has spoken about what I saw at the shopping centre. Mum is still just as pale as she was then.

I don't put the TV on and we sit there in silence until I hear my mum let out a big sigh.

'I'm so embarrassed that you had to find out. I'm so ashamed.'

'I don't know why I didn't see it before. You and Keith not wanting to move in with each other. Him not coming for Christmas. All the signs were there.'

She nods.

'You've been having an affair for years and his family have never twigged.'

She shakes her head.

'Have you ever asked him to leave her?'

'Never.' She puts her bowl down on the table and turns to me. 'It's not like that with Keith and me. I love spending time with him and he's a great companion, but I don't want him to live with me. One of the things that attracted me to him is the fact that I can't have him.'

'That doesn't make any sense,' I say, still so confused about everything.

'When I split up with your father, I was lost for a long time. Do you remember how I used to take you to Hazel's all the time and we'd spend weekends with the family?'

I nod. How could I forget?

'We had to go there as I couldn't cope. I'd been with your dad for so long and I couldn't remember who I was on my own anymore. I'd forgotten who I'd wanted to be.

'Hazel and Brian helped me get over your dad and reminded me how to have fun. They even helped me to get a job. I vowed then that I'd never lose myself again. That's why I didn't really date as I wasn't really interested. I didn't want another man to take over in my life the way I'd let your father.

'And then I met Keith through work and we'd flirt a lot and I enjoyed it. I knew it was harmless as I couldn't have him. And then one day we went out for coffee and I guess the affair started from there. It was like the best of both worlds for me. I got to have an occasional man friend but I got to keep my life too.'

I screw up my face as I try and come to terms with what she's said.

'But what about his wife? His family? What about hurting them?'

'To be honest I don't really think of them at all. I've tried to pretend that we have these separate lives and that he's just like me. I've not seen his wife before, I've never even seen a photo of her. I've never wanted to. It's not as if I didn't know she existed, but it makes it easier to pretend that she's not a real person, that they're not a real family. God, I sound like such an awful person.' She stops talking and pushes her ice cream round the bowl. 'I don't think I can pretend anymore. Seeing them, a happy family, I know that it's not right.'

'Don't you think you're selling yourself short? Not every man you meet is going to take away your identity. Not if you're with the right man.'

'I know, I'm sure they wouldn't, but I really was happy with it, a relationship and my independence.'

We sit there in silence once more, the ice cream melting, neither of us in a hurry to eat it.

'I'm sorry that you had to find out this way. I'm mortified.'

I take mum's hand.

'That must have been a really hard thing to see. Did you think that they were miserable in their marriage?'

'Keith and I never talked about it. I just assumed that it was a loveless marriage, but maybe I've had that all wrong. Not that it matters. I'll have to end it now that I've seen them all. I can't be the one who breaks up a family.'

I squeeze Mum's hand tighter.

'Are you going to be OK?'

'I'll be fine, darling. I know since your father left me that I'm stronger than that. Plus, this time round I'm happy just being me. I'll put the kettle on, shall I?'

She gets up and goes over to the kitchenette and I'm left struggling to process what went on.

My mum's been seeing an unavailable man because she didn't want to give up her life for a relationship and yet there was me doing the exact opposite. I was willing to give up my whole life for love, and as soon as I took that promotion I realised I couldn't go through with it.

I watch Mum making the tea and see she's pulled herself together already. Her words play over and over in my mind. *I'm just happy being me.* It's started to resonate with me as I've realised what's been the problem. I haven't been happy being me, but instead of fixing me and trying to be happy on my own I jumped at the chance of giving someone else the responsibility for making me happy.

My hands are shaking as I put my ice cream bowl down on the table. I might have lost Danny, but I can at least try to sort out the mess my life has got into. I can ace the probation period and get my promotion and I can find somewhere to live. At least that would be a step in the right direction.

'Are you all right, love?' says Mum, as she pops a steaming cup of hot tea down on the table.

'No, I don't think so. But I will be.'

I remember what my mum was like before my dad left. She was meek and mild and she didn't really seem to have an opinion about anything. I didn't really understand it then, but as I look back now I realise she did change and she blossomed – she really did become herself.

I've spent my whole life thinking that something was missing, that I needed something to complete me, but I've had it all wrong. I've got to make myself happy, and right now that means rebuilding my own life.

Chapter 29

My job is so surreal. Yesterday we had a conference for Heritage suppliers and I spent the day having to dodge an over-enthusiastic knight in a full suit of armour (luckily it was pretty noisy and I soon learnt to hide when I heard him clanking in my direction) and tonight I was working a party for your old firm. It was funny to think that if you'd never left London all those years ago you might have been at it.

Email; Lydia to Danny, October 2018

My mind is buzzing with ideas of how to sort my life out as I walk into work the next day. I need to sparkle in my job, which means making sure that my next events go more smoothly than Wednesday's. No more moping and feeling sorry for myself. That means when I'm at my desk I need to mean business. And it doesn't stop with work, I've lined up two viewings for flats tonight – it's time I stood on my own two feet.

Helen's back at her desk and she smiles at me when I sit down. 'Morning.'

'Morning,' I parrot back. I wish that I could say that she looked brighter today but her eyes are black rimmed and puffy. There's definitely something not right there and I don't know if I can ask her what it is.

'We had an email from the Family First team. They said that they were thrilled that the event went so well.'

'That's good to know,' I say, sighing with relief.

'Yeah, happy clients are always good. Did it go OK? It's just I was worried as Jenny was a bit funny about it when I asked her yesterday.'

I hesitate, wondering if I should tell her what happened. She doesn't look as if she's in the best place but if she did mix up two nights, then there's potential for another event going wrong.

'Well . . .' I say sitting down and taking a deep breath. 'It all went OK in the end, but there were a few things that weren't quite right. Or at least I don't think they were right. The venue was all set up like some kind of burlesque night – all black and purple. And then the Allbrite ladies turned up with dominatrix outfits. And the vodka luge was a pair of boobs.'

'What?' she says, gasping. 'That's not what was supposed to be there. All that stuff's for the Hotshots event next month. Oh, shit,' she says, picking up the file that's sitting on top of my desk and flicking it open. 'I don't know how I did it, but I've mixed the two events up. Shit, shit, shit. I've got a hundred and fifty men coming and they're going to be met with pink balloons and fully clothed silver-service waiting staff. Oh, Lydia. I'm so sorry.'

'It's fine, I coped,' I say, laughing at the memory of it.

Helen starts to well up. 'I'm so sorry, I just can't.'

'Everyone has an off moment, Helen. But is it something more than that? Are you OK?' I whisper. 'It's just with what happened at the Christmas event and now this. It's so not like you.'

She nods along and dabs at her eyes, stopping a tear from ruining her mascara.

'My mum's got cancer. She was diagnosed a couple of months ago and we all thought it was going to be OK, but it looks like it's got worse.'

'Oh, Helen,' I say leaning over and giving her a hug. 'You poor thing. I can't imagine what you're going through.'

'I don't know what to do. Mum needs to be cared for more and more and I'm already going there before and after work, and I've been trying to pop in on my lunch breaks, but she needs someone to be there all the time. My sister can't do it as she's got little kids and the nurses only pop in now and then. I just don't know what to do. I can't quit as I need to pay the mortgage.'

'We'll get something sorted. You've got to speak to Tracey.'

She nods her head. 'I didn't want it to affect my job, but it looks like it has anyway.'

'Come on,' I say standing up and leading her over to Tracey's office. I tap lightly on the door and she waves us in as she ends her phone conversation.

'Ladies, what can I do for you? Helen, are you OK?'

I keep holding Helen's hand and give her a little nod as she begins to explain what she just told me.

'Of course I understand that you need to take some time off. I'm sure you've got some holiday and overtime that need to be used up, for starters. Now, this must be stressful for you. Have you seen a doctor?'

'No, I don't need to see one. I'm not the one who's ill.'

'Helen,' she says gently. 'I think a doctor would be a good idea. I'm sure he'll see how much everything is affecting your health and how you're unable to work in this state.'

'Perhaps he'll give you a doctor's note,' I say reading between the lines.

'Yes, and then once you have your note signing you off work, we can go to HR with it,' says Tracey.

Helen nods as it finally dawns on her what Tracey's getting at. She then starts to sob and I put my arm around her for a hug.

'Thank you,' she says finally. 'I'll get my notes together and make sure that all my work's up to date.'

Tracey smiles. 'It's important for you to spend this time with your mum.'

'I can also make sure that I'm always contactable,' says Helen.

Tracey waves her hand. 'Don't worry about us, we'll be fine. Hand over your immediate work to Lydia and then we'll sort out the rest.'

Helen gets up and I can see the relief that's etched all over her face.

'Thank you, both of you,' she says as she leaves, her shoulders obviously that much lighter.

'I've been trying to work out for a while what's been going on with her,' says Tracey when it's just the two of us. 'Do you know she was drunk at the last Christmas party?'

'Was she?' I say, not doing a very good job of hiding the fact that I know, and Tracey raises an eyebrow – I'm fooling no one.

'Very out of character, but now it makes sense. Poor thing. I guess this leaves you in a bit of an awkward position as you've only just been promoted and now your workload is going to increase even more.'

'It'll be fine,' I say. 'I'm sure Helen's upcoming events will be meticulously planned.'

I try and ignore thoughts of Wednesday's mix-up.

'It's too much for one person, that's why we promoted you. I'll get involved with the planning and we'll see if we can get a freelancer to help run the events on the night. I know Roni who used to work here has her own business now, I wonder if she might be interested in working with us for a few months.'

I think back to Rob's Christmas party and I think she'd like that.

'The feedback from the client for the Family First event was that it went very well. And I heard from Fred and Jenny what happened. You did a fine job sorting it all out. I'm just sorry that we didn't promote you sooner.'

'Thanks,' I say thinking how much that means to me.

'It looks as if you're well on the way to making this promotion permanent.'

At least something is going right in my life.

I thank Tracey again and walk back over to my desk.

'Thanks, Lydia,' says Helen, turning to me as I sit down, 'for the support and for covering me the last few weeks. I don't know what I'd do without you here.'

'Well, that's lucky, as I'm going nowhere,' I say. I know that I should be pleased, that my professional life is the best it's ever been, but I can't help thinking of the new life I'm no longer going to have with Danny.

I try and push the thoughts of him out of my mind. This is about fixing me and pining over him isn't going to help.

Chapter 30

I've just finished having my kitchen redone and I thought of you today when I was fridge shopping. I was about to buy myself a super sleek black fridge with glass doors that was going to look great in my new kitchen. Only I realised it wasn't magnetic and then what would I have done with my very tacky fridge-magnet collection? There's also plenty of room for more . . .

Email; Danny to Lydia, November 2018

The lettings agent opens the door to the main flat and as I follow her in, I gasp. It's a corner flat and has almost panoramic views out over the common to the sea. I can see the ferries cruising across the harbour, the seagulls circling over the beach and dogs being walked. It takes me a moment or two to tear my eyes away from the view and take in the rest of the flat. To the rear of the room is the kitchen-diner that's separated by an open-partition wall.

I walk over into the lounge and I sit down on the leather sofa, which faces out towards the view. I don't think I'd ever get anything done if I lived here.

'Nice, huh?' says the agent.

'Just a bit.'

'The bathroom and the bedroom are through here.'

I reluctantly get up and walk in to see a nice modern bathroom, followed by a small but perfectly functional bedroom.

'It's great,' I say feeling as if this is a proper grown-up home to live in. It's the type of flat I should have rented when I broke up with Ross. I should have sorted everything out back then. 'What's the rental term?'

'Six months, but it's likely to be ongoing as the owner lives abroad.'

I look once more at the view. The sky is starting to turn pink as the sun begins to set.

'I'll take it,' I say. I've always loved it here down by the sea. Plus, it's only a fifteen-minute walk to Kerry and Jim's. Getting in and out of the city is going to be no worse than where I live now and there's underground parking, which is a rarity around here – it'll be refreshing not to be circling the streets having to parallel park miles away at stupid o'clock in the morning when I get home from an event.

'Great. So I'll email you the details of the holding deposit we'll need, and then I'll get the tenancy agreement together and we'll go from there.'

'Excellent,' I say as I look around the room again, imagining myself living here. It's small, but compared to where I am now it's a palace. And that view!

I park my car back on my street and smile properly for the first time in days. I'm only a few weeks away from having my very own seafront apartment. I walk into the granny annexe no longer feeling sad that I'm going to be leaving and I hear voices coming from Kerry's house. The door between my flat and their house is open.

I can hear my mum's cackle drifting down the stairs and it takes me a minute or two to realise that Hazel's there too.

I'm just about to turn round and walk out when Kerry shouts down.

'Lydia, is that you?'

I don't have time to make a bolt for it as suddenly she's walking down the stairs.

'I can't face seeing Hazel,' I say, knowing it'll undo all the good things that I've achieved getting my life on track.

'Come on, she's come a long way,' says Kerry. 'She's brought shortbread with her.'

I hesitate, but then I have zero willpower and I find myself up in the kitchen.

'Oh, Lydia, love,' says Hazel, wrapping me up in a hug. All I can do is bite my lip to stop myself from crying. 'Now what on earth is going on with you and Daniel, and why haven't you made up?'

'It's for the best,' I say. 'I think we were getting married for the wrong reasons. We were both searching for something that we thought marriage would help us find.'

'Well, I don't think there's anyone round this table who didn't think you were a little hasty in planning the wedding when you'd only just got together, but that doesn't mean that you have to break up. The two of you are so right for each other. You've always been so right for each other. We've known all along, haven't we, Linda?'

'Oh yes. And then we thought you'd finally got together at Kerry's wedding.'

'You knew about that?'

'Pur-lease,' says Hazel. 'It was written all over your faces at breakfast the next morning.'

So much for us being discreet.

'It doesn't matter though, does it? What happened in the past or even what happened between us now. He told me at the sten do that he can never trust me.'

'Why?' says Hazel. 'Because you kissed Stuart years ago?'

'I lied to him, or at least I didn't tell him the whole story. I was supposed to have quit my job and I hadn't. They'd offered me a promotion and I'd accepted it.'

'That's no reason not to be together. So you have a long-distance relationship.'

I shake my head. 'He said it proved we couldn't be together and I think he's right I wouldn't have chosen my job over him if I really loved him, would I?'

Kerry puts her hands on her hips.

'That proves nothing. We're not living in the 1950s anymore, your career is important and it's understandable that you didn't want to give everything up.'

'I'm sure Danny would have supported you,' says Hazel.

'It doesn't matter,' I say. 'I still think that he's in love with Victoria and he's kidding himself that he's not.'

'What?' says Hazel. 'Him and Victoria? Believe me there is nothing between them.'

'They kissed and she told him she loved him.'

'And did he tell you that he'd said it back?' says Hazel shaking her head. 'No, he doesn't love her.'

'But it still all seems to fit, that's why he was in such a hurry to marry me after we'd just got together; he was trying to forget about Victoria.'

'What? The reason he was in a hurry to marry you was because he's been in love with you for years, you idiot,' says Hazel almost laughing. 'Daniel was in love with you when you were teenagers and I'm guessing, giving the speed with which you two got engaged, that he never stopped.'

'Danny wasn't in love with me back then; we just had a heat-of-the moment kiss at a wedding. It was only as I was banging on about never having been in love that I think he felt obliged to make that silly pact with me.'

'Actually, that's not true,' pipes up my mum, who's been quiet up until now. 'Did you know that he cut his travelling short for you?'

'He what?'

'He flew back to London then caught a flight up to Newcastle to see you.'

I look over at Hazel for confirmation but it looks as if it's new information to her too.

'But I never saw him, why did he come all that way and not let me know he was there?'

'Well, he said that he saw you leaving your flat early one morning with a man with his arm around you and then I think he felt stupid for going all that way.'

'What guy? Hang on, during the holidays? That would have been my friend Tim, who's as camp as anything. He couldn't walk anywhere without looping his arms with whoever he was walking with. I can't believe Danny was there. How do you even know that?'

'He told me when we were sorting out your trip to Spain. It was his idea that you go.'

'What? But he didn't know I was going to be there,' I say as I think back to that moment in the lounge where I threw the can of mousse at his stomach.

'He did. He set it all up. He wanted you both to meet up somewhere neutral to see what happened.'

I think back to our time in Spain. He planned it. The whole thing. So much for it being fate.

I can't work out whether to be outraged or flattered.

'Why didn't he just ask me out?'

'Why do something the easy way when you can do it the hard way,' says Hazel, laughing.

'And you knew he was going to be there,' I say to her. She must have been a better actress than I thought as she seemed genuinely surprised to see me in Danny's lounge that night and I don't think it was only because I was near-naked.

'I didn't know then, but of course your mum filled me in later.'

I give my mum a look to suggest I wish she'd filled me in too.

'I think the bottom line is he's crazy about you,' says Hazel. 'Always has been, always will be. I mean, he sends you presents and cards for heaven's sake. I haven't got a birthday card in years and I'm lucky if he remembers to buy us a present at Christmas.'

'I've never known a guy who would go to the effort that he's done over the years to send you all that stuff,' says Kerry. 'Jim's idea of a thoughtful gift is a packet of Alka Seltzer after a curry.'

I think of all the presents: the magnets, the cards, the letters, and I slowly start to let it sink in that maybe what they're saying is true.

'Even if he did love me, he's not in love with me anymore. He was so mad at me after he found out about the kiss with Stuart and my promotion. I've never seen him so angry.'

'Then why hasn't he cancelled the wedding?'

'What?'

'The booking for the wedding is still standing, I phoned to double check yesterday,' says Hazel.

'Maybe he hasn't got round to it yet.'

'Or maybe he's hoping you'll sort it out,' she says, raising both her eyebrows at once.

I shake my head.

'This is all too much to take in,' I say. It was all such a whirlwind with Danny and I was using a relationship to fix what was wrong with my life. I feel the pain burning in my chest when I think of him.

'It wasn't real. None of it's real. We've built each other up in our heads over the years and we both thought we were people that we weren't. I don't think we really know each other properly at all.'

Hazel goes to open her mouth and I hold my hand up.

'I'm really touched that you came all this way to talk to me. I appreciate it, I really do, but Danny and I are not going to get married next week. He's going to get on with his life there and I'm going to get on with mine here.'

'But Lydia—'

'I can't do this,' I say getting up and walking away. 'I'm sorry.'

I walk down into my flat and grab my coat before walking out of my front door. I don't know where I'm going but I've got to get away from here. I don't pay any attention to where I am until the sea breeze hits me and nearly takes my breath away. It suits my mood perfectly.

I don't often walk along the prom in the dark but it's still relatively early and there are plenty of dog walkers and runners about.

I keep thinking over what Hazel was saying. Has he really always been in love with me?

I still keep seeing him standing there at the sten do – so hurt and angry – and I don't know if we'd ever get past that.

'Hey Lydia, are you OK?'

I look up to see Ross dressed in his running gear jogging on the spot in front of me. I didn't even notice him appear.

'I've been better,' I say honestly, and I start to cry.

'Hey, let's go for a drink,' he says. 'The Jolly Sailor's just over there.'

It makes me cry harder as he's being nice to me, even after we had that argument last week.

'So, I take it that there's trouble in paradise,' he says.

I go to turn back towards the seafront, 'Perhaps this wasn't a good idea after all.'

'Hey,' he says. 'I'm sorry. I promise I won't be such a dick. I'm sorry about the other night, for shouting at you. I was out of line. Look, what's happened?'

I take a deep breath and as we walk to the pub I tell him about Danny at the sten do and what Hazel's just told me.

By the time I'm finished, we've ordered drinks and are sitting in the window looking out over the common.

'I guess you probably think it's for the best that we've broken up. I know that you were never a fan.'

'That's not fair. It just hurt seeing you with Danny, but I think you're an idiot to have let him go.'

'You do?'

'I do,' he says sipping his drink. 'You've always been in love with him and I think I always knew that. Every time I saw you open one of those presents you used to get this look in your eye. I hated it. Whenever I bought you a present for your birthday or Christmas, I looked for the same look and it was never there.

'I wanted to marry you. Did you know that? I toyed with the idea of buying a ring not long after we moved in together, but something always stopped me. It's like what you said when we broke up: there was something missing between us and I couldn't work out what it was. We get on so well together. We have the same friends. We have a laugh. But that wasn't enough. And then when I saw you with Danny at the Dockyard I saw what was missing. You had this chemistry and I couldn't help but see it.

'That's why I was so pissed off at the pub the other week. I was jealous. I wanted us to have had that. Why couldn't we?'

'I don't know,' I say a little sadly. 'You know you used to drive me crazy when we were together as you never told me how you were feeling. Now look at you.'

'I know. It wouldn't have helped, though, would it?' he says shaking his head. 'I know that now.'

'You know you probably didn't look at me in the same way either,' I say. 'You know you stare at Jules when she's talking? And I don't think it's because she's talking so fast that you can't process it.'

He laughs. 'You get used to the way she talks. I just sort of zone out after the first question and tune in for the last.'

I smile back.

'But you're right, there is something there.'

'Do you think she's the one?'

He shifts uncomfortably in his seat.

'I don't know. I don't think we've been together long enough to know. Don't forget I haven't known her all my life. But, I think she has the potential to be though.'

I feel a burst of love for Ross, not in the way I used to, or the way I feel about Danny, but as a friend. I'm glad that he's found someone. He deserves to be happy.

'How do you know when someone's the one?' he asks.

'I don't know,' I say, shrugging sadly.

'Yes, you do. You knew Danny was the one. How? Lucy told me you tried to elope, so when you were standing there in Gretna Green, how did you know you wanted to spend the rest of your life with him?'

I close my eyes and imagine myself back on that day. I can feel Danny's hand clutching mine as if he never ever wanted to let me go. I picture his face when I walked out of the service station loos in my dress. I think of the feeling in my tummy when he kissed me when we stood outside the room we booked to get married in.

'I just knew,' I say a little dreamily as I open my eyes.

'Then there you go,' says Ross. 'So, what are you doing here talking to me when you could be talking to him?'

'He doesn't want me, not anymore.'

'Come on, Lydia. If he's been in love with you since you were teenagers he's not just going to have fallen out of love with you because of a misunderstanding.'

'But he can't trust me.'

'Then convince him he can. For fuck's sake, Lydia, we both spent years of our lives desperately trying to find a smidgen of the love that you two have got. Don't waste any more time without him.'

'When did you become such a relationship expert?'

He shrugs. 'I think Jules and her happy-ever-after rom-coms are rubbing off on me.'

'Good job too,' I say, pushing my wine away. If I'm going to be driving up to the Lakes, I don't want to be over the limit.

'So, are you going to go and sort out your mess?'

'I am. Thanks, Ross,' I say, leaning over and giving him a big hug.

'Go get 'em Tiger,' he says and I give him a look. That's the most unRoss thing I've ever heard him say. 'It's those bloody rom-coms.'

I laugh and wave goodbye.

I practically run all the way back to my house. I weave round a taxi parked in the middle of the road as I search for my keys. I'm in such a rush as I mentally run through a list of all the things I've got to pack to take with me that I don't notice at first the person standing on my doorstep.

'Oh, Lydia, thank God,' says Lucy. 'I just needed to check you were OK.'

'I'm fine,' I say. 'I've realised that I've been an idiot with Danny and I'm going to tell him I love him.'

'Oh good for you,' she says, beaming. 'I'm so glad you finally came to your senses.'

There's a beep of a horn and Lucy looks over my shoulder.

'Is that taxi for you?' I ask, not understanding what's going on.

'Uh-huh, I couldn't leave without telling you. Ed and I are eloping. You were right about what you said about thinking about what was important and you and Danny and the whole Gretna thing seemed like the right way to go. So we're flying to Vegas on the late flight tonight,' she says squealing.

'Oh my God, that's amazing.'

'I know; we're going to have a tacky wedding, just the two of us. Obviously, I wish you were coming too.'

'I think it's the best idea. Oh my God, Lucy,' I say wrapping her up in a hug. 'Although don't think it'll mean us missing out on a hen do.'

'Are you not off hen dos for life after last weekend?'

'As long as Ed doesn't come we should be fine,' I say with a wink.

The taxi beeps again and Ed sticks his head out the window.

'Lucy, come on, we're going to be late.'

'OK,' she says hugging me again. 'Let me know how it goes.'

'You too,' I shout as she runs off.

I watch Lucy heading off for her happy ever after and it spurs me on to get inside to get myself sorted. It's time for me to get mine.

Chapter 31

Merry Christmas! Thank you so much for my present. It was exactly what I needed. For the first year ever I've been feeling a bit bah-humbug. Maybe it's working all the Christmas parties or maybe it's just that life isn't working out how I'd planned it – that lucky rabbit foot doesn't seem to be working its magic. Yet who knew it would take seeing a skiing penguin playing Wham! to put a smile on my face. Hope you enjoy your present. See you in the New Year?

Email; Lydia to Danny, December 2018

I manage to make it up to the Lake District in almost record time, five and a half hours. I'm achy and knackered from the drive but my mind is wide awake and buzzing despite it being well after midnight.

I knock on Danny's door, it feels wrong to use the key he gave me, and start to shiver. I'm unsure whether it's from nerves or the cold.

It takes a few minutes for anything to happen – presumably I've woken him up – but then I see a light flick on and a fuzzy outline through the frosted glass followed by the sound of the lock being opened.

I take a deep breath but then see that it's Victoria standing on the other side.

I could weep. I've been planning my apology for the last few hours and here she is in his house. To think I believed him about there not being anything going on.

'I don't believe it,' I finally say as I shake my head and turn to walk away.

'Lydia, wait,' she says. 'This isn't what it looks like.'

I turn back as she struggles to pull her dressing gown over her bump.

'Look, I can explain, come in, it's bloody freezing out here.'

She's not wrong. There's steam coming out of her mouth as she's talking.

'Danny's not here, I'm alone,' she says. 'Come in.'

She smiles at me in the same warm way that she did my sister and I follow her inside.

'Bloody hell it's cold out. Was it icy driving up?'

Not really interested in the answer she heads up the stairs to the kitchen where she flicks the kettle on.

'Where's Danny?' I ask, as I prop myself up against the work surface.

'He's gone away. Somewhere up in Scotland, I think. He said he needed to get away. I think he just needed to clear his head.'

I nod. 'And what are you doing here?' I say, as I watch her moving around making the tea looking so at home.

'After everything that happened last weekend, I finally told Gaz what was going on. I didn't tell him that I'd told Dan I loved him, but I told him that I thought we were having problems. We had a big heart to heart and we've decided we needed a bit of space for a few days to think things through and Dan said I could stay here whilst he was away.'

She hands me a cup of tea and she points at the door leading upstairs to the lounge.

We walk up slowly and we both perch on the sofa. I almost feel as if I'm sitting down with a friend, she seems like a completely different person.

'I don't love Dan,' she says sighing. 'I mean, I love him like a brother, but I'm not *in* love with him, not really. Things are not right with Gaz, but that's all about us, not anyone else. I think that everything happened for us so quickly. We met and we were engaged within six months and then we got pregnant straight away. It's like we haven't had a chance to just be together. And then Dan's so nice and he listens so well and it just confused me. I felt stupid after I kissed him, I knew deep down that he didn't like me in that way and I thought that was the end of the matter. But then I saw how he was with you and it made me jealous. I thought it was because I wanted that with Dan but I think it's because it reminded me what Gaz and I were like in the beginning of our relationship and I wanted it back. Instead of working on it with him I started to convince myself that it was because I was with the wrong man.

'It all sounds so stupid to say it out loud. I love Gaz, I really do, it's just he drives me flipping nuts and I don't think all these baby hormones are helping.'

I look down at the bump and I wonder what kind of a home the baby is going to be born into.

'We're going to be OK,' she says rubbing the bump as if she knows what I'm thinking. 'I think it was probably best that we got this all out in the open before the baby comes as I can imagine that that's going to turn our lives upside down and if we're not on the same page beforehand then we're certainly not going to be when he or she arrives.'

Victoria blinks back a little tear. 'And I've been such a bitch to you and I'm sorry. You're really lovely, Lydia, and you are perfect for Dan. And I'm sure you'll get to know your way around the kitchen at some point.'

I laugh.

'Do you think we can start over and put this all down to a pregnancy blip, baby brain or whatever it is?'

'Of course,' I say. 'I'm glad you and Gaz are going to work things out. He was so upset at the go karting when he thought you were having an affair. He really loves you.'

'I know he does,' she says, wiping away a tear and almost laughing at the same time. 'I just think we forgot that. We'll be all right.'

It sort of feels like we should hug, but we don't and instead smile a little awkwardly.

'So, did you come to sort things out with Dan?'

'Yeah, I can't believe I drove for almost six hours and he's not here.'

'You could ring him in the morning, see where he is? You can't go anywhere tonight, not after that drive. You must be knackered.'

The adrenaline that was coursing through my veins on the drive up here has started to ebb away. She's right. It's late and I'm exhausted; emotionally and physically.

'I was asleep in the spare room, so you can have Dan's bed.'

'OK.' I nod.

'Get a good night's sleep and then phone him in the morning and see where he is. I've got an appointment first thing, so don't be alarmed if I'm not here when you get up. If you need any help, you can ring me. I'll leave my number on the kitchen table.'

'OK,' I say nodding. 'Thanks.'

I follow her downstairs and I go through the motions of cleaning my teeth in the bathroom. Then I head down to the bottom floor and stand alone in Danny's room. It smells so much like him that I have to stop myself from ringing him right now. Instead I strip off my clothes, put on a checked shirt of his that's lying by the laundry basket and climb into bed. Man, his bed's so comfortable and I barely have time to process what's gone on before I fall asleep.

The sound of the front door slamming wakes me up and it takes a second or two for me to come round. I was in a deep sleep and dreaming I was running through the cobbled streets in Spain trying to find Danny, only I kept finding myself at dead ends.

I rub my eyes.

That must be Victoria leaving for her appointment. I look up at the clock and am surprised to see that it's after eleven. I can't believe how long I've slept for.

The bedroom door bursts open and Danny rushes in heading straight for the wardrobes and for a second I think I'm imagining it. He bangs and crashes as he frantically searches for something.

'Hey,' I say, as he definitely hasn't realised I'm here.

'What the actual fuck?' he says, swinging round, a look of shock on his face. 'Lydia, what are you doing here?'

'I was looking for you,' I say.

'And you fell asleep?'

'Pretty much. You weren't here,' I say, shrugging.

'Fair enough. It's a comfy bed.'

'It certainly is,' I say, resisting the urge to do more bed angels. 'I got here in the middle of the night and I couldn't start looking for you until this morning.'

He nods, a hint of amusement on his face.

'So what were you looking for in such a tearing hurry?'

He pulls out a kilt and I wrinkle my face in confusion.

'Hang on,' he says, disappearing out into the hall and coming back with a Primark carrier bag.

He pulls out a reindeer onesie, not dissimilar to the one I already own.

'What the—' I say, confused.

'I was going to send you the onesie and the kilt and it was going to have a note saying, well, to be honest, I hadn't really worked out what it was going to say, but something along the lines of I'd marry you in fancy dress if it meant I got to marry you. Meet me in Gretna.' He shakes his head and frowns. 'Yeah, the words needed work. Do you know how long it took me to write each letter to you over the years? Sometimes I was there for days and went through a hundred drafts, but I just always wanted them to be perfect.'

I'm grinning because I'm enjoying Danny losing it.

'I don't always have the answers, Lydia, and I fuck things up too. I didn't leave my job because it was too high-pressured; I left because I fucked up. I made a massive mistake and I was fired. It was just coincidence that Gaz needed a business partner. A bit of luck.

I didn't tell you because I didn't want you to know I was a screw-up. So I get it, I get why you were embarrassed to tell me about some things. I also get what it means to have a job that you love and what a big part of your life that is. I don't want you to give all that up for me.'

'But I want to,' I say. 'I might not be able to for a while as I've not only got a promotion, and now I'm covering for Helen as well, because her mum is terminally ill, but I want to move up here, I want to be with you.'

'I can't ask you to do that.'

I'm confused, I'm still groggy from sleep and this isn't making sense.

'But I thought you said that you wanted to marry me.'

'I do. I do want to marry you, but you're not moving up here. I'm going to move to Portsmouth to be with you.'

'What? But how? What about the business?'

'We can run the business from anywhere, and these days it's doesn't matter if Gaz and I are in the same office or a thousand miles away. We can Skype and we share all the files on the cloud. We can even split the clients between us north and south, meaning that we have to travel less. I thought that I could rent this place out and we could rent in Portsmouth and perhaps one day we can move back up here or I could sell it.'

It slowly starts to sink in that he's got it all worked out.

'Why didn't we think of that before?' I say. It all makes sense.

'Because you never gave me the chance to think about it; you immediately said you'd move. But it makes more sense this way. I've only been up here eighteen months and I'm not settled like you are. Plus, I think Gaz and Victoria have a lot to sort out and I think they'll be better doing that when I'm out of the picture.'

'I spoke to her last night,' I say, nodding.

'Did she tell you she doesn't love me anymore? I mean, talk about fickle,' he says, jokingly. 'It was a rough week, first you didn't love me and then she didn't either.'

'Well, that's not true, is it?' I say sliding off the bed and walking up to him. 'Because I never stopped loving you.'

He looks at me and I imagine this is the look that Ross was talking about. I feel as if I'm being bathed in a warm glow. I try and look at him in the same way.

'What's wrong with you, have you got something in your eye?' he says.

I start to giggle and instead of explaining I lean up and kiss him. He wraps his arms around me and kisses me back. It isn't long before his hands start wandering under the shirt I'm wearing.

'So, am I going to be wearing this kilt next week?' he says as he pulls away.

'No,' I say.

'Phew, there's a relief. No one wants to see these knobbly knees. Back to the normal suit then.'

'Actually, Danny, there's not going to be a wedding next week.'

He looks wounded again.

'I want to marry you and I know I will marry you – I have absolutely no doubt on that score. It's just that I want us to get to know each other properly. I want us to be getting married because it's right, and not because of some pact that we made when were too young to know any better. I've waited so long to be with you and I know that I'm going to spend the rest of my life with you. What's the rush?'

Danny audibly sighs with relief.

'I'll marry you anywhere, any how, Lydia Stoker, and if that means I have to wait, I will. As long as I'm with you I don't care.'

'Great, because I definitely think you're onto something with the onesies. Now we both have them, and I reckon you'd look great dressed as a reindeer.'

Danny laughs and bends down to kiss me gently on the lips.

'I'll tell you something that doesn't look great on you,' he says, tugging at the shirt of his I'm wearing. 'It doesn't suit you at all.'

'Is that right?' I say raising an eyebrow.

'Uh-huh,' he says slowly undoing the buttons. 'I think we should do something about that.'

He's just pushing the shirt off my shoulders when the front door slams. Good timing, Victoria.

'Daniel, Daniel,' shouts Hazel before she bounds into the bedroom. 'For God's sake, you two,' she says laughing as Danny hastily grabs the shirt and pulls it round my front.

'What's going on?' says my mum bundling in behind her. 'Oh, Lydia, we were really worried about you. Kerry said you took off last night and you haven't been answering your phone.'

'I must have left it in the car,' I say.

'Well, at least you're OK and I see that you've made up. So that's good, we'll leave you to it, then. We don't want to interrupt that now, do we, Hazel? We're hoping for grandchildren sooner rather than later.'

I tut at my mum and she gives me a wink.

'We'll be at my house. Perhaps you can pop over later,' says Hazel.

'We'll be there,' says Danny giving me a look. 'Much later.'

And I can't help but squeal with delight.

Mum and Hazel clatter out of the house, chattering noisily, and I look up at Danny.

'You know we're never going to be rid of those two, don't you?'

'I know, but at least they're both as daft as each other,' he says.

'That's true. And they have both done their bit to try and get us together. Your mum came all the way down to see me and my mum told me that you came to Newcastle. You know that that wasn't what it looked like? The guy you saw was my flat mate.'

'It doesn't matter,' he says. 'That's all in the past now anyway. We've got a clean slate and a fresh start. We're not each other's back-up plan. We're not teenagers. We're just us.'

'Take it one step at a time and all that.'

'Exactly.'

He leans over and kisses me and it's unlike any other kiss we've had before. I'm left breathless as he lets me go and climbs off the bed.

'Where are you going?'

'To put the chain across the bloody door so that we don't have any more interruptions,' he says, laughing.

He comes back a few seconds later and practically jumps onto the bed. I can't help but think I'm the luckiest girl in the world. I might have realised how to be happy just being me, but that doesn't mean to say that I can't be bloody happy to have Danny in my life as well.

What Happened Next

Why our mothers insist on broadcasting our lives via round robin newsletters, instead of just doing sporadic bragging posts on social media like the rest of mankind, I will never know. But for once I'm glad as I've just come across a batch of them and it's made me all nostalgic.

Here are the best bits . . .

Lydia x

Summer 2019

Oh my days – where have the last six months gone? We're edging ever closer to Brian turning seventy!!! Of course, I've been sorting out my burlesque number for his party – it's going to have to be something pretty spectacular to beat what happened at the last one! Let's just hope there'll be no Janet Jackson wardrobe malfunctions this time . . . ;)

Well, this year has been certainly more dramatic than we expected. Daniel has FINALLY settled down – well, almost. For those that haven't heard the story: he nearly eloped to Gretna Green in January, booked a wedding for February and then rescheduled that wedding for next summer. But that isn't the exciting part. We're of course thrilled he's getting married, but we're even more thrilled about who he's getting married to: Lydia, as in my wonderful best friend Linda's daughter. To those of you that have been getting this letter as far back as the mid-eighties, I had hinted that this was a possibility then. I think my tarot card reader was wrong – my gift is not in reiki; it's in predicting the future. I'm going to look into doing a course next year. I think I'll have a fabulous little pop up tent at the wedding and I'll be able to predict the many, many babies that Daniel and Lydia are going to have.

The only down side to the whole thing is that Daniel has moved down to Portsmouth. He's managed to rent out his cottage and he and Lydia are renting a flat on the seafront. Unfortunately, it doesn't have a spare room – but luckily I can stay with Linda when I visit and it's closer than New York/Singapore/Tokyo.

Hazel x

Christmas 2019

Ho, Ho, Ho! Merry Christmas, everyone. Well, what a difference a year makes, huh? This time last year I was packing Lydia off to sunny Spain to give her a much needed nudge in the romance department, and here we are a year later and she's got a sparkly ring on her finger and the most wonderful fiancé to boot. We're over the moon about the impending nuptials, even if I have been given strict instructions of what I can and can't do at the wedding. Apparently, any form of dancing is out, as it is erotic poetry, and Olivia stole all the hula-hoops I was training to do some special tricks with – well, if I'm not allowed to use my snake hips for dancing . . .

It also turned out that Lydia wasn't the only one who put her Christmas present from me to good use. Thanks to a lovely romantic getaway I got Kerry and Jim, Olivia truly got the best present ever this year – a new baby sister! Luna Camille was born on 15th October. We are all smitten with her. I've been helping out quite a bit, as have Lydia and Danny, who are only a fifteen minute walk away.

Now this year I just need to think of a present for me that might just change my life . . . I have started writing my own novel. I gave it to Lydia to read and she handed it back to me after one page as she said her eyes were burning, so I took that to be a good thing – clearly it's sizzling in the right direction!

Linda x

Summer 2020

Stop the press! Daniel finally married Lydia – only twenty-eight years after their first marriage ;). Now, I know I'm a bit biased, as not only was it my son getting married, but it was also at my house, but it truly was the most wonderful wedding ever.

They got a married in a beautiful little church up here in the Lakes, with the reception in our barn. It looked stunning, as you can imagine. I went OTT with the fairy lights, candles and bunting. Lydia, of course, looked beautiful in the most simple dress and Daniel didn't scrub up too badly either. Olivia did an excellent reading followed by interpretive dance. My best friend Linda (aka mother-of-the-bride) did an excellent speech which had Lydia blushing throughout and ended in her throwing a bread roll at her head. And the ukulele band and I did an amazing rendition of 'Can't Help Falling in Love' – there wasn't a dry eye in the house! It's the first performance I've done at a family shindig where I've kept my clothes on for a long time! Seems to have worked wonders though as we've actually been booked for other weddings now. We think we're going to use our performances as a mini-business, rather than just as an excuse to go to the pub once a month and strum around in the snug. That almost sounds like a line out of one of Linda's novels. She's self-publishing in time for Christmas, so you know what you'll all be receiving as presents from me!

Hazel x

Christmas 2020

What a lovely year it's been. After all the excitement of the summer wedding, I did think that the rest of the year would quieten down, but I guess with my adorable little granddaughters to keep me on my toes that was never going to happen. Kerry's gone back to work and I'm doing 'Granny Day Care' once a week. I meet the other grannies at rhyme time and we head out from there for coffee – the bubbas have babyccinos – and then, if it's not blowing a gale or teaming down with rain, we push the prams along the prom for nap time. It's marvellous.

My books are also going strong – just like the heroes in them ;). I had planned to self-publish, but they've been snapped up by a digital publisher and my first book will be on your e-readers next month! You'll all have to buy it and make me rich of course – those babyccinos aren't cheap!

The newlyweds are still suitably loved up – and they're not the only ones. I've gone and met a man. Howard is mid-sixties, has two children (sons!) and is divorced. I made him show me the decree absolute on the first date! We're off to Spain for New Year. Hopefully the place will work it's magic on us like it did on Lydia and Danny!

Linda x

Summer 2021

I'm absolutely bursting to tell you the good news: Lydia and Daniel are having a baby! Little baby Whittaker is due at Christmas time!!! I have been wishing every time I've walked in on them in a compromising position – which has been surprisingly often – that it would at least result in a little bundle of joy, and at last it has! Linda and I couldn't be more excited. We did try and co-ordinate our knitting efforts before realising that neither of us could actually knit and instead we've decided to record a special disc of nursery rhymes for them. I'm on the ukulele and Linda's writing the lyrics, although she does sometimes fail to remember that she's no longer writing for her adult audience. Speaking of which – her last book became a bestseller in the ebook charts and she's been offered a new three book deal! Her and her new fiancé Howard jetted off to New York to celebrate!

Hazel x

Christmas 2022

What a year! I'm pleased to announce that just before hitting send, Maxwell Thomas Whittaker was born. Mother and baby are doing very well. I can confirm he is the cutest male baby the world has ever seen! He was a few days late, which gave Lydia and Danny extra time to get settled into the cottage up in the Lake District. Danny's renters moved out last month and the two of them jumped at the chance of spending Lydia's year of maternity leave living up there. Having seen how cosy they are in their little cottage, I get the impression that it might not be the temporary move they think it is. I would of course miss them immensely, but Howard and I have been thinking for a while about buying a little bolt hole up there. My books are doing rather well – who knew erotica for the over sixties would be so in demand – and Howard loves Hazel and Brian almost as much as I do. All we need to do now is convince Jim and Kerry to move and our lives would be perfect . . .

Linda x

Acknowledgements

Thank you to my lovely readers for picking up this book. I had so much fun writing it – and I completely fell head over heels for Lydia and Danny and I hope that you did too! Thank you for all the tweets, shares, reviews and emails that you send me. It means the world to me to know that I have such lovely, supportive readers. Also, to the wonderful blogging community that take the time to read the book, to review it and to share it on social media – I would be nowhere without you.

Thank you to my agent Hannah Ferguson for all her help with this book and much needed cheerleading when it got tough in the first draft. Thanks also to the rest of the team at Hardman and Swainson – Joanna, Caroline, Thérèse and Lindsey. Big thanks to everyone at Bonnier Zaffre for all you do behind the scenes to bring my book baby into the world. Special thanks to Sophie Orme, Claire Johnson-Creek and Bec Farrell for the notes and guidance, and replying patiently to all my plot changing emails.

In one draft Lydia and Danny snuck over the border from Spain and got married in Gibraltar, but I thought Hazel and Linda would have disowned them and the scenes had to be cut.

Thank you to Flora at Rock Occasions in Gibraltar for the help and guidance about getting married there. Thank you to Zeenat for your ideas and insight into events planning – I miss hearing those stories in the tea boat. Thanks to Ali for your help with research that again didn't make it into this one, but I'm going to save it for the next book. Also, a big thanks to Christie for checking things for me – again!

To all my friends and family, thank you for your continuing support and for feeding me and giving me wine when needed. Special mention to Debs for your ideas – and one day I'll write THAT book especially for you. To my new writer buddy Lorraine Wilson for our lovely meet-ups – they help keep me sane. But most of all, thanks to my lovely husband Steve. Thank you for everything, as per usual, and to the kids, despite the fact that they can't understand how mummy could write books that people actually read when I tell them the most boring made-up stories at bedtime.

Dear Reader,

Thank you so much for reading IF WE'RE NOT MARRIED BY THIRTY. I do hope that you enjoyed it!

Did any of you make one of those pacts when you were younger? I've found out that a lot of my friends had them and we've been having a lot of laughs imagining what their lives would have been if they'd gone through with them! I'm glad I found my husband before I turned thirty and never had to enact my back up plan – life might have been very different indeed!

I absolutely loved telling Lydia and Danny's story. It was so nice to write about a couple that were absolutely meant to be, but their lives had sent them in different directions. My favourite characters in the book, though, had to be the mums – Linda and Hazel. They were the type of characters that when I sat down at the keyboard they would write themselves – surprising and amusing me all the time.

Have you read my other books? THE BUCKET LIST TO MEND A BROKEN HEART and THE GOOD GIRLFRIEND'S GUIDE TO GETTING EVEN. They are both heart-warming and up-lifting and are great escapist reads. My most recent book, IT STARTED WITH A TWEET, is the story of social media obsessed Daisy who makes a catastrophic mistake at work that sends her life into free-fall. Her sister Rosie whisks her off to a tiny, isolated village in Cumbria for a digital detox. But village life isn't as quiet as she imagined, especially with Rodney the frisky farmer, Jack the grumpy, rugged next door neighbour and sexy Frenchman Alexis all helping and hindering her attempts to get back online. Will Daisy successfully sneak away to phone signal, or will she get used to life offline?

If you'd like to hear more about my next book or any future books beyond that you can visit www.bit/ly/AnnaBellClub where you can become part of the Anna Bell Readers' Club. It only takes a few moments to sign up and there's no catches or costs. Your data will be kept totally private and confidential, and it will never be passed on to a third party. I won't spam you with loads of emails, but will get in touch now and again with book news, and you can unsubscribe any time you want.

Do also stop by and say hello on Twitter @annabell_writes or find me on Facebook. It's so lovely to hear from readers! I'd also be absolutely thrilled if you'd take the time to review my book – on Amazon, Goodreads, on your blog or any other e-store. What better way to tell us what you thought of the book?

Thanks again for reading IF WE'RE NOT MARRIED BY THIRTY.

Best wishes,

Anna

If you love reading Anna Bell, why not try her brilliantly
heart-warming novel . . .

Abi's barely left her bed since Joseph, the love of her life,
dumped her, saying they were incompatible.

When Joseph leaves a box of her possessions on her
doorstep, she finds a bucket list of ten things she
never knew he wanted to do.

Will completing the action-packed list – no easy challenge
for the naturally timid Abi – be the way to win
back her man? Or might Abi just have
a surprise in store . . .

AVAILABLE IN EBOOK AND PAPERBACK NOW

And why not try Anna Bell's hilarious romantic comedy . . .

The Good Girlfriend's Guide to Getting Even

When Lexi's sport-mad boyfriend Will skips her friend's wedding to watch football – after pretending to have food poisoning – it might just be the final whistle for their relationship.

But fed up of just getting mad, Lexi decides to even the score. When a couple of lost tickets and an 'accidentally' broken television lead to them spending extra time together, she's delighted to realise that revenge might be the best thing that's happened to their relationship.

And if her clever acts of sabotage prove to be a popular subject for her blog, what harm can that do? It's not as if he'll ever find out . . .

AVAILABLE IN EBOOK AND PAPERBACK NOW

And don't miss her latest romantic offering . . .

Could *you* survive a digital detox?

Daisy Hobson lives her whole life online. But when her social media obsession causes her to make a catastrophic mistake at work, Daisy finds her life going into free-fall . . .

Her sister Rosie thinks she has the answer to all of Daisy's problems – a digital detox in a remote cottage in Cumbria. Soon Daisy meets a welcome distraction there in Jack, the rugged man-next-door.

But can this a London girl ever really settle into life in a tiny, isolated village?

And, more importantly, can she survive without her phone?

AVAILABLE IN EBOOK AND PAPERBACK NOW

Want to read
NEW BOOKS
before anyone else?

Like getting
FREE BOOKS?

Enjoy sharing your
OPINIONS?

Discover

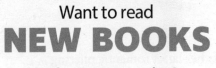

READERS
FIRST

Read. Love. Share.